CONNECTIONS IN DEATH

Lieutenant Eve Dallas and her husband Roarke are building a brand-new school and youth shelter, hoping to nudge kids away from dangerous paths. When Lyle Pickering, recovering drug addict and the brother of their newly appointed child psychologist Rochelle, is found dead of an overdose, it looks like a tragic accident. But Rochelle knows better, and so does homicide cop Eve. Lyle was murdered, and the evidence points back to his old street gang. As Eve and Roarke track the killer through New York City's dive bars, drug dens and strip joints, another body is discovered. With connections growing between the living and the dead, and the body count on the rise, Eve knows she needs to close this case fast, before the killer's lust for power turns the city's streets into a bloodbath.

CONNECTIONS IN DEATH

J. D. ROBB

LARGE
PRINT

First published in Great Britain 2019
by
Piatkus
an imprint of Little, Brown Book Group

First Isis Edition
published 2019
by arrangement with
Little, Brown Book Group
An Hachette UK Company

A catalogue record for this book is available
from the British Library.

ISBN 978–1–78541–774–0 (hb)
ISBN 978–1–78541–780–1 (pb)

Published by
F. A. Thorpe (Publishing)
Anstey, Leicestershire

Set by Words & Graphics Ltd.
Anstey, Leicestershire
Printed and bound in Great Britain by
T. J. International Ltd., Padstow, Cornwall

This book is printed on acid-free paper

All men are caught in an inescapable network of mutuality, tied in a single garment of destiny

MARTIN LUTHER KING, JR.

What atonement is there for blood spilt upon the earth?

AESCHYLUS

CHAPTER
ONE

The legalized torture of socializing lined right up with premeditated murder when you added the requirement of fancy shoes.

That was Lieutenant Eve Dallas's stand on it, and she should know. She was a murder cop in fancy shoes about to socialize.

Moreover . . .

Whoever decreed that fancy shoes for females required sky-high skinny-ass heels rendering said shoes useless for any practical purpose — including walking — should be immediately subjected to every known manner of torture, legal or otherwise.

Surely by the almost-spring of 2061, in the freaking United States of America, useless skinny-heeled shoes should be banned. Beat with hammers, set on fire, then banned.

She walked in those damn shoes toward a swank penthouse, a tall, lanky woman in a slinky jade dress that shimmered with her movements while a fat, teardrop diamond shot fire from the chain around her neck.

The short, choppy brown cap of her hair set off the diamonds winking none too quietly at her ears. Her long brown eyes narrowed with dark thoughts.

Just who came up with the concept of the cocktail party? Eve wondered. Whoever did, by her decree, should join the originator of fancy shoes in the torture chamber. Who the hell decided it would be a freaking fantastic idea to create a custom where people stood around, usually at the end of a workday, making small talk while balancing a drink in one hand and a plate of tiny, often unidentifiable food in the other?

And, oh yeah, whoever came up with small talk as a social imperative? Straight into the torture chamber.

And while we're at it, throw the sick bastard who added the requirement of a gift every freaking time you turned around right in there with the others.

Because a sane person didn't want to have to think about what the hell to buy somebody who invited them to a damn party. A sane person didn't want to *go* to a party at the end of a workday and stand around in shoes with stupid skinny heels and balance weird food while making idiotic small talk.

A sane person wanted to be home, wearing comfortable clothes and eating pizza.

"Finished yet?"

Eve glanced toward the ridiculously handsome face of her husband — the guy responsible for the slinky of a dress, the damn shoes, and all the diamonds. She noted the amusement in those killer blue eyes, in the easy smile on that perfectly sculpted mouth.

It occurred to her that not only would Roarke enjoy the upcoming torture, but he could have deemed and decreed all the rules of it himself.

He was lucky she didn't pop him one.

2

"Need a few more minutes for the internal monologue?" he asked, the Irish in his voice just adding more charm.

"It's probably the most sensible conversation I'll have all night."

"Well now, what a thing to say. Nadine's first party in her new home will be full of your friends. They, and she, are smart, interesting people."

"Smart people are home drinking a brew and watching the Knicks kick some Kings ass on-screen."

"There'll be plenty of games yet to come." He gave her butt an affectionate pat as they approached the outer doors of Nadine Furst's penthouse. "And," he added, "Nadine deserves a party."

Maybe, maybe she could concede that one. The ace on-screen reporter, bestselling author, and now freaking Oscar winner had earned a party. But she herself, murder cop, lieutenant murder cop, deserved maybe wishing a hot case had fallen in her lap at the last minute.

As Nadine had earned her cred on the crime beat, she ought to understand.

Eve turned to face him again — that carved-by-romantic-angel's face framed with black silk. In her fancy shoes they stood pretty much eye-to-eye.

"Why can't a party be brew and pizza and the round ball game on-screen?"

"It can." He leaned over to brush his lips on hers. "Just not this one."

When the doors opened, the quiet, classy corridor filled with voices, music. Quilla, Nadine's teenage intern, stood in a black dress with a silver buckle at the belted waist, short-heeled red booties. The purple streaks in her hair glittered.

"Hey. I'm supposed to say good evening and welcome. And can I — May I," she self-corrected with a roll of her eyes — "take your coats?"

"How do you know we're not crashing?"

"Besides how I know you?"

Eve nodded. "Besides."

"Because lobby security has the guest list and all, and you had to clear through it to get up here. And if you're some doof who slipped by or lives here or whatever, Nadine would have you booted. The place is full of cops."

"Good enough," Eve decided as Roarke handed over their coats.

"You look lovely tonight, Quilla."

She flushed a little. "Thanks. Um, now I'm supposed to tell you to go right in, have a wonderful evening. There's a bar and buffet in the dining area as well as waitstaff passing food and beverages."

Roarke smiled at her. "You did that very well."

"I've done it about a million times already. Nadine knows a shitload — I mean, a lot of people."

"'Shitload' covers it," Eve said. And as they moved through the foyer, through the open doors, was just a little horrified to see she knew most of them herself.

How did that happen?

"Dig the dress, Dallas. The color's, like, bang."

"It's green."

"Jade," Quilla qualified.

"Exactly." Roarke sent Quilla a wink.

"So anyway, I can take the gift, too, unless you want to give it to her, like, personally. We've got a gift table in the morning room."

" 'Morning room'?"

"I don't know why it's called that," Quilla said to Eve. "But we're putting the hostess gifts in there."

"Great." She shoved the fancy bag at Quilla.

"Chill. Okay, hope you have a kick."

"A kick at what?" Eve wondered as Quilla headed off.

"I think it means have a good time. Which should speak to you," Roarke added, "as you enjoy kicking things." He trailed his fingers down her back. "Let's get you a drink."

"Let's get me several."

The passage to the bar, however, proved fraught with obstacles: people she knew. And those people had something to say, which cornered her into saying something back.

She was spared cold-sober small talk by passing waitstaff and Roarke's quick hands.

His quick thinking and smooth moves also saved her from the chatty chat of one of Nadine's researchers. "Darling, there's Nadine. We need to say hello. Excuse us."

With a hand on the small of Eve's back, he steered her away.

Nadine stepped in from the terrace. Eve deduced the party do — lots of tumbling curls — as Trina's handiwork. Though far from Nadine's usual polished, professional style, Eve supposed the streaky blond curls suited the dress. Strapless, short, snug, in hot-tamale red.

Those cat-green eyes scanned, landed on Eve and Roarke. She met them halfway, rose to the toes of her skyscraper red heels, and kissed Roarke enthusiastically.

"I'd say this proves our place is perfect for entertaining."

" 'Our place'?"

Nadine smiled at Eve. "Well, it is Roarke's building. A lot of your crew's out on the terrace. It's heated, and there's a small bar setup, another buffet."

Despite the fact that friendship often baffled her, Eve knew her job. "So where is it?"

Nadine fluffed her hair, batted her cat-green eyes. "Where's what?"

"Well, if you don't want to show it off —"

"I do. Yes, I do." Laughing, Nadine grabbed Eve's hand. With the skill of a running back, she snaked through people, wove around furniture, bolted up the curve of stairs and into her pretty damn swank home office. It held a couple of sofas in classy blue, chairs that picked up the classy blue in a swirly pattern on white, tables in slate gray that matched the T-shaped workstation in front of a killer view of New York City.

A square, recessed fireplace flickered in the left wall. The gold statue stood on the mantel above it. Eve moved closer, studied it. Weird-looking dickless gold dude, she thought, but the nameplate read NADINE FURST, and that's what counted.

But if they weren't going to give him a dick, why didn't they give him pants?

"Nice." Curious, she lifted, it, glanced over her shoulder. "It's got weight. Blunt-force trauma waiting to happen."

"Only you." Nadine slid an arm around Eve's waist. "I meant what I said in my acceptance speech."

"Oh, did you say something?"

Nadine added a solid hip bump and, with a laugh, Eve set the award down again.

"It's all yours, pal."

"Not nearly, but — I get to look at it every freaking day. So." Turning, she reached out a hand for Roarke's. "Let's go down and drink lots of champagne."

Jake Kincade stepped into the doorway. The rock star, and Nadine's heartthrob, said, "Hey."

His dark hair spilled and swept around a strong face currently sporting a three-day scruff. He wore black — not a suit, but black jeans with a studded belt, black shirt, and black boots Eve admired because they looked sturdy and comfortable.

How come, she wondered, *he* got to dress like a real person?

"How's it going?" he said to Roarke as they shook hands. "Looking prime, Dallas. Got to gander the gold guy? He's shiny, but you gotta wonder. If they weren't going to suit him up, why not give him his works? One or the other."

"Good God," Roarke murmured.

Jake flicked him a glance. "Sorry."

"No, not at all. It's only, I know my wife and have no doubt she thought exactly the same."

"Maybe. More or less. It's a reasonable question."

"At least Jake didn't look at it and see a murder weapon."

The creases in his cheeks deepening, Jake grinned down at Nadine. "Maybe. More or less. Anyway, you got another wave coming in, Lois. How does anybody know so many people?"

Now Roarke laughed, took Eve's hand. "I'm beginning to think it's a good thing I saw her first."

"Lots of cops," Jake said as they started out. "Other than that trip to Central, I haven't seen so many cops since . . ." He looked at Eve. "I probably shouldn't mention the time I was sixteen and used fake ID to get a gig in this club that got raided."

"Did you kill anybody?"

"Nope."

"We'll let it pass."

"Speaking of cops, did you know Santiago can rock a keyboard?"

"Ah . . . he plays piano?"

"Wicked," Jake confirmed. "Renn brought his keys — the whole band's here — and the chick cop pushed Santiago into getting down. Chick cop's got pipes."

"She can sing," Nadine interpreted for Eve. "And that's Detective Carmichael, Jake. I asked Morris to bring his sax," Nadine added.

"Let me tell you, the dead doc can smoke that sax. Hey, there's one of my breed."

8

Looking down as Jake did, Eve saw Mavis, a fountain of pale, pale blue hair, a frothy pink dress with a short, flippy skirt, blue shoes with towering heels fashioned out of a trio of shining silver balls.

Beside her, Leonardo resembled some sort of ancient pagan priest in a flowing vest shades deeper than his copper skin. His hair showered down to his shoulders in what looked like hundreds of thin braids. At the moment, Mavis talked to — bubbled over, more like — a tight little group.

Feeney — the captain of the Electronic Detectives Division — wore the same rumpled, shit-brown suit he'd worn to work. Beside him stood Bebe Hewitt, Nadine's big boss, in shimmery silver pants and a long red jacket, looking fascinated. Then big-eyed teenage Quilla, towered over by Crack. The sex-club owner also wore a vest. His stopped at his waist with lethal-looking studs on the shoulders, leaving his chest and torso bare except for muscles and tattoos.

Beside him, a woman — unknown — smiled easily. She wore classic New York black and had a face made exotic by knife-edged cheekbones and heavy-lidded eyes.

"The kid's a little young for a cocktail party," Eve commented.

"You're never too young to learn how to host an event, or how to behave at one," Nadine countered. She glided down the rest of the steps and over to greet Mavis.

"The kid's all right," Jake said to Eve. "Giving Nadine a run."

"Is she?"

He grinned with it. "Big-time. Campaigned to come tonight, and tossed out how she could do a three-minute vid report on the party — soft-news clip. The Quill's got it going." He tapped his temple. "I got a couple earsful of your An Didean project, Roarke. She's keeping her own ear to the ground there. I'd like to talk to you about that sometime."

"Anytime at all."

"Hey, Dallas." Mavis did a little dance on her silver balls, grabbed Eve in a hug. "This party is whipping it." She added a squeeze for Roarke, for Jake. "All my fave people, add food and adult beverage, and it's going on. I heard there's jamming on the terrace. Am I going to get in on that?"

"Counting on it," Jake told her. "How about we check out the venue?"

"I'm in."

"I'll get the drinks," Leonardo said.

After Leonardo kissed the top of her fountain of hair, Mavis beamed up at him. "Thanks, Honey Bear. Check you all later."

"I'm heading to the music." Feeney shot a finger at Eve. "Did you know Santiago can burn up the keys?"

"I heard that."

"Light under a bushel." With a shake of his head, Feeney took his rumpled suit out to the terrace.

"Bushel of what?" Eve wondered.

"I'll explain later. It's lovely to see you, Bebe."

"And both of you. I'm grateful, Lieutenant, for the work you and your detectives did in the Larinda Mars investigation."

"That's the job."

Bebe nodded, looked down into her drink. "We all have one. Excuse me."

"She's taking on too much of the blame." Nadine looked after her as Bebe slipped away.

"It wasn't on her."

"No." Nadine nodded at Eve. "But she's the boss. I'm just going to smooth that out. And send somebody with another round of drinks."

Crack shot his eyebrows up. "Cops do bring a party down."

The woman beside him gave him a sharp elbow. "Wilson!"

He only laughed. "You looking fine for a skinny white girl cop."

"You don't look half bad for a big black man dive owner."

"Down and Dirty ain't no dive. It's a joint. Yo, Roarke. I want you to meet my beautiful lady. This is Rochelle Pickering."

Rochelle extended a hand to Eve, then to Roarke. "I'm so happy to meet both of you. I've followed your work, Lieutenant, and yours, Roarke. Especially in regard to Dochas and An Didean."

"She's a shrink," Quilla announced, and Crack grinned at her.

"Kid shrink. Watch those steps, shortie, or she could come for you."

"As if," Quilla muttered, but melted away into the crowd.

"Wilson." Rochelle rolled her eyes. "I'm a psychologist, specializing in children. I've actually consulted at Dochas."

"I'm aware," Roarke told her, which had her blinking at him.

"That's . . . unexpected."

"Our head counselor speaks highly of you."

"She's a marvel."

As promised, another tray of drinks arrived.

"I just have to take a moment," Rochelle continued. "It hardly seems real I'm standing in this amazing space. That I'm meeting both of you. I met Nadine Furst and Jake Kincade, God, Mavis Freestone — who's exactly, just exactly, as delightful as I'd hoped she would be. And Leonardo, someone whose work I drool over. And I'm drinking champagne."

"Stick with me," Crack told her. "The sky's got no limits."

Eve had questions, a lot of questions. Such as, she'd never known anyone to call Crack by his given name. What made this woman different? And how did a kid shrink hook up with the streetwise owner of the D&D? And when did Crack go all — what was the word? Smitten, she decided, the word was *smitten*. When did he go all smitten?

She could see the appeal. The woman was built and beautiful, but . . . just who was she anyway?

Thinking, she made her way to Mira. It took a shrink, she considered, to shrink a shrink. And nobody beat the NYPSD's top profiler.

12

Mira rose from the arm of a sofa where she'd perched, kissed Eve's cheek. As usual, she looked perfect. The dress, the color of the deep red wine being passed around, floated down to her knees and ended in a thin border of some fancy lacework that matched the elbow-length sleeves. She'd swept back her mink-colored hair — now highlighted with subtle copper streaks courtesy of Trina (whom Eve, so far, had managed to avoid).

"Nadine's really made this place her own. Stylish, yes, but eclectic and comfortable. She looks happy."

"The gold dude upstairs and the rock star out on the terrace play in."

"They certainly do. I like him — the Oscar, of course, but Jake. I like him."

Eve glanced toward the terrace. Through the glass she saw Jake and Mavis, nearly nose to nose as they sang while Jake's fingers flew over the guitar.

"Yeah, he works. Sort of speaking of that. Do you know anything about this Rochelle Pickering who's glued to Crack?"

Mira's eyebrows lifted. "A little. Problem?"

"You tell me."

"None I'm aware of. I volunteer at Dochas a few times a year. I met her briefly when we were both there some months back. She struck me as very stable and dedicated. A serious woman."

"Yeah, so what's she doing with Crack?"

Mira looked over to where Crack and Rochelle swayed to the music on the terrace. "Apparently enjoying herself. It's a party, Eve. It's what people do at parties. And here's Dennis to prove it."

Dennis Mira walked toward them with a plate of finger food. He wore a black suit with a crisp white shirt and a striped tie. His tie was crooked, and his gray hair windblown. His eyes, the softest, sweetest green, smiled at Eve.

Her heart went into meltdown.

"You have to try one of these."

He took something off the plate, held it up to Eve's lips. She saw what looked like a heap of little chopped-up vegetables, all glossy with something and piled on a thick slice of zucchini. Something she'd have avoided putting anywhere near her mouth, much less in it, at all costs.

But those soft, sweet green eyes had her opening her mouth, letting him feed it to her.

"Delicious, isn't it?"

She managed an "Mmm" as the meltdown completed.

She thought if everyone had a Dennis Mira in their lives, she'd be out of work. No one would have another violent thought.

"Let me get you a plate."

"No." She swallowed, decided her veg quota was complete for a month. "I'm good." And found herself just a little disappointed when Mira straightened his tie.

"Such a happy party, isn't it?" he continued. "So many interesting and diverse people in one space. I always think the same when you and Roarke have a party. It takes interesting people to gather so many of the same together." He gave her that smile. "You look very pretty. Doesn't she, Charlie?"

If Eve had owned a blush, she'd have used it.

Roarke slipped up beside her — more chitchat — then the four of them wandered out to the terrace. She'd avoided the terrace, because that way lay Trina. But she couldn't be a coward all evening.

The music blasted over New York. Eve decided if anyone called a cop over noise violations, they'd find a whole bunch of them busting that reg, including her entire squad, a chunk of EDD — and the commander.

At the moment, Commander Whitney was dancing with Assistant Prosecuting Attorney Cher Reo. A lot of shoulder shaking and hip rocking was involved. Eve's partner, Detective Delia Peabody, executed some sort of wild swing and hop in time with her main man and EDD ace McNab.

Baxter, slick suit, no tie, flirted with the terrifying Trina, which was no problem, as Detective Horndog flirted with any and all females. Reineke and Jenkinson clicked glasses as they joined in on the chorus of whatever girl duet Detective Carmichael and Mavis belted out.

It seemed Carmichael did indeed have pipes. And Jenkinson's tie glowed like the moons that covered it.

Standing spread-legged, Santiago ran his fingers over a keyboard. What came out was definitely music. Who knew? Trueheart, Baxter's earnest young partner, sat with his girlfriend and Feeney. Eve swore Feeney's eyes shone — or glowed like Jenkinson's tie — as he watched the Avenue A drummer bang and crash the drums.

She spotted Garnet DeWinter. The forensic anthropologist huddled in conversation with the commander's wife while Morris made his sax wail.

EDD Callendar rushed out on the terrace, giving a "Woo!" as she dragged a laughing Charles with her into the shaking bodies. Eve supposed dancing skills had once been a job requirement for the former licensed companion. Dr. Louise Dimatto, his wife, hooked an arm through Eve's.

"I'd say this house is warmed."

"It's a heated terrace."

"No." On a laugh, Louise lifted her glass. "Housewarming, Dallas. This house is definitely warmed. So, who's that stunning woman dancing with Crack?"

"That's what I'd like to know." Eve shrugged. "Kid shrink."

"Really. I love her lip dye. If I tried that color, I'd look like a zombie. Is that — That's Detective Carmichael singing with Mavis."

"Yeah. She has pipes."

"I'll say. Well, since Callendar stole my man, I'm going to steal someone else's." She circled a finger in the air. "Feeney," she decided, and circled the dancers.

Roarke brought Eve another drink that washed away even the memory of zucchini. When they took the music down to slow and he turned her into his arms, she swayed with him under the swimming slice of moon.

Yeah, she thought, this house is warmed.

★ ★ ★

16

And if, on the drive home, she took out her PPC and did a quick little run on Rochelle Pickering, so what?

Roarke stretched out his legs in the back of the limo. "What are you up to there, Lieutenant?"

"Just checking something."

He waited only a beat. "Don't tell me you're running Rochelle."

"Okay."

"Eve, Crack's a big boy. Literally."

"Uh-huh."

"Eve," he said again, and laid a hand on hers. "You should know I've already run her."

"What? You're not a cop, and —"

"And she's not a suspect. She is, however, the top contender for the head therapist at An Didean."

"I thought you had one of those already."

"I did. She had a personal issue come up just last week, and is moving to East Washington to be with her son. I'm vetting the position again. Dr. Pickering was already a leading candidate when I went with Dr. Po."

"Does she know that?"

"Unlikely. I can tell you she's highly qualified, experienced, dedicated, comes strongly recommended. And has no criminal record."

"That you found. Okay, okay," she mumbled after his quiet stare. "If she had one, you'd have found it." She shrugged with it. "Save me time then."

"She's the only daughter and second child. Three siblings. Her father did time — twice — for assault, for illegals. Her younger brother did time, as a juvenile, for theft, possession — and as an adult for the same. He belonged to the Bangers."

"That's bad business. Their turf's narrowed, but they're still bad business."

"Most gangs are. He's been out of prison two years — just — completed rehab and, by all accounts, is clean and no longer affiliated with the Bangers."

Eve put that aside for later. Though the Bangers weren't as big and bad as they'd once been, they didn't just let go, either.

"Her father died in a prison incident when she was fifteen," Roarke continued, "and her mother self-terminated shortly thereafter. From that point — and reading between the lines, to a great extent prior — they were raised by their maternal grandmother. They grew up in the Bowery," Roarke added. "The roughest part of it."

"Banger turf."

"Yes. The oldest brother went to trade school, and has his own business — plumbing — in Tribeca. He's married, has a three-year-old daughter and another child on the way. The youngest is in law school, Columbia, on scholarship. The middle brother's been gainfully employed at Casa del Sol, Lower West Side, as a cook — a trade he apparently learned in prison — since he got out. He reports to his parole officer, attends regular AA meetings and, with his sister, volunteers at a local shelter twice a month."

"The Bangers don't let go."

"The Bangers are in the Bowery. Rochelle lives with her brother in a two-bedroom apartment in the Lower

West, well outside their territory. She had a hard and difficult childhood — something you and I know a great deal about. She overcame. It's hardly a coincidence she devoted her skills to the emotional welfare of children."

She knew his tones, his inflections. Knew him.

"You're going to hire her."

"It strikes me as a happy twist of fate we happened to meet her tonight. I'd already planned to contact her Monday morning to set up an interview. If I'm satisfied after that, and she's interested, I'll offer her the position, yes."

He shifted, trailed a finger down the shallow dent in her chin. "Unless you give me a solid reason not to."

She hissed out a breath. "I can't. I'm not going to knock her because one of her brothers was an asshole, because her father was another."

Maybe it worried her a little. But Roarke had a point. Crack was a big boy.

CHAPTER
TWO

To counteract the party, socializing, small talk, and fancy shoes, Eve had a quiet, off-duty Sunday. With no fresh murders landing in her lap, she spent the day sensibly. She slept late, banged Roarke like a hammer, ate crepes, took a three-mile virtual run on the beach, pumped iron until her muscles begged for mercy. To cap it off, she took a session with the master in the dojo, followed it up with a swim and pool sex.

Then she took a nap with the cat.

Afterward, she indulged herself with an hour on the shooting range — determined that next time she and Roarke went head-to-head there, she'd crush his fine Irish ass. Following a leisurely dinner by the fire, she snuggled up with that fine Irish ass and a bowl of butter-soaked popcorn to watch a vid where lots of stuff blew up.

To celebrate the end of a day without Dispatch butting in, she let Roarke bang her like a hammer. Then slept like a baby.

Refreshed, renewed, and feeling just a little guilty she'd chosen the nap instead of carving through her backlog of paperwork, she headed into Cop Central early on Monday.

Not early enough to avoid the snapping, snarling traffic or the average driver who lost any moderate skill behind the wheel due to a thin rain whipped by a blasting March wind. Still, she figured the nasty was just the thing to start off a day of cop work.

Plus, the ferocity of the wind grounded the ad blimps. It made a nice change to inch her way downtown without hearing the blasts about early spring sales and discounts on late winter cruises to wherever the hell.

Which was it, anyway? Early spring or late winter? Why couldn't March make up its mind?

She could be an optimist and go with early spring. It wasn't snowing or sleeting or shitting out ice. On the other hand, it was still freaking cold in that screaming wind, and those skies could decide to dump out snow anytime now.

Plus, optimists usually got their faces rubbed in the dirt of disappointment.

Late winter it was then, she decided as she pulled into her slot in Central's garage. She headed up, pleased to have a full hour before the change of shifts.

She found Santiago at his desk in the Homicide bullpen.

"Catch one?"

He looked up with tired cop's eyes. "Yeah. Carmichael's in the break room getting us some atomic coffee. Street LC picks up a john who wants a BJ. The transaction's cut short when they move to a doorway off Canal often used for same, and find a DB. John takes off, but the LC does her duty, finds a beat droid."

21

"Who's the DB?"

"Low-rent illegals dealer, and one who made considerable use of his own product. The LC recognized him from around the streets, and she'd seen him arguing with a local junkie about an hour before when she came out of the flop she uses next door for more involved services. But she doesn't know the junkie's name. Anyway, we got pulled in."

He glanced back as Detective Carmichael came out of the break room with two steaming mugs of cop coffee. "Ah yeah, my life for you." Santiago snagged one, gulped some down. "When we got there, a couple of other LCs got in on it. They're shooting the shit, and one of them pops up a name. He says he's pretty sure the first LC means Dobber. Loser type, according to the wit, who moved in — the same damn building as the doorway — a couple months before."

Santiago signaled for Carmichael to take over.

"So we leave the beat droids — we called in another — with the DB and the wit, head in to check out this Dobber. He's in his flop, flying high on the happy poppers he took off the dealer after he stabbed him in the throat. Asshole's still got the sticker, LT."

"Jabbed at her with it," Santiago added. "So we add that to the charges even though he fell on his face."

"Tripped over his own feet. Blood on the sticker matches the vic. Asshole confessed in under ten in Interview, claiming he had to kill the guy because he was overcharging. It was a matter of principle."

"So it's wrapped."

22

"And tight," Carmichael agreed. "Mope's got a sheet as long as your legs. Just got out after doing a nickel for assault. Add all that, he's in for life this time around."

"Good work."

"LCs did most of it. You're in early. Something up?"

"Paperwork." Eve started to step back, get to it, then frowned at Santiago. "I thought you played ball, not the . . ." She wiggled her fingers over imaginary keys.

"Both. I wanted baseball — practically lived for it. So the 'rents said, No problem, play all you want. As long as you keep your grades up, stay out of trouble, and take a year of piano lessons from your aunt. My aunt's a pain in the ass, so striking the deal showed I wanted ball. Turned out I liked the music, too, so I stuck with it."

"Now you're a cop."

"A base-running, keyboard-smoking cop who got to jam with Avenue freaking A."

"And you sing," she said to Carmichael.

"I kill when I can get to open mic night. And now I've sung duets with Mavis and Jake. Big night, right, partner?"

Santiago rapped his mug to hers. "Hey, we should start a cop band. Call it The Badge."

Eve retreated.

In her quiet office she programmed coffee from her AutoChef, then settled down at her desk. Because cop work wasn't only about locking up assholes who killed over happy poppers, she dug into schedules, requisitions, reports, budgets. The budget part required more coffee, but she felt she'd made solid headway before she heard Peabody's clomping stride heading toward her door.

"Santiago said you came in early."

"Paperwork."

"I'm going to finish up the report on the double we closed Friday. Man, I'm glad we wrapped that before Nadine's party. What a night."

Rather than the glittery, boob-hoisting number she'd worn for "what a night," Peabody now stood in sturdy trousers and a sensible jacket, with her dark hair in the weird little flip she'd taken to wearing rather than all swirled around.

"I hardly got to talk to you," Peabody added.

"You were busy shaking your ass most of the night."

"The more you shake your ass, the looser your pants. Plus, fun!"

Eve's communicator signaled. She saw Dispatch on the readout. "Fun's over."

Within twenty minutes, Eve stood with Peabody over the body crumpled on the second floor landing of a multitenant building. From the looks of it, the building had once been a warehouse, now converted to apartments. Working-class, primarily, and was, in Eve's estimation, decently maintained and poorly secured.

Neighbors identified the dead guy as Stuart Adler, apartment 305. With the uniforms keeping those neighbors back, Eve crouched down to confirm ID with her pad.

"Victim is confirmed as Adler, Stuart, age thirty-eight, of this address. Single. Divorced, no offspring.

Got some bumps here for drunk and disorderly, public drunkenness. Two rounds of mandatory rehab, and since it's not yet nine A.M. and I can smell the booze on him, that didn't stick."

His eyes, pale blue and shot with blood, stared up at her as she examined the body. "Neck's broken. From the head wound, the blood spatter, it looks like he took a hard fall down the steps. Then add the knife still sticking out of his abdomen."

"Stick him," Peabody suggested, "give him a good push. Down he goes. Except . . ."

"Yeah, except. The sticking — with an open pocketknife — came after the fall or there'd be more blood from the gut wound. Not much of a blade, not much of a gut wound."

"Gary did it!" somebody shouted from above.

"What? Are you crazy?"

At the sounds of a scuffle, Eve straightened. "Stay with the body," she told Peabody. "See if you can lift any prints off the knife. And bag that apple in the corner."

She went up the stairs, where a half dozen people were shouting at each other.

"Knock it off!" She jabbed a warning finger toward a woman with wild eyes and a helmet of hair that even the bluster of March wind wouldn't move. "Who's Gary?"

"I'm Gary." The man who raised his hand had a small beard, a shock of brown hair tipped gold at the ends. He wore a tweed jacket with a loosened tie and his shirt unbuttoned at the neck. "Gary Phizer. 304.

Across the hall from . . . from Stuart. I called the police. I called them. I was leaving for school — I'm a teacher — and I saw him. I ran down to him, but I could see . . ."

"You were fighting last night!" Helmet Hair glared at Gary. "You threatened to break his neck."

"I threatened to break his screen, Mildred, if he didn't turn down the volume. He was drunk, again," he said to Eve. "And he had some vid on — a lot of shouting, crashing, whatever. I live right across the hall. It was two in the damn morning when we got into it. I'd already asked him twice. He'd turn it down, then turn it up again. I was just trying to get some sleep."

"You had an altercation."

Nervously now, Gary shifted. "Well . . . I guess. He took a swing at me. He missed, and nearly fell over. And, okay, I nearly punched him, and I've never punched anybody in my life. But he was drunk and stupid. Yeah, I was pissed off, so we had some words. I told him if he didn't turn the screen down, I'd get a damn hammer and break it to pieces."

"You didn't think to call the police about the noise?"

Now he sighed. "I have before — and I'm not the only one. What're they going to do? They tell him to turn it down, he turns it down, maybe keeps it down a few days. Then he gets drunk again, and around and around we go."

"That's the truth." A woman, still in her pajamas, jiggled a baby. "My husband and I finally ended up soundproofing the wall. We're in 303. When Stu fell off the wagon — which was at least once a week — he got obnoxious. Gary didn't kill anybody, Mildred, and you know it. Any more than my Rolo did, and Rolo had plenty of words with Stu about the noise before we gave it up and soundproofed that wall."

She wagged the finger of her free hand at Mildred Helmet Hair. "So did you, Mildred, and the rest of us. So did the family in the apartment below his because he'd stomp around half the night when he was drinking. Or he'd crash into things. Didn't you have to call the MTs, Mildred, just last month when you heard a crash and found him sprawled out right here in the hall? Tripped," she told Eve, "broke his nose that time. Either knocked himself unconscious or passed out from the drink."

Mildred crossed her arms over prodigious breasts. "I'm not saying he wasn't a drunken idiot, but he didn't stab himself in the belly."

"Or he did," Eve countered. "Peabody! Bring up that apple."

Peabody brought up the evidence bag holding a sad-looking apple going sickly brown where the peel dangled away from the fruit.

"Did Gary like apples?"

Mildred's wild eyes teared up. " 'Apple a day.' That's what he'd say. He liked to peel them, try to get the peel off in one run. Said it was good luck if you did."

"What did he peel them with?"

"His pocketknife usually, I guess. But Gary —"

"Did you get prints off the pocketknife from the body, Detective?"

"Yes, sir. The victim's."

"We have work yet to do, but I'm going to tell you that — with the evidence and statements given thus far — this doesn't look like a homicide. It reads, at this point, like an accident. Mr. Adler was drunk, he was using his pocketknife to peel an apple as he started down the stairs. Your elevator's out of order."

"For four days now," Mildred said bitterly. "The landlord —"

"Ma'am, save that," Eve advised. "He trips, loses his balance, takes a bad fall. When he lands, breaking his neck, fracturing his skull, he also has the misfortune of landing on his open pocketknife."

"It sounds just like him," the woman with the baby muttered.

"Why don't you all go back in your apartments, let us do our job."

"I'm glad I didn't punch him," Gary said quietly. "I'm sorry I called him an asshole last night, but I'm glad I didn't punch him."

Accident or not, death had to be investigated, evidence gathered, statements taken. All that took a bite out of the morning. By the time Eve sat back down at her desk in Cop Central to write the report, Roarke's admin, Caro, led Rochelle into his office in Midtown.

Rochelle tried not to goggle. She'd never seen an office so big, so classy. When the man himself stood up from his really important desk, with that heart-stopping framework of New York behind him, and crossed that plush carpet to shake her hand, she let out a breathless laugh.

"I never expected to meet you at all, much less twice in a matter of days."

"I appreciate you coming in, and so quickly."

"Curiosity's a big motivator."

"How about some coffee? Or tea?"

"Whatever you're having's fine. Thanks."

"I'll take care of that."

The admin looked as classy as the office, to Rochelle's mind, with her gorgeous hair the color of fresh snow, the sharp suit that made Rochelle's — now in its third season — feel just sad.

"Let's have a seat." Roarke steered her to a sofa as plush as the rest of the place.

Wilson had assured her Roarke was "a regular dude," but come on! This was Roarke. Billionaire business-man, philanthropist, innovator. And toss in the outright mouthwatering.

His eyes really were as blue as they looked on-screen.

"You enjoyed the party."

"So much! I saw Avenue A in concert when I was in college. Nosebleed seats, but it was wonderful. As wonderful as it was, that impromptu concert on Nadine's terrace? Well, I run out of words. I've seen Mavis in concert, too, and now it's an entirely different perspective."

"You like music."

"All kinds." She looked at Caro as the admin brought over a tray of coffee, cups, cream, sugar. "Thanks so much."

"You're very welcome. How do you take it?"

"A little cream, one sugar." Of course, both were fake in her world.

"Thank you, Caro," Roarke said after she'd doctored the coffee.

As Caro closed the doors behind her, Rochelle lifted her cup. "I assume you want to talk about . . ." She trailed off as she took a sip. "Oh," she said. "My." She took another sip. "My entire system just stood up and cheered. There were some mentions in the Icove book and vid about your coffee. Now I know."

"I often think it's how I convinced my cop to marry me."

"It may have been a factor. In any case, I assume you want to talk to me about some of my work at Dochas. I know you take an active interest."

"It's a factor," he said, and smiled at her. "You're aware of the youth facility we're completing in Hell's Kitchen."

"Of course. Do you really believe you'll have it ready for students by May?"

He appreciated the term *students* — another point in her favor. "We're on track for that. I'm aware that in addition to the consulting you've done at Dochas, you've been on staff at the Family Counseling Center downtown for the past five years."

"Yes."

"No ambition to open your own practice?"

She shifted, met his eyes easily, smiled with it. "That takes more wherewithal than I have available, frankly. And, moreover, I prefer being part of a team. When you are, you use that team, pull on their strengths to help you do better work, to help treat the whole patient. From what I understand, that's exactly what An Didean will do. Counsel, educate, rehabilitate, provide structure and safety and, not the least of it, a community where young people can connect with each other, with adults who want to guide them toward a good, healthy, productive life."

"That's precisely it. The work over the past months hasn't only focused on rehabbing, remodeling the building itself, but in gathering a staff that not only understands the purpose, has the training and dedication to fulfill that purpose, but believes in it. I'm confident you check all those boxes."

He waited a beat, watched her eyebrows draw together. "Are you interested in having me consult at An Didean when needed as I do at Dochas?"

"Actually, I'm hoping you'd be interested in coming on staff in the position of head therapist."

"I — I'm sorry." Because the cup rattled in the saucer, Rochelle put her coffee down carefully. "I was under the impression Dr. Susann Po had accepted that position. Mr. Roarke —"

"Just Roarke."

"I have tremendous respect for Dr. Po, professionally and personally. While I appreciate — While I'm very flattered you'd consider me for the position, I could never undermine someone with Dr. Po's skills and reputation."

"Dr. Po would never have been offered the position if I didn't share your respect. Unfortunately, she's dealing with a family emergency, and is relocating to East

Washington, perhaps permanently. She regretfully resigned from the position late last week."

"Oh, I see. I hadn't heard. I'm very sorry. I . . ." Rochelle picked up her cup again, drank more coffee. Took a very careful breath.

"Dr. Po has nearly thirty years' experience in youth psychology and counseling. I have barely ten. It feels ungracious to ask, but I have to ask: Does this offer have to do with my relationship with Wilson?"

"Last fall when I offered Dr. Po the position — a key position in a project that's very important to me, to my wife — I did so because of her experience, reputation, and a variety of other reasons. There were five names, five highly qualified people I considered before making that offer. You were second on that list."

"Oh."

"I don't believe you were in a relationship with . . . Wilson at that time."

"No, no we weren't. That is, we met near the end of December. So we've known each other for a few months. But we didn't begin to . . . We didn't get involved right away."

"I can assure you, I wasn't aware you knew each other at all. In fact, it was an interesting surprise for me to meet you Saturday at Nadine's party, with Wilson, as I had decided only that morning to ask you to come in, to speak to you about the position."

"I'm very glad to hear that. If I'd known this was an interview for such a vital position, I'd have come more prepared."

"We've already had most of the interview." Because he sensed genuine nerves now, Roarke smiled at her again. "Saturday night, and over coffee here. Rochelle, you wouldn't have been on the list last fall if I hadn't already done my due diligence. I'm aware of your educational qualifications, your professional work and reputation, your volunteer work, including the hours you've given to Dochas. Either I personally or Caro has spoken with a number of your colleagues, your superiors, your professors, and so on. As with everyone else who'll be a part of An Didean, I complete this process as we are here. A face-to-face."

The way her stomach jittered, she almost expected to see the skirt of her suit bounce. "A man with your — let's say reach — would be aware that my father died in prison. He was an addict, a troubled, often violent man. And that my mother's addiction to him and to the substances he introduced her to contributed to her suicide."

"I am. We make our choices, don't we, to overcome the brutality of our youth or to follow that path into the cycle of it. I don't need your skills to intuit that the path you took was influenced by your own childhood, and the desire to help the vulnerable, the defenseless. I've added that to your list of qualifications.

"More coffee?"

Now her throat wanted to close. "Actually, I could use a glass of water."

"Of course." He rose, strolled across the room to a little alcove, took a bottle of water from a cold box, poured a glass. "If you have an interest in the position, we can discuss more details. Job description, structure, salary, and so on."

"That would be . . ." She took the water he brought her, took three careful sips. "It's an important decision, life changing really. I should take some time, think it through before we . . ."

She set the water down, turned to him. "Am I crazy? Am I stupid? No, I'm not either of those things." She let out a rolling laugh. "Of course I'm interested. I'm staggered and flattered and working up to giddy while I'm trying to be sober and dignified."

She had to stop, laugh again, pat a hand on her heart while he smiled at her.

"And, yes, I'd like very much to talk about the details of your amazing offer. I'd really like to tour the building. I'd like to see where the children will live, the educational and recreational facilities, the group and individual counseling areas. All of it."

"Of course," he said again. "How about now?"

Her eyes widened, blinked. "How about . . . *now?*"

"We can discuss those details while I give you a tour. I'm interested in what you think."

She picked up the water, drank again. "Now works."

After the tour, and the handshake that concluded it, Roarke went back to his headquarters. He stopped by Caro's office.

"You can send the contract, as is, to Dr. Pickering, Caro."

"I'm glad to hear that. She's extremely qualified, clearly has the passion. And while I know you're sorry to lose someone of Dr. Po's standing, Rochelle Pickering's relative youth may add something. Plus, I got a good feeling from her."

"Did you?"

"She was overwhelmed, and struggling not to show it. Grateful for the opportunity, and not afraid to show that. I liked the mix."

"So did I. You can start juggling in those meetings you juggled out, Caro."

"You've got the 'link conference with Hitch in San Francisco and Castor's team in Baltimore in . . ." She checked her wrist unit. "Eight minutes. I juggled that back in when you texted you were on the way back."

"What would I do without you?"

"To prove your point, I switched your lunch meeting to the executive dining room. Why go out in that ugly weather again? And it'll save you the time you lost this morning."

"Perfect, as usual. Are you due for a raise?"

She fluttered her lashes. "Always."

He laughed, walked to his office.

By the time he got home that night, the rain had sputtered out, and the wind had toned down to stiff with the occasional angry gust. It flapped at his topcoat — a treasured Christmas gift from Eve — streamed through his hair, and made him grateful for the warmth of home.

Summerset, always at the ready, took his coat while the cat wound pudgily through his legs.

"An evening made for a whiskey by the fire," Summerset commented.

"You're not wrong." He had work yet, Roarke thought, but he'd get to it. "Let's have one."

He wandered into the parlor, dealt with the fire while Summerset poured the whiskey.

He had a fondness for this room, the rich colors, the gleam of antiques, the art he'd chosen. He settled into it while the wind rattled the bare branches of the trees outside the windows.

Summerset — his father in all but name, and the person who ran the house as efficiently as Caro ran his office — sat across from him.

He had thick hair the color of good pewter; dark, canny eyes; a thin, angular face of deep hollows Eve liked to call ghoulish. And had, once upon a time, saved a ragged Dublin street rat from a life of misery, and worse.

Roarke lifted his whiskey in a toast. "*Sláinte*. And how was your day?"

"Wet this morning for the marketing. But that afforded me and our friend there," he added as Galahad leaped onto Roarke's lap, and sprawled — belly up — over it, "an enjoyable afternoon in the kitchen. I had a yen to make fresh pasta, which I haven't done in some time."

At Roarke's puzzled look, Summerset sighed. "The noodles themselves, boy. Fresh. I've made up some capellini in a sauce with some bite. I think the lieutenant might enjoy it."

"We'll try it tonight."

"Speaking of the lieutenant, I did a bit of laundry as well. The sweatshirt, or what's left of it, from the Academy —"

"Isn't worth your life," Roarke interrupted.

"It's a rag."

"A sentimental one." He sipped his whiskey, lazily scratched the cat's belly with his other hand. And thought of the gray button he kept in his pocket. "We all need our talismans, don't we? On another front, I met with Dr. Pickering this morning, and gave her a tour of An Didean. She's taking the position."

"I'll make a note of it. She strikes me, from the reports I've read, as very suitable. And the progress on An Didean?"

"On schedule. They've finished the main kitchen, nearly completed all the bathrooms and the training kitchen. Most of the work's down to cosmetics now. We should have the Use and Occupancy in about a month, time enough for the staff to set up, for us to load in furniture, supplies, and so on."

"It'll be a fine thing for the children who'll make their home there."

"It will." Roarke set his glass aside, nudged the cat. "I've some work to finish up before Eve gets home."

"Whenever that might be."

"Whenever. Finish your whiskey, and thanks in advance for the pasta."

When Roarke went out, the cat obviously considered his options, then decided on Summerset's lap.

As Roarke had done, Summerset sipped his whiskey and scratched Galahad's belly.

"Will she have made it through the day without getting bloodied, do you think? Well, we'll hope for it."

CHAPTER
THREE

She came home unbloodied, but with her brain scorched. Why, why had she opted to end her day as she'd started it? With paperwork, with numbers, percentages, reports?

Whatever smug satisfaction she gained from being completely caught up would die within twenty-four hours when it piled up again.

She stepped in out of the whoosh of wind to face the looming presence of Summerset.

"Neither late nor bleeding." His eyebrows shot up in mock surprise. "One expects a tympani."

She didn't know what the hell a tympani was, but knew damn well he'd had that one ready. Two could play. She studied him as she shrugged out of her coat and the cat did his greeting wind and rub.

"Did you go out in this today?"

"I had marketing."

"That explains the reports of a flying skeleton." She tossed her outdoor gear on the newel post and, considering it a draw, headed upstairs with Galahad trotting behind her.

She considered going straight to the bedroom, ditching the work clothes, but habit sent her to her home office. She heard Roarke's voice from his adjoining office. Something about numbers — why was it always numbers? At least she didn't have to decipher these.

He'd turned on the fire, and that made a nice welcome home. She decided the next step of welcome equaled a really big glass of wine.

As she chose one, opened it, it occurred to her she hadn't had much taste for wine pre-Roarke. Could be, she thought, due to the fact that the wine she could afford in those days had been one dubious step up from horse piss.

She poured two glasses — Roarke's Italian label because she had a yen for spaghetti and meatballs — and wandered into his office. She'd intended to simply set his glass on his desk and leave him to finish up the 'link meeting, but he signaled her to wait.

She noted the two people — one male, one female — on-screen. Everybody talked about those numbers, and margins and whatever the fuck. So she sipped her wine — definitely not horse piss — and walked over to his windows.

A fresh gust had the trees, right now still as bony as Summerset, bowing and swaying. She could see the lights of the city beyond the gates. Right then, from that vantage, it seemed more fanciful than the house she lived in.

Only minutes before she'd been in the thick of it, pushing and shoving her way through traffic, watching the sea of pedestrians surge through intersections.

Every one of them, she thought, in a desperate rush to get somewhere.

Now she was out of it, and somewhere — exactly where — she wanted to be. Added to it, an evening without murder clawing at her brain.

Maybe she should pull out a cold case at random, see if fresh eyes and new angles could heat it up.

"All right then," Roarke concluded. "I'll have a look at the revised proposal tomorrow. Enjoy your evening." He ended transmission. "Though you'll be working through the evening if you want this to fly." He waited for Eve to turn, then lifted his wine. "Thanks. You read my mind."

"I wanted wine because my brain's fried from spending two big hunks of my day with numbers and reports. You're drinking it because you're half celebrating dealing with them."

"Isn't it lovely that wine covers both? Since you had two hunks of your day free to deal with numbers and reports, I assume you've no new case."

"Caught one, closed it."

"There's my clever cop." He swiveled his chair, patted his knee in invitation. "Let's hear about it."

She gave him a stony look, then opted to ease a hip onto the side of his workstation as he often did on hers. "Drunk tripped going down the stairs in his apartment building while peeling an apple with his pocketknife. Broke his neck and stabbed himself in the gut. Pretty much simultaneously according to the ME. Tox came back with a .20 BAC. Rotgut brew on top of it. He took the spill before nine this morning."

"There's a sorry end. My own morning held what I believe will be a happy beginning. I met with Rochelle Pickering, offered her the position and a tour of An Didean. She accepted."

"That's really quick. Are you sure —"

"I am, yes," he said. "But I have her file right here. Why don't you look it over before dinner? If we're agreed, I'll send her copy of the signed contract."

Really damn quick, she thought. "You signed it?"

"Signed by her, and witnessed, late this afternoon after she had it looked over. Signed by me, and witnessed, before I left for home. But not yet sent, so not yet official."

He studied her, his cynical cop, over another sip of wine. Behind her hung a portrait she'd given him of the two of them on their wedding day.

"This is your place as much as it's mine, so I waited until you could weigh in."

"I'm not going to . . ." She searched for a word, fell back on one of his. "Bollocks this up. You've vetted her."

"Read the file." He patted his lap again.

"That's a sneaky way of getting me to sit on your lap."

"If I didn't have sneaky ways, neither of us would be in this very pleasant office space."

He had her there. Hell, he had her everywhere anyway. She sat on his lap. And when he brought up his reports on Rochelle, she began to read.

It took less than fifteen minutes for her to admit she was being a hard-ass. "Okay, okay." She waved at the report on-screen. "She bangs the drum. You need a top shrink, and the kids deserve one not only with the chops, but who cares."

"They do. I'll add I liked her quite a lot. As did Caro."

Two people, Eve admitted, who read people well and didn't fall for bullshit easily.

"I'd still like to know where some seriously educated kid shrink met the bust-your-balls owner of a sex club."

"I asked her about that today. Interestingly, at a memorial service, as you and I met as well."

"One of her patients?"

"No, a friend of one of her patients. The girl, not yet sixteen, took her own life. Rochelle went to the service with her patient. Crack knew the girl and her family, as well as Rochelle's patient and his family. This was Christmas week."

"Suicide Central," Eve murmured.

"Sadly enough. Rochelle saw how the boy related to Crack, and asked if he'd consider training as a mentor for disadvantaged and/or troubled youths."

"Huh. He'd be good at it."

"So she thought. He thought not, then later reconsidered, and they met to talk about it. They clicked on several levels. She was very open about her middle brother, and believes that while Crack isn't his mentor, he's been another steadying influence. So?"

"Send the contract. She's probably pacing the floor waiting for it. Send it, and let's go eat spaghetti and drink more wine."

He kissed the back of her neck, sent the contract. "As it happens, pasta's just what I'd planned for tonight. Summerset made fresh."

"Meatballs?"

"The pasta — the actual noodles."

"You can do that? Why do that?"

"I can't tell you, but it apparently pleases him. It's capellini — spicy."

"Does it have meatballs?"

"We'll find out."

While Eve discovered zucchini — again? — instead of meatballs, Rochelle let out a wild scream in the tiny corner of her bedroom she'd used for office space since Lyle moved in.

She followed it with a whoop, then a dance.

She whirled around when Lyle rushed in.

"What the hell, Ro?"

"Oh! I didn't know you were home."

"Just walked in. I thought you were fighting off a rapist or some shit."

"No. Nothing." She laughed, waved a hand. "You've got the night off. I forgot."

"First night off in eight straight." Frowning at her, he leaned on her doorjamb.

He'd put back on the weight he'd lost to illegals and prison, and had a fit, healthy look that warmed her heart. And though she liked him clean shaven — he was handsome! — she didn't mind the strip of scruff around his jawline. He wore his hair in short dreads.

Best of all, his eyes, nearly the same shade as hers, remained clear. A little tired, maybe, but clear.

"I'll fix you something to eat."

He pointed at her. "You're dressed fancy again."

"Not really fancy." She did have on her second-best dress — the blue one with the banded cuffs — but she didn't think it rated fancy. "I'm taking Wilson to dinner, but I've got time to fix you something."

"I'm a cook, remember?"

Yes, he was, she thought — and it thrilled her.

"A cook with a night off. Missed having you around," she added and walked over to hug him. There'd been a time he wouldn't have returned the hug, but he did now, even lifted her a scant inch off the floor along with it.

"Why'd you scream?"

"I was just — Oh, I can't hold it in. Why should I? It's . . ."

He took a hard grip when her eyes filled. "You tell me what's wrong, Ro. Right now."

"Not wrong. Perfect. Look at my face! I'm just so damn happy. It's why I screamed, why I forgot about your night off. Why I can barely remember my name, except it's right there, on the contract."

He glanced toward her miniscreen. "What contract?"

"For my new job. For my dream job. Hell, here I go again."

She screamed, grabbed him, and danced.

"You've got a job. You love your job. What dream job?"

"As head therapist at An Didean. The shelter and school."

"Yeah, I've heard something about that place. Funny name. Wait. That's a Roarke deal, right? You're going to work for Roarke and the cop skirt."

Grinning like a fool, Rochelle poked him in the chest. "She'd bust you for the skirt, but yes. You don't have a problem with that, do you?"

"Why would I? Man, Roarke turns shit into gold all the damn time. It must be a good place or you wouldn't go into it."

"It will be, a really good place. It's scheduled to open in May. I have so much work to do to get ready!"

"Wait, back up. You said head. Like chief? Like numero uno?"

"With a staff of eight counselors, therapists, and an administrative assistant." She put a hand to her ear as if listening. "Do you hear that word, Lyle? Staff!"

His whole face lit up, for her. "Jesus, Ro. This is a big fucking deal. Like monster fucking big. MFBFD."

"I can hardly get my breath. It's why I asked Wilson out to dinner. I wanted to tell him. You know what? I'll tell him to come over here, we'll order in and celebrate like maniacs."

"Oh hell no, you take your fancy ass out with your man, have a big night. I was figuring on cleaning up, heading to a meeting, then over to see Gram and the gang. I haven't seen her in a couple weeks, and she'll skin my ass if it's much longer. I'll be late for dinner, but she's always got leftovers. Then I thought I'd just bunk there or at Martin's tonight."

Or he did now, to give his sister and her man the place to themselves.

"Can I tell 'em?"

"Yes. Absolutely yes. And that I'll get in touch tomorrow. Oh, Lyle, you should see the place. I got a tour today — from the boss! It's just amazing. The thought and care that's going into it. We're going to change lives. We're going to save lives."

"You saved mine."

"No, honey, you —"

"You're a freaking wonder, Ro. I'm real proud."

"So am I, of you." She cupped his face. "So am I."

"Get going. Get your fancy on, and tell Crack I said to take you dancing. Maybe you come by tomorrow lunchtime. I'll cook you up something special."

"I'm going to do all of that." She grabbed her coat, stuck her arms in. "This is going to make a big difference for us, Lyle. Such a difference. You tell Gram to plan a big family dinner for your next night off. We're going to celebrate till we drop.

"Crap, I'm going to be late." She snagged a scarf and her purse on the run. "I love you, Lyle."

"Back at you squared, Ro."

She bubbled like a fountain all through dinner. Crack couldn't stop grinning at her as she told him about the meeting, the tour, the offer, the contract. Her plans — already so many plans.

It was one of the things he loved about her. She planned ahead. She had a skill for being in the moment, focused on that moment and the person, but she also knew how to plan ahead.

She knew how to see what was, and what could be.

"Who knew when I met Roarke on Saturday night I'd end up working for him? I think Nicci did. You know my supervisor, Wilson. I think she had a feeling. Anyway, she said she did. I felt I had to tell her I'd accepted the offer, and was just waiting for the contract on Roarke's end. She was happy for me, Wilson."

"Sure she was. She ain't no fool."

"I'm going to miss working with that team. But oh, I'm going to have a new team, and with the tools we'll have, the financing, the educators, it's going to —" She broke off, laughing. "You need to stop me because I can't stop myself."

"Not in this lifetime. My Dr. Ro, head of the head shrinkers." He put his big hand over hers. "How 'bout I get a tour of the place."

"Yes, you *have* to see it. It's so well planned, so inclusive. It has such heart. Wilson, you remember that awful thing about all those girls, the remains they found when they started the work there?"

"I remember."

"They've got a roof garden, so the students can plant and grow things, so they can have places to go sit outside. They've put a memorial to those poor girls up there. It's sad, but it's also uplifting. Their lives mattered, and they're remembered. It's beautiful, Wilson."

"I told you before we went to Nadine's how they're about the best people I know. Don't know how I'd've gotten through after that crazy bastard killed my sister, my baby."

Now Rochelle brought that big hand to her cheek, cradled it.

"That skinny white girl held on to me when I fell to pieces. She got justice for my baby. And the two of them, they planted that tree for her in the park. Kindest thing anybody ever did for me."

He gave her hand a squeeze, picked up his beer to steady himself. "Now I know they're smart enough to hire up the best. 'Cause that's what you are. I love you, Ro."

"Wilson." He made everything inside her feel light and right. "I love you, too. It's so strange, isn't it? We met at such a sad moment, and here we are, making something so good together. I feel my life's taking such a turn. Lyle finding himself again, you, now this. I can look back, remember, even *feel* how hard, scary, rocky things were. And now all this. I feel blessed, Wilson."

"You earned every blessing."

She smiled, leaned toward him. "How about we skip dessert?"

"You? My sweet-tooth lady?"

"Walt's at the dorm for sure. Lyle's staying at Martin's. We have the apartment to ourselves. All night."

"I'll get the check."

She giggled her way up the steps, grabbed him outside the apartment door for a steamy kiss. There was so much of him, all hard and cut and strong. He made her feel delicate when she was anything but.

She fumbled with her keys for the police-grade locks she'd paid to have installed. And reminded herself they'd be able to afford a better place, a better neighborhood, very soon.

Crack took the keys, unlocked the door. He swung her through with every intention of completing the circle until her back was against the closed door, and he could get good and started.

They both saw Lyle slumped in the chair in the tiny living space, vomit on his shirt, his eyes glazed and fixed, and the pressure syringe empty in his lap.

"No!" She started to leap forward, but Crack wrapped around her, held her firm against that closed door.

"You can't touch him, Ro. You can't touch anything."

"You let me go! Lyle. Oh my God, Lyle. Let me go, goddamn it."

She fought him, a strong, desperate woman. She cursed him, beat at him, but he held her back. Held her when she went limp. Held her as he lowered with her to the floor.

"No, no, no. Lyle. Please, please. Maybe he's —"

"Baby, my baby, he's gone. I'm so sorry. I'm so sorry, Ro."

"He wouldn't. He wasn't using, I swear it. He wouldn't do this. He'd never do this."

"I believe you. Look at me now. Just at me." When she did, tears streaming, he kept rocking, but kept his eyes on hers. "We need the cops. I'm going to get somebody you can trust. I'm going to get Dallas."

Eve nearly ignored the signal from her 'link. Dispatch would use the comm, and she really had nothing to say to anybody else. Especially since Roarke had accepted her shooting-range challenge.

She was going to take him down.

But she glanced at the readout, saw Crack's name. She figured in all the time she'd known him he'd tagged her maybe once, so something must be up.

She said, "Yo."

And Roarke, just unbuttoning his shirt to change for the challenge, saw the cop take over in the next finger snap.

"Don't touch anything. Don't approach the body. Go out, lock up. Wait for me outside the scene. I'm on my way."

Roarke had already buttoned his shirt again, and now handed her the weapon harness she'd taken off. "Who's dead?"

"Rochelle Pickering's brother, in their apartment. Looks like an OD."

"Ah, Christ." He thought of the woman who'd glowed as they'd toured An Didean, and felt sick at heart for her. "I'll drive. I have the address."

"Did she talk about him today?" Eve asked as they jogged downstairs.

"She did, yes." As they moved, he remoted her vehicle from the garage. "She was very open about him, the trouble he'd been in, his time in prison, in rehab."

He got the coats Summerset had tucked away, handed hers over. "He asked to live with her after this bout and his time in a halfway house, asked her to help him stay straight, to give him a year."

The car rolled up as they went out into the wind.

"She told me he got a job, hasn't missed a day of work. In fact, was given a raise just last month. He'd cut off all ties with the Bangers, goes regularly to meetings, mended fences with his brothers and the friends he'd had before he started using."

She could check the record on the way, but she knew Roarke would have researched Lyle Pickering already. She'd use him as her data source for now.

"Give me a sense of him."

Roarke rattled off the address to the in-dash as he drove to the gates. "If memory serves, he's about twenty-six. His trouble started in his early teens. Truancy, petty theft, tagging buildings. Then the illegals, the gang. A bust for possession and malicious mischief while still a minor. A stint in juvie, rehab, community service. He lived in one of the gang flops for a couple years. I think you'll find your Illegals division has considerable on him."

"Yeah." She'd be checking that.

"He took the last bust as an adult, in a fight with a rival gang member. Both had knives over the legal limit, and he had possession of Zeus, Erotica, and other substances with a street value of around six thousand on him."

"Which is likely what the fight was about."

"He went down harder for that one, and that hard time appeared to slap him straight. He completed rehab, got a cooking certificate and parole — the halfway-house bridge, then the condition that he live with a family member for a year, sought gainful employment, and so on. For the last year, he's met all the parole provisions, submitted to the random drug tests, and apparently, through his own initiative, meets the prison therapist about once a month over coffee."

"So on the surface, textbook rehabilitation. And now he's dead, with his works and vomit in his lap."

"So the cop thinks, beneath the surface: once a user — of illegals and people — always a user?"

"My closest friend was a grifter," she reminded him. "The cop thinks people can change. It's just, they don't more often than they do. Almost never do. And the cop has to see the DB, the scene before making any conclusions."

"You haven't pulled in Peabody."

"If, after observing the scene, examining the DB, establishing the timeline, my conclusions are he slipped, fell back, and OD'd, there's no need to. Otherwise, I'm going to spoil her night.

"Rough neighborhood," she added as she looked around the shadowy streets lined with tat parlors, sex clubs, prefab walk-ups tossed up after the Urban Wars.

"Yes. Between them, they make a decent living, but there are expenses. The younger brother's in law school, partial scholarship, part-time job, but Rochelle and her older brother are supplementing the tuition and dorm fees. It's considerable."

She spotted Crack — you couldn't miss a man his size — and Rochelle outside a five-story prefab. Roarke squeezed between a couple of junkers at the curb. In a neighborhood like this, she thought, the choice was junkers or mass trans.

Most couldn't afford the junker.

Crack opened her door, reached for her hand. "Thanks for this."

She met his eyes, the sorrow in them, nodded.

Roarke went directly to Rochelle and, because it was his way, put his arms around her. "I'm sorry. I'm so very sorry."

She fell to weeping. "He wouldn't do this. He wouldn't do this to himself, to us. He'd never —"

Because it was her way, Eve stepped forward. "This is hard for you, but I need to ask you a couple of questions. When did you last see your brother?"

"It was right before I left to meet Wilson for dinner. It was right after the contract came through. I think about seven. I think."

"Yes, I sent the contract about seven," Roarke confirmed.

"He'd just gotten home. He'd worked the lunch shift and the happy hour. He had his first night off in eight nights. He was tired and happy. He was happy. He was happy for me. And he said he was going to clean up, go to a meeting, then over to mooch leftovers from Gram, bunk at Martin's tonight. He wouldn't do this."

"Okay. I need you to go somewhere and wait. Crack, your place isn't far. Why don't you take Rochelle there?"

"No. Please. I need to be here. I can't leave him alone."

"You need to get out of the cold," Eve told her, "and wait. I'm going to look after Lyle. He won't be alone."

"You need to trust her, Ro. You come on home with me, then Dallas is going to come over in a little while. I've got the keys here." Crack pulled them out of his pocket, handed them to Eve.

Between her master and her master thief, she didn't need them, but she took them.

"I need to tell my brothers, my grandmother."

"Why don't you hold off on that? You'll be able to tell them more when I've finished here."

With visible effort, Rochelle pulled herself together, and her eyes went fierce as they met Eve's. "I know one thing I'll tell them. He didn't do this to himself. I know the signs like I know my own name. Depression, evasion, withdrawal, agitation, anger. I know what I saw in my brother, and he wasn't using again. Don't you go up there looking at him like he was some loser. Don't you do that."

"He's a victim, one way or the other. And he's mine now. I'll do my best for him."

"Come on now, Ro, we're going to walk awhile. It'll do you good to walk awhile." With an arm wrapped around her waist, Crack led her away.

Eve let out a breath, took the field kit Roarke had already retrieved from the trunk. "Whatever I find up there, it isn't going to be easy for her."

"You'll find the truth, and that's all she can ask for."

She studied the building. A squatting piece of crap with no cameras, no visible security, and what she assumed would be a couple of half-assed locks on the exterior doors. A buzz-in system to make even the half-assed locks useless.

A basement unit where litter scattered over the pad of concrete, and the streetlights left deep shadows.

The perfect place for dark deeds.

She noted a street LC picking up a john near the east corner, and the guy hovering in a doorway toward the west corner who was practically wearing a sign announcing: Illegals Dealer Waiting for a Mark.

A couple of boys trying to look tough swaggered by across the street, hoods up, hands in pockets. Aiming for the dealer, she concluded.

Might as well gum up those works.

"Hey!" She held up her badge. "NYPSD!"

The boys took off in a non-tough trot. The dealer melted away.

"You know they'll be back inside the hour."

"Sure." She shrugged that off. "But those assholes have to go change out of the pants they just pissed in first."

She walked to the building, shook her head at the locks. "Why bother?"

Before she could try one of the three keys, Roarke took out a tool, went through the locks in seconds.

The entranceway — small, dark, smelling of old piss — had a stairway straight up, and a chain over the skinny door of an elevator that likely hadn't operated since they'd thrown up the building.

"She's on the second floor," Roarke said as they started up a stairway just as dark and smelly as the entrance.

Someone had cared enough to try to paint over the graffiti tagging the walls, and she caught a whiff of something like bleach, so maybe the same somebody had tried to eradicate the stewing germs.

As they moved above the first floor she heard music banging, a screen show muttering, an argument in midstream.

On the second, she heard someone laughing in what sounded like genuine enjoyment, a buzz of voices.

She studied the locks on the Pickering door.

"They're decent." She engaged her recorder. "Dallas, Lieutenant Eve, and Roarke, entering the premises with the permission of the tenant to investigate a suspicious death."

For the record, she used the keys, opened the door.

It smelled of lemon-scented cleaner and death.

The lights were on full. The living area held a sofa, two chairs, a couple of tables, some photos, and dust catchers. It stretched — barely — to include a tiny eating area off what she assumed was a kitchen.

Lyle Pickering slumped in one of the chairs and, as Crack had told her, had a syringe in his lap, a homemade tourniquet on his left arm where the sleeve of his sweatshirt had been shoved up.

The sweatshirt announced him as a Knicks fan. He wore baggies and well-worn high-tops. Vomit, crusting, ran down the shirt.

She turned from him to study the locks. "No sign of forcing, locks or jamb. No signs of struggle in here."

Out of the kit, she took a can of Seal-It, sprayed her hands, her boots, handed it off to Roarke.

"Must I?"

"Yeah. Take a look at the kitchen, then the bedrooms while I deal with the body."

She went step-by-step, confirming ID. "Victim is identified as Pickering, Lyle, age twenty-six of this address."

"There's a glass of water overturned on the counter in the kitchen," Roarke told her. "And what I'd assume is the victim's 'link on the floor."

"That's interesting. Like this small, shallow nick on the vic's throat and the faint bruises on his wrist are interesting."

"Should I contact Peabody for you?"

Eve studied the body, especially that left arm where a gang tat — a fist encircled by the word *Bangers* — showed distinct signs of a removal process. Before she answered, she put on microgoggles, studied that arm.

And spotted the tiny — and fresh — needle mark on the first knuckle of the fist. The circular mark from the pressure syringe hit at the curled thumb.

"Yeah. Yeah, why don't you do that?"

She sat back on her heels. "How do you kill a recovering addict if you're bright but not real bright?"

Standing back, Roarke studied Rochelle's brother with pity. "You stage it to look like a self-inflicted overdose."

"Yeah. Better to have hit him on the street, make it look like a mugging, a gang retaliation, a wrong-place-wrong-time. Come here, into his home, shoot him up for his sister to find? Bright, not real bright. And personal."

She nodded, reached in her kit for the next tool. "Yeah, pull Peabody in. We're going from what looked like murder this morning and turned into accidental, to what looks like accidental OD but is murder."

CHAPTER
FOUR

After he contacted Peabody, Roarke skirted around Eve, moved down a short hallway toward the two facing bedrooms and the single bath at the end.

He identified Rochelle's not only from the floral spread on the bed and the frilly shade over the lone window but by the neatly made bed with no clothes scattered over it or the floor. She'd squeezed in a small desk for a work area in the corner.

He turned to the brother's room.

A thin, gray duvet covered the not-as-neatly made bed. In the closet, clothes heaped in a plastic basket or hung — a number crookedly — on a rail.

A two-drawer dresser held a framed copy of the Serenity Prayer. A stubby jar, empty, carried a handwritten label.

Save It!

The top drawer hung crooked, jammed a bit when Roarke pulled it open. On top of underwear and socks, a jumble of bandannas, was a second pressure syringe and a pair of dime vials he imagined the dealer Eve had rousted earlier sold routinely.

One of the vials was nearly empty.

He left them alone, for Eve's record, moved to the second drawer.

Tees, workout gear, sweatshirts.

In the drawer of the box of a nightstand he found a cheap e-book that opened at a swipe. He scanned the contents, replaced it, moved into the bathroom.

As he came out again he heard Eve calling in sweepers.

"There's another pressure syringe in his top dresser drawer, and two vials of illegals. All but in plain sight, Eve. Lying on top of his socks and boxers."

"Which makes it look like he's been using all along. Or at least he started up again."

"There's also a notebook in the bedside table. A journal of sorts that it appears he's kept faithfully for about two years. Some poetry, some recipes. It has his work schedule. And a kind of log — how much money he's banking every pay period, and what he spends on his share of the rent, food, his clothes, music, even what he puts in the jar at meetings. He has a jar on his dresser for saving — I'd suspect loose coin and credits. It's empty."

She listened as she replaced her tools, the evidence bags she'd used.

"Might as well take the money. The only thing in his pockets is his two-year chip, his keys, and a bandanna. No wallet, no loose coins. They may have lifted other things. We'll have Rochelle go through the place later."

"What do you see?"

Shoving at her hair, she turned to the door. "He let somebody in, and since TOD was nineteen-twenty-two, it couldn't have been long after his sister left."

"Someone watching the place then."

"Possibly, yeah." Almost had to be, she thought, because she didn't buy that kind of lucky timing. "So he lets them in. Someone he trusted, wasn't afraid of, or just wanted to deal with. Then he goes into the kitchen, pours a glass of water. Maybe he takes out his 'link — going to contact someone. They — because it's probably more than one — get him from behind. The bruises on his wrist look like hand grips. Somebody with muscle. Glass gets knocked over, 'link hits the floor. I figure they jab him with the needle — he's got a needle mark. Get him high or put him out. Pull him out here, stage the OD. He's got a little slice on the throat. Hold a knife there in case he fights or tries."

Roarke could see it, too. "He wouldn't have had much of a chance, would he?"

"No, and it wouldn't take long. Minutes, really. While he's dying, they plant the illegals and works where they're easy to find."

She moved back to the body, lifted the sweatshirt to expose the abdomen and lower ribs, and the bruising.

"Couldn't resist giving him a couple shots before they killed him. Personal. Could've been clean, but they're not as smart as they think."

She walked to the door again to answer a knock.

"Good timing," she said to Peabody — and McNab, who stood with her. "We've got a homicide staged, poorly, to look like an OD."

"Rochelle's brother?" Peabody looked beyond Eve to the body. "Man, that's rough."

"No cams out front or on the door. You got the god of e's already," McNab added. "But I can help if you need."

"You could knock on doors with Peabody. I don't think we'll have much luck, if any, but we need to check if anybody saw anything. I'm looking, particularly, for anybody who came into the building or approached this unit, left this unit between seven and seven forty-five tonight."

"Can do."

"Rochelle?" Peabody added.

"I had Crack take her to his place. They got back from dinner out about nine-fifteen, found him, tagged me. I'll fill you in later. Sweepers and dead wagon on the way. Try to dig me up a wit."

Even as she spoke, the door across the hall opened. A woman, mid-fifties, mixed race, streaked hair slicked back in a tail, stepped out.

"I saw something."

Eve eased the door behind her closed to block the view of the body. "Ma'am."

"You the police?"

"Yes, ma'am." All three drew out badges.

"Well, I'm not going to pretend I didn't listen through the door when I heard these two come up." She nodded her chin at Peabody and McNab. "Been more coming up the stairs tonight than I hear in a month or more."

Then she sighed. "Is that young Lyle in there, come to a bad end?"

"Yes. Could we have your name?"

"I'm Stasha-Jean Gregory. I'm going to say I got home from work right about six, got out of my work clothes, had a brew, fixed me some dinner. I heard Lyle come up — gets so you recognize the steps — and, plus, I heard him open the door there. I think that was about seven, maybe a little before, but not much. Then I heard that sweet Rochelle leaving not too long after. Figure she had a date because she was wearing heels. Couldn't've been more than ten minutes after Lyle went on in."

"And you heard someone else come up?" Eve prompted.

"I saw that one. I forgot how it's trash day tomorrow, so I had to run my bag down. She was coming up."

"She?"

"A girl. Had a hood on, had her head down, but I got a glimpse, and she had a girl body, you know what I mean. Breasts and such. Pink in her hair. I heard her knocking on Lyle's door, and kind of crying. Saying how she was ready for help, or needed help. Didn't pass her on my way back, so I figured he let her in."

"What time?"

"Rochelle couldn't've been gone five minutes."

"You didn't recognize this girl?"

"I think maybe I've seen her around outside before. Not up here. So, I'm hardly back inside my place when I hear more coming up. I think three." Ms. Gregory blew out a breath. "All right, I know three because I got nosy and looked out the peep."

"Did you recognize them?"

"Didn't see faces, as they were at the door when I snuck up to look. Big ones, big guys in hoodies. Was the girl let them in. Let them in and ducked right out herself and ran on down the steps."

She paused now, rubbed her hands over her face. "I liked that boy. I sprained my ankle last summer, and didn't he help me up these steps when he was around? Carted bags up for me, or down on trash night. I saw that gang tat on him last summer, though he tried to keep it covered, and he saw me see it. He said that was all finished, and how he was saving to have it removed."

She let out a puff of air. "If I'd known there was trouble for him, I'd've called the police. The man I had the bad sense to hook up with when I was younger than that boy in there had some run-ins with the police, and they weren't much good to me back then, either. But I'd have called you in to help Lyle and his sister."

"You're helping them now. Did you see them leave? The three who came?"

"I heard them. I settled in to watch some screen, and I heard them. Laughing and banging on down the stairs. They weren't in there very long. I guess it was still shy of seven-thirty, but I didn't get up to look. They were laughing," she said again, "and now you say that young Lyle's come to a bad end."

She stared at the door across the hall. "I wish I'd gotten up to look. I wish I had. I heard Rochelle come up with that big, handsome man she's seeing. Sounded like they were getting a little frisky out in the hall. I had a smile over that, and went on in to put my night things on. I didn't hear them leave. Is she in there? I think I've got some tea, maybe."

"No, she's not here now."

"Poor thing." Lips pressed, Ms. Gregory shook her head. "Poor thing. I heard you come, and I thought, What the hell's going on tonight? So I looked. I heard you say you were the police, and when you opened the door, I could just see that poor boy. So I stayed up, and listened."

"We appreciate that, Ms. Gregory. Do you think you'd recognize the female again, if you saw her picture? Or, failing that, work with a police artist?"

Now she puffed out her cheeks. "Never wanted much to do with the police, but I'll look at the pictures and whatnot. For young Lyle and Rochelle."

"Thank you. Peabody, why don't you go inside with Ms. Gregory, get a description. McNab, you can start knocking on doors. Maybe we'll get lucky again."

"They killed that boy, that's what they did, then they walked away laughing like it was one big joke." Ms. Gregory shook her head again, gestured Peabody inside.

By the time Eve knocked on Crack's door, she had the broad strokes of what she believed happened. She'd sent Peabody to Central to write up a preliminary. She had a vague description of the female from Ms. Gregory, and might need to pull in Yancy for a sketch.

But if Lyle knew the woman, odds were Rochelle did, too. She'd go there first.

Crack answered wearing the same conservative dinner-date black sweater and pants. No feathers, no beads, no tats on view.

The Down and Dirty pulled them in, and Crack — or Wilson — was nobody's fool of a businessman. So his apartment climbed several steep flights over Rochelle's.

Rochelle sat in his living room with its bold African art and the oversize furniture to suit the size of the man. She popped to her feet, her eyes rimmed with red, her face sallow with stress.

"He wouldn't have done this. Whatever you say, I *know* he wasn't using again. And he'd never bring illegals into our home."

"You're right. Or, my conclusion at this stage of the investigation lines up with yours."

"He —" The fists at Rochelle's sides unballed. She lowered shakily into the chair again. "What happened to my brother?"

"Y'all sit down. I don't have any of that coffee you like around, but I got Pepsi." As he spoke, Crack stroked his hand over Rochelle's curly wedge of hair. "That's your cold drink, right?"

"That'd be great."

"Roarke?"

"I'm fine with that, thanks."

"I'm sorry." Rochelle pressed a fist to her lips, fought to steady herself. "I haven't even thanked you for coming so quickly, for helping. I'm sorry."

"Don't worry about that." Eve sat so she and Rochelle were eye-to-eye. "Rochelle, Lyle had a jar on his dresser."

"His Save It fund. He'd toss loose change in there every night after work."

"How much would you say he had in it?"

"Oh, I don't know. I guess it was about half-full, maybe a little more."

"It was empty."

"No, that's not right. I saw it just tonight. His door was open — he keeps it open to show me he's got nothing to hide. I saw it when I went in to change for dinner with Wilson. It was loaded up at least halfway."

"It was empty," Eve repeated, "and in his top drawer we found a second pressure syringe, and two vials of what appear to be illegals, one nearly empty."

Those heavy-lidded eyes hardened like granite. "I don't believe you. Not for one minute."

"You should because I believe whoever emptied that jar planted the syringe and illegals. Whoever did that killed your brother and attempted to stage it like an overdose."

"Killed him. Killed him. Killed —"

"You breathe, Ro." Crack hurried in with the drinks. "You take your breaths." After setting the glasses down, he plucked her out of the chair, then sat and cradled her in his lap.

"I knew he didn't — but to hear . . . Murder. Somebody murdered Lyle. I can't think. I need a second. Hold on to me, Wilson."

"Don't you worry. I've got you."

Eve picked up the glass, took a welcome infusion of caffeine while she waited for Rochelle to steady herself again.

"He was so happy," she murmured. "He'd found himself again, found the real Lyle again. I have to be grateful for that, that he had this time to be himself. I said, when I left tonight, 'I love you,' and he said, 'Back at you squared.' We said that to each other, the last thing. I have to be grateful for that. Oh God, if I'd insisted on staying home, making that celebration meal —"

"They'd have come another time," Eve finished. "It reads like they waited for you to leave. It's likely they knew his schedule well enough to know he had the night off. Who'd want to hurt him, Rochelle?"

"I swear I don't know. If you'd asked me a couple years ago, I could've named a dozen. But he's been out of that life, and he's stayed away. He goes to work, to meetings, to see our brothers and Gram. He's not even dating yet. He just got his two-year chip for sobriety."

"We have a witness who saw a female go to your apartment door shortly after you left. She wore a hoodie, baggies, boots. All dark. The witness believes Caucasian, middle twenties, small build. Very thin. She described her — and she only caught a glimpse — as having a thin, hard face. Pink in her hair."

"It sounds like Dinnie."

"Dinnie?"

"Dinnie Duff. They lived together in that flop. She's one of the Banger Bitches. That's what they call themselves. He was with her before he got arrested.

She's done time, too. He wouldn't have started seeing her again. He'd violate his parole."

"We think he let her in tonight."

"God."

"The wit believes she was crying, said she needed or wanted help."

"That would do it," Rochelle confirmed. "He might have opened the door if she asked him for help. I think he did care about her, even when he was at his worst. She killed Lyle."

"I think she was sent in so she could let the ones who did into the apartment. She left as she let them in."

The fierceness flashed back. "She's just as guilty."

"Yes, she is. I'm going to pick her up when I leave here, and expect to charge her with accessory to murder."

Rochelle closed her eyes, let her head rest on Crack's shoulder. "I don't mean to keep snapping at you."

"Skinny white girl don't worry 'bout no snaps," Crack told her.

"If I did, I'd be in another line of work. I also expect, during interrogation, to get the names of the three men she let into your apartment."

"What did they look like? I might have seen them before. I might know."

"The witness didn't see their faces. That doesn't mean I won't find them. I will. In the meantime, your apartment's sealed. You should stay here tonight. I'm going to contact you tomorrow. I want you to go through your apartment with me, tell me if anything's missing or out of place. Anything at all."

"Yes, whenever you want. But I need to see Lyle. You were right, Wilson, you were right to stop me from going to him. But now, I have to see him."

"I'll arrange that for you tomorrow."

"Did you ask for Morris?"

Eve nodded at Crack. "Yes. Morris will take care of Lyle."

"That's just what he'll do, Ro. He'll take care. I'll go with you."

"My brothers — Martin and Walter — and our grandmother. I need to tell them. How do I tell them?" She turned her face into Crack's shoulder for a moment. "But I have to. Face-to-face. We need to be together."

"We'll go to Walt's school. I'll get us a car and we'll go get Walt, then we'll go over to Martin's."

"I'll arrange a car and driver for you," Roarke said.

"You don't have to do that."

"It's done. You're family," he told Crack. "And Rochelle is one of my people now. Lyle is Eve's. You'll have a car and driver at your disposal for as long as you need."

"I don't know how to thank you," Rochelle said. "This doesn't seem real, then it does, horribly real, then it doesn't. I have to tell them, even knowing how it'll hurt them."

"You won't be alone." Crack kissed her hair. "I'll be right with you."

As they walked back to the car, Eve dug up the last known address of Dinnie Duff. "Banger turf," she muttered. "Won't that be fun?" She slid into the car, keyed in the address. "I'm calling it in, getting backup from a couple of uniforms who work that area."

"You don't think we can handle it . . . skinny white girl?"

"Oh, we could handle it, scary Irish boy, but I'm not looking for a gang fight. They sent three to take out Lyle. That's not small change, that's not some petty bullshit. It's something else, and a whole lot more. Dinnie Duff not only knows the three who killed him, it's likely she knows who sent them."

"Would they have a captain?"

"Yeah." She considered the most probable setup as Roarke took the wheel. "And likely a handful of lieutenants and down the pecking order. But someone in charge, someone overseeing gang business — illegals, finances, sex trade. Then there's negotiations or hits on rival gangs. There's the protection racket, and so on."

"It's a business," Roarke commented.

"It's an excuse to kill, maim, steal, and terrorize. But yeah," she conceded, "a business. So you don't put out a hit on a former member because he's living his life outside. You do that because you've got a personal grudge, or because he did something while living his life that messed with gang business."

"There may be something that at least hints at that in his journal."

"I'll be looking. But if Duff was with Lyle back in his gang time, and she's still with the Bangers, she'll know something."

They wound their way into the bowels of the Bowery. While most of the sector had been gentrified and

72

revitalized after the Urbans, this seedy handful of blocks seemed to prefer squalor.

Upscale here meant the obscenities tagged on the walls of buildings were grammatically correct.

Many who worked for a living here earned their pay in the clubs, dives, and hellholes underground. Those with no basic skills and the need for food or a fix tended to sell their bodies there, for individual use or for groups in sex games.

The Bangers ruled this tiny slice of the underground, routinely warring with the Chinatown Dragons in an attempt to expand their territory.

On the streets and sidewalks, they mugged tourists foolish enough to wander onto their turf looking for color, and catered to addicts and the street whores who couldn't meet the regs for a license.

Shopkeepers who balked at paying out protection money usually found their places of business burned out or their stock destroyed by homemade boomers. Often with the recalcitrant shopkeeper still inside.

As far as Eve knew, the only building off-limits was Most Holy Redeemer Church on East Third. Off-limits not because Bangers respected a house of worship, but because many of their mothers and grandmothers prayed there for the souls of their offspring — souls those offspring had already sold to the lowest bidder.

Eve scanned the streets — windows barred or boarded, steel gates locked tight and tagged, husks of burned-out vehicles.

Given the cold, the wind, most business and entertainment went underground, but a few packs wandered with gang colors — black and red — displayed on hoods, on bandannas snaking out of pockets, on wristbands.

"You carrying?" Eve asked casually as Roarke pulled over.

"Not to worry." He gave her hand a pat before they got out on either side.

She saw the looks from the pack — three male, one female — a couple of yards down. And when they switched directions, started to swagger back toward her, she flipped back her coat, put a hand — very overtly — on her weapon.

And smiled, showing her teeth. "Keep moving," she advised.

The tallest one — skinny as a stick, pasty white with a scatter of old acne scars — grinned back. "Come on now, baby. Why'n you roll with us? We'll show you how it's done."

When he rubbed his crotch, his companions howled with hilarity. Egged on, Eve noted, as their pupils were big as moons, by the chemicals dancing in their bloodstreams.

"With that little thing?" She cocked her head. "My cat's got a better package. Keep moving," she repeated. "Or I'll haul your brain-dead asses in for use of illegals, possession of same, and interfering with a law officer."

"Yeah?" This was a big one, massive shoulders, as black as his companion was white. The Bangers did go for diversity. "You and what army, bitch?"

Eve cocked her head again, this time toward Roarke. That brought on more hilarity.

"He's pretty." The lone female, mixed race, hair a flying flag of gang colors, licked her lips, wagged her tongue with its silver stud. "I want a taste of that meat."

Roarke glanced casually at Eve, but the blue of his eyes cut as sharp as the wind. "Are these the Bangers then?"

"Ooooh, he even talks pretty."

"Where I come from bangers are sausages. That doesn't seem far off, really. If you've more brains than a sausage, you'd use them to move along as the lieutenant suggested. Otherwise, you lot will end up bloodied before you land in a cage."

"Fuck you, limey prick." Howling with more hilarity, the third male — squat as a barrel, long bleached-white hair flying — heaved the rock in his pocket at the car.

It ricocheted off the security shield Roarke had engaged and smacked into the grinning face of the female. She dropped like, well, a rock.

"I'm Irish, by the way." Roarke braced for an assault. Eve drew her weapon.

A black-and-white rolled up with a quick one-two of sirens.

The two cops who got out — one male, one female — made the big Banger look like the runt of the litter.

The female cop shouldered her air rifle. It wouldn't kill anybody, but a blast from it would hurt like holy hell.

"Causing trouble again, Shake 'n Bake?"

Pasty Guy obviously didn't care for the nickname, and snarled at her. "We're just walking. We can walk where the fuck we want in a free fucking country."

"Then pick up Little Easy there and keep doing that. Unless you'd like to assume the position and have us go through your pockets."

"Fucking cops is wheeze."

But the big one hauled up the dazed female, and they all kept walking.

The male officer watched them go. "That bunch is mostly just bullshit and noise. Got plenty of worse around here. What're you after down here, Lieutenant?"

"I'm after Dinnie Duff." Eve gestured to a four-story building with a street-level tat-and-piercing parlor. It made Rochelle's apartment building look like a palace. "Last known address."

"Current Banger HQ. She mostly flops there." The female frowned at the building. "And some of the worse my astute partner mentioned does, too. She may be working the underground this time of night, but if we're going down there, we're going to want more cops."

"Ten-four," her partner agreed. "Worst of the worst."

"We'll check the flop. She had a busy night, so she may be in."

"We got your back. What're you pulling her for?"

"She's a prime suspect on accessory to murder."

Both uniforms stared. The female found her voice. "Dinnie? She's a user, a skank, and as useless as bull tits, but I wouldn't peg her on murder."

"How long have you worked this sector?" Eve asked.

"Eight years. Zutter here has seven."

"Do you know Lyle Pickering?"

"Sure. We busted him a time or two. Addict, asshole, had some violence in there, but it was mostly the Go."

Zutter nodded. "He sure liked his Go. He's out. Last I heard he was giving the straight way a try. We even had breakfast at Casa del Sol about a month ago, where he cooks. Seemed to be doing okay."

"He was — got his two-year chip, worked the job. And tonight, I have reason to believe Duff gained entrance to his apartment, assisted three unknown males into same. And now he's dead."

"Dinnie." Zutter puffed his cheeks, shook his head. "Dumber than a splintered post and half-crazy with it. Too bad about Pick. Too damn bad. Well." He rolled his shoulders. "Ready, Norton?"

"Born ready," she said. "Raised to roll."

They approached the door emblazoned with the Banger fist.

CHAPTER
FIVE

Zutter stepped up. "They've got a secret knock for the guard inside."

Eve stared at him. "No joke?"

"No joke." Zutter banged his fist in a quick one, two, three — pause — one, two — pause — one.

"And an unbreakable code, too."

Zutter spread his lips in a grin. "Door guards aren't usually their best and brightest."

To prove it, the guard who opened the door boasted more fat than muscle, a bull ring in his nose that would cause him serious pain when anyone with sense yanked it in a fight, and a monster matching game still *grring* on his PPC.

"Don't need no cops."

"Slice wants to confab."

"Slice wants?"

"Smelled some Dragon breath. What the what, Toro, you axe the zombies first. Ice pick them crawlers, grab up the torches for frying vamps."

Toro frowned down at the game. "Zombies first?"

While he puzzled over that, Zutter nudged the bulk of him aside to clear a path for the stairs. "*Monster Hunter,*" Zutter said as they walked up. "My eight-year-old kid plays it. Like I said, not the brightest."

Eve heard banging music, throaty moans, exaggerated gasps. It didn't take seeing the action to recognize a porn vid in play.

The stairs opened into a line of living quarters. Most stood open — a number didn't have doors to close in the first place.

The one on the left boasted doubles, both open. The bump and grind of porn music rolled out.

"That's Slice's flop. He's top captain," Norton explained. "Well, the only captain now, since recruiting's way down, busts are up. Second-gen Banger."

"How many flop here?"

"Hard to say. Maybe twenty, twenty-five regulars. But you could have double that before a strike. Their territory's shrunk, and they're clinging to what they've got, pushing to take back what they lost. A lot of them would die for it. Some do."

Eve stepped to the opening. Across a wide living area on a ten-foot screen, numerous people in masks engaged in various acts of sex in some sort of fancy ballroom. The music, provided by an on-stage band, hit heavy on the bass.

She judged the living space owed its size to the removal of walls to combine a couple of flops into one. Most of the furniture ran to low-rise gel sofas in shiny red and black, and most were currently occupied by couples — or threesomes — trying to mimic the action on-screen.

In the single oversize sleep chair, two women — obviously stoned — pawed and crawled lugubriously over a male. He gave tits and ass absent strokes with one hand, worked his PPC with the other.

Zoner smoke, with a chaser of Erotica, hung in the air like dreamy fog.

A dozen people, Eve counted, with most too naked to conceal any weapon. Still, she kept a hand on her own when she rapped a fist against the jamb.

"NYPSD."

The few people not completely dazed with drugs or sex, scrambled. The man in the chair just shoved one of the women to the floor, waved away the second. And with a half smile, adjusted his erection back in his pants.

Mixed race, with skin the color of Peabody's coffee regular, he had hard dark eyes and a long, thin scar down his left cheek, a tat of a blade dripping blood on the other.

He wore his hair in tight black-and-red braids that rained down his back from a band at his nape. The black long-sleeved tee didn't quite hide another slicing scar down the side of his throat.

She saw one of the naked guys start to reach under the gel couch, then freeze when both air rifles gave their cocking snicks.

"Yo now, everybody just chill it, all right?" Slice spoke in a gravelly baritone, kept that half smile in place. "We got us some company. I know you." He pointed a long finger, bumpy at the knuckles, at Eve. "Sure I do. Seen you right up there."

He gestured to the screen and a close-up of swollen genitalia hard at work.

"Y'all bring me a famous cop and her rich man. We need some refreshments! Bulge, get some clothes on and go on down there and pull Toro off the door. Mofo doesn't have the sense to tell us we got company."

"Everybody's fine right where they are," Eve said. "We're looking for Dinnie Duff."

"What you want with that little ho?"

"I'll talk to her about that."

"Now, she's a ho for sure, but she's my ho. We look after our own, don't we?" he said to the room at large. "You here to give her trouble?"

"Is she in the house?"

Slice bared his teeth at her, a grin and a challenge all at once. "Got your hard-ass on tonight, do you?"

"It's always on. Is she worth a raid? There's enough Zoner hanging in the air for me to haul every one of you in."

"We be out again in a flash."

"Yeah, maybe, but considering I'd have probable cause to look for more?" She scanned the room, noted that more than a couple of people in the room knew that flash wouldn't work for them. "Maybe not. Dinnie Duff."

"Fuck all." He shrugged it off, shoved the second woman to the floor. "Likely she's working under at Wet Dreams. I ain't seen her."

"How about we look?"

"How about I see a warrant?"

Now Eve smiled. "I can get one in under five minutes. I doubt that'd give you time to move out all the illegals and weapons, and anybody underage in here. But we can play it out and see."

"Fuck all and you with it." No longer smiling, he got to his feet. "Bolt, you've been banging that bitch most recently. Where's she at?"

"Work, she said. She needs the scratch."

The one called Bolt took his time pulling on pants, scratching his naked belly. The look in his eyes, Eve thought, was fierce despite the lazy movements.

Pissed, Eve thought. This one's pissed he got caught with his pants down and no weapon in his hand.

He was white with a tough, compact boxer's build, spiky red hair, his gang tat over his heart. Two lightning-bolt tats jagged down his arms.

"When did you last see her?"

"I don't keep a leash on that bitch." As if to prove it, Bolt reached over to squeeze the closest breast. Hard enough that the owner of the breast yelped. "Said how she needed some scratch, had shit to do, and couldn't party tonight."

"Which is her flop?"

"Man, she ain't got her own. Why she needs the scratch, so? She's been flopping with me for the banging. What the fuck, Slice? We don't need to put up with this shit. We got rights and shit. You gotta stand up, man, tell this bitch to suck it."

"I know what I got," Slice snapped back. "I ain't taking no shit from cops in our place."

Eve took out her badge, held it up, and aimed a cold stare at Slice. "You said you know me, then you know I'm a murder cop. Do you think I'm here to roust your ho for off-license sex work, for illegals?"

"Don't know why the fuck you're here."

"I'm here because Dinnie Duff is a person of interest in a murder investigation. You keep up this bullshit, you'll be one, too. Where is she?"

He laughed, and as if on signal, a few of the others joined in.

"You gotta be smoking something good if you're looking at that bitch for some murder. She squeaks if she sees a bloody thumb. She ain't killed nobody."

"Lyle Pickering would disagree if he could, but he's dead."

Slice's face went stony, and the lingering laughter cut off. "You saying Pick's dead? You saying he's dead and Dinnie did him?"

"I'm saying he's dead, and I need to talk to her. Where is she?"

"How's he dead?"

"Where is Dinnie Duff?"

"We said she ain't here. And ain't no way she'd do something to end Pick. Bangers stick, and that boy was a Banger." He booted one of the women on the floor. "Loose, you know where she's at? You say it straight."

"Must be working, Slice. She said, like Bolt said, she had shit to do, needed scratch. She ain't paid up her share for flop in a while. You said . . ."

"Go ahead."

"You said she had to pay up or find someplace else, 'cause spreading it for Bolt wasn't enough for her share. She said she had shit to do. That's all."

"That's right, I did." He nodded slowly, looked back at Eve. "Bitches gotta pay same as anybody, and fucking only pays so far. Pick's dead, you oughta look at the Dragons. We don't kill our own."

"He'd disavowed you."

"Disavowed's shit." Slice's eyes fired out hate — a violent, frustrated hate. "He wants to live his life like a sack, that's on him. But once you take the oath, you're one of us. Even that ho Dinnie knows how it is."

She considered pushing, but she'd planted the seeds, formed her impressions.

"I will find her. If anything happens to her in the meantime, I'll be coming for you."

"Come all you want, bitch. I've taken on harder asses than you."

At that Roarke let out a quick laugh. "Keep thinking that," he advised, then turned with Eve toward the steps.

Outside, Zutter puffed out his cheeks. "He'll send some boys to find her. If you want to get to her first, we need to go under. We're going to need more cops."

"How well do you know Slice?"

"I watched him fight his way up to top dog," Norton said. "The gang's what he's got."

"Would he put a hit on her for what I told him?"

Zutter rubbed his chin as he and Norton studied each other. They both shook their heads.

"He'd want to talk to her, squeeze what she knows out of her."

"If he ordered the hit on Lyle, he already knows," Eve pointed out. "And if he did, she followed his orders. Would he take her out now?"

"More get her out," Norton said. "Maybe he did already. Get her gone somewhere until he figures things settle."

"So, either way, he's not going to execute her." Eve stood in the wind, calculating while the neon on the tat parlor began to buzz like a small swarm of bees. "If he didn't order the hit, squeezes out she was part of it, does he follow the code, have a trial?"

"That's how he rolls. He'll gut her himself if it comes to that, but not before they stand her up, make her blubber first."

"Okay. Sit on the place, tag me if you see anybody leave and head to the underground. That's a couple blocks west, right?"

"Affirmative."

"And where's Wet Dreams from that entrance?"

Now Zutter pushed back his uniform cap, scratched his head. "First tunnel to the right, next left. It's not down deep. LT, you shouldn't oughta go down there without a force."

"Just getting the lay. Appreciate the assist."

"It's what we do in this little piece of heaven on earth, right, Zut?"

"You got it."

Roarke slid behind the wheel. "A couple blocks west, is it?"

"Yeah, then we'll take a trip to Wet Dreams."

"Darling Eve, life with you is a never-ending series of them."

"Funny."

She directed him to park in a loading zone, switched on the On Duty sign. From the trunk, she studied her choices, and took out two serrated-edged knives, passed one to Roarke.

"Thank you, darling. It's just my size."

She knew him, knew he could handle himself. Knew he'd enjoy it.

"What're you carrying?"

He opened his coat, took from the inside pocket a police-issue stunner.

"Jesus, I should arrest you."

"Promise you will when we get home." He leaned in to kiss her. "You know how it thrills me."

"Still funny," she muttered. "Keep it handy."

"You think he might just order that hit?"

"The minute I went in looking for her, she was in the crosshairs. I lean toward the uniforms' opinion," she added. "If she was following his orders on Pickering, he'll hide her until things cool off. But . . ."

"You're thinking of his reaction, weighing whether it was genuine."

"It felt real, so if she went rogue, she's finished. But he has his code, so it's more likely he'll try to get to her before I do, haul her in for a trial. And whether or not he ordered the hit, he has to make it look like he's following the code."

She took the tag from Norton.

"He's got three of his crew heading out now," Eve told Roarke, then rolled her shoulders. "Let's do this."

It smelled of human waste and rot and worse. In the echoing dark, shadows slunk away from the penlight Eve held in her left hand. A few huddled against the wall, too stoned to slink anywhere, eyes glassy with whatever they'd ingested or popped.

She skirted around them, then rammed an elbow into the throat of one who leaped forward. As he dropped, she pivoted in time to see Roarke use nearly the same maneuver — though his elbow struck nose cartilage.

"He had a friend," Roarke said easily, and smiled.

Yeah, she thought again, he enjoys it.

"Sometimes they pair up close to the entrances, hoping for a quick score."

She took the left tunnel. In the distance music thumped, and a few lights glimmered. In the faint glint of them a male, pants around his ankles, hairy ass pumping, pinned a female to the wall. His raspy grunts punctuated each frantic thrust.

Rather than appearing appalled or aroused, the woman merely looked bored. But when her gaze skimmed over Eve and Roarke, she bared what was left of her teeth in something approximating a smile.

"Soon's done here, give ya a double for half."

"There's an offer you don't get every day," Roarke murmured as they moved on.

"And the STD comes free." Eve stepped over a fresh splat of vomit, took the next tunnel.

More lights here as the underground clubs popped up, with some retail scattered. Bondage World boasted live models hyping their products.

A woman with enormous man-made breasts exposed by the cutouts in her fake leather skin suit moaned impressively as a second woman with a vibrating strap-on demonstrated the proper way to attach the looping chains of nipple clamps to wall hooks.

A couple of bruisers with full-body tats discouraged any potential customers from attempting to take an active part in the demo.

They passed Bang-O-Rama, a bar where volunteers paid for the privilege of being gangbanged onstage. At the moment, a group of women hooted and cheered on somebody named Coco, who had the stage — and writhed as sex workers penetrated every orifice in her body.

She wore nothing but a tiara proclaiming her as the BRIDE TO BE.

"A whole new meaning to girls' night out," Roarke commented.

Farther down the tunnel someone screamed in a way that didn't translate into pleasure on any level. Just as the laughter that followed didn't sound of humor.

Ignoring both, Eve aimed for Wet Dreams.

Smaller than most of the others, it amounted to a hole-in-the-wall with bad lighting, smoky air, recorded music. Eve assumed the lighting was an attempt to disguise the fact that the staff consisted of junkies going through the motions to earn enough for the next fix.

Then again, from her scan, a good portion of the clientele ran the same. Some of the glazed looks might have come from ingesting the Zoner smoke hazing the room.

A couple of women on the platform — too small to rate the term *stage* — pawed each other mechanically while a third attempted a clumsy routine on a pole.

Behind the bar a single male wearing nipple rings, possibly purchased at Bondage World, poured liquid the color of sludge into stingy glasses. The guy on a stool downed one while getting a lap dance from a sex worker so bony Eve could count his ribs.

If he'd seen his eighteenth birthday, she'd eat her badge.

A woman in a red skin suit approached. Pasty flesh sagged out of the open lacing running down both sides while another pair of man-made tits rose improbably high from the snug bodice.

She wore a coal-black wig with a sweep down the left side that didn't quite hide the puckering burn scars on her cheek.

"Looking for a table or a private room?" She had a voice like the smoke — thick and mildly drugged out.

"Neither. Dinnie Duff."

"If you're looking for personal service, I got better."

Eve pulled out her badge. "Dinnie Duff."

The woman hissed. "Just put that thing away. Business is bad enough around here. She ain't working tonight. She ain't come in for a couple, three nights."

"Is this your place?"

"Shit no. I run what there is of it."

"Name."

"Taffy Pull. I had it changed legal when I was working the stage."

"Okay, Taffy, Which is it, a couple or three since Duff's been in?"

"Well, shit." When the woman scratched her head, the wig shifted. "Monday night's slow. Hell, most nights is slow, but we do decent on the weekend. I coulda used her over the weekend, but she didn't show. So I guess she ain't been in since last . . . maybe Thursday night she was in and working. Maybe the night before. I figured she musta made enough to hold her over or she got herself busted."

"She told a couple people she was working here tonight."

"Well, she ain't. Look, it's no skin off mine if you bust her ass. She works, she gets paid." The shoulder shrug didn't move the breasts by a fraction. "She don't work, somebody else gets paid. It's all the same to me."

"How long has she worked here?"

"Jesus, I guess about three years. On and off. And plenty of off. You find her, you tell her she's off for good. I can't have cops coming around here. Ain't good for business."

Eve caught sight of the three Bangers heading down the tunnel, led by Bolt. "If I find out you're bullshitting me, I'll shut this place down."

The woman gave another shrug. "Got no reason to bullshit over some junkie whore too lazy to work. And this place — no big loss, right? You shut it down, there's always another place."

Eve left it at that.

Bolt stopped, eyed her up and down. "Bad shit happens to cops underground."

"Worse shit happens to people who start something with a cop who has a stunner aimed at them."

"One cop," Roarke added. "Two stunners."

This time when he looked down, she had the stunner in her hand, as did Roarke. Bolt smirked at them, but kept walking.

"That one has a very poor attitude," Roarke commented.

"Yeah, I guess he flunked out of Manners 101. Too bad he's only about five-seven and doesn't fit the description of big from the wit's statement."

"Well, he appears to make up for his lack of stature by being a flaming fuckhole. But back to our charming hostess. I don't believe she knows her former employee's whereabouts."

"No, neither do I. 'Flaming fuckhole,'" she repeated. "I've got to remember that one."

She ignored the cheers as another member of the wedding party stumbled up to the stage in Bang-O-Rama. Then the Bondage World demo of the Electric O, which made her think of a battery-operated cattle prod. And the howls of humanity in a chosen hell as they worked their way back through, and up to the street.

"Well now, after this fascinating evening, I could do with a good, long shower."

"Sick bastards. What kind of sick bastard wants somebody to slap a shock stick across his balls?"

"Don't look at me." Roarke opened the car door for her. "So if neither the Banger chief nor the curiously named Taffy Pull is bullshitting, that only leaves a couple of possibilities."

"Yeah, she's pulled a rabbit, or she's dead."

Roarke walked around, slid behind the wheel. "She might have managed to score. She could've been paid for betraying Pickering. She got high and flopped elsewhere."

"Not impossible," she conceded. "Maybe Slice has it right, and it was a hit by one of the rival gangs. They recruited her, she helped with the hit, and now she's flopping with them. But . . ."

"Why would a rival gang order a hit on a former Banger?"

"Why would anybody? It makes him more important than he seems." And that was the puzzle. "I need to know more about the players."

She pulled out her PPC, started runs.

"She actually did change her name legally. Rita Razowitz to Taffy Pull. Worked the sex clubs — a couple of high-end ones back in the day. A few bumps along the way, but nothing major. About twelve years ago she got into it with one of the other SWs over some dude. The rival set her hair on fire."

"That's love for you," Roarke said.

"It explains the wig, the scars. Spiraled down — a taste for opiates of any description, busted for illegals, for unlicensed solicitation. Blah-blah. She's been running that place for about four years.

"Can't think the dude was worth it," Eve considered. "No marriages, no cohabs, no offspring, and no criminal in the last four that shows."

"The sad life and times of Rita Razowitz."

People make their choices, Eve thought. Who knows why?

"She's not going to lie to cover for a junkie who works on and off. Slice is, legally, Marcus Jones Junior. Looks like Senior, street name Rock, was not only a Banger but a captain. Didn't cohab with the mother, did some time. Got himself beaten half to death about ten years ago."

"A job risk for a gangster."

"That took Jones Senior out. I'm reading severe head trauma, brain damage. He's in a medical facility for same. The mother spent Jones Junior's childhood in and out of lockup, so he was raised primarily by his maternal grandmother."

Roarke glanced over. "So he had something in common with Lyle Pickering."

"Yeah. Huh. He owns the building, the flop. Or a percentage of it — and the same with Wet Dreams, and a couple other enterprises. Like the tat parlor in the building, a strip joint. Owns them with a Samuel Cohen and an Eldena Vinn.

"Any bells from those two?" she asked.

"Sorry, no. But that's very interesting."

"Yeah, it's got my attention. I'll look at his partners. Jones has brains, skill, or luck. Maybe all. He's been pulled in for questioning plenty, but nothing's stuck to him since he did six months when he was eighteen."

"Brains would sell that underground pit and put enough change into that apartment building to charge actual rent — which tells me if he does have brains, he's not using them for more than show."

"Such as money laundering, the illegals trade, fraud, fencing, and so on." She continued to work as Roarke wove through traffic. "Okay, his partner, Cohen, was a lawyer."

"'Was'?"

"Disbarred, eight years back. Currently lists himself as a consultant. He's forty-three, also listed as owner of his residence: Lower East, a few blocks — important blocks — from Banger HQ. Working-class area. Cohabs with Eldena Vinn, twenty-five, employed at Bump and Bang — the strip club Jones, Cohen, and Vinn also own. She's listed her profession as dancer, which reads as stripper."

Eve sat back as — at long last — Roarke drove through the gates, and the lights of home glinted up ahead.

"How do a gangbanger, a disbarred lawyer, and a stripper become business partners?"

"I have no doubt you'll find out."

"Yeah, I will. It may or may not be relevant to Pickering's murder, but I'll find out. I smell dirty deeds."

"It may just be the fragrant remnants of our interesting night on the town. Christ Jesus, I want that shower."

When they got to the bedroom, he noted Galahad sprawled diagonally across the big bed, all four feet stretched out, belly up.

Enjoy it while you can, Roarke thought as he began to strip.

He also noted the wheels turning behind his wife's eyes as she unhooked her weapon harness, pulled off her boots.

He decided, as a dutiful husband, he should take her mind off work so she could get a good night's sleep.

He waited until she'd stripped it all down and reached for a sleep shirt. And scooped her off her feet.

"Hey!"

"We need that shower."

"I'll catch one in the morning. I know your pervy games, pal."

"Maybe I have some new pervy games." In the bath he ordered the jets on several degrees hotter than his own preference. And took her mouth with his as he stepped with her into the pulsing spray.

She decided a shower wasn't a bad idea after all, so she wrapped around him when he set her on her feet. Steam already pumped, and the pulsing hot beat of the jets felt nearly as good as the glide of his hands on her naked skin.

To get back some of her own, she backed him against the slick, wet tiles and got busy with her own hands, her own mouth.

No, not a bad idea at all, she thought as she gripped and dug into tight, rippling muscle, as she felt his heart trip against hers. She used her teeth, quick, hungry bites, as wet flesh slipped and slithered against wet flesh.

Hitting the dispenser, she filled her palm with liquid soap. Slicked and stroked it over him, around him. Down the solid wall of his chest, down the narrow cut of torso, down the taut belly.

Down.

She might have guided him into her, taken the moment, taken him, but he spun her around. With one arm chained around her waist, pinning her back against him, he glided his hand, the silky soap over her breasts, cupping them, thumb stroking the nipple while he feasted on the back and side of her neck.

Down that long, lean torso while his blood beat hot as the jets. A tease along the blades of hips as those hips began to pump in invitation.

Not yet, not yet, though he could have devoured her like a man starving. Instead, he trailed his fingers over her belly, felt the quiver of her need. A light stroke, to torment them both, down the inside of those smooth, strong thighs.

On a moan she reached back to hook her arm around his neck, trembling now, trembling for him.

Ready and open and his.

A brush, just a brush over her center, lightly cupping her there while her body arched against his restraining arm. And inside her, light, almost lazy while her quickened breath escaped in gasps.

Slow, he thought, slow though his own needs pounded. Slow as he felt her fall into the pleasure, melt in it, surrender to it.

It saturated her, seemed to turn even her bones to butter. She sank into it, all those honeyed sensations, floated through them on the thick, steamy air. And when they lifted her, up, up, she clung to the heights, then embraced the staggering fall.

"Ride it," he urged her when she went limp. "Just ride it."

He could take her up again, and would. Not so slow now, not so light.

Nothing, nothing aroused him more than having his tough, hard-eyed cop steeped in what he could give her. Once more, he thought as his own muscles quivered, just once more as he felt it build inside her again.

When he felt her shuddering on that edge, her body bow-taut, he whipped her around. With her back to the tiles, he plunged into her, hard, fast, deep. Held there, chained himself there while her cry of release echoed.

"God. God." Her head dropped to his shoulder as she fought for air.

No air, she thought, dazed and drugged, just heat.

Then he began to move again.

"There's more," he said as she lifted her head.

His eyes, impossibly blue, so intense, so focused on her. Only her. Love speared like an arrow, burst through lust so the mix of both overwhelmed her.

Her breath in tatters like his, she gripped the wet silk of his hair, dragged his mouth to hers. Fed there while all the wild and wonderful needs spread again.

Bracing her hands on his shoulders, she looked into that miraculous blue once more. "I can take it as long as you can."

She boosted up, wrapped her legs around his waist. "Now you ride it."

He couldn't stop. Tossing aside any semblance of control, he drove into her, again, again, with a blind, nearly brutal desperation. He heard her cries as he thrust, as his fingers dug into her hips. Not cries of surrender, not this time. But of triumph.

Now it was he who was lost, undone, conquered. When his release came, it slashed like blades to open him, to empty him.

He nearly staggered, had to brace a hand to the wall, pin Eve there with his body to keep them both upright. Then he gave that up, just slid both of them to the floor of the shower and tried to catch his breath.

Steam puffed and plumed. Jets of water sliced through the thickened air and rained down on them. He should turn that off, he thought idly as Eve sprawled over him.

"Maybe you do have some new pervy games."

"What?"

"Some shower."

He managed a laugh. "We'll have to get up and out of it at some point."

"It feels good."

She nestled her head in the curve of his shoulder, as if — he thought — she intended to bed down right there for the night. "Do you know how to cook a frog?"

"Why would anybody want to cook a frog? And you don't cook anyway."

"You put it in a pot of water, and turn the heat on very low. The water heats, but it's a gradual thing, so the unfortunate frog doesn't try to get out of the pot because it doesn't realize it's being slowly boiled to death until it's done."

Her brows drew together. "You've cooked a frog?"

"It's an analogy. Right now we're the frog and, in this case, I'd say we're gradually being steamed to death. So."

He managed to shift her, to get them both sitting up. Then he smiled. "Wet's one of my favorite looks on you." He leaned over to kiss her between the eyes. "Jets off."

They pulled each other up. Eve stepped out and into the drying tube. Roarke grabbed a towel.

She eyed him through the warm whirl of air. "We have good sex, right?"

He glanced over, watched the air send her short chop of hair flying. "I think we just confirmed that."

"Right." She stepped out, walked back into the bedroom.

When he came out, she'd pulled on a sleep shirt, had pulled back the duvet in an attempt to dislodge the cat — who ignored her.

So she crawled in, giving the sprawling lump of cat a solid nudge toward Roarke's side. Roarke lifted an eyebrow, solved the matter by hauling Galahad up, and dumping him at the foot of the bed.

Sliding in, he hooked an arm around Eve, drew her back to him.

"We even have, like, adventurous sex."

"Again, just confirmed. What's in that mind of yours?"

"I figure people can do whatever they want, sex wise, as long as everybody's an adult and willing. As long as nobody ends up on a slab. But . . ."

She turned over, and since he hadn't yet called for lights off, looked him in those eyes again. "I'm never going to whack your balls with a shock stick to get you off."

"It's difficult to find the proper words to express my gratitude for that."

"Okay. And I don't want you clamping any weird toys on my nipples."

"I can agree to that."

"Okay then. We're good."

"We're very good." He kissed her again. "Lights out."

"I'm not eating frog, either."

"Off the menu. Go to sleep."

He smiled into the dark, stroking her back until he felt her drift off. And thought again, they were very good.

CHAPTER
SIX

When she woke, Roarke, in his usual spot in the sitting area, was watching the financial reports on mute. The cat was sleeping in front of the fire that simmered low.

She smelled coffee and thought the scent, the view of Roarke in one of his business god suits, and the cat snoring by a low fire equaled a pretty solid way to wake up.

She rolled out of bed, headed straight to the AutoChef because the smell of coffee wasn't enough.

"Good morning."

She gulped coffee, glancing toward the window. "Might be. Nothing's falling out of the sky yet."

"And not forecasted to," Roarke told her. "You should be cheered to know the forecast included a good hint of spring. It's a chilly start, but due to climb into the sixties this afternoon."

"Huh." That perked her up nearly as much as the coffee.

"And as they're calling for a few days, at least, of this warming trend, they'll start excavation on the pond today."

"'The pond'?" It took her a minute to remember the walk they'd taken on the grounds months before.

Somehow they'd decided to put in a little pond, picked the spot. "We're really doing that?"

"It'll be pleasant, won't it, when spring decides to come and stay awhile to wander out and sit by the water."

"Yeah, it will. When does the whole thing about March happen?"

"Which thing is that?"

She circled a finger in the air as she gulped more coffee. "The one about the sheep lying down with the lion."

"Lamb. The lion lies down with the lamb."

"A lamb's a sheep, and the lion's lying down to eat the stupid sheep. I don't get what it has to do with March."

"Because it has nothing to do with it. I think you mean March comes in like a lion and goes out like a sheep. A lamb," he corrected, dragging his fingers through his hair. "It's a bloody lamb."

"Yeah, it would be if it's hanging around with a lion."

He watched her walk into the adjoining bath and thought, Well, she has a point.

He had breakfast waiting under warming domes when she came out. When he lifted the domes, she cocked her head.

"No oatmeal?"

"To celebrate the warming trend."

"Let's hear it for spring."

He had gone for a full Irish because who knew when or if she'd take time for a decent meal during the day.

102

In lieu of the black pudding, which she disliked intensely, he'd selected a small yogurt and fruit parfait.

She sat, dug in. "So after your predawn 'link or holo or whatever meetings, you're probably headed out for more."

"I have a thing or two."

"You've got that revised whatsit report you ordered up yesterday."

"Signed off this morning. And you, I expect, will be on the hunt."

"Yeah." Curious, she studied a bite of sausage. "Why do you call them bangers?"

"I'm not entirely sure, something about how they sound when they're being fried up. I think."

"Huh. Well, they're good whatever they're called." She ate the sausage, continued, "Anyway, I can hope we get a hit from the BOLO on Duff. Either way, I'm heading to the morgue this morning. I want a conversation with the sleazy ex-lawyer at some point, and a closer look at the Banger Duff was banging."

"Bolt," Roarke recalled. "He has killer in his eyes."

"Yeah, he does. I also need a conversation with whoever's riding cases on the Bangers. I should probably talk to Lyle's brothers, his grandmother. He might have said something to them he didn't say to Rochelle."

She crunched into bacon. "If he was going to meetings, earned his second-year chip, he probably has a sponsor. Another conversation. I've got to set up the board and book, write up a report on the visit to the Banger HQ, the underground."

"On the hunt," he repeated.

"Yeah, and I won't be slogging through snow or crap rain doing it."

Thinking of it, when she finished breakfast, she took a simple white shirt out of her closet. No need for a sweater. Then she stopped, abruptly flummoxed by the rails of pants, of jackets, the shelves of boots.

She'd gotten so used to hauling out cold-weather clothes, she wasn't quite sure what to grab.

She wasn't going to ask Roarke or use the closet comp (He'd hear that, wouldn't he?). She knew how the hell to dress herself. It was just . . . long winter.

She grabbed pants. Brown. Not Feeney's shit brown, but a chocolate brown that reminded her to check the ceiling tile in her office, make sure the candy bar she'd booby-trapped was still there. Then she snagged a navy jacket because it had that brown leather piped at the cuffs and down the side seams.

She studied her selection of boots, the number of which continued to be an embarrassment for her. Milder embarrassment than it once had been, but still.

She started to grab brown ones, but she knew damn well the navy ones with the brown leather down the sides went with the damn jacket, and if she took the plain brown, Roarke would switch them out anyway.

Why give him the satisfaction?

She pulled on the pants, a support tank, reached for the shirt.

And damn if Roarke didn't stroll in, take it, replace it with another white shirt.

"You're just fucking with me now."

"Though that's one of my favorite things, it's simply a matter of the softer white — dare I say oatmeal color — being a better choice than the other."

"Fine. Whatever." She put it on. It fit as if it had been tailored for her — which she assumed it had.

She didn't argue — what was the point? — when he offered her a navy belt.

"You know, murdering bastards don't care if I coordinate."

She carried the jacket, the boots out into the bedroom.

"And yet it adds to the intimidation factor when you present a strong, competent appearance."

"Maybe." She hooked on her weapon harness, added her pocket and belt paraphernalia. "A solid left jab adds intimidation."

"You'll look well dressed when you deliver one." He nodded approval as she put on the jacket, the boots. "Strong and competent," he repeated as he stepped over, kissed her. "That's my cop. You take care of her today."

"Don't bitch if I get blood on the boots."

"Have I ever?"

"No." And because he hadn't, she kissed him back. "We're good," she said as she walked out. "See you later."

It definitely felt like the lion, Eve thought when she walked outside. The air had bite, and the wind held a low, throaty roar. She hopped into her waiting car, grateful for the blast of the heater.

As she headed toward the gates then through them, she sent Peabody a voice text to report to the morgue.

The air blimps were back, blasting out their hype from a blissfully blue sky. No ice, no rain to dampen New York drivers' competence at the wheel down to zero, no gritty gray piles of snow heaped at the curbs.

Maybe the lion really was getting ready to lie down.

Of course the lack of gray and gloom, rain and sleet didn't stop the traffic heading downtown from tangling, clogging, or breaking noise-pollution laws with screaming horns.

But she'd take it.

The sun actually glared — enough that she dug into the center console, and was pleasantly surprised to locate a pair of sunshades.

As she bullied her way downtown, she thought over her impressions of Marcus Jones, aka Slice.

A badass, no question, and one likely to end up dead on the street or spending a lot of quality time in a cage. But not completely stupid. Smart and badass enough to work his way up to a command post in the Bangers, and, more, to have outside business interests.

A landlord, a property owner with business partners. Sleazy ones, but non-gang member business partners.

So where had he gotten the scratch to buy into real estate?

Illegals, identity theft, the protection racket. Could be some skimming off the top — or bottom — of gang business involved. Or some side deals — a little blackmail maybe, some solo illegals action.

Considering, she sent a memo to a contact in Illegals. Detective Strong — solid cop — who might be able to fill in some blanks.

One thing stood out for her, and she replayed it in her head as she parked. Slice's reaction when he heard Lyle Pickering had been murdered.

Shock — that had read genuine — and anger. Not the smirking smugness she might have expected, not the dismissive shrug. Maybe, just maybe, he possessed the acting skills that could earn him one of Nadine's dickless gold guys. But why trot them out?

If he hadn't arranged the hit on Pickering — and she had to give that a fifty-fifty at this point — who had?

And why?

She stuffed the shades in her coat pocket as she started down the white-tiled tunnel of the morgue. She smelled bad coffee, somebody's breakfast burrito, chemical cleaner, and the death none of those other scents could quite smother.

As she reached Morris's double doors, she heard the familiar clomp heading her way. Peabody sort of trotted down the tunnel. Not in her fuzzy-topped pink snow boots, but in the pink cowgirl boots Eve — in a moment of weakness — had allowed Roarke to persuade her made a fine souvenir gift for her partner.

Then there was the pink magic coat, another moment of weakness. The color, Eve thought, not the magic. Another scarf worked the pink into what Eve assumed stood as spring green.

At least the pants were a dignified black, even if she'd styled her hair into a short yet jaunty tail.

"Good morning!" Peabody all but sang it. "Isn't that a beautiful sky out there? And we're heading up into the sixties today."

"I'm sure the dead guy on the slab in there shares your joy."

"Aw." Then Peabody did a couple of shoulder bounces. "He's dead either way, but we get to hunt down his killer under blue skies."

Hard to argue, Eve decided. And since it was, she pushed through the doors.

Under his protective cloak, the chief medical examiner wore a suit not the color of Peabody's beautiful sky, but softer, more the tone it would take on as dusk crept in. He'd paired it with a shirt the color of the salmon Galahad favored.

Which, she had to admit, was a kind of pink.

His tie matched the suit, as did the cord woven through the black braid down his back. Though blood streaked his sealed hands, his dark eyes warmed as he looked up — and paused in the act of weighing some internal organs.

Kidneys, Eve decided.

"Ah, two of my favorite people, and my first live visitors of this gorgeous day."

His tone matched the — damn it — jaunty music on his speakers. She began to worry that spring wasn't such a winner after all.

He ordered the music's volume lower, turned away to clean his bloody hands.

"A good catch on the needle mark, Dallas. It's all but obscured by what's left of his gang ink. We'd have caught it in the PM, of course, but finding it on scene gave us all a head start."

"What was it? Do you have that yet?"

"I put a rush on the tox. Hopefully, it won't take long. I can tell you the fresh needle mark, the fresh mark from the pressure syringe are the only signs on the body of drug use. Added to the health of his internal organs, his skin tone, and so on, I'd judge him as clean before the overdose."

"The bruises on his wrists."

"I agree with your on-site there, too. Gripped by good-sized hands, with some force behind them. From the angle" — he ordered a close-up on-screen, enhanced it — "You can see the bruising from the thumbs, from the fingers. From the angle," he repeated, "he was gripped from behind."

"Grab his wrists from behind, keep him locked while a second assailant jabs the needle in to take him out. It'll be a barbiturate of some kind. Some kind of tranq."

"Most likely, yes, and again, I agree. I found microscopic bits of fabric in the needle mark. The lab will, no doubt, confirm they came from his shirt. So they injected him right through his shirt."

"In a hurry. Get him down, or at least compliant, then you can stage the self-induced. The tourniquet to pop the vein, the pressure syringe, overloaded. Plant illegals in his room."

"Just another addict losing the battle," Peabody said. "They'd figure that's what the cops would see, would say."

"They're not as smart as we are, are they, Peabody?"

She nodded at Morris. "Not even close."

"It's sloppy," Eve added. "Surface smart, maybe, but not thought through. Bad tactics. Rushed, maybe. Because if you wanted him dead, send the three guys to beat the crap out of him one night when he's heading to a meeting, or coming home from work. It's . . . a cop bias on top of it. It's thinking, Cops won't look past the obvious show. He's just another junkie. Stupid to jab him with a tranq — but without it, he's going to put up a fight. And the slice on his throat. Just in case he struggled, even under the tranq, hold a knife to his throat as you shoot him up."

She slid her hands into her pockets, rocking on her heels as she studied the body. "It's lousy tactics. I don't see how you climb up to command status in a gang by using crap tactics. You take him in his apartment, you kill him with the substance he's worked hard to kick? There's personal in there. Sloppy, rushed, personal."

She pulled her hands out along with her communicator as it signaled. "Dispatch," she said. "Maybe something on the BOLO.

"Dallas."

Dallas, Lieutenant Eve, the body of the subject of your BOLO, Duff, Dinnie, has been found on East Broadway under the Manhattan Bridge underpass. See the officers at that location. Probable homicide.

"Copy that. Detective Peabody and I are on our way. Damn it," she added, stuffing the comm back in her pocket. "I'll be sending you another body, Morris."

"We're here to serve."

"Let me know, will you, when this vic is ready for his family to come in?"

"Why don't I contact Rochelle directly, save you that time?"

"Appreciate it. Let's move, Peabody."

"Moving." At the doors, Peabody glanced back. "You totally smoked the sax at Nadine's, Morris."

He smiled at her. "Happier times." When the doors closed, he sighed and looked down at the body. "Let's see what we can do for you."

Peabody trotted to catch up. "You didn't seem surprised about Dead Duff."

"Because I wasn't. She had to be dead or in the wind, and dead was the better bet. Junkies are unreliable, so you use one to kill, you'd get rid of her before she gets picked up for something and blabs to try to get out of it. Or blabs the next time she's high, or blabs to try to broker a high."

"You figure she was dead, essentially, the minute she opened the door of Pickering's apartment."

"Yeah." Eve slid behind the wheel. "She was mostly an easy lay. Just one more junkie who'd trade sex for a flop or a fix. Her usefulness here was the connection to Pickering."

Eve pushed into crosstown traffic. "And that usefulness ended when she opened the door. Turned her into a liability. Shaky tactics again."

"Why — Wait." Peabody narrowed her eyes, let it work through. "Because a better one would be to kill her right there in the apartment, same way as

111

Pickering. Then it looks like they got high together, and went too far."

"Got it in one. Whoever ordered it didn't count on somebody looking out and seeing the three Duff let in, but even then, if they'd done them both, it could read as a party where two partied too hard. You leave more illegals sitting around, right with the bodies, maybe some booze. Strip them down some so it looks like they were at least planning to have some sex along with the high."

"It's a good plan. Good thing you're on our side."

"First mistake was jabbing him with a tranq, second was letting Duff slip out so you had to kill her later. We need to know more about Marcus Jones. Here's what we've got so far."

She filled Peabody in as she drove.

"I'm not sorry I missed the trip to the underground. What stands out is Jones having enough money to go into a real estate partnership. Sure, the area where he has property is mostly dumps, but you still have to have enough to lay down."

"Yeah, and I can't give him more than fifty-fifty on arranging these hits. Figuring out real estate will generate income, getting enough to lay down for it, working a partnership, and so on. It takes calculation and some brains. And some forward thinking. These hits?"

"Sloppy," Peabody finished.

Eve wound her way to the windy, pitted litter trap where the road above echoed and vibrated with traffic.

As she got out she flashed her badge to one of the four uniforms securing the scene.

Two droids, two live, she thought. Smart as, if she had it right, they stood pretty much on the border between Banger and Dragon territories.

"Officer Grogan, Lieutenant."

She got her field kit out of the trunk, then ducked under the police barricade. "What do you know, Officer?"

"Nancy Nuts found her. That's Nancy Tobias, sir. Around here, she's Nancy Nuts. Sidewalk sleeper, scavenges for junk, sets out a hat now and then, does a song and dance for booze money. My partner and I just came on, and she rolls her basket up to us, says there's a dead girl down here, and how is she supposed to get herself an audience if there's a dead girl? We had her show us. Vic's messed up pretty bad, and no ID on her. We got her thumb on the pad, hit your BOLO."

"Where's Nancy?"

"We got her to sit down outside on the street, bought her an egg pocket. They won't let her in the café there. She's pretty ripe, so you can't blame them. The droid's got her."

"Peabody, why don't you go talk to her. Find out if she saw anything besides the DB, where she slept last night. You know what to do."

She started toward the body with Grogan. "This would be the crossroads, more or less, between Banger and Dragon turf. Is that right?"

"About. This is neutral territory because it's not worth spit. They use it sometimes when they stage a challenge. Assholes fighting for a leadership position, or the champion of one gang taking on the champion of another. She's not the first DB we've found here."

Eve looked down at the body. It might have been, in some distant past, Dinnie Duff had some pretty to her. The ID shot Eve had studied had shown considerable wear and tear for a woman of twenty-four, but some remnants of that distant past.

Her killer or killers had beaten even that out of her.

Her face was a mass of black-and-purple bruises, dried blood, gashes, swelling. As she wore no coat, no shirt, more bruising — black along the ribs — bloomed on the bone-thin torso.

One of her bare feet cocked crookedly, and had likely been stomped on. Her tights, covered with bleeding hearts, bagged around her ankles while a short strip of skirt fluttered over her abdomen and left the violent bruising on her thighs, her genitals, exposed.

"Seen her around now and again," Grogan said, "even rousted her a few times for begging without a license. Popped her for possession last summer. She didn't have much of a life, but they sure as hell crushed what she had out of her."

"Yeah, they did."

"It's a violation of the neutral zone," he added. "It comes out Dragons did this, we're going to have a gang war."

Considering, she turned, looked at him. "Is this the sort of thing the Dragons do?"

"It seems to me if she crossed some line and they decided to beat her to death, rape her with it, then they

114

wouldn't leave the body here. They'd dump it over in Banger territory. Leaving her here, in violation, messing her up this bad when everybody knows she's a Banger Bitch? You're asking for a war."

Interesting, Eve thought, crouching and opening her kit.

She verified ID, recording the body in situ. "Evidence of rape, possibly multiple rapes. Victim has been beaten — face, torso, abdomen. Her left foot and ankle appear to be broken. She has no identification, no coat or shirt, no shoes. The tears on her earlobes indicate she'd been wearing earrings, and an assailant ripped them from her ears. Bruises on her throat indicate strangulation. Manual choking."

Carefully, Eve ran her sealed hands over the blood-matted hair, around the back of the head. "Skull's crushed. Pounded it into the ground," she added. "That's what they did.

"Lure her in here. Got some good stuff, payment for the job you did tonight. Start punching. She's got deep bruises around her mouth. Hold a hand over her mouth so she can't scream. It'll be the same three who did Pickering. It's going to be the same three."

Three big males against one underweight female. Brave bastards, a credit to their gang.

Fuckers.

"Beat, kick, rape. Take turns there. Choke her. Beat her head against the concrete. Take her coat, her boots. Her shirt's going to be ripped most likely, why take her shirt? Take her 'link if she has one, anything else, rip the fucking earrings out of her ears, and leave her."

She took out her gauge, checked for time of death.

"Just before twenty-two-thirty. About the time we got to Banger HQ. She's already here getting the shit beat out of her when we're talking to Slice."

"Are you thinking Slice ordered this, Lieutenant?"

She pushed to her feet. "You don't?"

"Well, you're Homicide, but . . ."

"But you work this area."

"I sure do."

"So, tell me why you don't think Slice ordered this."

"I don't see him wanting a gang war, not this way. He wants more turf, sure."

"Turf's pride," Eve put in. "It's power and money."

"That's right. But you're asking for just what you've got this way. A bunch of cops asking all kinds of questions. Like I said, leaving her here is a violation. I'm not saying he's a humanitarian, but if he'd ordered her hit, it'd be cleaner."

He swiped a finger across his throat. "He likes the sharps. Beating and raping her takes time. He'd want it quick and done. Dump her somewhere, maybe in the river. Looks more like a sex deal gone wrong, a mugging, whatever. Keep away from his turf. Cops'll ask questions, but not like we will now, and not a spit away from his HQ."

His take ran on the same track as hers.

"You've got points, Grogan. Right down the line. I need you and your partner to do a canvass. TOD is just before twenty-two-thirty, but it wasn't quick. We're looking for anything from twenty-one to twenty-three. Do you know if she had any friends?"

"I don't know much about her, Lieutenant. She had some crazy in her — not, you know, benign like Nancy Nuts. A mean streak of crazy. I can't remember seeing her hang out with anyone much. She struck me as more a hanger-on than part of the inner circle, if you get me."

"I get you. Stay with the body," she ordered the droids, and called for the sweepers and the dead wagon.

CHAPTER
SEVEN

As Eve wrapped up, Peabody came back with a torn, bloody shirt in an evidence bag.

"Pretty sure this is the vic's," she said. "Nancy had it. She said how it was just lying there, and she could use it. I bartered an energy bar for it."

"Good catch. It's been compromised now, but we'll send it to the lab. Did she have boots or shoes, a coat?"

"No. What she has is mostly broken stuff, a couple stray socks, hubcaps. Junk. She did say she'd seen the girl with the purple face around."

Peabody glanced at the body. "Purple face is pretty accurate at this point. She recognized the hair, the pink hair, and figured it was Meanie who got dead. That's what she called Duff, because she was mean."

"Officer Grogan concurs."

"She said mean things to Nancy — who really ought to be in a shelter. She won't go, Dallas. She likes camping out. Sidewalk sleeping's camping out to her."

"How much did you give her?"

Peabody sighed. "Twenty. I know it's pissing in the wind, but —"

"No, it's not. She'll get a couple of decent meals out of it." And some rotgut, Eve thought, but why say so? "Put in a chit for it."

"Thanks, but it was personal. I liked her. She called me Officer Puppy. She said I have puppy eyes."

"She's not far off. And we're not far off from Banger HQ. Let's go chat with Jones."

"He said he didn't order the hit on Pickering," Peabody began as they walked back to the car. "Could he have ordered this one? Payback for her part in Pickering?"

"The timing's off, unless he found out before we told him. If we'd found her floating in the East River, or with her throat slit well inside or well outside Banger territory, I'd lean harder that way. The beat cop says the kill zone's neutral territory, and the kill violates the code. The kind of violation that can start a gang war."

As Eve settled behind the wheel Peabody considered. "Maybe he wants one. He wants more territory, and there's nothing like blood and war to cement a commander's cred."

"I'd lean harder that way if we didn't know he has business interests that could end up burned out or attacked in a war. The beat cop gave me a pretty clear idea of the politics. And I've got a tag in to Detective Strong to see what she knows or can find out about the illegals trade on Banger turf."

"She'll dig in. She's a good one. Maybe the Dragons worked this to put Jones and the Bangers on the hot seat. Tie them up with cops, erode power. You hit their HQ last night, and we're going back this morning. That seat's pretty hot."

"I could lean there. But . . ." She pulled to the curb near Banger HQ. "Pickering strikes me as personal. So he's turned his back on the gang," she added as they got out of the car. "And that might earn a slap, a threat, or a beating followed by derision, not a hit. He went inside and didn't name names, didn't give up his gang family. That earns serious cred. You'd think enough to buy him safety."

At the door, she repeated the secret knock. The one who opened it gave her the hard eye. "Got a warrant?"

Not as easy a mark as the one the night before, Eve calculated. More muscle than fat, a tat of a snake coiling over his shaved head. And a look of at least average intelligence in that hard eye.

"We need to talk to Slice."

"He ain't receiving visitors today. Especially cunt cops."

"Why don't you let him know Lieutenant Dallas is here, see what he says?"

"Fuck you."

When he started to shut the door, she slammed her shoulder against it. The force, and the surprise, took him back a couple steps. She didn't figure that would last.

"Fine. I'll just tag the PA's office for that warrant. My partner and I will take a stroll around the block."

"A nice day for a stroll," Peabody added.

"Yeah. And when we get back, we'll haul Marcus Jones — that's Slice, by the way — into Cop Central for an interview on suspicion of murder. Two counts."

"Bullshit, bitch."

She pulled out her 'link, keyed in. "Yeah, Reo," she began as she strolled away. "I need a warrant. Actually two," she continued, letting her voice carry back. "The first a search and seizure."

"Try it, bitch!" he called out. "You'll end up bloody."

Deliberately, she stopped, turned back to face the door guard. "Make that three. Might as well have one ready for obstruction and assault on a police officer. What's your name, asshole?"

"Fuck you!"

He slammed the door.

"So, Reo."

"I'm barely into my first cup of at-the-office coffee," Reo complained. "And somebody's already yelling fuck you."

"Well, I've got two bodies in under twelve hours, had a trip to the underground, and I'm currently exchanging insults with the door guard at the Banger HQ in the Bowery."

"Okay, you win." Reo, a classy blonde and fierce litigator with a hint of magnolia, rolled her eyes. "You're looking to search and seize at Banger HQ? And anticipating an altercation?"

"It might come to that. Let's give it a minute. So . . ." Eve dug for small talk. "How are things?"

On the 'link screen, Reo stared. "You're asking me 'how are things?'"

"I'm killing a minute. It's the small talk. I say, how are things. You say, good or, they blow. I say, great or, gee, that sucks. Then you say, how about you, and I say — Never mind," she finished when Jones opened the door. "Minute's DOA. I'll tag you back."

He stood in black baggies, bare chested and barefooted, with annoyance simmering in sleep-clouded eyes.

"The fuck you want now?"

"Dinnie Duff's dead. We can talk about that out here, in there, or down at Central. Pick, and now."

"How's she dead?"

"Pick," Eve repeated. "Now."

"Shit." He rubbed a hand hard over his face. "Gimme five."

When he shut the door, Eve glanced at her wrist unit. "If he goes over five, tag Reo back, get her started on the warrants."

"You know he's probably having illegal substances, weapons, and other questionable items scooped and moved out the back."

"If he has brains, he did at least some of that last night after our conversation. Right now, he needs to get dressed because he doesn't want to talk about Duff inside, or out on the street. He sure as hell doesn't want me to pin his ass in Central."

"What's his other choice?"

"We'll see."

"Okay." Peabody waited a beat. "So, how's it going?"

Eve couldn't stop the quick laugh. "Better way to kill the five, dig into Duff, find out next of kin for notification. Movement at a couple windows on the second level — third's boarded, but we've got a couple people awake enough to watch us out here."

"Slice works out. He's got a mag bod going. I don't think much of the one-armed tat sleeve personally."

"This is why small talk is useless and annoying."

"Not entirely. I also noted his gang tat's the same design and in the same place as the one Pickering was having removed — even while admiring his six-pack abs."

"Okay, that earns you a point."

"Duff has a mother in Jersey City, age forty-eight, domestic worker. And a father in Attica, a lifer. They didn't make it legal. One sib, male, age twenty-six, with an Atlanta address — employed at a construction firm, same father listed."

"We'll go with the mother."

"No criminal there. Father's a bad seed, in and out, and now in for good this time for aggravated assault. Looks like the brother had some issues as a juvenile, got straightened out. He's been in Georgia for eight years, employed at the same firm for the last five. No recent bumps.

"Duff, on the other hand."

"Yeah, I skimmed hers. Illegals, possession, possession with intent to distribute, unlicensed solicitation. A long line of petty shit. No real violent crimes on her sheet."

"Now she's dead, and if she wasn't dead, she'd be looking at charges of accessory to murder."

Jones made it out in about three, red hoodie, black pants, scarred high-tops.

Black, Eve noted, but not Lightning brand.

"I want some breakfast."

Since he kept walking, Eve signaled Peabody, fell into step with him.

"I have to hand it to you. I don't know if I'd have an appetite if I had the cops coming around asking about the murders of two people I'm connected to."

"I ain't worried about it."

He turned into a grease trap called 24 Hour Eats.

It smelled like overcooked onions, tremendously bad coffee, and fake meat sopped in that grease.

The decor ran to walls painted screaming orange, decorated with blissfully optimistic pictures of food. The yellowing white of the counter had scorch scars, and the handful of backless stools carried strips of duct tape along the seats.

The line of booths looked no more promising, but Jones swaggered back to the last, a corner, slid in, tapped a hand on the scarred laminate of the table like he owned the place.

Which he did, Eve thought. At least a share thereof.

A waitress, somewhere in her forties, Eve gauged, with a lot of tits straining against an atomic-yellow uniform, shuffled right over with a coffeepot.

"How's it going, Slice?"

She poured what pretended to be coffee into the brown mug he turned over. Eve waved a hand in a no signal over hers. Peabody shook her head.

"Get me the cheese grits, Melba, and three eggs scrambled soft, sausage, and toast."

"I'll put that right in for you."

She shuffled off, pausing to fill the mugs of a couple of men who looked more like they were ending the night than starting the morning.

The counter waitress slapped a plate in front of a solo female Eve tagged as street level.

Jones added three containers of nondairy creamer and three packets of fake sugar to his coffee.

124

"How'd Dinnie get herself dead?"

"Probably by letting three murdering goons into Lyle Pickering's apartment. She finished that up getting beaten to death, raped repeatedly, choked, and stomped on. Her assailants stole her shoes, her coat, her 'link if she had one, ripped her earrings out of her ears, and left her under the Manhattan Bridge overpass."

He hadn't shown any reaction to Eve's listing of the violence, but his face lit with fury at the location.

"Fucking Dragons."

"I don't think so."

"Fuck you know?"

"I know she, reportedly, told at least two of your crew she intended to go to work, needed the scratch. But she never showed, and hasn't worked there in days. I know she went to Pickering's apartment for the specific purpose of aiding his killers with entry."

"She had the softs for Pick." He jabbed a finger on the table. "I say bullshit she helped him get dead."

"Yet that's exactly what she did, and a few hours later, in fact, about the time you and I had our first conversation, she was being gang-raped — and not onstage for pay — and beaten, kicked, having bones broken and her skull fractured."

"If she did that to Pick, she earned it. If she did that, she went in with the Dragons, that's what."

"Unless you can give me a solid reason why the Dragons would order a hit on Pickering, and Duff would work with them on it, I'm not buying they killed her."

"Dragons don't need a reason." But his tone lacked conviction. Then it turned ugly. "Chinks talking Chink more'n they talk American. Why don't you go over to Chinktown and bang at that mofo Fan Ho instead of getting on my ass."

"We'll table your racism for now. Who had it in for Pick?"

"I said, you talk to Fan Ho about that, 'cause it ain't none of mine. Now, some maybe don't like how Pick didn't come back when he got out, but you don't kill a brother over that. Now, maybe Dinnie got her ass up seeing he didn't come back to her, neither. Maybe she got high and got pissed and got some fuckers to do him."

"You just said she was soft on him, wouldn't have a part in killing him."

"Maybe she didn't mean to." He shrugged, drank coffee. "Maybe just give him a good taste of what he'd been missing. That boy loved his Go. Maybe she figures she gets him back on it, he comes back to her." He shrugged again. "How the fuck I know?"

She leaned in, ignoring the waitress who set down his plate — grits as orange as the walls, runny powdered eggs, sausage that smelled like something pigs wallowed in, and toast as thin as paper.

"I the fuck know the men who entered Pickering's apartment entered with the intent to kill him."

"Pick?" The waitress squeaked it out, then trotted rather than shuffled away when Jones aimed a hard look at her.

"You don't know shit about what's in their heads."

126

"They came up behind him, restrained him, jabbed a needle right through his shirt to tranq him. They set him up so it would look, if you didn't look close, like he pumped himself full of that Go, planted more in his room.

"Duff got that started, and now she's dead, too. And you know what I'm going to find? I'm going to find the same three who killed Pickering killed Duff. To shut her mouth. I'm going to find those three are three of yours."

"The fuck you will."

"Count on it. Who wants a war with the Dragons? Who wants one enough to violate your neutral zone with rape and murder?"

"Ask the Dragons. If they want one, they'll get one."

Eve watched his face while he squeezed anemic ketchup on his runny powdered eggs. "There's a lot of collateral damage in wars. People hunker down at home, don't go out to eat or shop. They don't look to move into the area. Wars are bad for business, aren't they, Slice, and you've got considerable business in this sector."

He began to eat, his eyes on his plate now rather than on her. "My business is my business."

"Where'd you get the scratch to buy into the building where you flop? And this place? And Wet Dreams?"

"My business" — he scooped up more eggs — "is my business."

"Banger business mostly runs to illegals, sex work, the protection racket, a little identity theft, a little fraud.

127

You'd pull in a share of that, a top-level share, but it's hard to see that share spreading out enough to buy into property."

"We in the security business. We offer up security to locals, help keep the neighborhood safe."

He gestured to the waitress. "We keep the neighborhood safe around here, Melba?"

She smiled like a woman with a stunner at her throat. "You sure do, Slice."

"We got licenses for the sex work," he continued. "We got those who flop at one of our places paying rent for it. If I got business, it don't mean I ain't loyal to my crew."

It wasn't only temper under his tone, barely controlled, but nerves. He didn't like her pushing on his outside enterprises.

So she pushed again.

"Maybe you don't see taking a little extra off the top as disloyal. Others may disagree. In fact, some in your crew might wonder how it is you can buy property with a disgraced lawyer and his skirt — then charge rent."

She could smell the nerves on him now, the way she could smell what passed as sausage on his plate.

"Owning shit's no crime. Seems to me you're saying all this was to spark off a war, and how I got business interests that could get squeezed by a war. Makes no sense for me to get it going."

"Maybe, maybe not. Property values go down, you buy it up cheaper. All kind of angles here, Slice."

"Screw your angles." He flicked his eyes, filled with rage now, up to hers. "I got nothing more to say."

"Then think about this while you're finishing your breakfast. If you didn't order these hits, somebody in your crew went around you and ordered them. Who wants a war?" she repeated, and slid out of the booth.

"Something to think about," she added, leaving him to his runny eggs and orange grits.

"You don't think he ordered either hit," Peabody said as they walked back to the car.

"Fifty-fifty's down to sixty-forty against. Both kills were sloppy. I don't think he'd be that sloppy. He's a killer, and if he had reason, he'd have taken both of them out."

Once again, she got behind the wheel, studied the HQ. "Then there's that forty. Maybe the sloppy had purpose. Maybe he's got an eye to buy up more, scare people into selling or moving. You fight your way up to top ranks because you want power. You go into business because you want to make money. Right now, he's got both going."

She started to pull out when her 'link signaled. She took it on her wrist unit as she drove. "Dallas."

"Strong. I just got in — had an op closing up — and got your message. Lyle Pickering."

"In the morgue. So is his onetime skirt, Dinne Duff. What do you know?"

"I know we need to talk. I can come to you."

Something in Strong's tone had Eve deciding to skip the trip to Casa del Sol to talk to Pickering's boss and coworkers. "I'm heading into Central. Give me thirty."

"I'll see you in your office in thirty."

"I'll want Peabody, so the lounge might be better."

"Your office, sir. Please."

"Okay then. In thirty. Something there," Eve mused. "For now, Peabody, check in with EDD on Pickering's 'link. He had to have a sponsor. Let's see if we can pin that down, and have him or her come in to Central. Seems to me a recovering addict might tell another recovering addict more than he does his family. Add the family to the list, too. We need to have conversations. They come to us or we go to them, whichever works."

While Peabody worked, Eve mulled. She turned over what she knew with what she believed. Juggled it all again, turned it over again.

By the time she pulled into the garage at Central, she figured she had about fifteen of her thirty left to set up her board, her book.

"Okay, EDD ID'd the sponsor from the frequency of transmissions and the content of same as Matthew Fenster. Forty-one, he's employed at the Clean House rehabilitation center and also helps run their halfway house — where Pickering did his stint after making parole."

"That makes it an even closer connection."

"He's got one marriage — divorced. One offspring. Bumps for possession, for fraud. Lost his position at a financial investment firm due to that fraud. Went into a white-collar prison nine years ago — when his son was two. Did three years — during which time his wife divorced him. Completed mandatory rehab, did a voluntary stint when he got out at Clean House, lived in their halfway house. Looks like he took some courses on counseling. He joined the staff three years ago."

She scrolled more as they headed to the elevator. "His earnings took a dive. Before he got axed and locked up, he earned high six figures, not including some nice bonuses. Currently, well, I make more. He has a resident's apartment in CH, included in his salary. No bumps since his release."

"Contact him while I set things up, see if he'll come in. If he balks, we'll pay him a visit at work."

Eve pushed out of the elevator, headed for the glides after one stop due to the crazy eyes of a woman in restraints between two uniforms.

She didn't want any distractions.

When she turned into her bullpen, she regretted leaving the sunshades in her car. They might have prevented her eyes bleeding from a glance at Jenkinson's latest tie, featuring jagged blue sperm squiggles over a field the color of chili peppers. If you infused them with plutonium.

"Bring Strong in when she gets here," she told Peabody, and escaped to her office.

She tossed her coat aside, programmed coffee. As she began to set up her board she considered that only the day before she'd spent several loose hours at her desk tackling paperwork.

Now she had two unquestionably connected murders, a potential gang war in the offing, and a whole lot of questions.

At the center, Lyle Pickering, recovering addict. A man who had appeared to drive himself to a fresh start. The system had worked in his case. Crime, punishment, rehabilitation.

Now it would be her job to make certain that system continued to work for him, and find him justice.

Dinnie Duff. Eve pinned the ID shot, one of a worn-looking woman wearing a pound or two of eye gunk and pink streaks in her hair, and beside it the crime scene shots of the battered, bloodied dead.

An addict, one who'd sold her body and likely any remaining portion of her heart and soul for the next fix or a place to flop. In and out of lockup, part-time underground sex worker, and one complicit in the murder of Lyle Pickering.

And still the system she'd slithered around would work to find her that same justice.

Marcus "Slice" Jones. A bad dude, she considered as she added his photo. Maybe, maybe not behind the murders, but a bad dude nonetheless, and one she didn't doubt had killed or ordered hits.

Not an addict, she mused. Likely sucked down some Zoner now and again, downed his share of brews, but he showed no signs of abusing his own products.

Too smart for that, she decided. He had some brains in there, and some canny with it. If he'd used those qualities on the right side of the law, he'd probably have earned some reasonable success and a decent life. And he wouldn't have her determined to slap him in a cage.

Because that's where he belonged.

She added the tox report on Pickering as it came through her incoming. Enough Go in his system to kill him twice — and a solid, souped-up dose of Out, like an injected mickey.

Wouldn't a man, one with brains, one who trafficked in illegals, know that heavy of a tranq would show up in autopsy?

Would he care? she wondered. If not, why go through the motions to set it up to look like an OD?

Sloppy, sloppy, she thought as she added to the board. Maybe even impulsive. Slice struck her as more calculating than impulsive.

With more coffee, she sat at her desk, started her murder book. She'd barely begun when she heard the clomp of Peabody's cowgirl boots.

Detective Lilah Strong stepped in with her.

Eve's first thought was the Illegals detective looked tired, with shadows under the eyes, against the toffee-colored skin. She'd let her hair grow some, but unlike Peabody's jaunty little tail, Strong let hers explode in a cloud of curls around her face.

She wore a rust-colored jacket over her service weapon, serviceable boots, and a grim expression.

It deepened when Strong's tired eyes scanned the murder board.

"Lieutenant."

"Detective." Eve gave Peabody the come-ahead as she rose. "Close the door, Peabody. You want coffee, Detective Strong?"

"As strong and black as you've got it, thanks. I was finishing up a long one, didn't get your message until . . . Damn it, Lyle."

"You knew him." Eve handed Strong her black coffee, Peabody her coffee regular. So the three women stood with their mugs, facing the board. "You worked on the bust that sent him in the last time, with Officers Zutter and Norton."

"Yeah. He was high and stupid, I was undercover. He tried to sell me Go, with a downer chaser to bring me down after the high. Then he ran, then he got in a pretty solid roundhouse before we got him under control. You know, later, he told me that was the best thing that ever happened to him."

Eve could hear it. Not just regret, but grief. "You kept up with him?"

"He contacted me from prison, asked me to come talk to him. I figured maybe he had some info, wanted to turn it for some privileges or early parole. What he wanted? To apologize for the punch, and the uncomplimentary names he called me. Part of his twelve steps. I'm going to say I didn't buy it right off, figured he had some angle."

She drank some coffee. "But he didn't ask me for anything, just said he was going to try to stay clean. He knew he had work to do, knew it wouldn't be easy.

"Anyway, it made me curious enough to talk to the warden, and the prison addiction counselor. Both said they felt he'd turned a corner, or at least was standing on one. Still, I didn't so much buy it."

"When did you start to buy it?"

"At his parole hearing. His family was there, his sister spoke. She would let him move in with her, on the condition he finished his halfway-house term with no issues, he went to regular meetings, got work, and kept clear of anyone in the Bangers. You could see she wasn't a pushover. It wasn't blind faith so much as hope. And . . . grit," Strong decided. "She wanted her brother back. Lyle spoke of remorse, of getting and staying clean, learning to cook, and finding self-worth and pride in learning a skill."

Strong let out a breath. "God, he was really proud he could cook. Then he said what turned a key for me. He said with his sister's help and the help of the prison shrink, he'd come to understand his addiction to illegals was connected to his addiction to the gang. He'd used illegals as an excuse not to face life as it was, and the gang as a way to distance himself from the family he was hurting. So he had to work, every day, not to fall back and use, either. It didn't sound like bullshit."

"After he got out?"

"I kept track. I wondered, because it didn't sound like bullshit, if he could walk the walk. I dropped by the place he worked, and he came out on his break. I could see he was still clean, could see how the waitress — old enough to be his mother — doted on him. That's when he told me getting busted, getting locked up tight, had been the best thing that ever happened to him."

Strong stopped, rubbed at the back of her neck. "Goddamn it. He said he had his family, he had a job. Sometimes when he got really tired or low, he thought how easy it would be to get a little boost. How he'd tell himself maybe he would — after he went to a meeting. If it was a bad maybe, he'd tag his sponsor."

Strong looked down at her mug. "Any chance of another hit? Getting the real's a big moment."

"Sure." Eve signaled to Peabody.

"I asked him if any of the Bangers gave him grief. He sort of brushed it off as no big. Yeah, a couple times some had come around wanting to hang or get high or pull him back. If it shook him, he tagged his sponsor, or went to see his younger brother, maybe his grandmother."

Strong took the refilled mug, gestured to Duff's photo. "That one there? He told me — not that first time, but later — she'd come around looking to pick things up with him — sex and drugs. He cared about her, that was the problem. He gave her information about rehab — and Clean House, where his sponsor works. Tried to get her to go to a meeting with him, that sort of thing. And I'm pretty sure he gave her a little money now and then when she came crying."

"When did you turn him?" Eve asked. Strong sighed.

"I'm still not sure if I turned him or he turned himself. Some of both, I guess, some of both. But for the last ten months he's been one of my confidential informants. And I'm sick, just sick, Dallas, thinking that might be why he's up there on your board."

CHAPTER
EIGHT

Eve eased a hip onto her desk. "At this point I can't tell you why he's up there. I know how. I know Duff's one of the whos, but I don't have clear motive."

"Could be I just gave it to you. I don't know."

"Why did you take him on as a CI?"

"He contacted me, asked me to meet him. That's close to a year ago. He didn't want to meet where he worked, but at this place near his grandmother's. Near one of his meeting sites, too. Fake-coffee place a lot of those in recovery go to after meetings. Well out of Banger territory, a good clip from where he works."

Eve nodded. "So you realized he didn't want to be seen with you by someone he knew?"

"Yeah, had to figure it. He looked stressed, said he'd been to a meeting, and he was going to another after he talked to me. Or maybe he'd just go hang with his sponsor. But he'd wrestled with telling me what he was going to tell me, and he couldn't go back to work if he just swallowed it down."

"Why don't you sit down?" Eve said. "Take the desk chair. The other's a killer."

"Thanks." As she sat, Strong took another moment, gathering her thoughts. "The waitress I told you about had a kid still at home, her youngest. Sixteen. So, Lyle tells me the kid sees a couple of Bangers trying to sell this boy's cousin — and that one's fourteen — some junk. Sort of pushing him around, saying how he might as well because if he doesn't, they'll just take whatever he has on him, and his shoes, and he'll get nothing. So the older boy heads over to get his cousin, tells him to take off and go home. And ends up getting the crap beat out of him. Ended up in the hospital. Messed him up good."

"Lyle knew the kid."

"Yeah, and he knew the two Bangers. The kid was afraid to give the cops a description, but he told Lyle."

"And Lyle told you."

"Yeah." She paused again, drank more coffee. "I want to say it wasn't easy for him to rat them out, but he'd — he'd really turned that corner, Dallas. They'd beat that kid down for protecting his cousin, and Lyle wouldn't just stand by, you know?"

"The kid mattered to him. The kid's mother."

"Yeah. And doing the right thing mattered, too. He said if we busted them for this, it would come back on the kid, maybe the cousin, maybe the mom, too. But couldn't I do something?"

"You did something."

"This was back when Oberman still had Illegals in her pocket, so I had to do something on the down low. I had a lot more free time back then, as our squad was basically Oberman's cover, so I used it to watch the two Lyle identified. It didn't even take long for me to catch them making a deal. Another minor, apparently their

138

specialty. I didn't bust them for the assault, but for possession, and intent to sell to a minor and within fifty feet of a school. That wrapped them."

"He was grateful," Eve prompted.

Strong looked back at the board, at Lyle. "He baked me cupcakes, fancy ones. Damn good, too. I took advantage of that, Lieutenant. I took advantage."

"You did your job, Detective."

"Ah, fuck me." After setting the coffee down, Strong pressed her fingers to her tired eyes. "The whole Oberman deal — I knew she was a dirty cop, worse than dirty. But I couldn't do a damn thing. It stewed in me, and here I saw a way to do my job, like you said, and work around her. I never listed him as my CI. Never told her or anybody, not at first, I had a source. One I started milking. He was grateful," she murmured. "He'd developed a genuine moral code, you could say. So he'd feed me bits — a lot he'd pick up from Duff. Mostly they turned out to be good bits, and I could use them. Small-time, mostly, but we both felt good about it."

"I think it probably helped him," Peabody put in. "Gave him something, like his cooking. He was making restitution."

"I guess. You know he was getting his gang tat removed. He'd show me the progress. Slow — it costs more to get them off than to ink them on. He introduced me to his sponsor, Matt Fenster."

Strong let out another breath. "Ah, I'd better disclose Matt and I have sort of been seeing each other recently."

"Okay."

"I just want to be up front on that. Have you notified him?"

"Not yet."

"Would you let me do that? I'd like to tell him in person. He's going to take it hard, LT. He was really proud of Lyle, and they, well, they had a real connection."

"Peabody, did you reach him?"

"Yes, sir. I asked if he could come in, and he said he'd be here before noon. I didn't tell him why."

"You take a few minutes with him, Detective."

"Appreciate it." Steadier, Strong picked up the coffee again. "After we took Oberman down, that bitch, and got the dirt out of the squad, I still kept Lyle on the DL for a while. I just wanted to get a good feel for the new LT, the transfers. I didn't tell my boss about it until a few weeks ago when — between what I got from Lyle, what I was able to put together from pattern, from some buzz — I thought I hit on a fairly major illegals buy.

"We busted three Bangers, got a couple of flunkies buying up the junk for an asshole trust-fund baby on Long Island. Got him, too, but he got a deal." On a scowl of disgust, Strong gestured with her mug. "Money talks."

"I heard about that. Good bust. Isn't the trust-fund asshole doing six months — minimum-security rehab palace, but six months in?"

"Yeah. The Bangers are doing a dime each, and he gets a knuckle rap. But it's something. I thought I had enough shields up, Dallas, to cover Lyle, but if I didn't . . ."

"He made a choice, a courageous one. Don't take that from him."

Strong turned her gaze to Eve. "I need to be in on this. He was mine. I need to be in on this."

"I thought that was understood."

Eve knew Strong to be tough, so the swirl of tears in her eyes brought some concern. "Okay, listen —"

But Strong waved a hand, battled back the tears. "I'll copy you on all my files where he played a part. How they'd get to him?"

Eve ran it through, gave Strong a minute to absorb it.

"Yeah, yeah, he'd have let her in. It's the first I know about her going to his place, going into his place. At least, he never told me she had. She'd hang outside the building, catching him coming or going to work. Sometimes she'd wait outside where he worked. Lately he didn't see her as much, and he heard she'd started flopping with a Banger called Bolt."

"Yeah, that sticks."

"He's a bad one, Dallas. Bolt, along with a female — not a Banger Bitch but a soldier — Tank, because she's built like one, and Riot are lieutenants for a reason."

Frowning, Strong studied her coffee before she drank. "It might be Duff hooked up with Bolt to try to get more stable status with the gang. Can't say for sure, but if she came around crying, asking for help, I see Lyle opening the door — even just to give her a couple bucks, get her gone."

"You don't see him being involved with her again?"

"Risk his parole, his job, the life he was building? Big no. He felt sorry for her on some levels. He saw her as caught in the same cycle he'd finally broken for himself. And they had a history, so he'd try to help her."

At a knock on her door, Eve moved over, opened it to Santiago.

"Sorry, LT. There's a Matthew Fenster out here. He says you asked him to come in."

"Yeah, thanks. Ask him to wait a minute. Peabody, check and see if we've got an open Interview room so Strong can talk to him in private. Tag me when you're ready, Detective," she told Strong. "Make it quick. I want his take on this."

When she had breathing room in her office again, Eve turned back to her board. Back to Dinnie Duff.

Why would Duff have betrayed such a soft touch? Addicts like her always needed money for the next fix, and it sounded like she'd been able to whine a few bucks out of Pickering routinely.

Then again, addicts like her could and would betray anyone.

Still.

Then again, Pickering wouldn't get high with her, have sex with her, hang out with her. All of those would be essential needs for someone like Duff.

He gave her a few bucks here and there, but otherwise, he'd cut off their connection. No banging, no partying.

Would that make him just another mark? No, she considered, more than just another. A mark, but one she wanted to pay back for casting her aside.

Maybe.

"Were you pissed off at him, Dinnie? Yeah, I bet you were. Fucker thought he was better than you, with his going-straight life and asshole job. Maybe some payback in there."

Maybe, maybe, but she could punch a dozen holes in that one, Eve mused. And the first would be if nothing turned out to be missing.

She sent a text to Rochelle.

She needed a walk-through of the crime scene.

When she got the buzz from Strong, she walked out to Peabody in the bullpen. "Where are they?"

"Interview B."

Eve waved Peabody down again. "I've got this. I need you to notify Duff's next of kin, and I want to know the last contact. You know the drill. I need you to run a search on Pickering's journal for any mentions of Strong, Duff, the Bangers. When we're done here, we're meeting Rochelle at the apartment."

She headed out, walked down, and opened the door of Interview B.

Strong sat beside a man who rivaled Feeney's explosion of ginger hair. He had pale green eyes to go with it that, right now, were blurred with clouds of grief. He had a long, sharp nose and a long, thin neck that made his face — between the explosion and the stem — look oddly oversized. A single silver stud glinted in his left ear.

"Matt, this is Lieutenant Dallas."

He got to his feet, a skinny guy in a gray sweatshirt, and extended his hand. "Lieutenant. Anything I can do to help you."

"I appreciate you coming in so quickly, Mr. Fenster."

"Matt. Just Matt."

She sat across from him. "I understand you were close to Lyle. I'm sorry for your loss. When did you last see or speak to him?"

"A couple of nights ago. Thursday night. We went to a meeting, had coffee after. We tried to hook up every week if we could. Just connect, talk."

"What did you talk about?"

"Work, on both sides. How things were going with me and Lilah — Detective Strong. His family. Sports." In a helpless gesture, Matt lifted his hands, let them fall again. "We were friends. We got to be friends."

"Did he mention Duff, or any concerns he had about other gang members?"

"Not Thursday night. I'm going to say I'd discouraged him from giving his hard-earned money to Dinnie. We didn't talk about it Thursday, but we had before, a few times. I tried to show him that he was, by trying to be kind, enabling her."

"He still had an attachment to her," Eve prompted.

"He had this hope she'd eventually come into Clean House, or go to a meeting with him. Basically, he wanted to save her, even knowing she had to save herself."

"He had feelings for her."

"Not romantic ones, but romanticized ones, if you follow me."

Because she did, Eve nodded. "Okay."

"I backed off there some because he had to make his own choices, and it felt like he was starting to see my point. She wouldn't let go, Lieutenant, and he had to. I think he would have, but . . ."

144

He lowered his head, took a grip on Strong's hand. "I never saw this coming. I knew she was trouble, but not like this. Now they're both dead."

"It's not on you, Matt."

"You, either," he said to Strong, pressing their joined hands to his heart. "It's not on you, Lilah. I warned her off once."

"Tell me about that."

"Just a couple weeks ago Lyle tagged me, said he felt like he needed a meeting after work, and could I meet him."

"Was that usual?" Eve asked.

"Not unusual. I still tag my sponsor when, for whatever reason, I'm feeling the pull. It's backup," he explained. "You get that. Sometimes you need backup."

"Sure."

"I went by the restaurant so we could walk to a meeting together, and she was out front. She was pissed because she knew she wouldn't get anything out of Lyle if I was around. She tried to shake me down instead."

Strong stared at him. "Jesus, Matt."

He only shrugged. "She said she needed rent money. If I didn't want her getting it from Lyle, I needed to cough it up — and offered me a BJ in exchange."

"I didn't hear about this," Strong muttered.

"Neither did Lyle. I didn't see the point. I asked her if she'd like me to call the cops, have her hauled in for unlicensed solicitation, unlicensed begging. Maybe I could get stalking tossed in there, too. We said a few uncomplimentary things to each other, but she left. Parting shot? Unless I was — sorry about the language

145

— 'sucking Lyle's dick,' she'd get him back, and I could go to hell."

"You should've told me, Matt."

"Babe, if I told you about every time I have hard words with an addict, it's all we'd talk about. She took off, Lyle and I went to the meeting, had coffee after. He thanked me for going with him, said he was feeling a little down."

"Did he tell you why?" Eve asked.

"Yeah. It was the anniversary of his mother's suicide. He got through it, and I felt like getting Dinnie off him that particular day was, well, meant, you know? He just didn't need that shit."

"Any other recent altercations with her, or anybody else in the gang?"

"No. I'm not in their territory. I do know Slice went into Lyle's work right after Lyle got the job. They go back, you know, to when they were kids. Slice figured he'd come back to the gang, Lyle said he was done with that life. They got into it a little, but Lyle said Slice backed off — in a 'fuck you then' kind of way."

"Any return visits?"

"I don't think so. I really believe he'd have told me if Slice kept at him."

Matt reached for Strong's hand again, obviously needing the connection. "Lyle contacted me after that time, needed to talk. I know he told his parole officer, and his boss backed him up on it. Some of the other Bangers went in off and on in the first few weeks, trying to get a rise. He didn't give them one. He stuck."

Matt scrubbed a hand over his face. "It's not easy, Lieutenant, to stick, to push back your old life, the people in it, to stay straight and sober every day when somebody's tempting you otherwise. But he stuck."

That picture came through clear enough, Eve thought. "How about the prison shrink? Lyle met with him on and off, too. Do you know him?"

"Sure."

"Would Lyle have told him anything he wouldn't tell you or Detective Strong?"

"I can't say, but from what I know Lyle just wanted to keep that connection open. He credited Ned with helping him turn the corner while he was inside."

Matt shifted, leaned forward a little, met Eve's eyes straight-on.

"Addicts are liars, Lieutenant. I spent a good part of my life smoking, popping, drinking anything I could get my hands on, and lying about it. I'm spending this part of my life dealing with people who are either doing the same thing or trying to break the cycle. I'm probably nearly as good at spotting a liar as both of you. And I believe Lyle told me whatever weighed on him, whatever lifted him, worried him, made him proud. Being a CI made him proud, but he'd never have done it if they hadn't put that boy in the hospital. He talked to me about it before he made the call."

He looked at Strong, smiled a little. "Backup," he repeated. "I was his backup, so I said how it might've been him. Not in the hospital, but putting some kid in there. Beating on some kid just because he could. And until he'd gotten straight, he wouldn't have given a damn. Kid should mind his own, right? Shouldn't get in front of Banger business. Asking for it. He saw things different now."

"Okay. If you think of anything else, let me know. Detective Strong, I'll be in touch."

When she rose, so did Matt. "Lieutenant? Is it all right if I go see Lyle's grandmother? I know the family. Hell, they invited me to Thanksgiving dinner. I'd like to go see them, do something."

"I've got no problem with it. Keep his CI status out of it, for now."

Eve went to get her coat, her partner. "Lyle's sponsor comes off solid and steady. It's clear they had a tight, personal friendship, also solid and steady."

"How's Strong holding up?"

"She'll stand. Did you make notification on Duff?"

"Yeah. Duff's mother took it like she'd been waiting for notification most of Duff's life. Sad, resigned, unsurprised."

They headed out of the bullpen as Peabody ran it through.

"She said she hadn't spoken to Duff in more than a year. Duff'd gone home, claiming she was in trouble, needed to come home to get well, and so on. Not for the first time," Peabody added. "A couple of days in, the mother comes home from work, the daughter's gone, the living room screen, costume jewelry, and the cash gone with her."

"That couldn't have been a big surprise, either," Eve said as they rode down to the garage.

148

"Not really. The mother had taken her in with the warning if she screwed up again, she'd never let her come back. She screwed up. The mom had all the locks changed, and told her neighbors if they saw her daughter, they should get the police. And she left a message saying the same on the 'link number she had."

They worked their way down to the garage.

"She said her daughter didn't have friends. She had losers and thugs. Always blamed everybody else when something went wrong, started using when she was about fourteen. Took off whenever she liked, would come back crying, being sorry, making promises, then do it all again. Took up with the Bangers, and the mother laid down the law. If she ran with that type, she couldn't come home. Anyway, she didn't know who she ran with, specifically, just the gang, the type."

And that picture, Eve thought, also came though clear enough. "Okay."

"On the journal search," Peabody said as she settled into the car, "there are mentions of Duff, of the gang, Slice and other members, of Strong, his sponsor — but, at a glance, he doesn't write about being a CI."

"Kept it confidential, even from his journal. It wasn't passcoded, probably to show his sister he had nothing to hide, but he's careful. Maybe somebody breaks in, takes it, reads it."

"He didn't have any trouble writing down his thoughts about Duff. You go back a few months, they're conflicted. She needs help. Maybe he can help, that sort of thing. But I read an entry he put in just a few days ago where he wrote about deciding he had to cut her off, all the way off, and why. What he said to her, what she said."

"That jibes with the sponsor's take. What was the why?"

"He finally realized what his sponsor, the prison shrink, his family, his boss, the waitress at work had been telling him all along. He wasn't helping, but enabling. In the case of his boss, it was a little more direct. She was a junkie whore, and just because he wasn't doing her didn't mean she wasn't screwing him, and he paid her for it."

"Sounds like his boss had it right. But Lyle still let her into his apartment."

"From some I skimmed in the journal?" Peabody began. "He had a lot of soft spots. The wit said she was crying, and how she needed help. In the journal, Lyle wrote he told her she could come to him if she was ready to admit she needed help — for her addiction. He'd help her get into Clean House, take her to meetings, ask his sponsor to sponsor her. Otherwise, blow basically. If she kept coming around, high or jonesing to get high, he'd call the cops."

"So she comes to his place, says she needs help. Maybe says he had it right, she's ready to ask for help. Please help. He buys it, opens the door. She can spin him a load of bullshit, but she has to get him out of the room long enough for her to let the muscle in. So, can she have some water — crying, shaking. He goes into the kitchen to get it, takes out his 'link. Likely to tag his sponsor. And that's that."

150

As she thought it through, Eve drummed her fingers on the wheel. "But how does the junkie whore come up with a plan to get into the apartment, when Lyle's alone, and distract him enough to get all that muscle in there — with the tranq, with the illegals. And why, if she set it all up, doesn't she hang around and watch it go down? If this is her payback for him cutting her off, wouldn't she want a bigger piece of it?"

She glanced over at Peabody's thoughtful face. "Don't you want to stay, make sure it's done right? And where did she get the illegals, or the money to buy them?"

"All good and valid points," Peabody conceded, "but we've got enough to confirm that's how it went down."

"We've got enough to confirm she got him to open the door, then she let in the killers. What all this says to me? She's the bait. Maybe she wanted him dead, too — but then again, why did she leave?"

"She didn't want to see the rest."

Eve waved that off. "I'm not giving her the credit of actual feelings. She left, I think, because she'd done what she came to do. What someone with enough punch — and access to illegals — ordered up. Add in, they don't kill him in a fight, don't beat the crap out of him in payback or to teach him a lesson. Because it wasn't so much payback. It was . . . business," she decided.

"Sloppy, poorly planned, but business. Personal business. With Duff as the bait. And once that business was done, they — what is it? — cut off bait."

"Just cut. Cut bait."

"Whatever." Eve pulled up in front of the apartment building on the edge of Tribeca.

"Yeah, and 'whatever' makes sense." Peabody angled in her seat. "Duff whines to the right person — or the wrong one — about Lyle's cutting her off, even threatening her. And that person sees an opportunity. Take the ex-Banger out — who does he think he is? — and use the junkie who can't keep her mouth shut to do it, then take her out. The gang-war angle, Dallas," she continued as they got out of the car. "Jones said he's not looking for that, but maybe he is — the property-value angle you played with. Or maybe one or more of his lieutenants are trying for a coup."

"Dissention in the ranks, very possible. Or Jones saw this as a way to cement his authority." She needed to think about that, the ins and outs of that.

They went inside, started up. "Sacrificing an ex-member and an easy lay isn't much of a sacrifice."

"Like pawns in chess."

Eve considered, rolled it around. "Yeah, like that."

They found Rochelle already on her apartment level, in the arms of the witness across the hall.

A young man Eve recognized from the ID shots as the younger brother stood a few steps away.

"I'm so sorry, Ro, just so sorry. When I think I watched those awful people go right in there . . ."

"If you hadn't, we might not know what they did. So I'm grateful. We're all grateful."

"He was a good boy. He'd come back to you a good boy," Ms. Gregory said as she moved back. "You let me know when you're having his memorial. I'm going to be there." She let out a sigh as she nodded toward Eve.

"I've got to get to work. You let me know if you need anything."

"If I could have just a minute, Ms. Gregory? Peabody, why don't you take Rochelle and her brother inside?"

"I just feel sick about all this," the woman said when she and Eve stood alone in the narrow hallway.

"I just want to confirm what you told us yesterday. You saw the woman we've identified as Dinnie Duff on the stairs."

"I did, and heard her knocking on Lyle's door. Calling and crying."

"Do you recall what she said?"

"Something about needing help, asking him to help her, crying her crocodile tears and saying she couldn't keep on, was ready for help."

"'Couldn't keep on.'"

"'Can't keep on like this' — something like that. Saying how he promised to help. I didn't hear it all. I was heading down, like I said. Trash night."

"Yes. But you also saw the three she let in — through your peep. You're sure they were males?"

"Big guys. I saw 'em from behind, but you don't see many women with those builds."

She thought of the female Strong had mentioned — built like a tank.

Maybe.

"Anything about them, anything at all, stand out? Something they said, a gesture, clothing?"

"Didn't say a word in the few seconds I looked out. Just standing there in the dark hoodies — hoods up — and baggies. I just didn't see . . ."

She frowned, poking her bottom lip out, then pulling on it while she thought back. "Well, now that I think about it again, one of them had the jitteries."

"'Jitteries'?"

"Couldn't stand still." She demonstrated, bopping her shoulders, a little shuffling of her feet. "And he kept —" She held her arms down by her sides, started snapping her fingers, one hand, the other, and back again. "I didn't think of that last night. I guess it was like he was listening to music. Might've been. Then that bitch opened the door, and they went right in, she snuck right out. I don't know how that helps you any."

"It's very helpful. If anything else comes to you, let me know."

"I can promise you that. I have to go. I had my morning off, but I'm due in right now."

"Thank you again."

As Ms. Gregory hurried down the stairs, Eve went into the Pickering apartment. She could still smell fading death and the lingering whiff of the sweepers' chemicals.

"I don't see anything out of place in here," Rochelle was saying. She stopped, turned to Eve. "Everything in here looks like it always does. In the kitchen, too. I'm sorry, this is my brother Walter. Walt, this is Lieutenant Dallas."

He kept his hair cropped close to the skull and his face clean shaven. Like his sister, he had heavy-lidded eyes. At the moment, they looked sleep starved.

"I read the book, saw the vid." He didn't smile when he said it, but extended a hand. "I hope you're as good as they made you out to be."

154

"Walt." Rochelle spoke quietly, laid a hand on his shoulder.

"I didn't mean it as an insult."

"Why don't we go through the rest of the apartment," Eve suggested. "Rochelle, you'll be most familiar with your own room. Let's start there."

They walked down — another narrow hallway.

"It looks like I left it."

"Why don't you check the closet, the dresser drawers, the desk drawers."

"All right. I really don't have anything worth stealing. I always try to keep twenty dollars in emergency cash in the pocket of this jacket. And here it is. I don't see . . ."

Exactly, Eve thought. "What don't you see?"

"I was going to say I don't see anything missing, but my red purse is gone. I've had this old red purse for years. I always had it hanging on this hook. Gram bought it for me — remember, Walt? — when I got the job. She said red's good luck. I still use it sometimes. It's not here."

"Can you describe it?"

"It's just a red purse — bright, shiny red — pretend patent leather, you know, nothing extravagant. It has a silver chain if you want to wear it on your shoulder, and a magnet clasp. It's what you call an envelope bag, I guess. About a foot long, maybe, and I don't know, eight inches wide. It's not worth anything."

"Bright red, silver chain. Caught the eye. Anything else?"

"No." She pressed a hand to her temple. "I loved that damn purse."

Eyes a little blurry, she walked out, yanked open a dresser drawer. "They killed my brother, and I'm getting upset thinking they came into my room, pawed my things."

"Ro." Walter moved behind her, rubbed her back. "It's natural."

"Nothing feels natural." She pulled a long, thin black box from the top drawer. And opening it, let out a choked gasp. "Oh, Walter, they took Mama's brooch. That terrible, gaudy old pin. And oh, the earrings Wilson gave me for Valentine's Day. And, oh God, just a cheap bangle bracelet I picked up on the street one time. It's just costume jewelry, but they took it anyway."

"Do you have pictures of anything that was taken?"

"I — God." Rochelle framed her face with her hands, pushed in with them. "My mind's just drained out. I took a selfie on Valentine's Day, wearing the earrings. One of me and Wilson together. It's on my 'link."

Because her hand shook, Walter took her 'link when she pulled it from her pocket. "I'll find it, Ro. You should sit down."

"I just need to move a minute." She paced the little room, struggled to regulate her breathing. "I never wore the brooch. It was cheap and gaudy, but it was my mother's so I kept it."

"Gram has a picture of her wearing it."

She stopped, looked at Walter. "Of course she does. I forgot."

"Can you get that to me?"

"I'll take care of it," Walter said, and held out the 'link to his sister. "Is this the one?"

"Yes, yes, that's it. They're so pretty."

And shiny, Eve thought as she studied the photo on-screen. Gold dangles glittering with heart-shaped red and clear drops.

"Peabody."

Peabody moved to Walter, gave him the codes to send a copy of the photo.

"I don't think I have one of the bangle."

"Describe it."

"It's about an inch wide, I guess, three circles of colored stones. Like cabochons, in ah, purple and green and amber. It's not worth the stealing, but I liked it."

"Check the rest."

Once she had, Rochelle shook her head. "I don't see anything else."

"Let's check Lyle's room."

Rochelle gripped Walter's hand before they crossed the hall.

"His Save It jar. I know that was at least half-full." She moved to his closet. Her voice had thickened, but she managed to keep it steady. "His good high-tops are gone. He didn't wear them to work — grease and spills. He only wore them when he went out, over to Martin's, or sometimes when he went to church with Gram."

"Earned his points," Walter murmured and shared a smile with his sister.

"That's right. Grammy points. Black Lightning high-tops, with the white lightning bolt down the back. Size . . . I think size ten."

She walked to the dresser. "I don't know what he had, I mean, what he might've kept in his dresser."

"Is there anything you know he had that might be missing? Something shiny, say, like your jewelry, or eye-catching like your purse. Or usable like the shoes?"

"I don't really —"

"Did he have his earbuds on him?" Walter asked. "He'd have had them in his pocket, or if he was going to shower and change like he told Ro, he'd have put them on the dresser."

"We don't have earbuds in his effects."

"They're good ones. Martin and Clara gave them to him for Christmas. Bodell buds. Black. The Exec level. He prized them. And they're worth something."

Eve had them search, but already knew they were gone.

"We'll follow up on the missing items," Eve told them. "If they try to pawn anything, we'll trace it back. This is very helpful."

"I just don't understand." Rochelle ran a hand over her face, over her thick wedge of hair, down to the back of her neck. "If they tried to make it look like Lyle was using again and overdosed, why did they take anything? We'd have known somebody stole those things."

"If you'd believed Lyle was using again, what would you think when you found your jewelry missing?"

As she lowered her restless hand, Rochelle sighed. "That he'd taken it to get money for illegals. If I'd believed the first, I'd believe the second. But neither's true."

"Exactly, and now we have more lines to tug. The apartment's clear for you to stay."

"Actually, I'm going to pack some things. I'm going to stay at Wilson's for a few days, and spend time with my family. We're going to see Lyle later today."

"You can go ahead and pack what you need. Walter, why don't we talk out in the other room?"

"Are you okay, Ro?"

"Yes. You go ahead, Walt."

He hugged her first, held on a minute, then walked out to leave her alone to pack.

CHAPTER
NINE

"I'm going to see if Ro has anything cold. You want?"

"Sure."

He walked into the kitchen — needed composing time himself, Eve thought, though he'd held up well for his sister.

"She's got that bug juice — health crap. I wouldn't go there. A few Cokes because that was Lyle's . . . That was Lyle's poison, especially since he gave up drinking."

"I wouldn't mind the bug juice," Peabody told him.

"Okay, that's on you. I'm going for a hit of one of the Cokes."

"I'll go with that." Eve watched him from the doorway. He knew where everything was, didn't have to hunt. "You ever bunk here?"

"I lived here before college. Ro got the place after she got the job, and we went in on this two-bedroom. I live on campus now, but sometimes I flop on the couch since Lyle . . ."

He stopped pouring, braced his hands on the counter. "Rochelle, she needs to cry for a few minutes, then she'll steady it up. She's a goddamn rock."

"You're doing pretty well yourself."

"She's never going to feel okay living here again. That's okay, she should find a better, safer place. With the new job, she can do that. Shine's off that, right now, but it'll come back."

He finished pouring. "I wasn't sure about her letting him move in, not at first, even after he got the clear from the halfway house."

"It takes time to rebuild trust."

"It was just that Ro would be here alone with him, and if he slipped back?"

He looked over his shoulder at Eve with the eyes he shared with his sister. "I believed he was clean, you could see it, but I thought he should stay in the halfway longer first. Rochelle wouldn't have it, and she was right. Being here, with her, it helped him with that next transition. He told me that himself. Having Ro be here for him, having her to talk to, knowing she believed he could do it, it helped him."

He handed Eve a glass, and with a shake of his head, offered Peabody another filled with army-green liquid. "Don't say I didn't warn you."

He went in, sat down. "You want to know the last time I talked to him, so I'll just start there. He tagged me the night he died. He said he was heading home from work, had the night off and was planning to go see Gram, in case I could make it. I had to study, so I passed."

"How often did you see or talk to each other?"

"We talked or texted every couple of days. He liked to know how things were going. Sometimes he'd come by if I had free time, and we'd hang or go catch a vid.

Now and again, he'd flop in my dorm if we stayed up late talking."

"You were close." Peabody gave him a sympathetic smile. "I've got sibs. I know how it is."

Walter stared at his drink. "We hadn't been, but we worked on it. We got there. I guess I'd say he could tell me things he didn't want to tell Martin, maybe even Ro. Martin can be a little it's black or it's white."

"What kind of things?" Eve prompted. "Dinnie Duff?"

"Yeah. He felt sort of responsible for her. She was into all that shit before they hooked up, but after they did, he made it easier for her to get the junk, to work the streets — or not work. He took care of her, and he saw that as helping push her down. And under it? He cared about her. They had this common ground, since her father used to smack her around, even raped her when she was like sixteen, so —"

He broke off when Eve held up a hand. "Duff's father left long before she turned sixteen. He'd have been in prison when she was sixteen."

"But she told him . . ."

"Addicts lie."

"I know that." Obviously shaken, Walter dragged a hand over his hair. "I know it, but she told him all this, and he believed her. She told him her mother was a drunk who turned tricks and was in lockup half the time so she had nobody, had to live on the streets half the time."

"Her mother's a domestic worker, with no criminal record or any indication of alcohol abuse. Duff has an older brother in Atlanta living a decent life."

162

"Jesus, she played him. He believed her. He wasn't lying to me, Lieutenant. He believed her and felt sorry for her."

"I know it."

"It made her seem vulnerable, even helpless," Peabody added. "It made her a victim, gave them that common ground. Could he have found out the truth?"

"I don't know. I just don't. I know he finally decided he had to stop giving her money, listening to her bitching. He seemed a little pissed, I guess, but he didn't say he found out it was all bullshit. I was just glad he'd decided to stop with her, so I didn't ask too many questions."

He rubbed both hands over his face. "Clean break, he said. Screw that shit. Is that why she killed him?"

"We're looking at all the angles."

"He missed her — not just the sex, but her. Having somebody to be with. He missed sex, too." Walter smiled a little. "He said he missed having a woman, but he wasn't going to go there yet. I knew it wasn't easy for him to keep turning Dinnie away. He could've had the bang and walked away — but he didn't want to risk it."

"Did he talk to you about the gang?"

"Some, when he first got out, not so much in the last few months. He and Slice, they go back, so that was another hard one for him. I think the gang was easier to step back from, because he had family. But the individuals in it were harder. Slice, he was more of a brother to Lyle than Martin was, than I was, for a long

163

time. And Slice wanted him back, told Lyle he'd make him his next in command."

"Did he?" Eve asked.

"Yeah, right after Lyle got out, and again a few weeks later when he had the job. He asked me not to say anything to Ro, so I didn't. But it was hard for him to say no. He was somebody in the gang before he got busted. And after, he was still somebody because he kept his mouth shut and did the time. He knew he could walk back in there, especially with Slice backing him, and be important, be in charge. Have all the junk and women he wanted, walk down the street and see respect and fear. But he said no."

Walter lifted his glass, drank deep. "He took being a short-order cook in an all-night diner, living with his sister, going to meetings instead of hitting a club. Saving his pay instead of pocketing his share from the gang business."

Finally, Walter's voice broke, his eyes swam. "He was a goddamn hero. You find who did this, because Duff didn't do it alone. You find who shot my brother up with what he'd battled back every damn day. You make it matter."

"It does matter. He matters."

With effort, he pulled himself together before Rochelle came back, rose to take the small suitcase she carried.

"We can give you a lift," Eve offered.

"No, but thanks. I'm just going to drop this off at Wilson's, then we're going to pick up our family, and go see Lyle."

164

"We'll be in touch," Eve promised, and left them alone.

"I'll have the pictures of the two pieces we have sent out," Peabody said as they walked down and out to the car. "And descriptions of the rest. Big, stupid mistake to steal."

"Sloppy again. Crappy planning. The wit gave me more on one of the killers."

As Eve passed it on, Peabody noted it down. "Probably jonesing."

"Maybe. We're going to swing by and talk to Crack. Red purse, shiny jewelry. Catches the eye."

"Like magpies."

"Like what?"

"Magpies. You know, the bird that's attracted to shiny objects, uses them in its nest."

Eve knew — sort of — what a magpie was because Roarke had pointed them out to her in Ireland. "Magpies," she murmured. "Yeah, at least one's like a magpie. The other stuff — the shoes, the buds? That's somebody who can use them, or knows who can. You can pawn the buds, sell the shoes, but more likely you use them or trade them. Send the beat cops — Zutter and Norton — the descriptions, the pictures. I want to know if they spot any of it."

She had to hunt for parking near the Down and Dirty. It did the bulk of its business after dark, but parking didn't get easier in the daylight.

When she found a slot two blocks down, she grabbed it.

"Feel that." On the sidewalk, Peabody lifted her face. "That's what sixty degrees feels like. And sun. Winter's done! It is over!"

"You say that and just ask for it to dump a round of wet snow on your sixty degrees."

But damn if it didn't feel good to walk without getting slapped in the face by the wind or slogging through the last round of wet whatever decided to fall.

"How about a soy dog? My treat."

Eve knew the street dogs were disgusting, but even Roarke's amazing menus had never killed her taste for them. "Loaded."

"Is there another way?" Peabody almost danced on her pink boots to the cart. "I'm getting a fizzy water. The bug juice was pretty good, but I can't get rid of the spinach aftertaste."

"Fizzy water's good." Because cart coffee? That, she had lost her taste for.

Chowing on loaded dogs, they walked toward the sex club.

"So, how serious do you figure Crack is about Rochelle?"

"Because that's really what's on my mind right now?"

Peabody took another bite, talked around it. "There's always room in the brain for romance. And, you know, spring."

"What's spring got to do with it?"

"It's romantic." Seriously beaming, Peabody licked a little mustard off her thumb. "People get romantic in springtime."

166

"I thought they got romantic in winter for the body heat."

"Not sex, romance. Although in spring you could have sex in a meadow, because romantic."

"Bugs, bees, possibly snakebites on bare asses."

Undeterred — because spring — Peabody pushed on. "He gave her pretty earrings for V-Day. That says serious."

"Right now he's connected through the earrings and the woman whose lobes they dangled from to a couple of pretty serious murders." Eve polished off the dog. "Let's stick with that."

The Down and Dirty was, as its owner stated, a joint, and that's just what it wanted to be. It did a solid, sordid business with a mixed clientele of shady characters, wide-eyed tourists who wanted a risky and risqué experience before they went back to humdrum, the horny who'd pay to get lucky in one of the private rooms, and the broody type who seemed content to drink the swill as long as the server was mostly naked.

She'd had her bachelorette party (stupid term) at the D&D, watched her friends get stupid drunk, and had foiled — barely — an attempt on her life by a wrong cop.

Good times.

When she walked in, a holo band had the stage. The lead singer, female, wore elaborate body paint with the fangs of some sort of jungle cat impaling her tits. A large bird — maybe a hawk — flew above her crotch, talons at the ready. Various other predators stalked, fought, and prowled over the rest of her.

Her bandmates wore G-strings and crotch-high boots while a couple of dancers — live and wearing strategically placed glitter — gyrated.

Since the dancers worked up a sweat, glitter ran in sparkly streams while the band banged out the chorus: "Gonna pump you like a well, gonna drill you down to hell."

Romance, Eve thought, and headed to the bar.

The single tender, a brute with arms like cut steel, sat on a stool playing with his PPC. Idly, Eve wondered if monsters fought on his screen. Whatever he played, he had the time, as only a scatter of customers drank the swill or watched the show.

"Is Crack around?"

"Busy." The bartender didn't bother to look up. "Drink or blow."

Since it was precisely the level of charming service Eve expected at the D&D on a spring afternoon, she palmed her badge rather than flashing it.

"Tell him Dallas and Peabody want a word."

He looked up, gave her one hard study, then nodded. "Shoulda said."

"I'm saying now."

"Back in the office. Hold it."

He got up, all rippling cut steel, a single blue braid spilling out from an otherwise shaved head, and went through a door behind the bar.

"How do they get bodies like that?" Peabody wondered. "Do they pump iron twenty hours a day? Eat some special protein? Sacrifice goats to some primeval god?"

The last got a snicker out of Eve.

"It's scary and exciting at the same time. I'm glad McNab's not built like that. I don't think I could handle being scared and excited every day."

Crack came out — more rippling cut steel. He wore a deep blue shirt, one that actually buttoned and made him almost look like a businessman.

"You get them?"

"Not yet. Can we talk?"

"Yeah." He gestured as he came around the bar, led the way to one of the privacy booths. Though it made Eve's back twitch a little when he lowered the dome, she didn't object. Especially when he hit Mute on the control, and the band noise dropped to a faint murmur.

"Dinnie Duff was killed last night."

"Son of a bitch. How?"

"Beaten to death, multiple rapes, some choking. Morris will confirm. He's my next stop. They left her in the neutral zone between Banger and Dragon turf."

"I heard a report on a body found there, but they didn't give a name or much else."

"They will now, since we've notified her next of kin."

"They killed her so she couldn't talk. Don't have to be no skinny-ass cop to figure it. How you gonna find those three motherfuckers now?"

"By doing the job. If being a skinny-ass cop was easy, everybody would do it."

"It's the job even when the cop doesn't have a skinny ass."

Crack managed a smile at Peabody. "You've got a fine ass, girl. I'm just worried about Rochelle, her family, too. Miss Deborah took it hard, real hard."

"The grandmother."

"She had her kids all back together, you see. She had the one everybody thought was lost come home. Really come home. And now . . . They're going to see him today, and I know how hard that is. But I thought it best I stayed back, let them go as a family. Maybe I should go. Maybe I should."

"I think you made the right decision," Peabody told him. "Give them this time, then you'll be there."

"We just left Rochelle and her brother Walter at the apartment. She was packing up some things."

He nodded at Eve. "She let me know she was gonna meet you, and we'd already talked about her staying with me. Not so much room over at Martin's place. I ain't going to let her go back to that apartment. That's a talk we'll have when she's settled some more."

"There were some things missing."

"They stole from her, too." His eyes, already hard, turned to stone. "What did they take?"

"They emptied out Lyle's coin jar, took his good shoes, his earbuds. I'm going to confirm the buds, make sure he didn't leave them at work."

"He wouldn't've. No way. It wasn't just because they were prime ones, but he got them from Martin. Martin was kinda a holdout on Lyle. He held back the longest, and the buds? Well, it was saying how he trusted Lyle again, had his back again. He'd never have left them somewhere."

"Rochelle had a red purse in her closet. It's gone."

"That little red job?" Obviously puzzled, he held his big hands out to indicate size. "It have money in it?"

"No. Just the purse."

"That don't make a spit worth of sense."

"It might. They took her mother's pin — brooch — from a box in her dresser, and a bangle bracelet."

"That makes more sense. They ain't worth anything, but if you're a fuckhead you could think they're worth something. That pin was sentiment. I hope you can get it back."

"They took the earrings you gave her for Valentine's Day."

"Well, shit." He punched the menu, ordered a brew. "Want a drink?"

"No, we're good. The other jewelry was costume, no real value. I'm betting the earrings were the real deal, whatever Rochelle thinks."

"If I said how they're real, she'd be too nervous to wear them."

"Are they insured?"

"Yeah, yeah." As his big hand tapped, tapped, tapped on the table, he scowled through the dome. "I look like a fool to you?"

"You look like a big, hard-bodied black man gone soft over a woman to me."

Without turning his head, he shifted that scowl to Eve.

"If they're insured, you have the exact description," she continued, unfazed, "the carat weight on the rubies and diamonds."

"Diamonds. Rubies." Peabody hunched her shoulders at the twin looks from her companions. "Sorry. Just wow."

"Just little ones," Crack responded. "I liked the look of them, that's all."

"What are they insured for?"

"Ten."

"Th — thousand?" Peabody hunched again. "Sorry!"

"I'll need that information. They'll probably try to pawn them. Taking easily identified items from the crime scene's a stupid mistake. I have to lean toward taking the jewelry's something they might think gets blamed on Lyle — if they figure cops are stupid enough to buy the OD. But the purse tells me something else. Peabody's magpie theory."

"Bright, shiny things." Crack's brew finally eased out of the serve slot. "Might be they aren't looking to pawn. Gonna keep it for their nest, or give it to some skank."

"And when the beat cops see some gang skank sporting diamonds and rubies, we'll have them. We have one more lead. The woman across the hall remembered something else. One of the three couldn't stand still. Like maybe he had music in his head. Makes me think of the geeks in EDD — always moving. And this one had his arms down by his sides, snapping his fingers.

"You have a lot of the shady come in here, and you're not far out of Banger territory. Maybe you've seen someone like that in here."

"I'd tell you if I had, and I'll be asking my people to watch. I leave the customers be, unless they get out of line. Then?" He mimed cracking heads together. "We get some Bangers in here now and then." He shrugged.

172

"They know they cause trouble in my place, I give them more and worse."

He took a long, slow pull of his brew. "I know you do the job, both of you. And you're about to say something to me about not doing something I think should be done if I see some Banger snapping his fingers, or some skank wearing my Ro's earrings. You don't have to. You took care of the fucker who took my Alicia from me. You'll take care of those who took Ro's baby brother from her. Anyway, she wouldn't like it if I did what I maybe think I should do.

"If I did something, it would piss you off and disappoint her. I ain't aiming to piss off skinny-ass or fine-ass cops, or disappoint my woman. Especially when I'm going to ask her to cohab with me."

"Cohab," Eve echoed, as stunned as Peabody had been about diamonds and rubies.

"I've had my share of fine women." He kicked back in the chair, looking up at the top of the dome as if seeing a parade of those fine women.

"I'm gonna tell you not one of them would say I didn't treat her good, treat her right. The first time I sat down talking to Rochelle, I knew, right then, she wasn't a fine woman. No, she wasn't. She was *the* fine woman. Not much puts a scare into a head-cracker like me, but knowing that gave me — you call it a pause. Yeah, I had a pause."

Peabody all but swooned. "That's so romantic."

He shot her a grin. "Ain't it just? After the pause, I thought, Well, that's gonna be that. I've been taking it slow because *the* fine woman, she's worth the time. I wanted to ask her to live with me for a while now, but I knew she had to give Lyle all she could. I was thinking I could look into getting a bigger place, and they could both move in, but now . . . Anyway, she ain't going back to that apartment."

He slapped a finger on the table, ran it across the surface. "That's a line right there. We'll have a talk about that line, but I won't be taking no on it. Right now she needs her grieving time, and you need your cop time."

He took another pull. "I'll get you that insurance stuff."

"Okay. One last thing. Did Lyle say anything to you about cutting Duff off? Telling her he'd call the cops if she kept hassling him?"

"No. We got along fine, me and Lyle, but I'm not the one he'd talk to about that. Did he?"

"It looks that way."

"Now he's dead, and if that's the why of it, I'm gonna be more pissed, and I'm running out of pissed room. And still, goddamn it, I'm glad he laid that line. A man's gotta lay his line. Women, too," he said with a glittery look. "So don't get bitchy."

"Getting bitchy *is* one of my lines. We'll be in touch." Eve gestured at the dome.

When he lifted it, Peabody rose, then hesitated. "I know you're feeling like there's nothing much you can do to help. You are helping by being there for Rochelle. If you want something, I don't know, more tangible . . . People bring food for death. You could have food sent

174

over to where her family lives so they don't have to think about it. It would just be there."

"That's a fine idea, Peabody. I thank you for it." They left him brooding into his brew while the holo band banged and the dancers gyrated.

"That was a good thought, Peabody," Eve said when they walked back to the car. "It gives him something to do."

"He looked so sad. Pissed, yeah, but sad, too. He loves her — I mean the big *L*. Jeez, he gave her ten-thousand-dollar earrings for V-Day." She gave Eve an elbow bump. "What did I say about romance? Spring!"

"V-Day's in the winter." Eve returned the jab. "Shiny gifts equal follow-up sex, which equals body heat for some types. So what did I say?"

"Damn it. No, I've got better." Peabody shot a finger in the air. "Romance knows no season."

"We're heading to the morgue. See what that does to romance."

"It'll still be spring."

CHAPTER
TEN

Dinnie Duff wouldn't see spring, not this one or any other.

She lay on the slab with Morris's precise Y-cut closed with his equally precise stitches.

He swiveled around from a short counter where he'd been working, rose.

"And here we three meet again, without the thunder, lightning, or the rain."

"I know that." Peabody lifted a finger. "Shakespeare, right?"

"It is indeed." He crossed to the body on the slab. "Unfortunately for young Duff, she didn't have the same outcome as the bard's Macduff."

Since Eve didn't know what the hell they were talking about, she focused on the body. "COD confirmed?"

"While several of these injuries, particularly the combined injuries, would likely have caused death left untreated, it was, as you noted in your on-site, the skull fracture. The repeated slamming of same against the concrete and gravel. She had several pieces of both in the wounds. Broken ribs — and a punctured lung from the breaks. Broken nose, detached retina, fractured cheekbones — both — the bruising on her neck indicates repeated chokings."

"Choke, let her come around, choke again. Probably during the rapes."

"I can't tell you how many violated her, as they suited up, but she was repeatedly and forcibly violated. At least once postmortem."

"Sick fucks."

"I can't disagree, though the sick fucks might not have fully realized she was dead. I'm finishing the report now, but I can tell you, in technical terms, they beat the crap out of her, raped the crap out of her, and killed her by beating her head against the ground until her skull cracked like an egg."

"Suited up." She'd held out a little hope they'd gone into her bare. "Either because they worried she'd give them an STD or because they were smart enough to worry about DNA. Or both. Did she fight back, get a piece of one of them?"

Morris gestured so they lowered their heads together over the body. "The bruising on the arms, the legs — mostly calf area or close to ankles?"

"One goes in, the others hold her down."

"Yes. And though it's hard to make out without goggles due to the extent of the facial damage, I also conclude a hand over her mouth at some point. Squeezing. And then the choking would have also prevented calling for help. I can't tell you how many, as I said, but I'd say no less than three."

"It'll be the same three she let into Pickering's apartment. Cut bait," Eve murmured.

"Her tox came back positive for Zoner and Funk. I found no sign she'd been a habitual user of Funk, at least not long term."

"Wanted her compliant," Eve mused. "Maybe told her it was her usual mix."

"A stingy amount of both, so while I agree on the compliance, they also wanted her awake and aware. And while they suited up, I found some hair, some fiber. No DNA match on record on my scan for the hair, but I've sent it all to the hair and fiber queen."

"Harvo will run it down if it can be run." And faster, Eve knew, than anyone else on- or off-planet. "Chilly last night. Why undress when you can just unzip? Sloppy again. If you're smart, you pump her with the junk like you did Pickering, but hey, what's the fun in that?"

Because it had told her all it had to tell, she stepped back from the body. "These were hits, both of them, carried out by thugs. Underlings. And both of them personal. Maybe doing her where they did, leaving her there has a side benefit of stirring up gang tensions, but it's personal."

"I doubt this poor, doomed woman would disagree. She would have suffered. I gauge the first blows occurred about an hour before death." Morris looked back down at Duff's face. "A very long hour for her."

"Yeah. She was dead when Lyle opened the door, but a long hour."

When they walked outside, Peabody took a deep gulp of air. "Still spring, even if that put a damper on it.

Bigger damper would be you saying we're going back to Banger HQ."

"We'll let the beat cops keep an eye out there for now. Whoever ordered this wanted her to suffer, wanted her hurting and violated. Personal. She was flopping with the one named Bolt, one of the lieutenants. Let's find out more about him."

"I'll see what I can dig up."

While Eve drove, Peabody dug.

"Okay, got him. Kenneth Jorgenson's a very bad boy. Age twenty-five, bad boy son of Oliver Jorgenson and Pauline Grant, who ended their eleven-year marriage shortly after Oliver — also a bad boy — went in for fraud, embezzlement, and money laundering. One sibling, Jessica, age twenty-eight. That's Staff Sergeant Grant — she took her mother's maiden — U.S. Army, currently based in Nevada, ten years in. She enlisted at eighteen."

"Where's the mother?"

"Two residences — Palm Beach, Florida, and Bar Harbor, Maine. Married, seven years, to Humphrey Merkle, no offspring from that relationship. He's loaded — founder of Bertinili's Frozen Pizza."

"That's assembly-line shit."

"And sells. They also do pastas and all that. Anyway, loaded."

"So the Banger comes from money."

"Well, he started off with it." Digging, Peabody toggled and scrolled. "Everything went south when the father went down. They had to downsize, big-time. Mom went to work for — ha! — Bertinili's company, worked her way up the chain, and married the big guy. But by then, she'd spent considerable time dealing with the bad boy. Or not dealing — hard to say."

"What kind of bad?"

"Since his juvie record's already unsealed, I can tell you he's got truancy, destruction of property, shoplifting, trespassing, possession of illegals, possession of a knife over the legal limit, and assault."

Eyebrows lifted, Peabody glanced over at Eve. "That's all before he hit thirteen."

"That's bad enough, and cruising toward worse."

"Yeah. The mother actually tried a military school. He got kicked out. Then we've got more assaults, some B and E, illegals, more destruction of property, and so on. That's just what stuck before sixteen."

"Cruised to the worse," Eve decided.

"And kept going. He's got a rape charge in here that didn't stick — victim recanted. Looks like he was already a Banger by that time."

Peabody continued to scroll as Eve drove into the garage at Central. "Whoa. Dallas, he went after his mother — physical assault — and the sister kicked his ass. You go. Looks like he was about seventeen."

"Let's get the report on that. I want the details."

"Will do. He's done some stints. Been out now for about four years. Been hauled in a few times, but wiggled out."

"Could be he wants a higher rank than he has, more power than he's got. Let's pull all we can on him."

"Jesus, Dallas." The beaming that spring had brought on had dimmed by the time Peabody got in the elevator. "He beat on his own mother. What if the sister hadn't been there to stop him? That's more than bad boy. I mean, if you'd punch your own mom —"

"Why quibble about killing your fuck buddy?"

A woman with a sweep of winter-white hair and a sour expression stepped on. "Language!" she snapped at Eve.

"Yes, ma'am, that was language."

"Are you a police officer?"

"That's right."

She jabbed a long, red-tipped finger into Eve's chest, repeatedly.

"Ma'am, I'm going to ask you to stop that."

She jabbed again. "I pay your salary, young lady, and I don't expect officers of the law to use such language."

As she spoke, jabbing that finger, the doors opened on the next level and let in a pair of uniforms discussing the dickwad they'd just brought in.

The woman actually said, "Harrumph!" then stalked off the elevator.

"Must be her first trip to a cop shop." Eve rubbed idly where that finger had tried to poke through flesh, and waited another level before jumping off.

"Get those reports on Jorgenson," she said as they used the glides. "He's not a big guy — and the wit's firm on that. Unlikely, if he's involved, he's one of the three who killed Lyle. As an LT, he'd probably have access to the illegals stash, be able to cut out enough to take Lyle out, to plant the rest."

"To pass the junk to Dinnie, too."

"Yeah, he's a definite possibility."

"Could he do all that without Jones knowing?"

Eve replayed the visit to HQ, and Jorgenson's reactions. Pushing Jones, pushing at him to stand up, to strike back.

"That's something else to find out."

In her office, Eve hit routine. Coffee, updating board and book. Then she sat, boots on desk, coffee in hand, for some thinking time.

The evidence, and every instinct, said both murders came through the Bangers, with Lyle Pickering as the primary target. The method, the setup on Pickering read as an attempt to mask murder with accidental overdose. An addict surrendering to old habits.

That method also read personal grudge. Easier to jump him on the street one night after a late shift, if taking him out was the only goal.

The why of taking him out, Eve mused. Gang pride? He'd cut himself off from his "family," even started the process of removing his gang tat.

Not enough, she thought. Enough for a beatdown, possibly, but not enough to kill. Or to spend so much valuable product in the cover-up attempt.

But more than enough, she considered, if someone in the gang discovered Pickering's connection to Strong.

And yet, wouldn't that rate a beatdown, a serious beatdown, followed by an execution? Not a relatively tame OD?

He'd betrayed that family, worked with the enemy. And for that, death — but in this case a relatively painless one.

Because the cover-up rated as high, or possibly higher, than the crime?

She pushed up, paced as she rolled, rolled, rolled it around.

Then she broke her own rule — really, it would only take a minute — and tagged Mira on her personal 'link.

"Eve."

She led with "I'm sorry. This isn't personal, but I figured if you were in a session or a consult you wouldn't answer."

"I'm actually about to leave for the day — early. Dentist appointment. Routine, she says, hopefully, as always."

Instinctively, Eve ran her tongue over her own teeth. "Yeah, good luck. It's about the gang-related murders. I sent you the reports, and realize you probably haven't read them yet."

"I did glance at them. You hadn't flagged them for me as urgent, but after meeting Rochelle, I wanted to see what I could do. Why don't I come to you? I have a little time before I have to leave for the appointment."

"Great. Thanks."

"It'll take my mind off the dentist chair. Five minutes."

Eve used it to make herself a kind of chart, working the connections, victims, suspects, players, witnesses.

A lot of links there, she decided, and added the chart to her board.

She turned at the sound of Mira's heels.

Maybe Peabody had it right about spring, she mused. Mira had certainly dressed for it, going for sunny yellow in one of her sleek suits. And the heels made her think of Peabody's meadow with flowers blooming from toe to spike. She carried a light topcoat in pale, pale blue over her arm.

"Thanks for the time."

"It's not a problem." Mira laid the coat on the visitor's chair. "I liked Rochelle quite a bit. I'm so sorry she's going through this."

As she spoke, she walked to the board, studied it. "Have you told her he was Detective Strong's CI?"

"Not yet. If that was the motive, or part of the motive, I'd like to keep it quiet for now."

"Do you think he told someone, other than his sponsor?"

"I think the chances are low. I still have to give his journal a thorough read, but we didn't find any mentions there. If he didn't write it in his personal journal, didn't tell his sister, it's hard to see him talking about it. That doesn't mean somebody didn't find out, or suspect."

Mira's eyes, softly blue, studied Eve's chart. "If they did, that sort of betrayal would almost certainly equal a death sentence."

"Who planned it, ordered it, and picked the three to carry it out? Because I'm not buying Duff, who ends up beaten to death only hours later. She had no standing in the gang, no pull. Add in she was a serious addict. So it's hard for me to buy she'd not only have access to the illegals, but would leave them behind to try to cover up the murder. But . . ."

Eve circled. "She was pissed at him. He'd recently given her the heave. Get lost or I turn you in. You can bet she whined about that. To the other Banger Bitches, to this guy." Eve tapped Jorgenson's ID shot. "Since she was trading him sex for flop space."

"Which would give her motivation to help exact punishment on Pickering," Mira agreed. "Murder seems extreme if she or the others didn't know about his CI status."

Eve tapped again — Slice and Bolt. "These two. Jones is currently top dog, and he and Pickering went back. Similar enough backgrounds, and what might have been a genuine friendship at one time. He offered Pickering second in command if he came back, and that tells me he valued Pickering."

"Second in command?" Mira eased a hip on Eve's desk, nodded. "That's more than friendship, I agree. Yes, I'd say he valued Pickering, trusted and respected him, to make such an offer."

"Then we come back to the question mark. If he subsequently learned Pickering was a CI, he'd be honor bound to take him out. Would he go to the more elaborate OD cover-up — which was poorly executed — instead of having the traitor hauled in, then taken out and messed up, killed?"

"To carry out the execution this way, because of their history. It's possible. Kill, humiliate, attempt to set a scene that makes the victim appear to have lied and cheated. This punishes him, and his family."

Eve pointed, nodded. "That's right, and there's some strategy there. Still, smarter to do it somewhere else, leave the body with some illegals on him as well as in him.

"Jones doesn't strike me as stupid," Eve added. "He's a killer. It's right there in his eyes."

"It is, isn't it?" Mira murmured. "You can't always see it, but just from this? He takes pride in what he is."

"You're not wrong. But he's survived this long because he's not altogether stupid. Hell, he's making a decent living in real estate with his partners — and I'm going to have a talk with them later. That says backup plan. When his days as top dog are over, he's got the cushion."

Mira angled her head, studied Eve now. "At the base of it, you don't believe he ordered a hit on Pickering."

"It'd be easier if I did," Eve admitted. "He's a killer who takes pride in it, and I want to slap him in a cage and lock the door. But, I don't. Every time I put it together, it doesn't fit."

"Why?"

"First, right off the top? His reaction when I told him about Pickering was outrage. Some shock tossed in, but outrage. He's a good liar, no question, but I buy the outrage."

"Because someone went over his head and took a former Banger out. Someone disrespected the chain of command."

"That's it." Eve banged a fist on the side of her thigh. "Exactly it. One of my detectives goes over my head, I'm going to kick some ass. And that's what I saw. The idea that maybe someone had. And that would put him out of the hit on Duff, because why? Plus, the timing's too close. She's dead because she served her purpose, and had a big, whiny mouth on top of it."

"The other one? Jorgenson. You're leaning toward him."

"He's in the running, and right now leading the pack. He's got a hot head, and made a point of pushing at Jones while we were there. And he's got a long sheet, a lot of violence on it."

She studied his ID shot again. "Still, I need to do runs and get a feel for other lieutenants or up-and-comers. I need to take a look at the case files, see if I can find a close connection in the gang for the ones Strong put away using her CI. And one more."

Eve stopped, checked the time. "I'm holding you up."

"I've got a couple more. Finish it out."

"Okay, I get taking Duff out, and quick. But it was overkill. They beat the shit out of her, raped the shit out of her. Pickering they tranq, then pump full of junk. He probably never felt anything after that first grab and stick."

"That could come down to basic misogyny," Mira pointed out. "The former gang member — male — who fought the fight, who did time, wore the colors, is given an easy death. The female who outlived her usefulness, which was primarily sex — and there are others to provide that — is brutalized. Just another whore."

Mira crossed her very fine legs at the ankles. "So, from my scan of your reports, the look of your board, and this conversation, my initial profile would be a true believer. The gang first, last, always. And one with ambition and some clout. Enough to have three men — or two if he joined them — and Duff do what he told them. Enough to have access to the illegals used and planted. He's impulsive. More thought, more careful thought, would have plugged the obvious holes. But Pickering had to be punished, humiliated, the reputation and trust he'd fought to earn back shattered.

"If he's not top dog with every intention of staying there, he intends to be. If not Jones, someone who had the additional motive of killing one of Jones's old friends."

"And adding some turmoil."

"Yes, particularly with the second killing — that brutality, the location. Stir up trouble, help put the trouble out — like an arsonist who joins in the fire line."

"Gain more cred."

"Yes. Ambitious, impulsive, brutal, and loyal above all to the gang — as he sees it. If, again, it's not Jones, it's someone who's already working to depose him. Women are to be used however he chooses to use them. He may have watched his father or another male authority figure abuse and/or humiliate his mother. If she tolerated it, she's a whore. If she didn't, she's a bitch."

"Peabody's digging into a report right now. Jorgenson went after his mother, physically. His sister — military — stopped him."

Mira's eyebrows lifted. "That's certainly interesting, and certainly fits. Attacking his mother, being stopped

188

by his sister? It's likely he has a very skewed view of women."

With obvious reluctance, Mira pushed off the desk. "I'm going to take a closer look at your reports after I'm done at the — absolutely routine — dentist." She picked up her coat. "I'll write up a more cohesive profile once I have."

"Thanks. And the good luck thing again."

"I'll take it. Eve, when you speak to Rochelle, please give her my sympathy. And let her know, though she probably has her own contacts, if she wants the names of grief counselors, I can help there."

"I will."

As Mira clicked away on her garden shoes, Eve turned back to her board.

She spent the next hour going over the data Peabody sent her on Jorgenson, picking through Strong's case files for connections still in the gang to anyone she busted. And after a quick tag, had Strong send her the best guess on the Banger chain of command.

With that, she started runs, played with probabilities.

Glancing over when her comp signaled an incoming, she seized on Harvo's report.

"All hail the fucking queen!"

She hit her 'link, made the tags while she worked out the steps in her head. Then, swinging on her coat, headed out to the bullpen.

"Officers Carmichael, Shelby, suit up. We're moving, Peabody. Harvo came through."

"We got one?"

"Barry Aimes, aka Fist. Reo's getting the warrant. Dug down into his juvenile for the DNA match on one of the hairs Morris found on Duff. No luck on a second sample. Aimes is only seventeen. Got booted from school for fighting, did a little short time in kid jail for same. And he left his hair on Duff."

She showed Peabody the image on her 'link screen. "Wears it long, and it's currently dyed red. He's got a job listed — stocking shelves at a mini — and a residence. We'll hit the mini first."

"Seventeen." Peabody shoved her arms in her coat. "And he's already killed twice."

"Bad boy," Eve said, looking forward to sweating his co-killers' names out of him once she had him in the box. "Here's how we're going to roll it out."

CHAPTER
ELEVEN

Eve didn't care about double-parking on police business, but in this case, she had a purpose to pissing off drivers when she slid next to the beater at the curb in front of the mini-mart.

If Aimes managed to get by her out the front, she'd pursue on foot while Peabody jumped back in the car to cut him off.

If he tried the back, she had her two uniforms waiting.

A big guy at six-three and two-sixty, she'd reminded her takedown team — and one who likely carried sharps and couldn't be expected to go quietly.

With Peabody, she walked into the mini, a quick shop approximately the size of her closet. Its wares included snack packs of junk food, some canned goods, candy, condoms, a section of cheap makeup and hair dye. She imagined the lottery tickets and black-market tobacco products sold illegally under the table kept the place afloat.

She didn't see Aimes — and it would've been impossible to miss him in a space that size with the only occupants one middle-aged male wearing a do-rag and a sour expression behind the counter, and a lone female with an infant in a sling, a dented basket in her hand.

Eve approached the counter with its short stock of candy bars inside a locked case.

"Help ya?"

"We're looking for Barry Aimes."

"Yeah?" His sour expression soured further. "Let me know when you find his lazy punk ass so I can fire it. He hasn't been in for two days running."

Too busy killing people, Eve thought. "Is that usual?"

"It's not unusual, right? You cops?"

Eve took out her badge. "You don't seem surprised cops would be looking for your employee."

"Employees show up for work, right? What he is, is the lazy punk-ass nephew of my woman's cousin, so she nags me shitless to give him a job. What he do this time?"

"Do you know where he might be?"

"Hell." After shoving at his do-rag, the man let out a long-suffering sigh. "Probably out getting high or at home, where he mooches off his old lady — who works for a living — sleeping off his last high. You find him, you tell him he's done here. Last time he showed up I come up sixty short. He's done, and if the Banger trash he runs with don't like it, screw 'em."

"Do the Bangers extort money from you for their questionable protection?"

"This place ain't much, but it's my ain't much. I got nothing to say about that. But that don't mean I have to put up with Barry's lazy punk ass anymore."

"All right. Could I have your name?"

"Ain't you got one of your own?" He actually grinned at his own humor. "Hoobie. Kent Hoobie."

192

"Mr. Hoobie, if he comes in, or you see him, I'd appreciate you not mentioning this visit — and contacting me."

When she passed him a card, Hoobie started to stuff it in his pocket, then he stopped, eyes narrowed. "Homicide? Jumping Jesus, did that stupid kid kill somebody?"

"We need to speak with him" was all Eve said.

Outside, she contacted her uniforms, told them to come around. "Peabody, did you dig up the exact location of the apartment?"

"Fifth floor, east side. My map shows an alley between the building and the one directly east."

"Okay. Suspect hasn't come into work the last two days," she told the uniforms. "So here's how we roll on the residence."

A few blocks later, Eve double-parked again. They'd moved beyond Banger turf, into the sort of borderland between the badlands and the solid middle class.

Working-class building, she judged, with a single entrance cam that might even work. She mastered in while the uniforms took the alley.

Inside the lobby with its dull beige walls stood two elevators with dull green doors.

She took the stairs.

"Five flights," Peabody grumbled. "Loose pants. His mother works as a sales clerk at Trendy, a chain store in the Sky Mall. Long commute."

"Rent's cheaper here."

She could hear music and muffled voices from screen shows, some baby sending out wild screams as if being eaten by wolves. And a lot of quiet. Working class, she thought again. Too early for most to be home.

"It's 516," Peabody said as, breathing a little heavy, she reached the fifth floor.

Eve approached, noted the additional lock and another cam that might actually work.

She rapped the side of her fist on the door, listened hard for any sound, any movement. Heard nothing. Pounded harder.

The door just down the hall opened. A girl of about fourteen, wearing a teenager's bored disgust, poked her head out. "What's the what, duet? Nobody's in there, okay? Some people are trying to do their homework."

"We're looking for Barry Aimes. Have you seen him?"

The girl, a lot of wavy brown hair with fading blue streaks, eased out a little more. "No. Why would I want to? If he was in there, he'd have the music or the screen on. Probably both, so I have to put on my headphones to get my homework done. So he's not in there. Maybe at work. Probably not, but maybe."

"When's the last time you saw him, or heard him?"

"Awhile, I guess. My mom thinks he moved out. Hope so. I'm never supposed to open the door to him, even if she's home. She says he's trouble. What do you want him for anyway?"

Eve held up her badge. "He's trouble."

The girl looked mildly impressed with the badge, and eased up for a closer look at it.

"Man, how come she's always right? If you're a cop, how come you have that rocking coat? And she has those chill boots?"

"If you're a kid, why aren't you in school?"

"Yo, school let out *hours* ago."

The accompanying eye roll, Eve had to admit, was practiced and perfect.

"My mom says Mrs. Aimes works really hard, and tries her best and doesn't deserve trouble like her son, and how he's going to end up dead or in jail. I bet you put him in jail so she'll be right again."

Eve dug out a card. "If you hear him come back, contact me. Don't speak to him and, like your mother said, don't open the door."

"I don't speak to him anyway — and if my mom knew how he looked at me a couple of times, she'd . . ." She looked up from the card, clever blue eyes narrowing. "I know what Homicide is. I need to tag my mom. She's at work. I don't want her walking home by herself if that pervy jerk's killed somebody."

"Tag your mom. Otherwise, keep this quiet. Do you know when his mother usually gets home?"

"I think around seven or eight most nights. Except Fridays and Saturdays she works late and it's more like eleven, I guess. She works at the Sky Mall at Trendy. She gives me discount vouchers sometimes. She's nice. I need to tag my mom. She'll be starting home soon."

"What's your name?"

"Carrie Dru."

"Carrie, we have a warrant for Aimes's arrest, and it includes entry into his residence. So we're going inside."

"Can you do that?"

Eve tapped her badge. "Yeah. You go inside, stay inside."

Without another word, Carrie popped inside, closed the door. Eve heard locks click.

Engaging her recorder, Eve moved back to Aimes's apartment door. "Dallas, Lieutenant Eve, and Peabody, Detective Delia, mastering into suspect's apartment."

She drew her weapon, and did just that.

"Clear it. He may be lying low, or sleeping off a high."

The living area, clean, neat without being crazy about it, held decent furniture without a lot of fuss, the standard entertainment screen, a scatter of photographs, including one she took to be the suspect as a toddler.

The kitchen off the living space — also clean — told her the kid next door had it right. Even lying low or high, if a teenage killer was in residence, there'd be dirty dishes.

The mother's bedroom, neat and spare, faced one with a lock drilled into it, and a handwritten sign.

KEEP OUTTA MY SPACE!

"Not today, Barry."

Eve mastered through.

The smell told her the mother obeyed the sign. It stank of stale Zoner from the minute butts of same littering a small plate; of sweaty, who-needs-a-shower male; and of the remnants of a days-old burrito.

Dirty clothes littered the floor along with discarded, empty tubes of Cola Blast and a couple of foggy brown bottles of what she deduced had been cheap, homemade brew.

She doubted the sheets had been changed this year, and from the varying stains decorating them, she had to be grateful she wouldn't be the one dealing with them.

Peabody made a soft gagging sound. "I don't know if it's scientifically possible, but I swear there's about six months' worth of trapped boy-farts in this room."

"Oh, it's possible," Eve said, breathing through her teeth. "It's possible."

With more reluctance than she'd have felt approaching a mangled corpse, Eve stepped to the narrow closet, nudged it fully open with an elbow.

And spotted a bright, shiny red bag hanging by its silver chain.

"Field kit, Peabody."

"I got a mini can of sealant right here." Peabody passed it to her, and Eve sealed her hands, passed it back so Peabody could do the same.

"Looks like most of his clothes are gone from in here — if he ever actually used the closet. But he leaves this."

"He could be flopping somewhere else and doesn't want anybody else to see it," Peabody suggested. "Maybe even at Banger HQ."

"Yeah, we could try there, see if Reo can expand the warrant for entry. We might get him, but we'd send up a flag to the other two, and whoever put out the hit. He might be there, but he's in the wind if he's lucky, dead if he's not."

She took the purse off the hook, opened it.

"And look here."

Peabody looked inside, saw the pair of oversize hoop earrings in gaudy fake gold. "Jesus, Dallas, he didn't even clean her blood off them."

"They're Duff's, but we'll send them to the lab, confirm. Unless you've got evidence bags in your pocket, we're going to need a kit."

"Loose pants," Peabody said, and took off.

"Tell the uniforms to stand down, but hold," Eve called out.

She took the earrings out, studied them. Not just blood, she noted, little bits of flesh, too.

Shiny things, she mused as she stepped out of the closet, scanning the room. Would this particular murderous magpie leave his shiny things behind if he ran?

Dirty clothes left, and a couple of shirts, on the ragged side, on the closet floor. No shoes.

Holding the purse carefully, she got down, looked under the bed. A few more scattered clothes, a lot of dirt and dust, another plate holding a moldy smear of God knew what.

No shoes.

She opened one of his three dresser drawers, found a pair of truly filthy socks that hadn't made it to the floor.

Peabody hustled back in. "Gave up, took the elevator. I justified it because it's quicker."

"Bag the earrings, then put them back inside the purse, bag that. No shoes in his room."

"He might only have one pair," Peabody pointed out as she bagged the evidence, marked and sealed it.

"Yeah, maybe. Here's what we're going to do. We get the two cops from last night to sit on the place, that's Officers Zutter and Norton. See if he goes in or out. Make that happen — and while you're at it, ask them if they know the finger-snapping guy. Maybe we can push there."

She paced as she thought it through. "He's going to have a 'link, and he's seventeen years old. He's going to use it, unless he's dead. Let's put EDD on that. See if they can locate him. I'll do that. You find out who in the bullpen's not working something hot. Bring them up to speed. Let's get them out to the Sky Mall to talk to the mother."

"If the kid had the time right, she might be on her way home."

Eve glanced at her wrist unit, said, "Shit. You're right. Long commute. We'll get them to sit on this place, talk to the mother when she gets home. She hasn't been in his room, not for weeks anyway, and not likely since he put in the lock. She doesn't know where he is, but she might know something.

"Christ, who could live with this smell?"

She walked out, left the door open and unlocked.

Outside, she cut Carmichael and Shelby loose.

"We can sit on the place, Lieutenant," Carmichael told her. "Until you get another team on. It's a nice night for a stakeout, right, Shelby?"

"You got that. Sir, we've got the suspect's ID on the 'links. We can generate copies if you want us to ask around."

"Not yet. He's bound to have one person around here who doesn't think he's a pervy jerk or a lazy punk ass. If he's just chilling somewhere, we'd spook him. Just sit on it for now."

As she drove back to Central, Eve contacted EDD.

"Feeney, I need a trace and target."

"I need a brew and the game on-screen. Damn it, it's the wife's girls' night. I'm picking up pizza on the way home, with freaking anchovies."

"Ditch it on McNab. I've still got Peabody, so he's at Central most likely. Or somebody. Just a trace and target. The name's Aimes, Barry." She rattled off the address. "It might be under his mother's name. She's —"

"You think I can't find some asshole's mother's name? Stop wasting my time. Anchovies." His droopy eyes took on a little shine. "I can't even have them in the house when the wife's in it. The boy'll tag you back when he gets what you need."

"We should do a girls' night," Peabody said. "Go to a club and — no, a piano bar! Classy. We could all have fancy drinks, and —"

"Consider this conversation the closest you'll ever get me to a piano bar with a bunch of women drunk on fancy drinks. Who's on the mother?"

"Santiago and Carmichael, so — hee hee — Carmichael's going to relieve Carmichael. Zutter and Norton are checking with their LT on sitting on Banger HQ, don't see an issue. And Zutter said he's seen this finger-snapper. Pretty sure. They don't have a name, don't think he's an official Banger unless he's new, but they've seen him around, hanging with some of the lower levels. Big guy, they say about six-two, maybe two-sixty. Black, late teens to twenty. They'll ask around — they know how."

Another killer in his teens, Eve thought.

"What he did — whoever he is — is pull on the lower levels, young, stupid. The type who'd do what he said, want to impress, make their mark. So, sloppy."

She pulled into Central. "Write it up. If McNab hits the target, let me know asap. Otherwise, when you're done, the two of you swing by Casa del Sol, talk to Pickering's boss, coworkers, then take this home."

"You're going home?"

"I'm going to see a sleazy, disbarred lawyer."

"I'm up for that."

"In this case, I'm going to see if I can hook in somebody who knows sleazy lawyers. Write it up — copy Mira. It might add to her profile."

"All over it. How about I see if Reo can expand the warrant — just in case?"

"Do that. Out."

Eve plugged in the sleazy lawyer's address, pulled out. And tried Roarke on the in-dash.

"Lieutenant. I'm just on my way home, and assume you're not."

"I'm not. We ID'd one of the killers."

"Quick work."

"Depends," she decided, and brought him up to date.

"That's quite a bit packed into your day," he commented. "And more to come?"

"Yeah. I could've done without the stinky memory of trapped boy-farts at the end, but that's the job."

"I'm doing my best to be grateful you've shared that particular experience with me."

"The telling doesn't come close to the experiencing, trust me. So we've got a BOLO out on Aimes, and I'm going to tug another line. How about taking a detour, adding a tug of your own?"

He smiled. "Where?"

"I'm going to pay a visit to Samuel Cohen, Jones's business partner in real estate."

"Ah yes, the ambitious, enterprising street gangster. Makes me nostalgic."

"I bet. Which is why I thought you'd be handy when I talk to the partner."

She swung well away from a lumbering maxibus, cut nimbly back in front of it to take the next turn.

"The disbarred lawyer, remember? Who lives with a stripper about half his age."

"That may make up for the disbarred."

"Yeah, most people with dicks would think that."

"Darling, that's sexist. I'm sure there are some lovely lesbians who'd think the same."

"Okay, got me there. Hold on."

Punching it a little, Eve threaded the needle between a double-parked cargo van and a crew jackhammering a section of the cross street. And nipped through the intersection seconds before pedestrians surged across.

"Anyway —"

"Are those shouted expletives aimed at you?"

"Maybe. The stripper's name's on the papers, too. They've got a place on the Lower East Side."

"Give me the address, I'll meet you."

She did, added, "Make sure you're wearing your intimidating rich bastard suit."

"I have no other kind. I'll see you shortly."

She pushed through traffic along with what seemed like half the city of New York, and thought of Barry Aimes's mother's long commute. Air tram or commuter bus, Eve figured, and likely close to an hour both ways unless she got lucky.

And while Mom stood on her feet most of the day dealing with customers, then dragging herself home after a day at the mall — which right there should qualify for combat pay — her son was fat-assing and farting in his filthy room smoking Zoner, or out killing people.

How would she react, what would she think when she got home and found the cops at the door?

Resigned, defensive, weepy?

Could be any of those, Eve thought, but odds are shocked wouldn't make the list.

What bad boy Aimes's hardworking mother ought to do is find herself a little apartment near the mall. Though Eve admitted she'd rather stun herself multiple times than nestle into the 'burbs. But once he was in a cage — and he damn well would be unless he ended up on Morris's slab — it didn't make any sense to add a couple hours onto a workday so you could afford a two-bedroom in Manhattan to accommodate your lazy-ass son who disrespected you enough to put a lock and a sign on the bedroom door you paid for.

She put it aside — not her problem — and began the hunt for parking. When she spied a sedan nosing out from the curb, she hit vertical, zipped forward, and hovered while the overly cautious driver inched, waited, inched, waited.

The second his rear bumper cleared, she punched down, destroying the hopes of a compact all-terrain that tried to beat her claim.

Satisfying, Eve thought, then stepped out on the busy crosstown street. Pedestrians streamed by as she stepped onto the sidewalk. In light jackets, many in shirtsleeves, they took advantage of the evening balm. She smelled the gyros and skewered meats from a Greek place with its door open and a pair of tables, already occupied, flanking the door.

A far cry from the handful of blocks that hosted Banger HQ.

As she began to walk, traffic hitched and honked, hampered by a delivery truck hogging the bulk of the street. A couple of women hurried by, chattering about somebody named Julio who thought he was God's gift as they turned into an after-work watering hole.

Some kid with a demon grin zoomed by on an airboard. The odds of a pack of roaming street rats knocking him off and stealing it in this neighborhood ranked low.

She paused outside Cohen's building. A nice four-stack — two up, two down, with the faded red bricks, the doors all snowy white. Decent security on all four units, to her eye, and with privacy screens engaged on all the windows.

According to the data, Cohen/Vinn had both west-side units. Which in this quietly mid to almost upscale neighborhood wouldn't come cheap.

She spotted Roarke strolling her way, waited. More than a couple of heads turned. She saw one woman nudge her companion, then pat a hand on her heart.

Yeah, he had a way of tripping up the heartbeat.

He stepped up to her, took her hand, and kissed it before she could stop him.

"On duty."

"And look it," he said. "Every inch. It's a lovely evening, isn't it, to grill suspects."

"It's always a lovely evening for grilling suspects, but I'm going at Cohen more as a connection. He's in business with Jones. Is he in business with the Bangers? How much does he know? It's worth a conversation. He's got both units on this side."

She walked up to the door, pressed the buzzer.

Seconds later the intercom hummed, then let out a cheerful female voice. "Wow, Jimmy, that was fast! Be right there."

"Might be Vinn," Eve said. "Eldena. The stripper."

"You must've flown. I didn't — Oh."

She had the body for the job, Eve thought. At the moment a snug black tank and cropped black skin pants covered the curvy inches. She had her hair, roasted chestnut, scooped back in a tail from a face dominated by wide brown eyes and currently devoid of enhancements.

Her bare feet had the toenails painted bright green. She looked young and dewy, and surprised.

"I'm sorry, I thought you were Jimmy with the Chinese."

"I'm Lieutenant Dallas, with the NYPSD."

Eldena frowned at the badge Eve offered. "Can I help —" She broke off, wide eyes going even wider as they focused on Roarke. "Oh, oh! Dallas. Dallas and Roarke. God, I loved *The Icove Agenda*. I mean, you think that couldn't happen, but it did. This is even better than Red Dragon's noodles, and they're mag. Do you want to come in?"

"As a matter of fact."

"Sorry, I was working on some choreography, so I'm a mess. I'm a dancer. Come in and sit down. I'll take your coats. Can I get you a drink?"

"We're good. Ms. Vinn —"

"Oh, please, call me El."

"We're here on police business, and would like to speak with you and Mr. Cohen."

"Oh. Sure. Sorry, I'm just thrown off. Sam's back in his office. I'll go get him. Are you sure I can't get you a drink?"

"We're good," Eve said again.

"Well, make yourselves at home. I'll be right back."

As she hurried out, chestnut ponytail bouncing, Eve shook her head. "See? See? What did I say? The Oscar thing just makes it worse. Cop at your door, and you're all, Oh, I loved the vid. Jesus."

In mock sympathy, Roarke patted her back. "A brutally heavy cross to bear."

"Bite me," she muttered and took stock of the living area.

She supposed she expected more of the ornate from a stripper and a sleazy ex-lawyer. But the walls, a quiet, muted green, held a few cheerful floral prints. The furniture ran to the simple, even tasteful in the wide, U-shaped sofa in cream — covered with bright, fussy pillows, of course. The chairs had a geometric design that picked up the green and cream.

A lot of matchy, sort of studied, but . . . average, she decided.

"Not your usual den of iniquity," Roarke commented, smiling at her. "I think you're a bit disappointed."

"No, but it's interesting. The fact it comes off ordinary."

She turned when she heard Eldena hurrying back in her house skids. "He's on the 'link — just wrapping up. Please, have a seat."

She sat herself, crossed her excellent legs. "Is there anything I can help with? I hope there hasn't been any trouble in the neighborhood. We haven't had any."

"I'd like to talk about your business partnership with Marcus Jones."

"Who?"

"Marcus Jones," Eve repeated. "Maybe you know him as Slice."

"I don't think so. I don't have any business partnerships." She smiled, obviously puzzled but willing. "I'm a dancer."

"During the course of an investigation, I've read the documents, your business connection with Jones, the ownership — Jones, Mr. Cohen, yourself — of several buildings in New York."

She actually laughed. "Oh, that's not right. I'm sorry. We don't own any buildings. I wish!"

Not lying, Eve thought. More interesting. She pulled out her PPC, keyed up the file with the papers for Banger HQ. Rising, she offered it to Eldena. "Is that your signature?"

"I . . . It sure looks like it."

Eve scrolled to papers on another property. "And this?"

"I don't understand. This is . . ." She looked up at Eve.

Wide eyes, sure, Eve thought, but not stupid. "I need to know what this is about, all right? What investigation?"

"Murder, Ms. Vinn. Two of them."

Every ounce of color drained. "Murder. Who? How? It can't have anything to do with me and Sam. It just can't. I don't understand."

Someone else came hurrying down the hall. "Now, who's here, cutie-pie, who's so special?"

Sam Cohen's big white smile died away the instant he turned into the room. He struggled to put it back in place. "El, you should've told me the police were here."

"I wanted to surprise you." She stared at him with those wide eyes gone cold. "Surprise."

CHAPTER
TWELVE

He kept the smile going, though it looked a little sickly to Eve's eye. He hit about five-eight, carried a soft belly under a white shirt and navy sport coat. His gilded hair showed no gray as it swept back from a high forehead. His eyes, blue, looked both worried and calculating.

He said, "Ha ha!" Then seemed to recover his balance as he strode into the room. "El, sweetie, how about you get the house droid to make some coffee for our guests."

"We're not here for coffee."

At Eve's flat statement his balance teetered a bit, but he kept up the jovial tone. "Well then! Let's take this back to my office."

"Here's good. We're here, Mr. Cohen, to discuss your business relationship with Marcus Jones."

"Business is business. Excuse us, El."

"She stays," Eve said. "As Ms. Vinn's name is on the paperwork in the real estate holdings with you and Mr. Jones, we have questions for her, too."

"Yeah, how'd that happen, Sam?" Eldena's voice, no longer cheerful, dripped with venom. "How is it we have *real estate*, we own *buildings*, but I'm taking my clothes off five nights a week at the Bump and Bang so we can pay the freaking rent?"

"It's complicated, baby, complicated. We've got some investments. I'm looking out for our future. I'm —"

She jabbed a finger in the air that cut off his words as if she'd sliced his throat.

"You said the only way we could get by, could live in a decent place, was for me to stick with the club while you worked to establish your consulting business. And now there's real estate, partners with some guy I never heard of. My signature's on the papers, but you never told me any of this."

"We'll talk about all that, don't you worry, sweetie." He moved to give her hand a pat, but she jerked away. "What's the problem?" he demanded of Eve. "It's not against the law to own property."

"Your business partner, Marcus Jones, is the current leader of the urban gang known as the Bangers, who are known to traffic in illegals, identify theft, the protection racket, and the unlicensed sex trade."

"Oh my God, Sam." Horror replaced venom. "Oh my God!"

"Jones is currently a suspect in two murders."

"None of that has anything to do with me." He actually flicked his hands in the air as if brushing it all away. "I'm not legally culpable in any way for the alleged criminal actions of an individual who has a minor interest in my real estate holdings."

"Including the holding where Jones and his gang have their headquarters?"

"I think I'm going to be sick." Pale as death, Eldena pressed a hand to her stomach.

"Just be quiet, Eldena!" Cohen snapped, and her color flooded back.

"Excuse me?" She fisted her hands on her hips. "Excuse the hell right out of me."

"This is a legal matter, El." Though he calmed it, Cohen put authority into his tone. "It's best for you to say nothing. Someone's at the door," he added when the buzzer sounded.

Eldena merely folded her arms across her chest and stayed planted.

"Fine then, fine! I'll get it."

"I'll go with you." Roarke rose, his smile ice sharp. "Just in case you find a need to take the air."

"Don't be ridiculous."

When Cohen stomped out, Roarke strolled after him.

"I didn't know anything about this." Turning, Eldena held out her hands to Eve, a pleading gesture. "Any of this, I swear."

"I believe you," Eve said.

"But, but, but . . ." Squeezing her eyes shut for a moment, she fisted those hands, tapped her own chest. "I've signed papers without actually reading them, which makes me an idiot. Sam takes care of things like taxes and insurance, and I don't know. He says, Sign this, sweetie. Oh my God."

Cohen stomped back in, dumped the take-out bags on a table. "Eldena, these people don't have your best interest at heart. Let me handle this, then you and I will talk privately."

"Why don't you tell me how you became acquainted with Marcus Jones?" Eve asked.

"Through a client."

"That would be former client, seeing as you've been disbarred."

In his eyes came a quick, keen rage. "That's neither here nor there, and is something I intend to rectify. My relationship with Jones is strictly business. I learned he had an interest in purchasing the property downtown, and as I was looking for an investment, we formed the partnership. There's nothing more to it."

"You were aware of his criminal history and gang affiliation?"

"Neither here nor there," he repeated with another flick of his hand. "Strictly business."

"It's both here and there that Jones gets his money to invest with you through criminal activities."

"Then prove same and arrest him."

"When did you last see or speak with Mr. Jones?"

"We have no need to communicate unless it concerns one of the properties."

"That's not an answer."

He aimed a stony stare at the wall. "I can't recall."

"You can't recall the last time you saw or spoke to a business partner with whom you own several million dollars of real estate?"

"Millions," Eldena breathed out.

"That's on paper, sweetie. You don't understand how business works. I know nothing about Mr. Jones's personal life, and since I can't help you with your investigation, I have nothing more to say."

"Try this. Where you were last night between six and ten P.M.?"

"This is outrageous! And I was home, with Eldena."

"He was from six to at least eight," Eldena confirmed. "I left about eight — to *work* for a living. But he was here at least until then."

"What time did you get back home, Ms. Vinn?"

"About three. Sam was in bed, as usual, when I got home after I spent hours naked or getting naked, and giving lap dances to assholes because I get a percentage of the fee."

"That's all going to be over soon," Cohen began.

"Too bad for you." Eve decided to twist the knife. "Since you and Jones, and apparently Ms. Vinn, own the club where she works."

"You —" Eldena lost her breath, pushed the heel of her hand up her chest as if to find it. "How *could* you? How could you do that?"

"I'll explain it all, I'll explain."

"So you have no alibi between the hours of eight P.M. and three A.M.?" Eve interrupted.

Cohen sent Eve a disgusted look, or tried, as panic jittered in his eyes. "I was home, and have no need for an alibi."

"Think again," she advised.

"It's interesting, isn't it?" Roarke said conversationally. "That someone with a legal background, however nefarious, would enter into multiple partnerships with someone they claim to know little to nothing about? It would make that person either a fool or a liar."

"Could be both," Eve added.

"It could, yes. Plus, one more. This person may also have a financial interest in the partner's — also nefarious — other business ventures. Of the illegal sort."

"This interview is over." Cohen surged to his feet. "If you want to speak to me again, it'll be through my lawyer."

"You can count on it." Eve rose, dug out a card, handed it to Eldena. "If you think of anything more, you can contact me."

"Thank you. I'll walk you to the door."

"There's no need to —"

Eldena rounded on Cohen. "Now you be quiet."

When she opened the door, Roarke touched a hand to her arm. "The lieutenant likely feels unable to give you any advice at this time. I'm not as hampered. You should get your own lawyer. A good one."

"Thank you. You can count on it."

As they walked away, Eve glanced over at Roarke. "That last bit — to him, not her? Good timing on that. And nice, what is it, derision."

"Heartfelt." He paused by the car. "You know how you often say, after I've done a bit of something, that you owe me one?"

"Yeah."

"I'd like to collect."

"How exactly?"

"You need to let me dig into this bloody bloke, and bury him once I have. He'll have more tucked away here and there, and possibly some of that will help your case. Regardless, I want to dig, and deep. I shouldn't need the unregistered, but if I do, I do. That's the payment."

"If you need the unregistered, tell me. If you get anything there that does play into the investigation, I need to know how to deal with it."

"Agreed. You drive. I'm going to get started."

Since he pulled out his PPC as soon as he got into the car, she gave him quiet to work. She had plenty to think about.

She had no doubt Cohen was as dirty as they came — a liar, a cheat, very likely into some fraud, tax evasion. It wouldn't surprise her in the least to learn he got a small percentage of Banger income.

The question was: How deep did it go? Just business? Did just business include accessory to murder?

Why put the woman's name on the documents? She'd have asked Roarke, but he was already muttering to himself as he worked.

She had a theory. The properties all carried mortgages. Was she cover? Something goes south, he leaves her holding the bag?

Considering that, she called in, ordered surveillance on the residence. If Cohen left, she wanted to know where he went.

"His partnership with Jones extends to a company," Roarke said as he continued to work. "CoJo Corp. They use it to bank rents, to pay for maintenance, taxes, insurance. All very standard, with each of them taking a percentage every month — of what they report, in any case."

"You've got more than that," Eve said as she drove through the gates.

"I do. I've found two buried accounts already in the time it's taken to get home, and that's on a bleeding portable. Sort of a pity, as playing with the unregistered would be a bit of fun. He's just not good enough at this to bother."

"Or you're too good to need to bother."

When they got out of the car, he skirted the hood, took both her hands. "I wish I didn't know, absolutely, you sign papers of ours without the reading of them."

"I give them a scan." Sometimes. "If you fucked me over, I'm a cop. I know how to make you pay without letting it show. Like, the one where I tranq your wine, dress you in a diaper and pasties, get you in your office, and transmit the image globally."

"You've given this some thought."

"Just in my free time." She gave his hands a squeeze before drawing hers away and laying them on his cheeks. "Bottom line? She wasn't wrong to trust a man she loves — because it has to be love. He's not rich or good-looking or powerful. She just loves the wrong man. I don't."

"Well now," he murmured, then leaned in to take her mouth in a soft, slow, sweet kiss.

"There's the one where I coat the inside of all your boxers with a biological that causes your works to develop festering boils."

216

It made him wince. "Christ Jesus, you obviously have far too much free time."

"I've got a whole list," she said as he opened the front door. "For him, too," she added, shooting a finger at Summerset.

Summerset merely cocked his eyebrows. "No visible injuries once again. We appear to be on a streak."

"For him I have the stick up his ass surgically removed, and without it, his whole body collapses into a puddle of ghoul."

She tossed her coat over the newel post. "You'll be too busy with festering boils to have him reanimated."

"Don't ask," Roarke told Summerset as Eve headed upstairs with the cat on her heels.

He went up after her.

"I want another thirty on this," he told her. "And you'll be wanting to set up your board."

"Thirty's good."

She dealt with her board. Two murders, she thought, and she hadn't had five minutes in her home office on either. That changed now.

Seated at her command center, she wrote up notes on the Cohen/Vinn interview. She circled a finger in the air when Roarke came in. "Need another five."

"And a meal."

He strolled into the kitchen, considered the options. By the time she'd finished he had the domed plates and a bottle of wine on the table.

"You know he never asked — like Vinn did — who died and how."

"I noticed." Roarke poured the wine, lifted the domes.

"Because he was part of it, heard about it, and/or Jones contacted him for some legal advice after our visit." She sat, added — in his opinion — entirely too much salt and butter to her mashed potatoes.

"Again, it could be all of the above."

"Could be." She sampled the potatoes, deemed them good, cut a slice of a pork medallion. "The real question is how much time he'll do and where — not if."

"I can give you tax evasion."

"Already?"

Roarke studied his wine, sipped. "I regret calling for payment on this one. But what's done is done. Shell companies — so thin I could've cracked them with a thought. He'll have fraudulent identification to access some of his six accounts."

"Six?"

"Not counting the legitimate ones, or the one with Jones. I'll give him some credit for knowing enough to live within Eldena's means, and to carefully file their taxes on what they report. What he doesn't report is considerably more. More rent than either of them show — which means you can likely slap Jones with tax evasion and so on. He also owns the residence — and makes a very nice rent from the other units, and from Eldena."

"I had a feeling. Is her name on that one, too?"

"It is. Jones's isn't, so he's kept that apart. It's mortgaged, you see, like the others. Cohen needed her income to float the loans. The rent more than covers the expenses, and he banks the profits. The bloody bastard takes most of her income — which I imagine he tells her is to pay rent and so on. Banks that as well. I'll give you hard numbers, but for the moment, we'll say he's very well set."

As he often did for her, Eve broke a dinner roll in half, handed him a share.

"Okay, fraud and tax evasion, good start, and an excellent way to sweat anything else out of him. I'll buy the connection with Jones through a client due to the sleaze factor. But he knows more than real estate holdings. He should've asked about the murders, should've at least tried to look shocked about a couple homicides."

Because he felt they'd both earned it, Roarke topped off their wineglasses. "I have to say, after so easily unearthing his system and accounts, he's not particularly smart. He sees himself as what my mates and I would've called a cute hoor. Someone who's getting the leg up on the quiet. But he's a bumbler. Canny or greedy enough to set this all up, not bright enough to do it very well. And tying himself to someone like Jones?"

Sincerely baffled by the ineptitude, Roarke shook his head over another sip of wine. "A violent gangster already known to the authorities. Jones runs afoul of those authorities, they begin to dig — as indeed happened — and Cohen's in the drink. Bleeding eejit."

Eve studied him as she ate. "You're really pissed. Because it was too easy, not enough fun?"

"That's a minor disappointment, but no. Eldena Vinn. He used her, stole from her, all while patting her head and telling her he'd take care of things. It's not the same, not nearly, as telling someone a loved one's dead, but, Eve, her world fell apart right then and there. You could see it. It fell apart because he valued his bank accounts more than a woman who loved him."

"Better she knows," Eve said simply. "Now we'll see what she does about it. I can't see her taking him a cake and a smile on visiting day or gearing up for a conjugal. Meanwhile, he's a non-cute hoor — which makes no sense in any language — a bleeding eejit, a sleazy, disbarred lawyer. But is he complicit in murder?"

"Are you asking yourself or me?"

"It can be both. Let's start with you."

As he ate, Roarke considered it. "He's small-time, basically a grifter running a long con on an easy mark — because she cares for him, trusts him, it's easy. Some part of him believes the con — he's taking care of things."

He sat back, gestured with the wine. "He got lucky, as I see it, having a young, attractive woman fall for him, and again making contact with someone like Jones. He gives each of them what they want or need from him."

"Which is?"

"For the woman, he's attentive, charming, he buys her little thoughtful gifts, I'd wager, makes her feel special. Meanwhile he plays to her hopes for a future. If she can just support him now — emotionally, financially — just until he reestablishes, he'll give her

220

everything she wants. He hates to ask, of course, hates to put such a burden on her. He's not worthy of her."

"Which makes her feel special, again. Puts her in a position of proving he's worthy."

"It's likely a Mira question on why she'd fall for it, but by all accounts, she did. With Jones, he's the professional. The smart guy, the lawyer. Disbarred, but that's just a technicality, and it gives him that leg up. He knows the ins and outs, the back doors, the underbelly. And if one of his gang has a little legal problem, he can step in, give advice on the side — those ins and outs. He gives Jones a way to own something, to look at these properties, and think: That's mine. That's powerful, take it from me."

Bouncing things off Roarke never failed, Eve thought. Because he really did know the ins and the outs.

"It's not just cutting Cohen in on a percentage of the action — that's business," she said. "It's the trust again. He's got a lawyer, one with connections, one who helps him out now and again, and one who isn't fussy about where the percentage comes from. Cohen's in it, too, and that builds trust. I go down, you go down."

"Again, I'd defer to Mira, but wouldn't that be the sort of bond Jones would trust? Add in profit, the tangible buildings. Jones may believe what he tells Cohen falls under attorney-client privilege."

"Wouldn't surprise me. It doesn't surprise me, either, we're on the same page. Cohen knows about the murders. Accessory before or after the fact yet to be determined."

And she'd damn well determine.

"How soon can you get me those hard numbers?"

"It won't take long."

"And put together in a way that gets me a warrant."

Now his eyebrows rose. "What? Like a report?"

"Not that formal, just clear so I can send it to Reo, so she can pump up a judge." She smiled. "I'll owe you one."

"I'll collect more carefully next time. Actually, free pass on it. I said I wanted to bugger the bastard, so there's the satisfaction."

"Hold that thought," she said when her comm signaled. "Dallas."

"Sir, Officer Trace. Cohen just left the residence with a small suitcase. He got in a Rapid. We're tailing."

"Keep on him, Officer. Let me know where he lands."

"Yes, sir."

"Gave him his walking papers," Roarke assumed when she clicked off. "And good on her."

"What does that even mean? Who needs papers to walk? But he's on the move, so we should do the same. I'll get Reo on tap, let her know you're sending hard data for the warrant."

"All right then." He rose, then frowned. "I think it must be like firing someone. The pink slip sort of thing. You know, you're done, start walking."

"Then why papers?" she insisted. "A pink slip — and nobody gets an actual pink slip — is a paper, not papers. So a walking paper. Why not say she told him to take a hike? And that doesn't work, either, because he got in a cab."

He decided he wanted a second glass of wine for the work, poured one, smiled at her. "I adore you, Eve."

"Yeah, yeah, start walking."

CHAPTER
THIRTEEN

Cohen didn't go far. He checked into a hotel about ten blocks from the residence.

So, Eve thought, he got his pink walking paper and took a hike in a Rapid.

Now she had to wait for the wheels to turn. Roarke to Reo, Reo to a judge, then back to her.

She got coffee, sat with her boots up, studied the board.

The simplest theory: Pickering slipped up somewhere, and his CI status leaked. Not only did he break with the gang, not only was he having his gang tat removed, going to lame meetings, working some shit-ass job, but he was ratting out his own brothers and sisters to the cops.

That's a pisser.

Instead of a trial, a beatdown, and a slit throat, Jones decides another way. Having so close a connection — friends since childhood — Pickering betraying his family looks bad on leadership. He tells Duff to set him up, enlists three young low-levels or wannabes to stage the OD. The OD for humiliation.

You humiliate me, I humiliate you to death.

She could see that. She'd have given Jones more credit for cunning, but she could see it.

Duff. Maybe she whines, or makes demands. Maybe she makes noises about telling someone. Have to take her out. Same three killers, and give them the go-ahead to have their fun with her while they're at it.

Harder to see that, harder to see the strategy in the location of the kill, but it could play.

It just didn't sit easy in her gut.

"If not you, who?" she wondered. And trained her eyes, her thoughts on Kenneth "Bolt" Jorgenson.

That one, she thought, just sat easy.

A violent criminal since childhood, with a father who goes to prison for nonviolent crimes — and erases the family stability.

One minute, Eve thought as she paced, you're a rich kid with all the perks. Nice digs, nice threads. You hook school when you feel like it, bully whoever you want to bully.

Then *bam*, your father's in a cage, your mother's looking for work. No more rich kid because your family sucks.

Eve circled back to Jorgenson's photo, and found, yeah, he just sat right in her gut.

He finds a new family, one more to his taste, with the Bangers. Gets into trouble, some real trouble — but he likes it. Likes trouble.

Then he physically attacks his own mother only to get his ass kicked by his sister. That had to sting.

He worked his way to lieutenant under Jones, she mused. But he wants more. Maybe — Mira territory — he was still looking for that status his father lost.

And — a kicker for her — he'd been trading a space in his flop with Duff for sex.

Roarke walked back in. "I sent the data to Reo, so my work is done. Though if you're going into Central to box Cohen, I'd very much like to watch."

"I want to, but it's smarter to let him sweat out the night. By the time the warrant comes through and I have him picked up, taken in, booked, and all that, it'll be too late for a bail hearing. So instead of watching porn and raiding the hotel AC, feeling sorry for himself, he'll sit in a holding cage feeling sorry for himself and trying to figure how much I know."

"He has just under four million in his accounts. That's not including the equity amassed in the real estate."

Eve shook her head. "No good to him. Ill-gotten gains. He won't be able to pull from that for a lawyer or for bail. Or it'll take time to sort out what's legit and what isn't, so he's stuck.

"I don't think it's Jones," she continued. "He just doesn't fit. I'm liking Jorgenson more because he does. But if not Jones, how does Cohen play in? Because he damn well knew something about something."

He could all but see her brain circling. "Let's have a walk."

"A what?"

"A walk, one not requiring papers. It's cooler, but still a lovely evening."

Frowning, she glanced toward the window. "It's dark."

"That's why we have lights. A walk will clear your head."

"I'm waiting for the warrant to —"

"Take your comm. Let's walk out, see what they've done on the pond."

She already had her comm — and her 'link, her badge, her weapon — but that didn't explain going outside to walk around in the dark. "You want to walk outside, in the dark, to look at a hole in the ground?"

"I do, yes." To get her away from the board and her thoughts for a few minutes, Roarke took her hand. "After all, it's our hole in the ground."

Because she had been, mostly, thinking in circles, she let him pull her out of the office and downstairs.

He got her coat out of the closet.

"Why does he hang this up when he's just going to put it back where I left it for the morning?"

"He has a tidy soul."

"Summerset has a soul?"

Roarke flicked a finger down the dent in her chin, then got his own coat. "We'll go out the side."

The house had a zillion rooms and easily three zillion doors. She let him navigate back toward the kitchen, then a left through what she knew he called the morning room with its glass wall and cushy sofas and little indoor garden.

She stopped, pointed. "Are those limes?"

"I believe they're lemons, with some ripening to do yet."

"You have lemons growing on a tree in the house."

"I doubt they'd take well to New York winters."

He opened the glass door in the glass wall where, outside, the grounds were already lit in all their glory.

"You can probably see this place from Mars."

He just took her hand again. "I'd hoped to check it out before dinner, but there will be criminals."

Okay, it wasn't bad. Cool, but not cold, and the lights beaming through all the still-bare trees threw everything into a kind of fascinating relief. Overhead, thin clouds whisked over the half slice of moon, and the sounds of the city, just a murmur really, assured her she wasn't walking in some weird-ass country woods.

"What was the first place you bought? Real estate."

"A small, seedy hotel in Dublin. A rattrap, really, and one my mates said I'd be better burning to the ground. But I wanted it. I could see the bones of it," he added as they walked. "And what it might be with some care and thought, and considerable investment."

"How'd you afford it?"

"Well now." He kissed her hair. "I stole a pearl necklace — three strands with a small ruby clasp. Then I took the ferry to Liverpool, to someone I knew, and hocked them. It was enough for the buy, but not for the rehab."

"Pearls."

"And quite nice ones," he recalled. "I took Summerset to see the property, told him what I wanted to do. He took a loan out for the rest. And in eight months, we opened the Green, a small, elegant hotel we marketed to tourists looking for personal service."

"How old were you?"

"About sixteen, more or less. I had enough from it in a couple years to pay him back the loan, but he wouldn't have it. So we own it together."

"Still?"

In the glow of the lights, his eyes hit a stunning blue as he glanced over at her. "Whatever I've bought and sold, there's only one first. When I walked through it the first time, when it was mine, with its damp walls and broken windows, it was a revelation. Something belonged to me, and I could tend to it. I could . . . change it into something more."

"You still stole the pearls."

"And put them to very good use. Ah, there it is. Our hole in the ground."

She saw the hole, a sort of oval, about twenty feet around, and the muscular digger parked nearby. Crossing to it with him, she looked down. Ten feet deep, maybe.

"You could bury a lot of bodies here."

"Let's try water lilies instead." He slid an arm around her. "I think we'll enjoy this, when there's time for a walk."

"What did they do with all the dirt?"

"Hauled it off for some other projects. Which reminds me, the Nebraska project's nearly finished. I'll have to show you the current pictures."

He turned her, kissed her. "And I didn't steal any pearls for this one."

"But you're still buying rat holes."

"That's the fun of it." He kissed her again. As she lifted her arms to wrap around him, her 'link signaled.

She pushed back, pulled it out. "Reo. Did you get it?"

She got her warrant, Roarke thought while she paced and stalked, confirming with Reo.

He listened with half an ear, imagining the pond as it would be in years to come while she switched from 'link to comm to snap orders at the uniform sitting on Cohen.

Water lilies, and some sort of flowering weeper with its branches trailing toward the water. A bench for sitting. Turning, he studied the house, rising up in the night sky. He remembered how the boy of sixteen had felt walking through a sad, battered old building, knowing it belonged to him.

And how the man had felt when he'd first walked through the house he'd made in New York, knowing it belonged to him.

It was nothing, he thought, compared to the now, looking at it now that he shared that house with his cop, this life with her. Knowing she belonged to him, and he to her.

"They're picking him up."

He looked at her then, and into those steady cop's eyes. "There wasn't a cop who could lay a finger on me, on that boy who stole the pearls, and so much before and after. Fists and boots, but they couldn't put me in a cage. And I wonder, if you and I had crossed our paths in the before, well, who would've won that one?"

"Justice, ace. I'd've dogged you for it."

No question she would have dogged him to the end. How could he not adore her?

"I'd have fallen in love with you regardless, and you with me." He moved to her, enfolded her. "It was meant."

"Feels like it. So . . . I'd have brought you a cake and a smile."

Laughing, he kissed her hair again. "Well, this was a nice walk, and it's a fine hole in the ground. Now it's back to work, is it?"

"I need to update Peabody. I want to start on Cohen in the morning. And I want confirmation from the uniforms when he's in custody."

"As I said." He took her hand, strolling back to the house. "It's to work."

She woke early and alone. Well, not alone, she thought groggily, as the cat curled his tubbiness at the small of her back. As she waited for her brain to wake up she considered the fact that the bed approached the size of Utah, and she routinely ended up sandwiched between Roarke and the cat.

Oddly enough, she was okay with that.

Because her brain was, mostly, awake, she opted to roll out of bed. She hit coffee first, downing it as she dragged on shorts, a tank, and running shoes.

She wanted to break a good sweat before she pulled Cohen into the box, so took the elevator straight down to the gym.

She programmed tropical for her run, but chose a hilly terrain rather than the flat beach. Her quads woke up and whined in the first half mile, so she kept the pace steady until they stopped complaining.

The sweat broke in mile two as she pushed herself up a hill into some sort of rain forest. In the thick, damp air, vegetation dripped green and madly colorful flowers rioted alongside her track.

Since, to her mind, it felt just a little creepy, she picked up her pace. Topping mile three she came to the base of a waterfall spewing down from a cliff and beating itself into a rushing blue river. A white bird with a wingspan as wide as a maxibus swooped down, skimmed the water. And came up with a flapping fish in its long, sharp bill.

As she judged the look in its eye definitely homicidal, she ran on. And with as much relief as satisfaction, saw that curving white beach and the rolling breakers below.

She aimed for it, leaving the drumming water behind, kept a steady pace while birds as bright as the flowers zipped overhead. Then ran flat out for the last half mile to reach the beach dripping like the vegetation in the hills.

She slowed, jogging lightly until her heart rate leveled again, cut back to a walk while she guzzled water.

Satisfied, she pumped weights for fifteen, stretched it out, then walked through Roarke's version of an indoor rain forest to the pool. Stripping down, she dived in.

After a few lazy laps, she rolled over to float and think about Cohen and connections. He hadn't resisted arrest, though he'd refused to unlock the hotel room door. Once the officers gained admittance he'd squawked — according to Officer Trace — about his civil rights, suits against the NYPSD and the individual officers, even the hotel.

He'd bitched — her word — all the way down to Central, through the booking process, and into his holding cell.

And somewhere in there he'd offered the booking officer his wrist unit and two hundred in cash to let him go.

So an additional charge of attempted bribery was added just to sweeten the pot.

He'd been allowed his single contact. And the report stated whoever he'd contacted hadn't come through. So there'd been a little blubbering as well as the squawking and bitching.

She'd lay money he'd contacted Vinn, begged for her help. A guy didn't blubber after tagging his lawyer.

Which made him — Officer Trace's words — a weak sister.

She ate weak sisters for breakfast.

Looking forward to it, she got out, dried off. And, wrapped in a robe, rode back to the bedroom, where Roarke programmed coffee.

"You're up early," he commented.

"Not as early as you, but then I only wanted a workout, not global domination." She took the coffee he held out to her. "I did about five miles in some jungle mountain beach place with killer birds and plants that looked like they ate small mammals. That's probably why I did the five in about forty-five."

"With that under your belt, you should be ready for breakfast."

"Quick shower first."

When she came out, she saw waffles, fruit, and the bacon that wasn't bacon but some sort of ham. And good.

"I imagine you're primed for Cohen," he said as she went about the business of drowning and smothering the waffles.

"I need a quick roundup with Whitney. The tax shit's federal, but I want the shot at him before they slap him down. And they're going to confiscate all his e-toys, so I want a look at them first."

"Holo with Whitney," Roarke suggested, "then you can get that first shot on the way to Central and Cohen."

"Huh."

"Better time management."

She told herself she hadn't thought of it herself because she wasn't used to the holo feature on her command center.

"It is." She got up, grabbed her 'link off the dresser, got busy sending texts. "Peabody can meet me at the residence, bring McNab. He can clear it with Feeney. I can holo from here with Whitney as soon as he sets a time. I'm already poking through the electronics and everything else by the time Whitney contacts the feds, starts laying it out. Plus, get the jump on Cohen."

She looked up as she finished. "This is why global domination is within your sights."

He only smiled. "Do you need a hand engaging the holo feature?"

"Why would I? I can figure out — Yes." Why fight it? She sat again, went after the waffles. "Thanks."

"You're welcome."

"Where's the cat?" she wondered. "There's ham on the plate, and he's not trying to sneak over and steal it."

"Early start for us. I imagine he's down with Summerset getting his belly full. He'll be disappointed he missed his chance here. Will you contact Eldena, let her know you're coming?"

"No point risking she has a change of heart and goes soft on Cohen. She's pissed, but people get over being pissed. Do you still want to watch when I have Cohen in the box?"

"Let me know when you're bringing him into Interview, and I'll see if I can manage it."

"Good enough."

She polished off breakfast, went into her closet to face wardrobe.

Spring tease or not, she wanted to look mean, and that said black to her. Black pants, black tee, black jacket in thin leather because leather said mean when you wore it right.

Add black boots and a scowl, and there you had it.

When she stepped out to strap on her weapon harness, Roarke lifted his eyebrows. "Going for the kill, are we?"

"That's exactly right." She snagged her 'link, read the text from Whitney. "Ten minutes. Shit."

"Plenty of time." He rose and went with her to her office.

"You'll want to stand, I imagine."

"Yeah."

"Where?"

"Ah . . ."

"With your command center at your back rather than the room itself. Work mode. Order open operations. I could do it, yes, but it'll stick better if you do it yourself."

"Yeah, yeah. Dallas, open operations."

The center flashed on. The D and C unit hummed and then went to waiting quiet.

"I assume Whitney's still at home?"

"Yeah, it's early."

"Then you need to order the holo option, follow that with when you want it to begin, and where you want the uplink."

She could do that, and did.

"All right then, last, as he's your superior, you tell it to wait for the uplink from Whitney, then proceed. If you were including others, you'd simply list the names and locations, and when you wanted to bring them in."

"Got it. Hold for uplink from Whitney, Commander Jack, then proceed with holo communication."

"Well done." He cupped her face in his hand, kissed her. "If you'd think of electronics as tools instead of the enemy, you'd have an easier time."

"They are tools, and the enemy."

"Well then, I'm in my office if you need help in the battle. When you're done, just tell it to disengage holo option."

"Good. Thanks."

Alone, she walked to her board, gave it a long study, then moved back into place when the comp announced:

Uplink from Whitney, Commander Jack, in progress.

His image formed, real as life. His suit, slate gray, fit well over strong, wide shoulders. The gray threaded through his dark, close-cropped hair read steely.

"Commander, I appreciate you meeting with me so quickly."

"I'm interested, Lieutenant, to learn how a disgraced lawyer facing charges of tax evasion and fraud connects to two gang murders."

"That's what I intend to find out, and why I need to interview Cohen before the feds take over. I believe Cohen and Jones have more than a business relationship, as outlined in my report. And, in fact, suspect Cohen may be acting as Jones's de facto legal counsel. As such, he may have information on the murders."

Though she'd sent him a written copy of her report, she laid out her theory.

"There's no question the murders connect, sir. If Cohen has any knowledge, using the current charges as weight will help break him. In addition, what he knows about the Banger organization will aid concurrent investigations into their illegals trade, suspected identity theft, their protection racket, and other criminal activities."

"They're a blight," Whitney said. "A relatively small one compared to what they were even a decade ago, but a blight. I'll contact the FBI, relay this information when I arrive at Central." He glanced deliberately at his wrist unit. "You've got a ninety-minute head start before that time, and likely an hour more before they move on Cohen. Make the most of it."

"Yes, sir."

"Any and all data relating to the tax evasion will be relayed to the federal authorities, Lieutenant."

"Absolutely, sir. If possible, Commander, Special Agent Teasdale might be a good FBI contact."

"She would." Whitney gave Eve the slightest of nods. "Get moving," he said, and faded away.

"Okay then." She started to turn away, remembered. "What was it again? Fuck. Wait. Ah, disengage holo option. And close operations."

Holo option disengaging.

The center shut down. "Not so hard," she mumbled, and swung into Roarke's office.

"Hold a moment, Peterby." His screen went to quiet blue when he swiveled to her. "Done?"

"Yeah, gotta move. Thanks for the assist."

"Not a problem." But he crooked a finger so she rolled her eyes, then leaned over his command center to meet his lips with hers.

"I'll tag you when I'm ready to sweat him."

"And I'll try to juggle things so I can watch and be entertained. If I can't, take care of my cop, and kick his sorry, cool hoor ass."

"Affirmative on both."

Leaving early gave her a head start on morning traffic, and whatever gods decided the vehicular luck of the day smiled down so she hit nearly every green. As a result, she hit the Lower East Side well ahead of the time she'd texted to Peabody.

Since she saw no point in waiting, she edged into a slot and hiked a couple of blocks to the four-stack in the cool March breeze.

Privacy screens engaged, she noted. Most likely Vinn was still sleeping. It never hurt, to Eve's mind, to catch somebody before they'd had their morning caffeine and started thinking clearly.

She buzzed, waited, watched a teenage type walk a trio of yap dogs who trotted along on stubby legs with ears flapping. Buzzed again, longer.

The door opened a crack, and an eye peered out. Not Vinn's brown one, but green and bloodshot.

"Do you know what the freak time it is?" The voice, rusty with sleep, matched the annoyance in the bloodshot eye.

"Yes." Eve held up her badge. "Lieutenant Dallas, NYPSD. I have a warrant to enter and search." Now she held up the copy she'd printed out.

"Man, hasn't that fuckhead caused El enough trouble and heartache? Whatcha want to mess with her for?"

The door opened a few inches wider so Eve studied the woman with sleep-tangled blue hair, wearing a wrinkled tee that skimmed just south of her crotch that identified her as an OFF-DUTY STRIPPER.

"I'm here to mess with the source of her trouble and heartache."

"Didn't ya get the cop memo, sister? Asshole's in jail."

"I know. I put him there."

The woman fisted a hand on her hip, which shifted the shirt a dangerous fraction north. "I'm liking you better." She opened the door fully, stepped back to let Eve in. "El tagged me up last night for some emotional support, and that included a couple bottles of wine. She's still out. What're ya searching for?"

"I'll know when I find it. If Ms. Vinn's sleeping in the room she shared with Cohen, I'm going to have to disturb her."

"Well, shit."

"Can I have your name?"

"Me? The real's Lisa Killagrew. Onstage I'm Tequila."

"Ms. Killagrew, if you could inform Ms. Vinn I'm here, with a duly authorized search warrant, we could get this done as quickly as possible."

"Should she, like, pull in her lawyer?"

"Has she hired an attorney?"

"Yeah, she hired Pete. He's a lawyer. He hired us a couple years ago for a private — his brother's stag party. He said she oughta — I'm probably not supposed to tell you what he said she oughta."

"Leese, who are you talking to?"

Eldena appeared at the top of the stairs looking impossibly young and pale in a little black nightie — sheer as air, with three red hearts strategically placed.

To add a touch of mystery? Eve wondered.

Staring at Eve, Eldena let out a gasp that ended on a choked sob.

"Oh God, are you here to arrest me?"

"No. I'm not —"

240

Bursting into tears, Eldena dropped down to sit on the steps. "I'm sorry. I'm a wreck."

"Now, you stop that crying." Lisa used a stern mother's tone Eve admired, and had Eldena sucking up the sobs. "Didn't Pete tell you everything was going to be all right?"

"I just feel so stupid."

"Then don't be stupid. You need coffee, that's what. Christ knows, I do. You want?" she began, turning to Eve, then shot a finger in the air. "Shit. Dallas."

Eve felt her stomach sink.

"El told me and all that, but my brain's not working all the way yet. Me and El went to a matinee to see the vid. I like how you kick ass. I'm going for coffee. El, remember what we said last night?"

Eldena gave a firm nod, even if she did sniffle with it. "Tough, strong, mean. It was easier with the wine," she said with a half smile as Lisa walked up to her.

"You don't wanna get walked over, don't be a doormat." After a pat on Eldena's shoulder, Lisa continued upstairs.

"I asked Lisa to come over. We were supposed to work last night, but she said we'd take a mental health break, and we drank a lot. Before that, I made Sam leave. I said he had to go somewhere else last night so I could think. We had a big fight about it, but I made him leave. Later, Pete — he's a lawyer — he said that was good because possession is nine-tenths and all that. And how I should have the locks changed."

"I couldn't agree more."

Eldena rose, scrubbed her face with her hands as she walked down to Eve. "I've got a locksmith guy coming this morning. Sam, he tagged me and said how he'd been arrested, and I had to help. How he'd need me to post bail, and . . . I told him to suck it."

"Wise words."

"I was so mad, and I'd had wine, and Leese was here helping me stay mad. Should I contact Pete? It's really early."

"You can do that. I'm going to tell you . . ." Eve trailed off as the buzzer sounded. "That's going to be my partner and an e-detective."

"Oh God."

"We have a search warrant."

She closed her eyes for a moment, then nodded and went to open the door.

McNab's eyes popped — Eve gave him credit for keeping his tongue from landing on his airboots.

"This is Detective Peabody and Detective McNab," Eve said. "Detective McNab will access your electronics. If you have the passcodes, that would save time."

"I only have my 'link and my PPC — and the separate tablet I use for working on choreography. They're not passcoded. I — I — I don't know Sam's passcodes. I'm sorry."

"It's all right. Detective Peabody, why don't you go upstairs with Ms. Vinn, get those devices while she gets dressed. She has a friend upstairs getting coffee."

"Sure. Ms. Vinn?"

"Okay, ah, the tablet's back in my studio, but the rest is upstairs. I think maybe I should contact Pete, even though it's early."

"Go ahead. Detective McNab and I will start down here."

"All right. Oh, Sam's office? He locks it. I don't have the key or the codes or any damn thing."

"I have a master." Eve waited until Peabody escorted Eldena upstairs. "If you drool, I won't wait for Peabody to kick your ass."

Deliberately, McNab swiped the back of his hand across his mouth. His grin was as bright and shiny as the range of hoops along his earlobe.

"You gotta look. Where do you want me to start?"

"We'll take the office." Since Cohen had come from the back, she gestured.

McNab pranced along beside her in his airboots, his knee-length electrified blue coat flapping over his egg-yolk-yellow baggies.

"She-Body caught me up. You figure the guy's linked to the murders, and right now you've got him on fraud and shit."

"And it's a lot of shit." Eve glanced toward the studio — two mirrored walls, a shelf holding bottles of water, a few rolled-up towels, and a little table.

"Her tablet's there on the table. We'll wait on that."

She turned instead to the locked door, mastered her way through.

Workstation, she noted, holding an upscale D and C unit, a nice fake leather desk chair. Office AC, friggie, wall screen. She spotted a half bath through an open door.

"He's got a lot more space than she does," McNab commented.

"He's a dick as well as a crook. Go ahead and get started. I'll take the upstairs first."

CHAPTER
FOURTEEN

She met Peabody on the steps.

"She's getting dressed," Peabody said. "Her friend's with her."

"Did she contact the lawyer?"

"She said she wanted to get dressed first, have the coffee, take a blocker for the hangover. Up there, you've got a good-sized master suite, a hangout room, and two other bedrooms, another bathroom, the kitchen, an eating area. Nice place."

"Yeah. Take those to McNab. You can handle the office while he's digging into the e's. Let's keep it moving."

"On it."

Eve continued up, glancing in the hangout room. Obviously from the empty wine bottles, glasses, remnants of the Chinese, the women had used the room for drinking and that emotional support.

She wandered the rest of the second floor, noted everything was neat except the kitchen, which showed recent activity.

She went back to the closed bedroom door, knocked.

"Yeah, come on in."

Eldena sat — skin pants, loose top, hair brushed and pulled back in a tail — while she drank coffee and ignored the bagel her friend had probably brought her.

Lisa had pulled on sweatpants and sat with her, chowing on her own bagel.

"I'm going to call Pete in a minute, but you should go ahead and look for whatever since you have a warrant. I was just saying to Lisa how the rent's due next week — Sam always handles it — but I have enough to cover it. I just need to find out where to send it."

Eve decided she could take a minute. "Eldena, you should inform your attorney that your name, along with Cohen's, is on the mortgage for this property."

"I'm sorry, what?"

"You're currently co-owners of this property, this building," Eve explained, since Eldena looked mystified. "I can tell you, he used what he told you was rent for his personal gain. Just as he used the rent from the tenants in the other half for his own gain. If your lawyer's any good, he should be able to secure this place for you."

Eldena held up a hand, and once again looked as if she needed to find her breath. "Are you saying this is my house?"

"I'm saying Cohen used your income and your name on the application to secure the mortgage for this property."

"Oh God, he's a lying liar." She pushed up, hands waving as she stalked around the room. "He said how I had to work in the club, just a few more months, then when it was a few more, he'd say just a few more. To pay the rent and everything. I gave up my dream because I *loved* the lying son of a bitch. I was in *Swing* on Broadway, twice! I made it to *Swing*, but he said how we needed the money."

She held her hands out, breathed deep. "But this could be my house?"

"Talk to your lawyer. It should be easy enough to prove your income is what's been paying the mortgage. Tell him we'll be happy to share any relevant information when we can."

"Thank you." She squared her shoulders. "Lisa, let's take this downstairs, get Pete on it, and leave Lieutenant Dallas to do what she has to do."

"That's the way, El."

Shoulders still squared, Eldena looked at Eve. "Sam's going to prison, isn't he?"

"I think you can count on it."

"I want to know, because even now I can't really believe he would. But I want to know if he had anything to do with those people dying. Come on, Leese."

Lisa rose, picked up the coffee and bagels as Eldena sailed out. "Kick his ass, and kick it hard."

She intended to, Eve thought. She fully intended to.

She found nothing of interest on the second level — and wasn't surprised Cohen used chemicals to get it up for his young lover. His business interests he kept locked in his office, and McNab hit a gold mine.

"It's all here," he told her. "He kept good records, didn't even try to hide them. I mean, you'd think he'd have tried a wipe or something when she kicked him out."

"He figured he'd talk his way back in. And I don't think she gave him the time or the space before she booted him out to try the wipe anyway. So he figures to get back in, then cover up whatever he can cover up once he is. He's stupid, and he figured she was naive and dumb and soft.

"Copy everything," she told McNab. "The feds'll roast him, but we're going to start the fire."

"Already copied."

"Good work. Let's move out. I want to hear anything you found on Jones and/or the Bangers when we're out of here."

She headed to Central with Peabody riding shotgun and McNab in the back. "Can I do the coffee thing?" he asked.

"Do it while you report."

"First, there's nothing that implicates Vinn re Jones. Oh, and I just want to say, skimming through her tablet — she's good." He only grinned at the cool look Peabody aimed over her shoulder. "Not just the sexy moves — which my She-Body has plenty of."

"Do not," Eve warned as her eye twitched. "Do not."

"She's got other stuff she recorded on there. Like, ballet stuff and tap and all that. And she's not stupid. On her PPC I found a small personal account. It's not a lot, but it looks to me like maybe she culled out some of her tip money — that's how it reads — and set up her own nest."

"Great. Can we move on to criminal behavior?"

"You bet. He keeps a calendar — appointments. And he has regular meetings with Jones. Once a month. And that coincides with deposits he makes. Meets Jones, stashes money.

"You said to keep it moving," McNab added, "so I didn't stick, more got an overview, right? And part of that is him also moving product for Jones. Illegals."

"Is that so?" Eve mused.

"Like I said, good records. My take? Jones skims some of the product, passes it to Cohen, Cohen sells it to his contacts, and they split the profit. Or they did."

"What does that mean?"

"That end's been falling off — from my skim — the last eight, nine months." From the back, McNab gestured with his coffee, downed some. "Less product passed, so less profit for Cohen. He has a client list — disbarred or not — and he lists Jones as a client, and the share from illegals as part of his rolling retainer for legal advice. About six months ago, he took on a client he names as Bang-Two, and it looks like he's working the same kind of deal. Smaller, but the same sort of deal, and with this one, he's pulling some from their sex trade."

"He gets a cut?" Eve demanded.

"Sort of. How it reads?" Now McNab scooted up in his seat. "Cops bust one of the sex workers, Cohen goes in as their representative. He doesn't have to be an accredited lawyer to do that, as long as the person represented is aware he's not. He takes a fee and lists that as part of his consulting business. It's tangled, Dallas, but it's all down there in his records."

"No mention of Pickering?"

"I ran a search of the name to speed it up, got nothing."

"Okay." She pulled into Central's garage. "I want you to fine-tune this while we take Cohen into Interview. Anything you get, anything, you pass on when you get it."

"It's a lot. I can ask the captain or maybe Callendar to jump in."

"Whatever it takes." She thought of her approach as they walked to the elevator. "Peabody, have him brought up. He can sweat in the box while I work this out a little. And I need to update Whitney. McNab, copy everything to my office comp."

"Already done."

"You're worth the coffee." Impatient with the elevator, she pushed off, hopped on a glide with Peabody trotting after her.

In her office she contacted Whitney, played it out, sent a quick text to Roarke that she was going in.

She wished she had time to read through, even skim through, what McNab had dug out, but the clock was ticking.

Bang-Two, she thought. He'd pulled another partner/ client from the Bangers, someone ambitious, looking to undermine Jones.

Jorgenson. He just kept fitting the bill.

Jones cuts back on Cohen's take, she thought, so Cohen's fine with the undermining.

Killing two people, putting the cops' target on Jones's back? Serious undermining. Just how much did Cohen know?

She put together a file — a nice, thick one — took time for another hit of coffee, then headed out.

"Let's burn his balls, Peabody."

Peabody aimed a look — the Officer Puppy look. "Do I have to be good cop?"

"Today? No good cops in the box."

"Woo! He's in Interview A."

"He's probably going to start bitching about false arrest, harassment, and other bollocks," Eve said as they walked. "When we get going, it's going to all be a big misunderstanding and how we're guilt-by-associationing him."

"Well, he is guilty by association."

"Oh yeah." Eve paused outside the Interview room. "Once he realizes we've got him on the tax evasion, the fraud, profiting from illegals, he's going to start talking deal."

"And we say screw that."

"Depends."

Peabody actually danced in place — the frustrated dance. "Aw, come on, Dallas."

"How much do we care about him doing time in some white-collar cage for the tax shit? That's the feds' worry — but we use it as a hammer on the murders."

"Ooooh! Squeeze him with the taxes, the fraud." Following, Peabody nodded and changed to a quick, satisfied shuffle. "Then dangle a deal, maybe, if he flips on the rest."

"Right. We use a deal, the idea of one, like the candy at the end of the stick."

"It's a carrot at the end of the stick."

"Who the hell wants a carrot when there's candy? Reo's up to date, on her way in. Let's see how it goes."

As they walked in, Eve noted Cohen looked a lot worse for wear, and the orange jumpsuit didn't do much for his sallow complexion.

"Record on. Dallas, Lieutenant Eve, and Peabody, Detective Delia, entering Interview with Cohen, Samuel."

She read off the applicable case files over his as-expected bitching.

Outrageous! Demands to speak to her superior. Threats to have her badge.

"Pipe down!" Peabody snapped, with enough lash in her voice to have Cohen goggling at her.

"Who do you think you are?" he managed when he recovered.

"Peabody, Detective Delia." She sat across from him. "Also known as your worst nightmare."

Eve might have rolled her eyes, but Peabody coming on strong and pissy left Cohen obviously shaken.

Eve sat, set down the file, and used a flat, cool tone in contrast. "Have you been read your rights, Mr. Cohen?"

"I will not be interrogated by a pair of underlings. I demand to speak to your superior and lodge a formal complaint."

"Okay then. Samuel Cohen, you have the right to remain silent."

As she read the Revised Miranda into the record, he talked over and around her. "Do you understand your rights and obligations in these matters?"

252

"I've been harassed, my reputation impugned. I spent the night in a *holding cell!*"

"Let the record show Mr. Cohen refuses to answer. This Interview will be postponed, and the subject returned to Holding until such time as a psychiatric evaluation can determine if subject is capable of understanding his constitutional rights.

"We're backed up on the psych evals, aren't we, Peabody?"

"Logjammed." Peabody gave Cohen a ferocious smile. "It'll be two, three days before they can get to him."

"I know what game you're playing," Cohen said as Eve rose, rattling his restraints as he folded his arms. "I'm not going back to a cell."

Eve slapped her palms on the table just hard enough to make Cohen jump. "You're trying to bust my balls over a basic yes-or-no question. Answer or you'll spend the next seventy-two in a cage, on the wait list for psych."

"Of course I know my rights and obligations. I'm a lawyer, for God's sake."

"And did you give legal advice to Marcus Jones, aka Slice, and/or any member of the gang known as the Bangers in exchange for financial remunerations, for goods, and/or for services?"

He did a decent imitation of an insulted scowl. "Don't be ridiculous."

"You are acquainted with Marcus Jones and, in fact, have a business partnership with him involving several real estate properties?"

He'd obviously had time to work on his outraged and impatient face in Holding, Eve thought.

"I've already explained that the very slight acquaintance with Jones is and has been business. A fact you twisted and used to upset and frighten my fiancée."

"It's a considerable financial partnership to form with a 'slight acquaintance,' and one even minimal vetting would have revealed as a gang member, and one who's served time."

"Forming such a partnership with a questionable character isn't illegal."

"No, neither is using money from your — and let me break the news — former fiancée to finance the partnership illegal. Unless, of course, you obtained that money through fraudulent means — which you did. And unless you then created shell companies and underground accounts to then conceal the profits from those ventures, thereby evading the taxes and fees due on same."

"That's preposterous. Eldena signed all the agreements and documents."

"That's something her lawyer — she's got one, by the way — will take up with you." As his mouth opened and closed, she continued, "But she didn't sign on to those shell companies, to those underground accounts."

His gaze slid away, pinned itself to the mirrored wall. "I have no idea what you're talking about."

"You keep really good records," Peabody said with another ferocious grin. (Somebody else has been practicing, Eve thought.) "Then you add in the stupid

254

by keeping the really good records right on your home-office comp."

The outrage came back, but this time with the first beads of sweat popping out. "El had no right, no authority, to allow you to compromise my office or the equipment therein. I'll file a motion to —"

He broke off when Eve opened the file, took out the warrant, pushed it across the table. "Duly authorized. We'll set aside — for Eldena's lawyer to pick up — the fraudulent manner in which you bilked a woman who had the poor judgment to trust you. But what I have in here . . ." She began to sift through the papers in the file. "Yeah, multiple accounts set up for the express purpose of tax evasion."

"Establishing tax shelters is perfectly legal."

"Not the way you did it — fake names, Sam, fake addresses. You know, *tsk*. Of course, the feds are going to do more than wag a finger at you over this."

"There's absolutely no need to involve the federal authorities." He patted a hand in the air as if to tell her to slow down. More beads of sweat popped over his top lip. "I'm sure we can come to an arrangement."

She kicked back, shot up her eyebrows at Peabody. "An arrangement?"

"It's a lot of money," Peabody speculated.

"I'm certainly willing to compensate you for keeping this matter — one that falls into a gray area — contained."

" 'Compensate'?" Peabody pursed her lips.

"We'll say five percent."

"Five percent of the monies held in all those accounts," Peabody qualified, "if we don't notify the FBI, and look the other way on the fraud?"

Smiling a little, Cohen spread his hands as far as his restraints allowed. "We all benefit."

"Just business," Eve said. "Except . . . That sounds like a bribe, doesn't it, Peabody?"

"It's got that ring to it. Just like the one he tried on the booking officer."

"That was a misunderstanding! You're misunderstanding me."

"No, you were really clear. For the record, that's a second count of attempting to bribe police officers. And we haven't even gotten to the fact that Jones, you, and the Bangers operate as organized crime, which brings in RICO. Your really good records list the percentages you took from their illegals dealing, from their unlicensed sex workers, their underground club, their protection racket, from their identity theft operation."

"I had nothing to do with any of that. Those are simply consultant fees for legal advice. I was not involved in any illegal activity."

"You profited from it, you were aware of it and failed to report these activities to the authorities."

"I — I was engaged as legal consultant, and therefore bound by confidentiality."

"Bullshit! Bullshit!" Peabody exploded, surging up to push her face into Cohen's. "You were disbarred in the first fucking place."

"That was a misunderstanding, and I intend to correct it. As a matter of integrity —"

256

Peabody made a grab for him — a feint — but even as Eve swallowed a laugh, she knew her role. She jumped up, held her partner back. "Easy now."

"This piece of *shit*'s talking integrity? He takes a percentage of money from selling illegals to addicts, to *kids*! From people just trying to run a business and afraid they'll get burned out or put in the hospital. And we haven't even gotten to two dead bodies."

She bared her teeth at Cohen. "What was your fee for that, you shitbag fuck? What's your percentage of two bodies in the morgue?"

"I had nothing to do with — I don't even know those people. You've lost your minds! You — you threatened me. I have nothing more to say. I'm going to engage legal counsel."

"With what?" Eve tossed back. "Your accounts are frozen."

"You can't do that!"

"Done. But since you're entitled to legal counsel, we'll arrange for a public defender."

"I don't accept that. I do not accept that. I invoke my right to counsel. I still have contacts. You're required to allow me to engage my own counsel."

"Sure, and good luck with that. Make sure you let whoever you try to rope in know they'll be defending you on accessory to murder charges — two counts — and various other state and federal crimes. Interview suspended while subject attempts to engage legal counsel."

She stepped out, signaled to a uniform, ordered him to take Cohen back to Holding and allow him to contact legal counsel.

"Did I go too far?" Peabody asked her. "I felt like I had it going, but then he calls for a lawyer."

"No, you were good. He was going to try to lawyer up sooner or later. He figured he could bullshit his way out of it, but kept digging himself a bigger hole."

She watched Detective Strong and Reo come out of Observation. Strong grinned, shot out a finger at Peabody. "Badass."

"Thanks."

"He may be able to tag up a lawyer as slimy as he is," Eve commented. "It isn't going to help. We're going to have the FBI horning in before we get him back in there, most likely. I need you to hold them off," she said to Reo.

"Already on that page. You gave me some nice ammo in there for that. We're handing them a platter loaded with goodies. I can wrangle you time to work some names out of him on the murders. He breaks, they get even more."

"He'll break."

Hell, Eve thought, she could already see the cracks forming.

"It's taking time because, Jesus, he's delusional. He believes his own bullshit. Just business, not involved, consulting fees. I figure we string that out some, then wrap him up in his own bullshit. Who consulted with him about taking out Pickering and Duff?"

She looked back at Reo. "When it gets through the delusional bullshit that he's wrapped, he's going to want a deal."

258

"He needs to go down for whatever part he played with Lyle," Strong insisted. "With Duff, too."

"Didn't say otherwise. How much will the feds deal?" she asked Reo. "If he rats out the gang — if they can get key players on racketeering."

"Dallas —"

"I've got an idea how to play this," she interrupted Strong. "I need some room for it. The asshole's tried two bribes already — one on the fucking record. It's how he thinks. Compensation. I want to offer him some compensation. Damn it."

She yanked out her comm when it signaled.

Dispatch, Dallas, Lieutenant Eve. See the officers at 21 Forsythe re: the body identified as Aimes, Barry.

"Responding now. Damn it, goddamn it," she muttered as she shoved her comm back in her pocket. "Reo, you work those feds. It's up to three bodies now. Strong, do you want in on this?"

"Damn right."

"Then let's move."

Forsythe's Chinatown," Peabody said when they reached the garage and climbed in Eve's vehicle.

"I know."

"So we've got a wannabe Banger dead inside what's probably Dragon territory."

"Somebody wants a gang war." The base of it, Eve thought, was just that simple. "It's a twofer. Snip off a loose end, like Duff, and push farther into the

259

competitor's territory. Somebody's beating the war drums, and that's stupid. Because we'll follow the beat right to him."

"Lieutenant," Strong began from the backseat, "I'm not going to second-guess you. I'd be one of the last who'd ever do that."

"But?" Eve prompted.

"Lyle was mine. He deserves justice. From what I saw in the box, from what we have on him, I don't see opening up a deal to Cohen needs to happen."

"Three dead, Detective. Two more who might be, and Christ knows how many will be if this does escalate into a war. A deal on the federal side gives me a lever with Cohen. He understands deals."

She flicked a glance in the rearview mirror at Strong's hard, unhappy face.

"Peabody, in the time we've worked together have you ever known me to advocate, much less push, for a deal that would deny the victims justice?"

"No." Peabody shifted, looked back at Strong. "No," she repeated.

"I'll run how I see the play through for you," Eve told Strong. "I'm going to want you on board."

She outlined her strategy as she pushed into Chinatown, wound through the traffic clogging the streets, the tourists taking advantage of a decent day to shop and take vids.

Rather than waste time looking for parking, she pulled into a no-parking zone, flipped up her On Duty light.

She saw the police barricade up ahead and the people crowded up to it, craning necks to see something exciting.

And the very bold street thief winding through the crowd like a quiet river while nimbly picking pockets.

"For Christ's sake," Eve grumbled.

She pushed through the crowd and, since the thief was in the act of lifting a wallet from a back pocket, she managed to grab him by the collar before he spotted her.

He tried a spin — nimbly — managed a backfist she avoided, almost completely. Annoyed by the almost completely, she swept his legs from under him and pinned him to the ground with her knee.

He let out a spate of what she assumed was Chinese, and one of the onlookers — female, fruity Brit accent — shouted, "Police! This woman attacked this young man. Police!"

"I am the police." Eve dragged out her badge and applied more pressure with her knee as her captive wiggled like a worm. "Sir," she said to the man directly in front of her, "you should put that recorder down and secure your wallet."

He frowned, reached back. His mouth dropped open. "Margo! He was picking my pocket! Holy cow this is exciting. Could you say your name, Officer, and say something, you know, official?"

A lot of somethings she couldn't say leaped to mind. "Peabody, get a uniform to handle this."

"Strong already moved on that."

As Eve slapped on restraints, the thief continued to wiggle, squirm, and protest in Chinese at the top of his lungs.

Several more people crowded in to record the moment for their social media pages and/or friends at home.

A uniformed officer strode through, ordering people to move aside. Then he looked down, shook his head. "Knock off the Mandarin, Charlie, you were born in New York. I've got this, Lieutenant, appreciate it. Working a crime scene, Charlie, you moron. Right down the block, sir, and to the alley on the left."

"Looked like he connected," Peabody said as they cleared the barricade.

"Barely." Still, Eve wiggled her jaw side to side. Barely, she thought, could still hurt like a bitch.

CHAPTER
FIFTEEN

Strong stepped up to the alley entrance.

"Family-owned restaurant, residence in the apartment above. Suzan Ho, female head of household, came down with some recyclables, found the body behind the container, does the screaming thing. Neighbor in the apartment across the alley — Mae-Ling Jacobs — pokes her head out the window, sees the situation, calls in the nine-one-one. Responders checked the prints, ID'd the DOB, secured the scene."

From the mouth of the alley, Eve took a quick scan. "Ho might be a fairly common name, but it's not going to be a coincidence the body was dumped in this particular alley. Jones kept banging about Fan Ho — Dragon leader."

"You'd be right. I haven't dealt with him myself, but I know the name. I'm pretty sure this is his family's restaurant."

They walked as they talked until Eve stopped by the body, one somebody had attempted, poorly, to conceal behind the commercial recycle unit.

On a tangled sheet of blood-smeared plastic, Aimes lay faceup, mouth open as if expressing surprise to find himself dead in a Chinatown alley. Blood from the deep gash across his throat had soaked through and dried over the grinning skull on his T-shirt.

"No spatter, no blood pool on the plastic," Eve noted. "They killed him somewhere else, half-assed wrapped him in the sheet, dumped him here."

Beside her, Peabody nodded. "It looks like they more or less rolled him behind the recycler, so he rolled out of the plastic."

In a hurry, Eve thought, and getting the body here was the main thing.

"Strong, you take Ho, Peabody take Jacobs. I've got the body. Peabody, get some uniforms to start a canvass. They had to have transpo to get a DB the size of this one from the kill site. And find out when the restaurant closed last night — the last time anyone used this recycle unit. Strong, notify the sweepers, the dead wagon."

Recorder on, Eve sealed up, then crouched down to verify the identification. For the record, she read off his data, the location, the names of the witnesses.

She slipped on microgoggles to examine the wound. "A deep slice, no visible hesitation marks. The absence of spatter and blood at the scene indicates this isn't where the victim died. Dump site. The victim has bruising on his knuckles, some swelling. It looks at least a day old to me. ME to confirm. My take is the bruising's from beating on Dinnie Duff."

Methodically, she searched his pockets, came up empty. He still had his shoes, she noted, but they were torn, worn, and worthless.

"Pierced left ear, but no ring in it. Big guy like this? Big, tough guy, he'd have put up a fight if he knew it was coming. Angle of the wound indicates the attack came from the front. If he was facing his attacker, he knew him, didn't feel threatened. And where's his sticker? He'd have had one."

She took out her gauge, got a reading. "TOD one-fifteen. So you didn't run, did you, Barry? I bet you hunkered down, got stoned. Maybe did some bragging on bagging a couple of kills. Maybe made some demands. So you had to go. Dump site's deliberate, right on the Dragon leader's doorstep. Because they're idiots," she said in disgust. "And they think we'll look local for the killers."

Easier places to make the dump, even if you wanted to point the finger at a rival gang. But somebody wanted to go for the top.

She sat back on her heels, closed her eyes, and imagined it.

"Attack from the front. Maybe, just maybe, a partner moving in from behind to get a grip, hold him still for a few seconds. It only takes a few seconds.

"Did they already have the plastic, already have it worked out, or was it of the moment? Doesn't matter to you, does it, Barry?" she said, looking down at the young, empty face.

"Roll him onto the sheet, wrap him up because you're going to transfer him to a vehicle, and you don't bother with that if you're going to boost one."

She straightened up. "No, you had access to a vehicle, and didn't want to get blood in the back of the truck, the van, in the trunk of the car. You had brains enough for that."

Calling over a couple of uniforms to help her turn the body, she finished her exam. As she packed up her kit, Strong came back.

"Ms. Jacobs and Ms. Ho are friends, and Jacobs works in the restaurant. So does her teenage son, on weekends. She'd gotten her kids — three — off to school, her husband had already left for work. He's a medical tech. She heard the screams, ran to the window, saw Ho, saw the body. She said she called out to Ho to go inside, that she was calling the police. Timing jibes.

"She worked last night until ten, but says the rest of the staff — the cleanup — would clock out about eleven. She and her husband went to bed by midnight, and her three kids were home and tucked in."

Strong looked up at the window, gauged the distance to the body.

"Jacobs thinks she heard some people arguing in the alley and some rattling around, but isn't sure of the time. She thinks it was around two, but she was half-asleep and can't say for sure."

"Okay."

"I asked her about gang activity. There's where she got evasive. She made a point of saying how her son — the one who works at the restaurant — is studying to be a doctor. How he's never been in trouble. Neither have her two girls — ages fourteen and eleven. But there was something."

"Yeah, there's something, since she's friends with and works for Fan Ho's mother. Let's see what Peabody's got."

They badged through the alley door, started up to the apartment.

"I did a quick run on Jacobs's son, and he's clean."

"It's going to be the restaurant. That's the tie-in."

She rapped on the door. When it opened, she saw the tie-in face-to-face.

She put him early twenties. Strongly built, dark, hard eyes in an action-vid-star's face. He wore his hair in a single short braid. A red-and-gold dragon tat breathed fire on his right biceps.

"Lieutenant Dallas, Detective Strong." She held up her badge. "Are you a member of the household?"

"Fan Ho. A lot of cops to talk to a woman, already shaken, about a body in the alley."

"How about I talk to you instead?"

He shrugged, dismissive. "The other girl cop's in the kitchen, pushing at my mother and grandparents, who came to be with her. They live across the hall."

Eve glanced at the facing apartment. "Anyone else over there now?"

"No."

"Why don't we move in there? Detective Strong, you can join Detective Peabody, let her know I'm getting Mr. Ho's statement in his grandparents' apartment."

"Yes, sir." And as she understood the unstated, Strong took out her PPC as she walked back and began the run.

Ho crossed the hall, tapped numbers into a lock pad, opened the door.

Inside, the apartment smelled of herbs and flowers, and held a quiet order and serenity despite its bold colors, shimmers of gold.

Other than the bold, the decor ran to family photos and a collection of statues of the smiling, big-bellied god she recognized as Buddha.

Ho dropped onto a red-and-gold couch, swiped a hand in the air by way of invitation.

"I already told the other cop I was sleeping. My room's on the other side of the apartment. I didn't hear anything until my mother came running in. She woke me up, told me somebody was dead in the alley."

"And what did you do?"

"I got up, went to the kitchen, leaned out the window to look. It wasn't anybody I knew, so nothing to do with me. I made her some tea because she was upset. That's it."

"Do you work in your family's restaurant?"

The shrug again. "I pitch in sometimes. It's not my deal."

"Where were you this morning between midnight and three A.M.?"

"Home for most of it. I was out with friends for a while, got home about twelve-thirty, one o'clock. My father was still up, working on taxes or something."

His tone, clipped, told her he'd talked to cops often enough to know not to elaborate, to give just enough information to cover.

But under it, she read a simmering fury. Someone had brought cops to his door. He didn't strike her as the type to let the insult pass.

"Did you see anyone?" she began, already knowing how he'd answer. "Anyone around the building?"

"Didn't see anything, don't know anything. Is that it?"

"No. What's your position within the Dragons?"

He leaned back, crossed his leg over his knee. "Who said I have one?"

"So you're ashamed or afraid to admit your affiliation."

That got a rise. His eyes fired — killing lights. "Do I look afraid of some cop with tits?"

"Ashamed then of the trouble and dishonor you bring to your family."

He surged to his feet, and she to hers. Those killing lights flared as he shifted toward a fighting stance.

"It would be a mistake to take me on in your grandparents' apartment. And your mother's already upset. I'd hate to tell her I had to haul her son into a cage."

"You?" He barked out a laugh. "I could get that stunner away from you in two seconds, give you a good jolt with it."

With her gaze cool against his heat, Eve placed her right fist into her left palm in *Bao Quan Li* before shifting her own body. "Try, and we'll finish this conversation at Central."

She could feel it vibrating from him — the need, almost a lust, to come at her, to cause pain. To win even though, perhaps because, he knew she baited him.

Then he dropped down again, flicked his fingers. "You're not worth it."

Some control then, she decided. And maybe some respect for his grandparents, his mother. More, he was more angry and upset about the body on his doorstep than he wanted to show.

"If you looked out the window, as you stated, unless there's something wrong with your eyes, you saw the Banger tat on the body. And unless you're an idiot, you knew cops would question you about your gang affiliation, your whereabouts, and whether or not you knew the victim."

"So you think I killed some Banger trash, then left him where my mother would fucking trip over him? Where it would bring cops to the door?"

"No."

His eyes sharpened at that, looking for a lie, a ploy.

"I think you know about the body left in the neutral zone, and if you were going to retaliate for that offense, you'd have left a message on Banger turf. Somebody wants you to do just that, and light the fuse that starts a war."

"Bangers want war, they'll get one."

This one and Jones, she thought, same mold.

"I didn't say Bangers want war. I said somebody. And if you're stupid enough to take the bait, you're giving him what he wants. And your family will grieve."

"I can handle myself."

"I bet you've got cousins, friends with mothers. And there's a restaurant downstairs that could be a target if you let it go that far. You? I don't give a rat's ass about you, but I do about the people who'd get caught up in the violence, and you ought to care what it'll do to your rep, to your profit margin, to your family's safety if you light the fuse somebody else primed."

"Dragons breathe fire." He tapped a finger on his gang tat. "They disrespected my family."

"Deliberately. Let it get under your skin, the blood's going to wash over you, and your family. Let me do my job, and whoever wants that blood will be in a cage."

"Your job?" He tried for mocking, but the rage won. "You mean nothing here. Whoever wants blood will see their own spill."

She walked to the door, paused. "I'm not interested in you, today. But sooner or later you'll come across my screen. If it's not because you're already in the morgue, I'll end up putting you in a cage."

She walked out, once again knocked on the door across the hall. And wondered how long it would be before she knocked on it to give Fan Ho's family notification.

They're a nice family, Dallas." As they drove back to Central, Peabody stared out the passenger window. "Kind, loving, hardworking. It shines through. And I know in my gut, the mother's first fear when she saw the body was her son had done it. She's afraid for him, that shines through, too. You have to wonder why he chose the life he has when he comes from such solid people."

"That's a Mira question. What I can tell you is, while he didn't kill Aimes, if he had, it wouldn't be his first."

"His given name's George," Strong supplied. "He uses Fan, which means *lethal* in Chinese. Trouble started with him, on record, pretty early. Truancy, destruction of property, fighting. He went after a teacher, laid her out right in class. He was eleven."

Unsurprised, Eve nodded. "You don't have to be Mira to see that while he probably loves his mother, his grandmother, outside of family he doesn't think much of women, and sure as hell doesn't respect any in authority."

"No illegals charges," Strong continued, "nothing on possession, use, distribution, which might be why he hasn't come across my screen. His sheet lists him as the captain of the Dragons. He did his time as a minor, and since then he's been pulled in on charges — and slipped the knots of them."

"He hates cops," Eve added. "Big surprise. Doesn't think much of women as actual human beings, and considers Bangers trash. He has a whole pot full of rage, but he does have some control. We'll hope he uses it while we shut this down."

"He was born in New York — his parents and grandparents were born here, too. But I've got a report here. He has a sister. It's believed she was seeing some guy she met in school, Hugh Lanigan, non-Chinese. The guy gets jumped one night after taking the sister home. Broken jaw, broken arm — football quarterback who'll never spiral a ball again. Can't or won't identify his attacker. But he broke things off with the sister, finished out his senior year — online."

"How long ago?" Eve asked as she pulled into the garage.

"Three years. The kid lost a football scholarship. He's in college in Miami. The sister's in college in Seattle."

"Three years and a few thousand miles might be enough," Eve considered. "Why don't you talk to him, see if his memory's cleared? Fan Ho needs to be locked away."

"Wouldn't that be sweet?"

"Peabody and I will go at Cohen again. Let's see if he managed to find a lawyer, and if another dead body shakes him any."

"Can I use a bullpen desk?" Strong asked Peabody as they walked to the elevator. "I'll see if I can persuade the sister's ex to cooperate."

"I'll set you up."

"Is Vending on your level as bad as ours?"

"At least."

Strong sighed, stepped into the elevator. "Oh well. I'll risk it."

"Write this up, Peabody. I need to talk to Reo, update the board."

Once on Homicide level, Strong scowled at Vending and Eve swung into her office to reach out to Reo.

"I'm still in the house," Reo told her. "I'll come to you."

While she waited, Eve added the new crime scene shots, pinned on Fan Ho's ID shot, the witnesses.

"Coffee, please," Reo said as she walked in, and Eve held up two fingers.

"Does your DB relate to the others?"

"He was part of the team who killed Pickering and Duff. They dumped him in the alley behind the family restaurant and residence of the captain of the Dragons."

"Not even subtle." Reo passed Eve the coffee and, knowing the dangers of the visitor's chair, sat at the desk. "Cohen hired an attorney, who came in to speak to his client. Quit in very short order. Cohen's now back to being a fool and representing himself."

"Should make the job easier. Feds?"

"My powers of persuasion?" Reo fluffed at her already fluffy hair. "Are awesome. In addition to that, after some mumbling and claim staking, they liked your plan. Didn't love, but liked. My awesome powers turned the tide."

"They'll leave Eldena Vinn out of it?"

Reo smiled. "Powers of persuasion. Awesome. She'll have to testify, but I've already had a talk with her lawyer. She's not only willing, she's eager. Agents should be, as we speak, at her place getting her statement, confiscating Cohen's electronics and records."

"Good. That keeps them busy while I lay a third body at Cohen's feet. This guy?" She tapped Aimes's photo on the board. "He murdered two people, participated in the brutal beating and gang rape of the woman who assisted in the first murder. He had her earrings, with her blood still on them from where he ripped them out of her ears, in a purse he stole from Rochelle's closet after murdering her brother."

Eve looked at Aimes — defiant young face in his ID shot, dead and drained at the dump site. "Lab's confirmed Duff's blood and tissue on the earrings. We'd have put him away for the rest of his life. Now he'll never see eighteen."

Hissing out a breath, Eve rubbed the back of her neck. "And now I've got to send cops and a grief counselor out to the fricking Sky Mall to notify his mother because I didn't scoop him up, lock him up, before somebody slit his throat."

"Are you looking at Jones for that?"

"If Jones found out Aimes went around him to kill Pickering and Duff, he'd execute Aimes. But I don't see him ordering the body dumped at the back door of a Dragon captain."

She gestured with her coffee. "Jones is a fake. Sure, he's beating the Banger drum — but he's cheating his fellow gang members while he's at it. Banking profits, going into a partnership outside the group to make more. For himself. He doesn't want attention focused on him, and sloppy murders tend to do just that."

"And if Cohen went into partnership with him, and Jones started cutting back on the percentage . . ."

"Cohen might have gone into a partnership with someone else," Eve finished. "Someone in the position to, and with the ambition to, take over if they could depose Jones."

This time Eve jabbed a finger on Jorgenson's ID shot. "It's going to be him. He wants the war. He wants to lead."

"If so, why not just kill Jones?"

"A harder target, but that may be coming." She polished off her coffee. "So. Time to get to it."

"I'm on tap if you need my awesome powers of persuasion."

They parted ways in the bullpen. From Trueheart's desk — he and Baxter were on their way to the Sky Mall — Strong signaled Eve.

"I know you want to get to Cohen, but I reached Ho's sister's ex-boyfriend. Good timing on that. Hugh Lanigan's younger brother's in his first year of college in Cambridge. Smart kid, got into Harvard. The parents moved to South Carolina a few months ago."

"You're going to tell me Ho threatened his family, so he kept his mouth shut."

"You should be a detective. Stay away from my sister, or you're dead. Go to the cops, and your little brother's dead. And, hey, your mom looks pretty good. Be a shame if somebody messed up her face."

"Now Lanigan figures they're out of reach so he can talk."

"He's ready to file charges, testify, do whatever it takes to put Ho away. He talked to his family about it just a few days ago, and they're behind him. He was just building up the guts for it."

"Reo's in Observation. Go get her, set this up."

With a nod, Strong rose. "Dallas, if this goes our way, we're going to put a hurting on two gangs. We won't wipe them out, but they'll hurt."

A nice side benefit, Eve thought as she tapped Peabody. "Let's break this prick."

"Snap! We're good with the feds?"

"They're with Vinn now."

She opened the door to Interview. If anything Cohen looked more miserable than he had that morning. "Record on. Dallas and Peabody resuming Interview with Cohen. I don't see your legal representative, Sam. Should we go find him for you?"

"On further consideration I've elected to represent myself in this witch hunt."

"Then, for the record, you're waiving your right to an attorney?"

"I am an attorney."

Eve merely sat, stared at him.

"All right, yes."

"Okay then. And, for the record, we're adding a third charge of accessory to murder."

"What? This is ridiculous. This is — this is bullshit!"

"Aimes, Barry, age seventeen." Eve mimed slitting her throat with her finger. "He's one of the assholes you enlisted to kill Pickering and Duff. You know what's bullshit, Sam? That there's honor among thieves. There's even less honor among murderers."

"I don't even know this person."

Casual, confident, Eve rocked back in her chair. "You know, I don't doubt you didn't know his name. His name wouldn't be important. Just that he do the job you wanted done. But you damn well know the name of the Banger who helped you set all this up. Give me the name, Sam. Even a half-assed attorney would advise his client to roll when he's facing three counts of murder."

"Even a half-assed cop would know I've been in custody since last night and couldn't have had anything to do with slitting some gang member's throat."

"Gosh, Sam, you've forgotten all about accessory before the fact. You maybe need to hit the law books again. Add this: The newest dead guy was part of your conspiracy to murder, and is now dead due to his part in that conspiracy."

"Buy a clue," Peabody added. "And give us the damn name. Even a half-assed murder suspect knows he who flips first gets the best deal."

At the hard, angry look Eve shot her, Peabody shrugged.

"Come on, Dallas, he can't be that dumb."

"What kind of deal? No, no," Cohen said immediately. "I don't want to hear it. I don't know anything about any of these killings. My partnership with Marcus Jones was real estate. How he earned his share of the investment has nothing to do with me. If he's a criminal, arrest him!"

"Maybe we'll put you in Holding together," Peabody speculated. "After we let him and the rest of the gang know why you're in here."

"Terrible accidents do happen in Holding sometimes," Eve added, shifting to Peabody. "Outside, too. Say, if somebody happened to make bail and got released, and word got out he'd spilled his guts to the cops . . . Terrible accident."

"You can't do that!"

"Do what?" Eve shifted back. "We're just talking here."

"I've told you nothing. Those people are violent criminals."

"You should've thought of that before you threw in with them. And don't start back up with the bullshit. Your records, for Christ's sake. Your records show your percentage of profits from illegal activity committed by Jones and his gang. So, yeah, we're going to wrap Jones up, using your records. And unless he hires an idiot for an attorney, he'll find out where we got our information. It's called discovery. Remember?"

"A guy like Jones'll probably break his spine for that alone," Peabody put in. "Unless we work it so Jones can't get to him. But we've got no incentive."

"Once we pull Jones in using the evidence gathered from Sam's records, it's done." Eve lifted her shoulders, let them fall. "Those terrible accidents? They increase exponentially in prison."

Cohen's eyes glittered, not from anger, but the beginning of tears. "This is my life you're talking about."

"Three people in the morgue, you fuck. Every one of them had a life. And that doesn't begin to count the scores of lives screwed up or ended because of your partner's criminal activities, from which you profited."

"I — I need some water. I need some water. And I need to think."

"Dallas and Peabody exiting to get the subject water and allow him thinking time. You've got ten minutes. Pause interview."

"I'll get the water," Peabody said. "You want coffee?"

"Pepsi." Eve dragged out tokens for Vending. "Don't use my code or the machines will spit out anything but."

"I thought he would spill it before now."

"First we had to break through his delusions — and they're pretty damn strong — that he could wiggle out. We finally got there."

As Peabody walked to Vending, Eve saw Roarke come out of Observation.

"I didn't know you were here."

"Only just. It appears I missed much of the show, and another murder. And . . ." He skimmed a fingertip over the faint bruise on her jaw.

She'd forgotten about it. "Come on, that doesn't even show."

"I know that face, every inch. A fight with a suspect?"

"No, and not a fight. A takedown. A street thief got in a glancing — and lucky — hit." Now that Roarke had reminded her, it pissed her off all over again. "The fun never ends."

"And with all the fun, I'll wager you've missed lunch."

"Been a little busy, and Vending sucks anyway."

With a shake of his head, he tapped a finger on the dent in her chin. "There's food you'll actually eat without complaint in your office AC."

"Right. I always forget. I'll get something after I break this son of a bitch. I figure you're here mostly because you feel sorry for Vinn, so I'll tell you: She stood up. She has a lawyer, she's cooperating with the feds, and apparently has a stripper pal who has her back and doesn't take any crap."

"Glad to hear it. Peabody," he said as she clomped back with the drinks. "You look both lovely and formidable."

Her eyes got a little sparkly as she passed Eve the tube of Pepsi. "Thanks. It's been a day so far."

"Plenty more to come." Eve cracked the tube. "Before the end of it we'll be busting a Dragon captain for aggravated assault, with a sweetener of threatening bodily harm. And we'll bust Jones for a whole — what do they call that? — plethora of charges. Plethora. It's got a ring."

She guzzled Pepsi. "And if we can finish breaking Cohen, somebody's going down for murder in the first, three counts."

"That's a very busy rest of the day," Roarke commented. "I hope to join some of it. I have about an hour now, then some things to see to. If I don't see you before, let me know when you start out."

So saying, he pulled a candy bar out of his pocket, broke it in half. "So the two of you keep your energy up."

"Loose pants or chocolate? Chocolate!" Peabody took the candy.

Eve eyed it narrowly. "Did you get that from my office?"

"I didn't, no. I brought it with me on the suspicion my cop — or cops in this case — hadn't eaten since breakfast."

"I had a mini oatmeal crunch power bar," Peabody said. "This is better."

Eve studied the wrapper, noted it didn't have the mark she'd put on her office stash. But that didn't mean she wouldn't check her hidey-hole later.

But for now she ate the chocolate, drank the Pepsi. And decided the quick energy boost couldn't hurt. She handed Roarke the empty tube. "See you later."

"I'd wish you good luck in there, but from the little I've seen you have all you need."

She would have, Eve thought as she opened the door to Interview, when she pried the damn name out of Cohen.

"Record on. Dallas and Peabody entering to resume interview."

She sat, noted Cohen's eyes were a little red against a face paler than before. Fear could squeeze out a few tears.

In one go he drank half the water Peabody set on the table.

"You've had your water and your thinking time."

"I . . . Hypothetically. If I had information regarding certain criminal activities and enterprises, and volunteered this information to the authorities, would this result in immunity from any inadvertent connection to those activities?"

" 'Immunity'? Are you serious?"

"By providing this information — again, hypothetically — I'd put my life in danger. With immunity, I'd be able to relocate out of harm's way."

An operator to the end, Eve thought. Just what she'd counted on. "You're going to relocate to prison. Stop wasting my time."

"Information I provide could and should lead to the convictions of multiple violent criminals." His voice took on a desperate edge now. "I'm sure the prosecuting attorney's office would be interested in this information. By granting immunity on the gray area of my business practices, the PA, and the federal government, would break the back of a notorious gang."

Frowning, Eve sat back. "I'm not going to be able to work immunity, not with the feds or the PA. At the end of the day, the Bangers are pretty small change."

"Three murders," Cohen insisted. "They want the people really responsible."

She frowned again, showing him the face of a cop conflicted between duty and dislike. And reluctantly letting duty win.

"I can cite cooperation, and push harder if that cooperation leads to arrest and conviction, but immunity's never going to happen. You've been cheating the federal government, Sam. They get really pissy about that."

He wiped his lips with the back of his hand. "If I knew the location of illegals with a street value of more than a hundred thousand dollars, and the equipment used to make false identifications and to conduct identity fraud, they might be less pissy."

Eve drummed her fingers on the table. "They might be marginally less pissy, but that won't get you immunity."

Peabody leaned over to whisper in Eve's ear, said the words "Witness Protection" just loud enough to carry.

Eve drummed her fingers again, then leaned back to Peabody. With a nod, Peabody rose.

"Peabody exiting Interview," Eve said. "We might be able to deal down some of the charges, depending on the information. Are you going to stipulate that Eldena Vinn was unaware of your activities in this matter, had no knowledge of the fraud or tax evasion, was, in fact, duped into signing documents, and that you took her money for same under false pretenses? Otherwise," Eve said when he hesitated, "the feds are going to haul her in and mine her for information, and that information's going to add weight to the charges already against you."

"There's no need for that. I can stipulate that I handled the household finances."

"Do better, or I won't even step up to the plate much less go to bat for you."

"She was unaware. I was looking out for her financial interests."

Eyes flat and steady, Eve leaned toward him. "Cop to this, Cohen, or I walk out of here, go pick up Jones, and that's the end of it."

"All right, all right. I used her, I'm not proud of it. It's not my fault she didn't read the papers I put in front of her."

"You defrauded her. You used funds you took from her under the guise of household expenses to fatten your own bank accounts and listed her income, without her knowledge, to secure loans for real property."

"I gave her a very good life," he began, then stumbled over his words as Eve started to rise. "I lied to her. I'll admit that. I used her income to secure loans

284

without her knowledge. My records are very clear on what monies I took from her, and she can have it back. Minus, of course, reasonable living expenses."

A few tears did swirl in his eyes as Eve started to stand again. "All of it! She can have all of it. It's not important. What does it matter? I'm prepared to give you information on much more. Valuable information. I'll take Witness Protection."

As if on cue, the door opened to Peabody and APA Cher Reo.

CHAPTER
SIXTEEN

"Detective Peabody entering Interview with APA Reo."

In her pretty pearl-gray suit, Reo sat, set down a cup of what Eve knew by the scent was her office coffee and a file.

She smiled as if sitting down to a fancy lunch with a friend. The APA looked like an easy mark. Young, blond, pretty, slight build.

No one noticed the fangs until after they'd sunk into their neck.

"Cher Reo, Mr. Cohen, with the prosecutor's office. I'm told you have information on gang activity and would like to proffer that for a deal regarding the various charges currently against you."

Seeing a mark rather than her fangs, Cohen reverted. "I want immunity from all charges, state and federal."

"Oh." Reo batted her pretty eyes. "Oh dear, I'm afraid there's been some miscommunication. Immunity isn't on the table. Lieutenant, I'm at Central coordinating an assault charge. I can't take time away from that to deal in fantasies. If Mr. Cohen gains a grip on reality, let me know."

"Just wait!"

Reo smiled again. "Mr. Cohen, I realize you're in a precarious situation, but there are only so many hours in a day. I simply can't waste any of mine."

"Wait!"

He snapped it out. The same tone, Eve thought, he'd used when telling Eldena Vinn to be quiet.

It wouldn't work here, either.

Reo glanced at her wrist unit, back at Cohen with the bitter cold of January. "Sixty seconds, starting now."

Eve decided he'd felt the first bite of the fangs when his tone turned wheedling.

"I can help you break the back of the Banger gang. You'd be able to confiscate thousands of dollars' worth of illegals, and weapons, and equipment. I can't go to prison. I might be killed! I want Witness Protection."

"Mr. Cohen, Witness Security is a federal program. I'm an assistant prosecutor for New York."

"You can work it," he insisted. "You can get the deal. The feds are going to confiscate the real estate and the funds anyway. Why care if I go to prison? Why care if I can give them bigger, a lot bigger, than me? I'm a legal consultant, that's all."

Reo's eyes widened as she picked up her coffee. "Like a consigliere?"

"Yes. No." He swiped the back of his hand over his mouth. "I consult, advise, that's all."

"And you claim, in that capacity, to have valuable knowledge that will lead to arrests and convictions?"

"Absolutely."

"Example?"

"I need a deal."

"Oops, ticktock." Another glance at her wrist unit. "I need an example. Demonstrate your knowledge, and we can talk deal. Otherwise . . ."

"There's an electronics shop on Broome — or was. When they refused to pay an increased protection fee, Jones ordered the place hit. A couple Molotov cocktails right before closing. The owner was still inside. He got out with minor injuries, but he lost everything."

"And how did you come by this knowledge?"

"After the fact." Earnestly now, Cohen patted his hands at the air. "Of course I'd have advised against destroying property, endangering lives. After the fact, one of the gang — Rufus Miller — was arrested. There was a witness who claimed they saw him light the place up. I was called in as his representative."

"When did this take place?"

"Last November."

Reo took out her PPC, keyed into it, scrolled. "Hmm. I see the witness recanted." Reo spent another minute scrolling. "I also see an Amber Alert on the witness's eight-year-old daughter, who was abducted on her way home from school — on the very day of Miller's arrest. She was returned, unharmed and unable to give any information on her abductor."

Another hint of fang showed now as Reo smiled. "Coincidence?"

Looking away, Cohen tugged at the neck of his jumpsuit. "I only know the witness recanted."

All three women remained silent, beat after beat.

"Okay, okay. Jones ordered it. He ordered the kid wasn't to be hurt, just scared. It was only a few hours.

That's an example. I need a deal, in writing, before I give you more. Bigger."

"Bigger than firebombing, kidnapping, witness intimidation? My, my."

Reo took a tablet out of her briefcase. "Let the record show I'm bringing in Special Agent Teasdale of the FBI. Let's see what we can do, Mr. Cohen."

Eve figured she deserved some acting props for pretending annoyance and disgust. She'd personally requested Teasdale for this part of the game plan. They'd worked together before, and she knew the woman shot straight.

Reo cued up the tablet, brought Teasdale's image on-screen.

"APA Reo."

"Special Agent Teasdale, good afternoon. As previously discussed we have Mr. Cohen in Interview, He's given a verified example of his inside knowledge of the Banger organization and their alleged activities that break state and federal laws."

"As discussed, the FBI currently has agents reviewing and logging Mr. Cohen's records. These records document his activities, which break state and federal laws."

"Understood. However . . ."

Reo laid it out; Teasdale pushed back. Cohen whined, promised names, dates, locations. As negotiations crept along, Eve lobbed objections.

Why not just give him an all-expenses-paid lifetime vacation in fucking Tahiti?

Peabody tossed in a derisive remark about Club Fed.

At one point, Eve stormed out. When she hit the bullpen, she started barking orders. "Everybody in the conference room in thirty for a two-pronged op briefing."

"What's up, Loo?" Baxter asked.

"We're taking on the Bangers and the Dragons. If you're on a hot, I need to hear about it. Otherwise, you're on this until it's done. Detective Strong, my office."

She hit the AC for coffee, gestured Strong to do the same.

"Put a team together," Eve told her. "Ho's your collar, and you'll head that op."

"I appreciate it."

"You worked it. You've got thirty, so move it. I need to update Whitney and get SWAT on board."

"Did he give you a name? On Lyle."

"That's coming, but he's already given us enough on Jones to lock him up for a nice long stretch. We'll see who else he flips on. Move it, Strong."

In fifteen, Eve stalked back into Interview. Cohen, not as pale now, sat with his head bowed while Teasdale and Reo worked out fine details.

"I need to pick where you relocate me."

"No." Teasdale's tone was flat and firm. "Unlike Lieutenant Dallas's trip to Tahiti, WITSEC is not a vacation. If all terms of the deal are met, if your information proves valid and results in arrests, you will be given a new identity and relocated where the federal government deems. You will then adhere to all terms of the program, or your status will be rescinded."

"But —"

"If those terms aren't agreeable to you, Mr. Cohen, I can promise you'll spend the next ten to twenty in a federal penitentiary — and it won't be Detective Peabody's insulting 'Club Fed.'"

"I need it in writing."

"You'll have it. APA Reo, as I'm currently occupied, can I send the completed agreement to Mr. Cohen through you?"

"Of course. In return I'll copy you on the information Mr. Cohen offers from our record."

"I appreciate the interagency cooperation. I'll send you the paperwork shortly."

When Teasdale signed off, Reo turned to Cohen.

"Mr. Cohen, do you understand the agreement, its terms, your obligations?"

"Yes." He sat up straight again, and the look in his eyes read smug. "I'm a lawyer, Ms. Reo. I understand the deal on the table."

"And you understand the statements you make, the information you give upon acceptance of the deal must be valid and truthful? If they prove otherwise, the deal is rescinded."

"I get it, okay? My life's on the line here. I get it. Can I get a sandwich and a Coke?"

Reo stared at him. "You want a sandwich?"

"I've barely eaten since they pulled me in."

"Detective Peabody, would you get Mr. Cohen a sandwich?"

"And a Coke," he added.

"For Christ's sake," Eve muttered as Peabody walked out scowling. "Peabody exiting Interview. Maybe you want some cookies, too."

He actually smirked at her. "I wouldn't say no."

"Don't push it, Mr. Cohen," Reo added.

Eve swung around to stare at her own reflection in the two-way glass. She wondered if Roarke was still in Observation. Doubted it. The negotiations had taken more than an hour, and despite them running exactly as she'd hoped, she had a small, nagging headache as a result.

In short order, she reminded herself, she'd be moving again.

"Agent Teasdale's efficient." Reo's tablet signaled incoming. She scanned the screen. Nodded, nodded, ordered the printout.

"You'll initial each page as you read through the agreement, Mr. Cohen. Agent Teasdale has already done so and pre-signed. Lieutenant Dallas, you'll witness Mr. Cohen's signature, as will I."

Eve said nothing.

Peabody came back, updated the record, tossed a Vending sandwich and a tube of Coke on the table. She sat, giving a very good impression of a steaming sulk.

Cohen unwrapped the sandwich, bit in — wrinkled his nose — but kept eating as Reo slid the papers and a pen across the table. With his bottom lip poked out in concentration, he read, initialed, read, drew his eyebrows together, initialed.

"It seems to be in order." He signed and gave Eve a quiet, satisfied smile.

"Very well, Mr. Cohen." Reo signed in turn, held the pen out to Eve.

Eve added a bad-tempered scrawl.

"I'm going to scan this document to Special Agent Teasdale. I will messenger her the original once this interview is concluded. At this point, I'm reopening the interview to Agent Teasdale. You will answer her questions, Mr. Cohen, answer mine, answer those of Lieutenant Dallas and/or Detective Peabody. Any and all questions asked, any and all answers you give or statements you make must, as agreed, be valid and truthful."

"Just hold on, goddamn it." Eve slapped a hand on the table. "I'm not standing around in here while some fed pokes at this asshole over transporting illegals over state lines or financial bullshit. I want a name. One question, one answer. Who ordered Lyle Pickering and Dinnie Duff's murders?"

"I don't know who actually did it. I want to stress I advised against this, strongly advised against it. I wasn't aware —"

"One question, one answer," Eve demanded. "Who ordered the murders?"

"Jones." He looked away, pressed his lips together. "Marcus Jones."

"Follow-up. Why?"

"He . . . he was angry Pickering wouldn't come back, wouldn't work for him. He wanted to make an example out of him, and make him look worthless. Then he could have the girl killed, point fingers at the Dragons. Cement his standing, take back some territory, bring the Bangers back to what they had been."

He looked back at Eve now, but never quite met her eyes.

"I told him it was crazy. I thought he listened. After, I was afraid to say anything. Afraid he'd kill me. He needs to be locked away. He's dangerous. You need to put him away."

"You knew two people were going to be murdered."

"I advised against it."

"You knew a third person, Barry Aimes, was going to be murdered."

"No, I swear." He sent her a look, direct and pleading. "I didn't know, exactly. Maybe he talked about dumping something right on Fan Ho's doorstep, but I didn't know."

"Come on, Peabody. I've had enough of this asshole. Dallas and Peabody exiting Interview."

Peabody trotted out after her.

"He was lying about Jones," Peabody said as she hurried toward the conference room Eve had booked.

"Yeah, he was. Good for you, Peabody."

"Well, he wasn't even very good at it. I just don't get why. Why lie when that kills the deal?"

"Because he's not just a sleazy disbarred lawyer, he's a lousy one — which is why he doesn't really understand what he agreed to. It's all not going in a cage for him. He thinks with what he gave us on Jones, what he'll give the feds, we'll have Jones wrapped up tight. Jones denies the murders, who's going to believe him? Why would we, in Cohen's opinion, actually dig

294

down and work the case? He gave us the killer, done and done.

"Get everything we have on Banger HQ and the players ready for the briefing," she said when they reached the conference room. "Strong's heading the Dragon end, so work in what she gets."

"All over it and back again in a freaking bow. What about the illegals and fraud equipment Cohen claims to know about outside the HQ?"

"That's Teasdale's."

"Yeah." Peabody huffed out a breath. "Is it okay I feel a little pissy about that?"

"Yeah, then swallow it down." Eve already had. "Because we're going to bag a bunch of bad guys."

While Peabody worked, Eve tagged Feeney.

He said, "Yo. Just caught me, heading out."

"You're going to want to head back. I need a couple of e-teams. Combat ready. We're hitting Bangers' and Dragons' HQs. We're going to have a party."

"I'll get my party hat."

"Conference room two, as soon as you can get here." She broke off with him, texted Roarke.

It's going down in about an hour. Going to brief the teams in about ten.

She contacted the commander, finished up as Roarke's response came through.

I'm with you, Lieutenant.

"Yeah," she murmured. "I know it."

She took the photos Peabody generated to the board. Jones, Ho — primary targets. Then the lieutenants. As she arranged them, Eve studied them again.

"This one here." She tapped a photo. "Put a ring around him."

"Which one is that?" Peabody shifted to read the name on the ID shot. "Jorgenson."

"He's the one I keep coming back to."

"Why him, especially?"

"Duff. She's flopping with him — she's broke, a used-up, burned-out, whiny addict. Plenty of others who aren't as far gone as she was, but he lets her flop with him. Connections, Peabody. She's connected to Pickering, and Pickering had a soft spot for her."

"And still he cut her off."

"Yeah, which made her prime to pay him back."

"We'll never be able to ask her," Peabody said, "but yeah, that's how I see it."

"The why for Jorgenson? Could be he got wind — through our pal Cohen — about how Jones is skimming, how he's fattening his own accounts, separate from the gang. Jones started putting some hurt on Cohen's take, so Cohen looks to someone who'd be grateful for some information, who'd be willing to take Jones out. Not directly. Jones has too much punch and pull. But you set the cops on him, shake some of that pull. Start a war — and if the cops don't have Jones in a cage, he ends up a casualty of war."

"Then Jorgenson steps in — with the advantage of knowing where Jones has his money buried."

"And Cohen ends up owning all that property. Big win for him."

"It could play like that," Peabody considered, "because Cohen lies and cheats like other people breathe. It's like an involuntary reflex. But Lyle Pickering's murder could track back to being Strong's CI, and that getting out somehow. And then —"

Peabody broke off when Strong came in. Both she and Eve let that end of the discussion die off.

"I pulled five from my squad," Strong told them, "and have a translator on tap in case any of the ones we pull in claim they don't speak English. My team's solid."

"Good enough. You'll have an e-team and Tactical added on. Work with Peabody on the targets. We'll hit Ho's headquarters. If we don't flush him out there, we hit his residence."

Baxter strolled in next. "Trueheart's letting his mom know we'll be late for dinner. Seriously," he added when Eve frowned. "His mom invited me over for a home-cooked."

He got bad cop coffee from the conference room AutoChef, drank it while he studied the board. "Bad dudes — and one dudette, though wow, she is one big mama. This'll be fun."

As the rest filed in, the room smelled of that bad cop coffee. When Jenkinson sat, she realized she'd managed to avoid looking directly at his madly pink polka dots over nuked green tie, until just that moment.

Now her eyes vibrated.

As they started to adjust, McNab bounced in along with Callendar and a couple more e-geeks dressed like circus performers.

Even when she closed her newly vibrating eyes, colors pulsed behind them.

Feeney shuffled in, soothing in wrinkled beige and brown. Then Commander Whitney with SWAT commander Lowenbaum. She gave everybody a moment to settle, then stepped up to the board.

"This will be a two-pronged operation. Detective Strong will head the team targeting this individual. George Ho, aka Fan Ho, is a leader of the Dragons organization. At this time he's charged with aggravated assault and threats to cause bodily harm. It's very likely there will be additional charges pending. Detective Strong's team will be assisted by EDD and Tactical. All team members will wear vests and helmets. This is a dangerous, violent individual. Assume he's armed, assume any with him are also armed and dangerous.

"Peabody, Dragon HQ on-screen."

She outlined positions, timing, added three experienced uniforms to Strong's team.

"Detective Strong, anything to add?"

"Yes, sir, a couple of things."

Roarke slipped in while Strong added some details.

He leaned against the back wall, watched his cop run the briefing as Strong finished up.

"My team will take Banger HQ and this primary target. Marcus Jones, aka Slice. He leads the gang. He's charged with conspiracy to kidnap, enforced imprisonment of a minor, witness intimidation. Also charged with destruction of property, attempted murder in ordering said property — with an individual inside — firebombed. There are numerous federal charges in addition. We're also looking for a male, indeterminate age and race. He snaps his fingers."

"'He snaps his fingers'?" Reineke repeated.

Eve demonstrated, holding her arms at her sides. "It's all we've got. He's a suspect in three murders. These five." She gestured to the lieutenants — four males, one female. "We bring them in. But this one." She pinned a finger to Jorgenson. "Kenneth Jorgenson, aka Bolt. He leads my parade on suspicion of ordering those three murders. Jones, Jorgenson, all of them are dangerous, violent. Assume they're armed. My team will be assisted by EDD and Tactical."

She nodded to Peabody, who brought Banger HQ on-screen.

"Here's how it's going to go."

It fascinated Roarke how she, like a general with a map, placed her troops, laid out the tactics, the steps, the timing.

She may not have the focus to run accessories on her own command center, but she knew how to plan and plot an operation.

He studied those troops as well, the attention paid, the slight nodding of Feeney's head as if saying: Yeah, that's how to bring it in.

Then he turned his attention to her board. She wanted Jones for a multitude of reasons, but not, he thought, for the murders that had brought them all to this point.

As a businessman, he agreed. Wars could be profitable, true enough, but a war in this case risked exposing the more lucrative business Jones had with Cohen.

He wouldn't want that, Roarke concluded. What Jones wanted was the status quo. Murders and swipes at a rival gang shook the status quo.

But an ambitious lieutenant, perhaps a bloodthirsty one, wanted nothing more than to upend that status quo.

He placed her pick easily enough as the one giving Duff a bed in exchange for sex, the one who'd said she'd gone to work on the night of her murder.

Which, in turn, linked him with the woman who'd set Pickering up for murder before her own brutal death.

And simple equations, he thought, often proved simple truths.

"Lieutenant Lowenbaum?"

He rose, took up a laser pointer to indicate on the map where he'd place his special weapons teams at both locations.

"Captain Feeney," Eve said, "I'll need you to split into two teams."

"Got that covered. I'll take Callendar and Stipper into Chinatown. That gives you Roarke, McNab, and Marley in the Bowery. We'll get you numbers and locations inside both buildings before you move in."

"That works. If anybody's got questions, now's the time. Then suit up," she said. "Full riot gear. Teams coordinate in the garage, level five, section one. Let's go kick some gangster ass."

As teams filed out, Peabody moved to her. "The magic coat counts, right, instead of a vest?"

"Button it, and keep it buttoned. And check out a clutch piece and an ankle holster."

"Okay. Prepare for the worst?"

"We're going to corner them. All of them are violent. Some of them are stupid. A lot of them are both. They've likely got some sort of protocol to handle a raid, and I don't think it's putting their hands in the air and saying we give up."

"So, worst."

"Get a clutch piece and a helmet," Eve repeated.

"For you, too."

"The helmet." Man, she hated them. "I've got a clutch piece. And a third helmet for the civilian consultant, and a sidearm. We'll take my ride, meet up with McNab and the van."

Eve walked to Roarke. "You're on e's, but you still gear up. Peabody's checking you out a helmet and a sidearm."

His lifted brows said it all.

"Use the department weapon if you're called to use one. Simplify. Don't take off your coat."

"And yours?"

"I'm going to get it."

"Then I'll walk with you."

"You'll ride with McNab," she told him as they started for her office. "Peabody and I will meet you."

"I missed the first part of the briefing, but I assume you got what you wanted from Cohen."

"I got a lie, and that's going to sink him. He fingered Jones, and it's not Jones." In her office, she put on her coat. "Unless I'm way off, Jones doesn't want a war or exposure, and the murders flirt with both."

"I doubt you're off at all. Pointing the finger at Jones eliminates his business partner. Cohen may have hopes he can recoup some of his funds and property."

She headed for the elevators to save time. "He was hard to crack. It's Mira territory, but I see it as he believes his own bullshit. Like he gave Vinn a good life, was just looking out for her, investing in their future. And all the way it was just business with Jones, just consulting. He didn't kill anybody, jeez. He just advised, just consulted. So you had to keep hacking away at that to expose the meat and draw some blood."

She tried to ignore the squeeze as more cops and support staff piled on.

"I don't know if that makes him a sociopath or just a really good bullshitter."

"Can be both." One of the females wedged in turned her head toward Eve. "I was married to one of those for three years, eight months, and fourteen days. It can be both."

"Yeah, it can be both. Your level," she told Roarke. "I'll see you there."

"Knock back a protein drink from your car AC." With the cramped car, she couldn't avoid the kiss on the forehead. "It'll give you a boost and clear up the headache."

The woman sighed as Roarke got off. "In three years, eight months, and fourteen days, that asshole never worried about my protein. And he *was* my headache. You're lucky."

She supposed she was.

When she got to the garage — finally — Eve opened her trunk, studied her mobile weaponry. She chose a combat knife, snapped it on her belt.

And hearing Peabody's cowgirl boots, got behind the wheel. Ready to roll.

CHAPTER
SEVENTEEN

Eve parked on the edge of Banger territory. Nightfall provided some cover as she and Peabody moved quickly across the blocks to the EDD van. She wanted a sense of the streets before they moved in.

Shops locking up, she noted, pulling down their steel doors. Bars open, the neon beginning to pulse. Lights on in apartments — many with riot bars over the windows even on high floors.

Not a lot of street action yet — too early.

She gave a one-two-three rap on the cargo doors of the van. McNab opened it.

"We're just setting up. Roarke's getting you some ears. Marley's working on the heat sensor."

Marley, Eve noted, looked about twelve with girlie ringlets — raven black tipped with Peabody pink — tumbling down her back. Her skin looked as smooth and creamy as chocolate mousse. She wore bibbed baggies in screaming red with zigzag blue trim over a skin shirt covered with big-eyed kittens.

"Bebopping, McNabber." She blew a purple bubble, snapped it back. "Got them some filters. Must be flush. Gonna zap them."

"She says they paid for some pretty good shields to —"

"I got it." Eve cut off McNab's translation.

"Solid." Marley tapped the heels of her hands together. "Take a mo. Ears up, Dreamcake?"

Roarke smiled at Marley with obvious delight. "Just about. Decent filters, but not prime."

"Nope, no primo."

McNab took a stool at a short counter, began to fiddle with dials and controls, his green eyes focused on the shuddering, spiking lines on a screen. "Let's go boost."

"Nicely done," Roarke told him. "We can get some sound," he said to Eve. "A portable at the site would give more, but we're amplifying. You might hear something useful."

"Zone in on where we talked to Jones."

"Just ahead of you." He tapped his headphones. "Basketball game on-screen, from the sound of it. Background noises." Tilting his head, he made some adjustments on his controls, closed his eyes. "Voices, a number of them. Some music, either at a lower volume or farther away."

"Got visual. One behind the door, sitting down. Moving on up," Marley continued. "Looks like a party. Got multiples."

"That's Jones's space." Eve edged closer, tracked the heat-generated images herself. "We've got a dozen in there."

"Got a couple over — Oooh, getting it going. Got sex, two on it. Got empty, empty, empty, got a sleeper."

She covered the floor, giving Eve a count of fifteen. Then moved up.

"Six. Two horizontal — sleeping likely. Four working, maybe eating. Sitting, but hands moving. Up one more. Nobody home. Uh-uh-uh." Lifting a hand, she wagged a finger back and forth. "Sneaky. Filtering there. Hold. You can't hide from the Marlimator. Cha-cha, gotcha. Three, standing, moving. And that's the wrap. Twenty-five human types from the door to the top."

"Can you get me ears in that top room?" Eve asked Roarke.

"Working on it," Roarke mumbled. "Filter — and some sound-proofing's my guess. Reinforced doors and walls, I'd wager. Bits coming through. Give us a boost here, Ian."

"I'm giving her all she's got, Cap'n!" McNab said in a thick burr and made Roarke laugh.

"*Star Trek*," Peabody murmured. "McNab's total on it."

"'Take him the fuck out. Fuck him up ... ' Response unclear. 'Ain't no leader. Time for Bangers to bang.' More indistinct. 'Fuck that shit, Bolt.'"

"That's it. Keep on it." Eve stepped back, contacted the team leaders. "We've got twenty-five inside this location. One at the door, fifteen on the next floor, six above, and three over that. Strong?"

"In position. Eighteen inside. Four just walked out."

"Go when you're ready. Helmet, Peabody."

"Here's yours."

"Helmets, e-geeks," Eve ordered as she strapped on hers. "And stay alert. If any get through us, they could spot the van, try for it."

Marley flipped one strap of the bib, patted her weapon. "We're good here."

Eve gave her a nod, looked at Roarke. "We're go. Move, move!"

Take care of my cop, Roarke thought as she pushed out the cargo doors.

She ran hard, weapon in hand. Signaled to the takedown team to hit the door with the battering ram.

The guard inside — the one from the first night, who now sported a black eye and a swollen lip — jumped to his feet. His PPC hit the floor as he reached behind his back.

"Pull it, you go down. Hands up!" Eve ordered. "Now! Take him," she snapped, and charged up the stairs. "Take the sex room," she told Peabody. "Baxter, Trueheart, this floor. Next team, up, up."

Someone fired a stream, then another out of Jones's flop. Eve returned fire to cover her men as they raced by.

"Marcus Jones, this is the police. You and your people are surrounded. Put down your weapons, and come out with your hands up."

The answer came in a shouted "Fuck you!" and more streams. Some idiot ran out with a knife and a war cry. Jenkinson dropped him with a mid-body stun.

"Dumb-ass," was Jenkinson's opinion.

Eve saw the homemade boomer fly out. She dived for it, then heaved it back.

On the explosion, the clouds of smoke, the ensuing screams, she and her team charged the room. In the chaos, she stunned two, shoved aside a shrieking, half-naked woman, dodged a knife swipe.

Some wild-eyed woman with biceps like soccer balls rushed her with a bat as the knifer tried again.

Tank, Eve thought. In the really big flesh.

Eve stunned her, which barely slowed her down, then slammed her boot into the kneecap of the knife-wielder behind her, which took him down.

A bat glanced off of Eve's helmet — and boy, did that make the ears ring. The fist Eve slammed in Tank's face had blood spurting, but the woman only grinned around it, swung again.

Tank — and she damn well fit the bill. Serious muscle, Eve thought as she ducked. Serious muscle on Zeus. She slammed her free hand to the floor, braced, and kicked up and back. The blow knocked her opponent back enough for her to spring up, fire another stream. Then wail in.

She took a few. More than a few, but the blows and the stuns took some of the juice out of those biceps. Leading with her helmet, she rammed her head into Tank's midsection, slammed down with the heel of her boot on the woman's instep.

The bat slapped Eve's shoulder, and though the force behind it lessened, she still felt it all the way to her fingertips as she pivoted, danced back, fired another stream.

Maybe she tasted her own blood in her mouth, but the goddamn *tank* finally went down jittering.

"Couldn't get to you, LT." Detective Carmichael, one eye swollen, dropped down, slapped restraints on the thick wrists. Then a second pair for good measure. "Couldn't get a clear stream."

"Jones?"

Carmichael pointed. "I'm on your six."

Slower now — of the twelve they'd seen in the room, seven were down and restrained — she moved through the mess of the living area toward what she took to be a kind of meeting room. Big table, chairs, a couple of wall screens.

A window stood open wide with the night wind blowing through. She gestured for Carmichael to hold, then crouched, rolled.

Jones stood planted, stunner raised. "You're done, bitch."

He fired, and from the quick slap and heat against her coat, she judged he'd bumped it to full, aimed at her heart.

It only took an instant for his fierce grin to fade in shock, and another for her to drop him.

"Looks like he's the bitch who's done," Carmichael said. "I've got to get me one of those coats."

"Lock him down, and let's clean up the rest of this mess."

She circled around, through another door to the hall. Found Baxter clearing the individual flops. "Your nose is bleeding, LT," he said with a glance at her.

"It's not broken."

"Bet it hurts anyway. Trueheart's hauling some of them out. We found a naked girl trying to hide in a bathtub. My boy's blushing, but he's getting her out and into the wagon."

"Good."

"They had a little more trouble than we did upstairs, so we gave them a hand. Got the three contained. All kinds of goodies up there, boss. Some cash money, ID maker, weapons, and enough illegals to keep you zoned out for a couple years."

"Also good. We get twenty-five?"

"Can't tell you for sure. We bagged eight."

"Jorgenson?"

"Oh yeah. He was the little bit more trouble upstairs."

"Very good." She swiped at the blood dripping from her nose. "Let's get a count. Where's Peabody?"

"Here I am."

Eve turned to see her partner hobbling up the stairs. She had blood seeping from several cuts and scrapes on her sheet-pale face.

"Ouch," Baxter said, then hurried to get a supporting arm around her.

"What the hell happened?"

"I sort of fell down the stairs — with the naked having-sex guy. He kind of went crazy, and I had to tackle him, then he pulled me down the stairs. But I got him. I got the naked guy."

"Jesus Christ."

"I got a little banged up. You, too."

"Did you break anything?"

"I don't think."

"I think she's a little shocky, Dallas."

Nodding at Baxter, Eve ran her hands over Peabody's arms, down her legs. Nothing felt broken. "Hold on."

She moved back into the living space. "Jenkinson, Reineke, get a team and clear the house, every room. Santiago, Carmichael, get the rest into the wagon."

"Some are going to need medical attention, Lieutenant."

"That's next." She tapped her comm. "Lowenbaum, we're controlled and clearing."

"Copy that. We got five who slipped out. A couple of them thought the van looked like a nice getaway. Didn't work out for them."

Five outside, she thought, eight from Baxter's count. She counted seven restrained or being restrained from the living area.

"Clean sweep. McNab, we need the MTs. Got some bad guys down. Listen, Peabody got a little banged up. We're bringing her out."

Like Baxter, she got an arm around Peabody, started taking her down the stairs. They hadn't gotten halfway when McNab charged up.

"Hey, hey!" He saw blood, bruises, dazed eyes. "Did you take a hit?"

"I hit lots of places when I fell down the stairs. My face."

"It's my best girl's face."

"Aw."

"I've got her." He put his arms around her. "Marley's pulling in medical. I've got her,"

"Go on back and help sweep it up," Eve told Baxter. "I need to check in with Strong, and the van. I'll be back."

She walked down behind McNab and the hobbling Peabody, then blinked when skinny-ass McNab picked Peabody up to carry her the rest of the way.

"Strong," she said into her comm. "Can you report?"

"Can and will. Ho and eight others are in custody. We got a few bumps, no serious injuries. Your team?"

"Bagged them all. Some bumps," she added as she watched McNab carry Peabody to a mobile medical. "Sweep the place, Strong. Good work. I'll see you back at Central."

She kept walking to the van, where a couple of men were still on the ground. One of the uniforms hauled one to his feet. The other, like Peabody, might need to be carried.

When she noticed the one now on his feet, hands restrained behind his back, begin to snap his fingers, she smiled.

She signaled a uniform over, gave instructions, then continued to the van just as Roarke stepped out.

"Peabody," he said.

"Banged up some. She's with McNab and the MTs. You had some trouble?"

Marley hopped out, held out a fist for Roarke to bump. "We gave the trouble. We are the freaking trouble. Dumb-asses thought they could jack the van? We said, Uh-uh. Dreamcake has a good pow!" Then Marley winced. "Looks like somebody got a couple pows in on you."

"I got in more. Go ahead and call in the sweepers, and we're going to need to coordinate confiscation of illegals, weapons, fraud equipment."

"On top, on bottom. Frosty working with you, Dreamcake."

"And with you, Detective Adorable."

As Marley hopped back in, Eve gestured toward the finger-snapper. "Is he one of your pows?"

"He was, actually. McNab and Marley handled the bulk of it — with assistance from Lowenbaum. That one thought he'd bull his way behind the wheel. He went down with one punch. He can't be more than sixteen."

"We'll find out. Look at his hands." Her smile came back. His fingers continued to snap as the uniform led him away.

"Ah, well now. I suddenly regret only punching him once. You've made quite a haul, Lieutenant, and I expect you'll be at this for a while. I'd like to have a look at Peabody before you start the next phase of this."

"She got tripped up by one of the bad guys. They both went down the steps the wrong way. She's lucid," Eve said as they crossed to the mobile. "I don't think she broke anything."

"And you?"

"Most of this is from a female with arms like concrete. They call her Tank for a reason. But she looks worse." There was, always, satisfaction in that. "Hey, that's Louise."

Roarke studied the woman applying ice patches to Peabody's face. "So it is. We know our Peabody's in good hands with Dr. Dimatto."

When he reached her, Roarke laid a gentle kiss on Peabody's forehead. "How's our girl?"

"Louise gave me really nice drugs."

"Yes, I did. And let's sling that arm until you get another pass with a healing wand. No breaks," Louise continued. "But a jammed shoulder, and her knee's going to need more treatment. My clinic's open."

She glanced around, studied Eve's face with cool gray eyes. "You're next."

"I'm fine."

"Which one of us has the medical degree?"

It seemed wise to change the subject. "What are you even doing here?"

"Word went out there were a lot of injuries in this location. Sit down, and I'll —"

But Eve's attention moved elsewhere. "Later. McNab, get Peabody to the clinic. Go with her." Eve was already moving.

She grabbed the arm of a woman being loaded into a wagon.

"Where'd you get the bracelet?"

"Fuck you!" The woman bared her teeth. The layers of eye makeup had bled down to smear below her eyes, costing the rage glittering in them some points.

"Book this one on accessory to murder, three counts."

"What?" She tried to break out of the uniform's hold, jerking one way, the other, and exposing even more of her left breast and its black rose tattoo. "I didn't do nothing!"

"The bracelet."

"What the fuck. Asshole wanted a BJ. I got the bracelet."

"Which asshole is that? Name, or three counts."

"Ticker. That's all I know. New guy."

"Hold on," Eve told the uniform, and went to get an evidence bag. "You're wearing stolen property." Carefully, she unhooked the bracelet with its large colorful stones, slid it into the bag. "When and where did you make the trade?"

"This is bullshit."

"I can add soliciting without a license."

"Last night, after I got off work."

"What time do you get off work?"

"Like, three. He's coming out of the house, and says give him a BJ and I can have the bracelet. So, what, he stole it? How'm I supposed to know?"

With a shake of her head, Eve walked back toward Roarke, held up the evidence bag.

"That would be Rochelle's."

"Matches her description, and it was on the wrist of some Banger Bitch who got it from a new recruit named Ticker in exchange for a BJ. He'll be in this sweep. I've got them. Just have to nail it down."

Roarke glanced around. Those in custody were still being loaded, or treated. Cops getting treated or swarming in and out of the building. People from the neighborhood crowded behind the barricades. And if he wasn't mistaken, a media copter hovering overhead recording the scene.

Add that to whatever Detective Strong had going at her location.

"Do you intend to manage the nailing tonight?"

Wouldn't that be just fine? Eve thought. But. "No. We need inventory on what we confiscate, all these people have to be processed. First, I want to see what's in the room with the extra filters. The one I believe BJ guy and the finger-snapper were in talking to Jorgenson.

"I need to ID this Ticker. Then I need to coordinate with Strong, write this up. Then we'll see."

"Somewhere in there you'll have a round with ice patches and a healing wand."

"Somewhere."

"And a meal."

She thought about it. "I could eat. But I want to see that room. You should go home."

"Then who'd handle the ice patches, healing wand, and the meal?"

"I can take care of it." The smirk she gave him stung her bloodied lip a little, but it was worth it. "Dreamcake."

He smiled at her. "Let's look at the room, and whatever else you need here. I'll go into Central with you. Then we'll see."

She could go with that, and started back to the house with him. She found Baxter coming down the stairs.

"Most of this place is a sty," he told her. "Individual flops high on the sty gauge. We're logging illegals, stickers, saps, black-market stunners. How's Peabody?"

"Should be at Dimatto's clinic by now. Sweepers are headed in. You can get Trueheart, go have your home-cooked."

"Yeah?"

"Briefing at seven-thirty tomorrow. We're going to be rotating cops and bad guys in and out of the box. It's going to take hours to process all of them tonight, not to mention to process what we take out of here."

"You sticking?" he asked as she started up.

"I just want a walk-through," she said, knowing if she said she was sticking, he'd stick, too.

"Okay. Catch you in the A.M. Nice haul, boss. Damn nice haul."

She'd consider it a nice haul when she charged three people with murder.

She found Jenkinson and Reineke, the latter with his own bloodied lip. As she talked to them, Roarke wandered. Baxter wasn't wrong about the sty. Beyond the broken furniture, the toppled tables, glasses, and chaos of what had obviously been a nasty fight lay the smell of unwashed bodies and clothing, stale sex, the Zoner smoke that had penetrated the walls over the years.

He'd had his times, Roarke thought, in places not much better. In some considerably worse. But even in those days had kept those visits brief. Summerset had ingrained standards into him, he supposed.

He took a scan of what he assumed to be Jones's bedroom. Cleaner than the flops and with a decent bed. As he hadn't sealed up, Roarke took care not to touch anything. He stood outside the closet, noted the clothes were newer, better, more plentiful — and used an elbow to move some aside.

Then he wandered back again to Eve.

"I believe you'll find a false wall in the closet. Jones's bedroom closet. And, no, I didn't touch it," he said, anticipating her.

317

"Somebody get me a kit!" she ordered, then headed for the bedroom.

In the closet she saw what Roarke had seen — a seam in the wall that had no place there, and a small keypad lock.

She grabbed the kit Reineke hustled in to her, sealed up. After a quick debate, passed the can to Roarke.

"Seal up, open it. No point in calling in Marley when you're right here."

"Try nineteen, twelve, nine, three, five."

"Why?"

"His name. Slice. They're barking morons, Eve. Try the numeral equivalent of his street name."

She did, and the lock disengaged. The door slid, shakily, into its pocket. Inside a mini D and C all but filled the small space.

"Barking morons," she agreed. "What do you bet his records — all his side deals, the Banger business — it's all on there?"

"I'd bet quite a bit on that."

"Reineke, tag this for EDD, and let the sweepers know to check for other panels, other false walls. This one is priority. Then you and Jenkinson can go home. Seven-thirty briefing in the morning."

Energized, she went straight up to the shielded room, and found Detectives Carmichael and Santiago.

Carmichael, hands on hips and sporting a black eye, looked on while Santiago, with blood on his shoes, manhandled a shelf away from the wall.

"Let me give you a hand there," Roarke began, but Carmichael waved him off.

"He got manly, bet me he could move it himself."

"Christ, Santiago." Eve could only shake her head. "You've got a problem."

"I can do this."

The shelf shuddered, squealed against the floor — which showed scars from previous shifts.

"You can see they've got setups for making false IDs," Carmichael continued as her partner struggled. "We already tagged the comps for EDD. We spotted the marks on the floor. Hell, a drunk, one-eyed rookie would've spotted them. So we figure, being detectives, there's something behind the shelf unit."

"Almost got it," Santiago claimed between gritted teeth.

"Speaking of eyes." Roarke took an ice patch out of his pocket.

"Hey, thanks." Carmichael cracked it, laid it against her eye. "You carry these around?"

"Tonight I do."

"Got it. See?"

Carmichael peered out of one eye. Grunted. "Huh! Big! Strong!"

Santiago just flicked his middle finger against his chin. "Keypad here."

Eve stepped to it. "It wouldn't be 'Slice' this time. This is for the gang, not Jones personally. Simple code the people authorized could remember. 'Fist'? That's their symbol."

When she started to count on her fingers, Roarke rattled the numbers off.

"Six, nine, nineteen, twenty. I've . . . played with codes in my time. It's a basic one."

And correct, Eve thought as the lock disengaged.

This panel opened out, and led to a reasonably organized storage space. Illegals in one section, ID supplies in another, a few wrapped stacks of cash, electronics — mostly tablets and PPCs, and likely stolen — a cache of weapons and jewelry, wrist units.

"Can't be more than five or six thousand street value on the illegals," Santiago commented. "Might be for personal use, or quick street sales."

"They've got another place for storing and distribution. The feds have that. This? This is like a pool. Everybody puts in, and the lieutenants pass out shares when needed."

"Stupid" was Carmichael's take. "Even a half-assed raid would find this. And we're going to find prints, DNA. The assholes are going into a cage because they're not smart enough to cover their assholes."

"I think they used to be smarter. Tag it," Eve added. "And go home. Briefing at seven-thirty. Santiago, is that your blood on your shoes?"

"What blood? Shit! These are almost new. No, it's not mine. Is Peabody okay? We heard she got banged up some."

"Some. She's all right. Seven-thirty," Eve repeated, and walked out with Roarke. " 'Barking morons.' I like that one, and it fits. A pack of wild dogs has more brains."

She detoured to talk to sweepers already ghosting on scene in their white suits and booties. She thought she might carve out time the next day for another walk-through when the place was empty of cops and CIs.

"You drive," she told Roarke. "I need to check on some things."

"Louise will take good care of her. It's our good luck Louise was nearby."

"Yeah. But that's not the only thing I need to check on."

Just the first. She tagged McNab.

"Hey." Relief breathed out in the single word. "No internal injuries, no breaks. Her shoulder's going to be sore for a couple days, but she won't need the sling. It's the knee that's bad. Louise treated it, and is giving us some stuff for it. She's going to have to wear a brace for a few days, and isn't real happy about it. Damn good thing she was wearing the helmet. The asshole that pulled her down with him has a concussion and about a dozen stitches in his head. Shattered his elbow, too. Ain't that a shame?"

"Okay, good. I'm briefing at seven-thirty tomorrow. If she's not up for it —"

"She will be. She needs to finish it out. The fall, well, it banged up her pride a little, too, you know?"

"Tell her not to be stupid. Seven-thirty."

She clicked off, let out a breath. And Roarke patted her hand as he got behind the wheel. Then he took the case of blockers he carried out of his pocket.

"No."

"You still have work," he pointed out. "Why be distracted by pain and discomfort?"

"Not distracted by it. Using it."

And using it, she contacted Commander Whitney.

CHAPTER
EIGHTEEN

Eve hit her AutoChef for coffee the instant she walked into her office. Roarke followed it up by programming her a pizza.

"Oh my God, nothing's ever smelled that good in the history of smells."

"See that you eat it, and use these." He set some ice patches on her desk.

"Okay, yeah. Want a couple slices before you head home?"

"I'm not heading home but up to EDD, where I wager I'll find Feeney, Callendar, and my new friend Marley. I'll order up there. Let me know when you're wrapping things up for the night."

Before she sat, he took her bruised face — gently, very gently — in his hands and laid his lips on hers.

Held there, just held there.

Understanding, she leaned in. "It probably looks worse than it is."

"Of all the women I've known in my life you're the only one who wouldn't have even troubled to look to see for herself."

She shrugged — felt the movement in various sore spots all the hell over her body. "Looking wouldn't change it, right?"

Again gently, he brushed a hand over her hair. "Eat your pizza."

"Count on it."

Alone, she took that first slice, bit in, just sighed and chewed. She downed the coffee, every drop, because she needed it, then remembered Roarke stocked Pepsi in her AC, ordered a tube.

If you couldn't have beer or wine, a Pepsi suited a pepperoni pizza just fine.

Eating with one hand, she contacted Reo.

The APA answered fast. "Good God, Dallas. You look terrible! How bad are you hurt?"

"It's nothing." Reo didn't look terrible, Eve noted. She'd taken off her face gunk and looked sort of fresh. "We got twenty-five. Strong got nine. I'm dead sure I got the two still alive who killed Pickering, Duff, and Aimes. And the one who set it up. I'm briefing at seven-thirty tomorrow. You're going to be filing a shit-ton of charges."

"Including assaulting an officer, from the look of your face."

"Yeah. With a deadly. Tank gets that."

"Do we have an actual name?"

"Somewhere."

"I'll find it."

"We can try for attempted murder of a police officer on Jones, as he fired on me — police stunner on full. That's some icing on a fat cake. We found illegals, weapons, what will turn out to be stolen property, fake ID equipment, the works. And EDD is working on electronics we confiscated."

"I'll alert my boss."

Eve polished off the slice, snagged another. "Cohen?"

"Sang like a bright yellow canary. You'll want to talk to Teasdale, but I got the heads-up the feds raided the building serving as warehouse — a property also held by Cohen, Jones, and Vinn — and scooped up plenty. Including a handful of unlicensed sex workers who were, at the time, employed.

"Should I tag up with Detective Strong?"

"Tomorrow's soon enough. We're going to be processing for a while yet."

"Then I'll fill in my boss, get my beauty sleep, and see you in the morning. Good bust, Dallas. Get some ice on that face."

"Right."

After she broke transmission, she pressed a couple of fingers to her jaw. Felt it go straight through her skull like a spike. Maybe the ice wasn't such a bad idea.

After she finished her second slice.

She exchanged reports with Teasdale, felt some solid satisfaction. Thought about a third slice as she set up to write her report. Looked around at the knock on her doorjamb.

"Officer Shelby. I didn't know you were still here."

"I was helping in processing, Lieutenant. Officer Quirk had the individual you told him to keep separate. He's Denby Washington, goes by Snapper."

"Of course he does."

"Lieutenant, he had earrings matching the description of those taken from the Pickering apartment on his person."

"You are fucking kidding me, Shelby."

"No, sir, I am not fucking kidding you. More, sir, he had a set of black Bodell Exec-level earbuds also on his person."

"Snap goes Snapper's cage door."

Shelby smiled a little. "I helped process an individual who goes by Ticker. Burke Chesterfield. And he had a brooch matching the description of the one taken from the Pickering apartment on his person. He was wearing —"

"Lightning high-tops," Eve said. "Black with a white lighting bolt down the back. Size ten."

"That's affirmative. Sir, we had their jackets sent to the lab, as they may match the fibers recovered from Duff's body. I also got DNA from Washington, as he's not in the database. I got him a tube of Coke, which he accepted. The empty tube's on its way to the lab."

Eve sat back, let it play through her mind. Since she'd caught the quick glance Shelby made toward the pizza, she gestured to it. "Want a slice?"

"Thank you, Lieutenant. I don't want to take your dinner."

"I'm good. Have a slice."

"Thanks." She took one, bit in, and Eve saw the same rush of gratitude and pleasure move over Shelby's face that had moved inside her own system. "This isn't eatery pizza."

326

"You bucking to make detective, Officer?"

"No, sir. I like the uniform. I'm learning a lot from Officer Carmichael. I want to say I'm grateful you put me with him. He's a solid cop."

"Yeah, he is. Do me a favor, Shelby, and make sure Washington and Chesterfield are kept away from each other. And both of them away from Jones and Kenneth Jorgenson."

"Can do, sir. Appreciate the slice."

"No problem. Take the rest."

"Oh, but —"

"I'm done." Eve held up the plate with the remaining slice. "Take it. Good work, Officer Shelby."

"Thank you, Lieutenant."

After a long breath, Eve turned to her computer. She had to set the anger aside but, as she'd told Roarke, she used the pain to push herself through the report.

When it was done, she sent a memo to Harvo at the lab to flag the jackets as priority. Sent one to Dickhead — the lab chief — to turn the DNA sample around fast.

She didn't bribe him as she often did to save time, but used the silent threat of adding Whitney to the memo.

She sent a quick memo to Reo, giving her the names of the suspects and, given the age of one, asking her to have Chesterfield treated as an adult.

She ordered herself to get up, to update her board, to just take the steps. Put together files for the briefing, reserve the conference room, book Interview rooms —

all of them — and assign rotating teams for those interviews.

She thought about contacting Crack, but that was personal. She had to hold on that.

Instead she contacted Nadine.

"Finally! A message returned. If I can get a statement — Whoa, Dallas, somebody got past your guard. A few times."

Unlike Reo, Nadine was in full makeup — camera ready. Eve imagined she'd been on camera, and would go back in front of it before her night ended.

After all, the NYPSD had just completed major busts on two urban gangs.

"You have to wait on the statement."

"Come on, Dallas, we're already running with the story — and congratulations, by the way. It's big. They pulled me back in to report on air. I just turned it over, but with a statement I can —"

"You have to wait."

The snap in Eve's voice had Nadine's eyes narrowing. "How bad are you hurt?"

"I'm fine. Peabody got worse."

"Peabody? What happened? Where is she? What —"

Eve cut Nadine off again. But she knew the friend asked, not the reporter.

"She's okay. Louise took care of her. It's not that. No statement tonight other than what the liaison's sending out because it's still in motion. I'm letting you know to get ready for tomorrow, and what I'm telling you goes nowhere until I give you the green."

"All right."

"This was a . . ." She trailed off, pressed her fingers to her eyes in an attempt to clear her head.

"Do you want me to come to you? Can I help?"

"No. No. This was a coordinated operation between the NYPSD and the FBI."

"The FBI? How close did you hold that one? Who —"

"Just wait, Nadine. Between the department and the bureau dozens of arrests were made, several thousand dollars — you need to get the hard numbers — of illegals have been confiscated along with weapons and blah-blah. You can get all that."

"Yes, I'll get it."

"In addition, the NYPSD recovered items stolen from Lyle Pickering's apartment. Items taken when he was murdered. These items were on the persons of Denby Washington, age eighteen, and Burke Chesterfield, age seventeen. We'll push to have Chesterfield interviewed, tried, and treated as an adult, and I don't expect we'll have any trouble there."

"Have you interviewed them?"

"Tomorrow. And tomorrow I'm going to tell you we've charged a third individual, Kenneth Jorgenson, age twenty-three, as well as Washington and Chesterfield, for the murders of Pickering, Dinnie Duff — who was an accessory in Pickering's murder — and in the murder of Barry Aimes who, along with the others named, murdered Pickering and Duff. A fourth man will be charged as accessory before and after the fact: Samuel Cohen."

"The raids were to dig these people out? Why? Why did all these people conspire to kill Rochelle's brother?"

"I'm going to find out. I need you to . . . I need you to —"

"Ask and it's done."

"No, no, it's not personal. The hell it isn't," Eve said on a breath. "The hell it isn't. Lyle Pickering was a confidential informant."

"Yours?"

"No. I need you to do what you do, Nadine. I need you to report his story. I need you to report the way he'd turned his life around, how he was doing everything right, working to earn back his family's trust. Risking his physical safety to work with the police. You know how to do all that."

"Yes, I do. And I will."

Yes, Eve thought. Yes, she would.

"I don't know how long we'll be at this tomorrow before I can give you the go."

"We've got plenty to report on. I want to share this with my researchers — you know you can trust them. I want as much on Lyle Pickering as we can get — before we talk to his family. After your go," Nadine added. "And I need what I can get on the people who killed him."

"Add Marcus Jones. I don't think he was in on the murders, but he's going down. That's it for now. I'm going home."

"Good. Put some ice on that face."

"People keep telling me that."

She clicked off, sat back. She should go up to EDD, see what they'd pulled out for herself. But she'd just run out, run down, been run through.

So she got her things, texted Roarke she'd meet him in the garage.

She got there ahead of him, took the passenger seat, put her head back, closed her eyes. If she could have, she'd have willed herself to sleep, into oblivion for a few hours. Then she could wake up and do what needed to be done without having her mind crowded with it all.

Because the fatigue she felt wasn't physical.

She kept her eyes closed when she heard Roarke open the driver's-side door. "Awake," she said. "Did you get anything I can use?"

He studied her a moment, and from what he saw — clearly — she hadn't used the ice patches. Well, he'd deal with that once they got home, but for now.

He took out his case. "Take a blocker now. Don't argue about it."

She considered it, just for spite, then realized how stupid that would be. She took the blocker, swallowed it. "What did you get?"

"All manner of data — and I have no doubt the FBI will want in on it. There's more to find, but we were just calling it for the night when you texted. Feeney and the rest will get back to it in the morning."

He glanced at her again as he drove. "It wasn't even a challenge, none of it. Some rudimentary IT knowledge and not much skill to marry with it. Like the false walls and keypads, child's play. The fact is, most children are better at such things."

He laid a hand over hers. "Tell me what's wrong."

She just shook her head. "Did you get more data from Jones's unit?"

"As you already believed, he had his records on the one hidden in his room. His profits and expenses with his Cohen partnership. How much he skimmed, Cohen's percentage of it. And he kept records on the gang's business as well. Illegals deals, their protection racket, who handled break-ins, burnings, beatings. All of it, Eve. And it looks like he was planning to relocate. To Aruba. He had searches on property there."

"So he's cheating his own gang with the goal of getting enough together to buy himself a place in the tropics. Fucking hypocrite."

"Well, yes, but I think hypocrisy is the least of his sins."

"Is it? Is it really? Isn't it all part of it? All fucking part of it?"

She shifted, so much anger rising up. "You ran with a gang in Dublin."

"I wouldn't say we thought of ourselves as a gang, but all right, loosely, yes."

"Would you have betrayed them for money, cheated any one of them for profit?"

"No, nor they me. But that may be a difference between a gang and mates."

"They pledge loyalty."

"And friends don't need a pledge, do they?"

She shook her head, sat back again. "What Jones was doing under it all laid the groundwork for all of this. His leadership sucked — and maybe we should be grateful for that because they weren't as powerful as they once were. He's skimming, so there's not as much for the whole to split. He's avoiding confrontation with rival gangs, isn't pushing for more territory, which is how they gain power and reputation. He's not because he's more interested in banking profits and dreaming of freaking Aruba."

"And so someone with more interest in power and rep plots ways to depose him and take over."

"Pickering. Someone who goes back with Jones. Someone who once pledged loyalty and now turned his back. Maybe his CI status leaked, I can't be sure. But . . . I think killing and humiliating Pickering to strike at Jones wouldn't have been enough if that got out."

"You think Lyle Pickering's murder was a personal hit at Jones?"

"I think that was part of it, yeah. And punishment for turning his back on the gang. Maybe even assurance that he couldn't change his mind, come back."

"Ah." Roarke followed her perfectly. "And compete for the leadership role."

"Yeah. It's Duff. It's Duff, how she was killed, where she was killed. It's Duff's murder they used to try to light the fuse for a gang war. Then Aimes."

Considering anger better than misery, he kept her talking. "You think he — Jorgenson — planned to kill Duff all along, even before he coerced, convinced, bribed her to aid in Pickering's murder."

"Pickering connects to Jones, Duff connects to Pickering. Yeah, she was always going to die. Pickering was more a kick in the balls. Cops are wheeze, right?

That's the word now. Cops see a junkie OD'd, file it, forget it. But Duff, that's going to bring on some attention, and it's something that can be used to rile up the troops. Dragons fuck with one of ours, we fuck with all of theirs."

As they drove through the gates she closed her eyes again.

"You know what to do tomorrow, what angles to take, what buttons to push."

"Yeah, I know what to do."

He didn't like hearing the discouragement in her tone, but let it go for now.

Despite the late hour, Summerset waited in the foyer.

"You know where to find the med kit," he said to Roarke.

"Yes, thanks."

"There have been numerous media reports on tonight's raids and arrests."

"Yeah, that's why we went in. For the screen time." Eve tossed her jacket over the newel post.

"I imagine there are people who have homes and shops in those areas, and see the reports, who'll sleep better tonight," Summerset added.

He waited until they'd started upstairs before picking up her coat, examining it.

Blood, of course — and from the look of her at least some of it her own. He'd gotten quite adept at removing bloodstains from leather. He took the coat with him to his quarters to see to it.

He had no doubt Roarke would see to the lieutenant.

The cat stretched across the bed, and stirred when they came in. His bicolored eyes blinked at her face as Eve unhooked her weapon harness. Then he leaped off the bed to rub against her legs, to butt his head against her calves.

She bent to give him a reassuring rub, and even with the blocker felt every muscle weep.

"I'm going to grab a shower."

"A soak in the tub might do better for you. And a glass of wine."

"Maybe. Yeah, maybe."

She went in to fill the tub, started to strip down. Roarke brought her a glass of wine, then took a glass jar from a shelf. He tossed a couple of scoops of pale blue salts into the water.

"It'll help with the bruising." While she stood watching him, he fixed ice patches to the worst of the damage to her face. "And so will that."

"Are you going to use one on your knuckles where you powed the finger-snapper?"

"He had a jaw like a marshmallow. Keep the jets on low."

"Yes, Doctor."

He kissed her lightly, and would have left her alone, but the cat leaped onto a stool, apparently to stand guard.

Eve finished stripping off, took a survey in the full-length mirror. A few got past her guard, as Nadine had said, a little bruising along the ribs, some on the arms from blocking. Definitely the face got the worst of it.

She met Galahad's eyes in the mirror. "I've had worse. You've been around when I've had worse. They called her Tank, get it? She had arms like steel beams. And a bat," she added when he seemed unimpressed.

"Screw it."

She slid into the tub, ordered the jets on low, and picked up the wine.

When she came out, Roarke had changed into what she thought of as rich-guy knock-around clothes: high-end sweatpants of cotton so soft clouds were jealous and a thin, roomy sweater.

He sat with his wine and his PPC, no doubt catching up on work. He looked up, gave her a close study, nodded. "All right, better. Let's finish it off."

After patting the cushion beside him, he took the healing wand out of the medical kit on the table.

"She had a bat. I might not have mentioned she had a bat."

"And biceps, as I recall, like concrete."

"That's no bullshit. I can show you her mug shot."

"I saw her on your board. And considering that, I believe you deserve another glass of wine."

He poured it for her, then began to stroke the wand over her face. "I'm very fond of this face," he said as he worked, "so I very much hope tonight's mug shot shows the wrath of my cop."

"I busted her nose. Had to be on Zeus because she just shook off the first couple of streams I hit her with."

"Concrete biceps, a bat, and Zeus. Turn a bit. There you are."

"Magic coat's magic. Jones hit me with a stream — and on full, I checked. That's going to be attempted murder of a police officer — maybe pled down to assault with a deadly, but we start with the high note. If Reo plays it right, when you add it all up, he could do the next seventy-five in a cage. More," she calculated. "He'll never turn that around."

"No tropical breezes for him."

"No."

After setting the wand down, Roarke cupped her chin. "Darling Eve, talk to me."

"I'm talking to you. Words are coming out of my mouth. I hear them."

He simply kept his eyes on hers, and the inexplicable sadness in them. "You put together two operations, successful ones, that may very well have broken the backs of two gangs. Multiple members will do time, and as you said, Jones himself could spend over three-quarters of a century in prison. I have no doubt that tomorrow you'll also break the three remaining who are responsible for Lyle Pickering, and Duff. And Aimes.

"Why are you sad?"

"I'm not sad. I'm . . . I don't know what I am."

She shoved up, pacing in a robe the color of apricots.

"We broke the backs, of the Bangers at least, because they're stupid, sloppy, poorly run. A bunch of what you said — barking morons. Why didn't we break them before? I don't know. Maybe because their territory had shrunk, maybe timing, maybe because people they preyed on didn't come to us.

"I don't know. Don't know. Maybe they stuck together better before Jones decided to go into business on the side."

She went back for her wine, took it with her as she paced again. "Most criminals are stupid. *Most*, I said," she repeated when Roarke arched his eyebrows. "They act on impulse, or they make mistakes. Some asshole decides to kill his wife, we're going to figure it out, almost every time. These assholes I'm boxing tomorrow are beyond stupid. They're — what are those words you use? Eejits, gits. Fuck-heads."

"All of those work," Roarke replied.

"And still, three people in the morgue. A family of decent people are never going to be the same. A couple of mothers lost children. They're not insane or diabolical. They're sure as hell not masterminds. They're just mean, vicious little bastards. And three people are dead."

Roarke said nothing because, finally, she was talking to him, finally she was saying what had lodged inside her and put that look in her eyes.

"You know what else?" She gestured with the wine, then gulped some down. "Rehabilitation is mostly a crock. Mostly. You lock somebody up, the odds of him coming out and staying on the straight are slim. Somebody like Pickering? Jesus, abusive father dies in prison, addict mother suicides. A serious gangster, an addict? Odds say he's going to go back in a cage, die on the street in some fight, or OD. He's never going to walk the line.

"But he did. He beat the odds, and was making something of himself. Goddamn it!"

Her voice rang with it — sorrow-coated outrage.

"You and I know how hard that is. He did everything right, Roarke. Everything right, and he's dead because some son of a bitch wanted to push his way to the top of the ranks.

"I told myself before that the system worked. Crime, punishment, rehabilitation. But it didn't, it didn't work for Lyle Pickering. The system failed him. We failed him."

There it was, Roarke thought, the root of the sadness. One he could dig out, and hopefully cast aside.

"On the contrary, you had it right the first time. The system saved him." He held up a hand before she could speak. "Now it's time to listen. I'm hardly the biggest fan of what you call the system, and I spent most of my life circumventing it, so I have a different perspective. Mine may be a bit more like Lyle's.

"Come, sit down. Listen to the perspective of someone who worked around the system instead of for it."

"He's dead," she said flatly, but she sat again.

"And between the time he went into prison — an addict, a violent man whose life appeared to have only one doomed path — and his death, he lived. He made a choice to live, and your system gave him the choice. Who taught him to cook, and to learn the satisfaction of having that skill? Who offered him counseling and help with his addiction? Who listened to him, helped to dig into the issues that sent him down that doomed path? Christ, who locked him up in the first place, forced him to make choices to accept the help and training or reject it?

"He made the choices," Roarke continued, "your system gave them to him to make. You demean the choices he made, Eve, the effort they took him, by thinking the system failed him."

He trailed his fingers, lightly, so lightly over her battered face.

And you fought for him, he thought, will fight for others like him. Again and again and again.

"Five people are responsible for his death," he reminded her, "and two of them have paid with their own lives. You and your system will see to it the other three pay, will demand justice for Lyle, and give solace to his family. A family, Eve, who will remember and cherish the man he began to be in prison, and not the one he was when he went inside."

"I feel it's . . . Do you really believe that?"

"Believe it? I'm proof of it." He skimmed a hand over her hair, down to the nape of her neck still tight with tension. "Do you think I work with you and the cops only for the entertainment? Not to downplay that value at all, as it's considerable. But since you — you and your system, no matter how I might push against it from time to time — I've seen what it can do and be in the right hands. And having a part in that? It's shown me that I can make a difference in my way. Maybe offset some of my darker deeds."

He kissed her bruised face. "I know a failed system, as it failed me as a boy and, Christ, it failed you. But you changed that, for yourself, for others. For me. The system you stand for didn't fail Lyle, Eve. And it's not failing him now."

She drew him closer, rested her head on his shoulder. And realized he'd given her what she hadn't been able to find for herself. Peace of mind.

"I'm going to remember all that, everything you just said, when I break them tomorrow."

"I'll regret not being there for that, but —"

"Somebody has to buy the next galaxy."

"Very true. Now, let's see to the rest of you. Lie down and I'll see what the bat-wielding, concrete-biceps-on-Zeus Tank has done to my cop."

"It's not too bad. Truth," she insisted when he took her hand, pulled her up.

"I'll be the judge of that." At the side of the bed, he circled a finger in the air. "Robe off, lie down."

"You just want to play doctor."

"A favorite of mine." To Galahad's annoyance, Roarke lifted his bulk from the bed and set him down in front of the fire he had simmering low.

Eve shrugged out of the robe, sat on the side of the bed. "See, not too bad. She got a couple of shots in the ribs — fist, not bat. The bat bashed my helmet, then sort of bounced off my shoulder."

"Mmm-hmm." He started wanding the thunderous rainbow of bruising on her shoulder. "And was she the only one you dealt with hand to hand?"

"Couple more, but they didn't really land anything. Carmichael's sporting a mouse, and Reineke got a little bloody. Nothing major. Peabody got the worst of it on our side. A bunch of them got the worst altogether. One of them tossed out a mini boomer," she remembered.

However casually she mentioned it, it still stopped his heart for a beat. "And no one was hurt?"

"On their side some because I fielded it and pitched it back in. Lucky for them it didn't have much juice." She turned her head, smiled at him. "I feel better."

"Good. There's some balm in the kit Summerset swears by. We'll try some on your face, but the rest, as you said, isn't too bad."

"I feel better," she repeated. "And I'm naked."

His gaze shifted to hers. "I had noticed, but I'm trying to maintain my medical ethics."

"Screw ethics," she said, and whipped a leg over, shoved him back, straddled him. "I soaked in the stuff, did the ice, got the wand. The least you can do is polish me off."

"When you put it that way."

"You could put it this way." She lifted his hands, pressed them to her breasts.

"You're definitely feeling better."

"Yeah. You're so pretty. I'm glad nobody punched you in the face." She leaned down, brushed her lips over his cheeks. "Dreamcake."

"I'm sorry, that nickname's taken. You have to think of your own."

"I'll come up with something. Meanwhile." She stripped off his sweater, ran her hands up that excellent torso, then up over his chest, his shoulders, into his hair as she leaned down to take his mouth with hers.

342

A long, quiet kiss, one that soothed the soul, a soul that had felt more battered than the rest of her. Eased now, she thought, by his words, by his faith in her.

It warmed her, this moment, this easy mating of lips and tongues. Centered her again. And all the violence faded away.

His hands glided over her, gently, lighting little sparks inside the warmth, little flickers of need inside the love.

He felt her give, felt her slough off the day with all its trials and tensions. Pressed his lips to the bruises on her shoulder, the war wound on the constant soldier.

Shifting, he stripped off his pants so they could twine flesh to flesh. Her skin carried the scent of her bath, of forest shadows and secrets. He drew it in as he pressed his lips to her throat, to the pulse that beat there, to her life.

"*My love, my own, my only*," he murmured in Irish.

The pulse quickened.

She took him in, slow, slow, slow, with a shuddering sigh. He filled her, beat by trembling beat, his hands skimming down her sides to cup her hips.

As she moved over him, and he in her, she felt the pleasure rise, felt it spread, felt it consume. All she was with all he was.

He came up to her to enfold her as they took each other, still slow, slow, slow. Wrapped around him, she found his lips again as that pleasure, a long, strong wave, rolled through her.

When her head fell back, she saw the moon, the white slice of it floating in the dark through the sky window. Beautiful and pure like the moment, like the easy mating.

And with him, only with him, reached for it.

Later, lying in the dark, curled against him and starting to drift toward sleep, she smiled. "You can be Dr. Sexpert."

"I don't think —"

"Just for tonight."

"Then never again."

He stroked her back to lull her the rest of the way to sleep, then felt the cat jump up to take his favorite spot. And so he brushed his lips over her forehead, and joined her in sleep.

CHAPTER
NINETEEN

She woke stiff, sore, and early. In the firelight Roarke stood, drinking coffee, watching the scroll on the wall screen as it reported from somewhere she assumed the stupid rotation of the planet made it later.

She thought, sleepily, he looked almost as good in a suit as he did naked. And that was saying something.

She started to roll out of bed, must have made some sound that acknowledged the annoyance of aches. He turned, studied her in the dim light.

"Feeling it this morning?"

"Maybe."

"We'll do another round of ice and wanding."

"Maybe." She eased out of bed, headed straight to the shower to pummel some of the aches into submission with hot jets.

It helped, as did the coffee Roarke handed her — along with a blocker — when she came out. "Swelling's down." He stroked a gentle finger down her jaw. "And the bruising lessened. Let's see what else we can do."

"It doesn't hurt to look like I got punched in the face during arrests on the record in Interview."

"Always a bright side."

When they sat, he placed the ice patches, glided the wand over her face. "Let's see the rest."

Rather than argue, she unbelted the robe, let him treat the shoulder, the ribs, her arms.

"You should try to take a break sometime during the day, do another round."

"Breaking those bastards is all the healing up I need."

"You could do me a favor," he said as he lifted the domes on breakfast. "Send me a running tally as you do."

Bacon, she noted — American style — an omelette, fruit, scones, and jam. Not bad.

"I can do that."

"What's your plan of attack?"

"After the briefing, I'm taking the one you punched first — and if Dickhead doesn't have the DNA, hasn't passed that to Harvo for the other hair found on Duff? I'm siccing Whitney on him. The finger-snapping guy's the asshole who had Rochelle's earrings and Lyle's earbuds in his idiot pocket. I break him, it all falls apart. And I get to tell Cohen even the bullshit deal he signed is rescinded."

"Why bullshit?"

"I didn't fill you in on that?" Breaking open a scone, Eve piled on enough butter and jam to delight any five-year-old. "The feds agreed to the Witness Protection — on the stipulation he told no falsehoods — *after* he'd faced prosecution on the accessories charges from us. So yeah, after he did fifty, minimum, on that, he could be Horace Dickwad of Bullshit, Iowa."

"He agreed to that?"

"Yeah, he did, because he's a crappy disbarred lawyer and he didn't read the fine print." She bit into the smothered scone. "Or maybe read it and just didn't understand it."

"It just keeps coming back to morons."

"Yeah, it does, and with Cohen lying — it's pathological with him. Since he lied about Jones, and probably more, no deal. He'll never see the outside again. When we're done with him, the feds slap him in a cage for the tax and fraud. Reo gets lots of points on how she handled this one."

It didn't shock her to find spinach in the omelette, but at least it was well disguised with cheese and herby stuff.

"I'll take the Ticker guy next. It's going to be his hair, his DNA."

"And save Jorgenson for the last of the three."

"He'll go down the hardest, if I can make that happen. And there's coordinating with the other interview teams as they take the rest. Strong and her teams."

"A big day."

"We took them down, now we wrap them up." She ate while Roarke paused to point a warning finger at the belly-crawling cat. Galahad rolled over, shot up a leg to wash.

The feline middle finger.

"And what's your plan of attack for the day?" Eve asked.

"Well now, I do have to finalize the purchase of that galaxy."

"Funny guy." Now she paused. "Not really, right?"

He smiled at her, then picked up a tablet he'd left on the table. "I'll be doing a bit more on this."

He opened it up, did something or other, and had the image on the tablet flashing on the wall screen.

Eve saw a sprawling house — white with blue trim, a lot of fields, what looked like landscaping in progress. "What is it?"

"Darling Eve, it's your farm in Nebraska."

"What —" How the hell had he managed to turn a scary dump into a postcard? Maybe still scary to her urban eyes with all that empty land, but . . .

"Still interior work going on, of course, though winding down. And the outbuildings . . ." He swiped at the tablet, did a run-through of a big red barn-thing, what she knew was a silo — another couple of buildings, fenced areas.

"You had to pour giant buckets of money into that place."

"It took an investment, yes, and some vision, some skilled workers. Still in progress, as I said, but on schedule. And though it's not yet on the market, I've had two offers. Or I should say you've had two offers. One's for twenty percent more than the outlay."

"People are just crazy." She scooped up more omelette. "Are you taking the offer?"

"That would be up to you, but I'd advise holding. Let them finish the work."

"You get off on this, don't you?"

Roarke did something else with the tablet, split screened the postcard house with the dump he bought — in her name — on a bet. "Who wouldn't?"

She considered as she ate. "I want to thank you."

"For the farm?"

"No, Jesus, because that's just nuts. For . . . what you said last night. I don't know, not exactly, why this one's hit so hard, why it just beat up something in me. I've dealt with worse. I'll deal with worse, maybe tomorrow. Who the hell knows? And I know you're going to have my back, like I have yours. Marriage Rules."

"And I'm such a stickler for rules."

"You are — when they're your rules. Anyway, it wasn't just that you pushed me to get it out, because that's in the rules. It was what you said about why you take time away from buying galaxies to work with me, with the squad and Feeney."

She shifted to him. "I never really thought about it, not that way, I mean. It mattered. It matters. Maybe even more because we don't always have the same lines, but we have the same purpose. That's the big one. I meant it when I said, when I go in today, do the job, I'll remember that."

He could think of nothing, so he framed her face, kissed her.

"There's one more. Maybe you should remember, you built Dochas, not because of rules or lines, but because of who you are. And you're doing the same with An Didean. That, well, that's your system. And it works."

"Eve. You undo me."

She took his hand, pressed it to her cheek. "That's all the sugary stuff I've got."

"It's more than enough."

"I've got to move." She rose, glanced toward her closet. "Hell. I want to look mean. Maybe, just this time, you could go get whatever makes me look mean."

He grinned, rose. "Not just mean. Arrogant and fearless."

"That sounds good."

He gestured for her to follow him into the closet. "Leather pants, black. No, not those," he said when she started to reach for a pair. "Those."

She wanted to ask what the hell was the difference, but she saw the subtle difference. The tough look of the metal button fly, the thick belt loops.

"Shirt, not sweater. Not white or black. This."

She frowned at it, noting the color mirrored the metal. Her frown deepened when he chose a black vest with a trio of thick metal hooks in lieu of buttons.

"Trust me," he told her. "Instead of a jacket, the vest. It'll show your weapon harness during Interview. Mean, arrogant, fearless. And bloody intimidating."

Last, he selected sturdy, mid-calf black boots with lacing that gave them a military look, and a black belt with a wide metal buckle.

"You'll scare the crap out of them," he promised.

Well, she'd asked for it, she reminded herself.

Once dressed, she took a look in the mirror. "Okay. Okay, you know your stuff."

At her back, he laid his hands on her shoulders. "Go get 'em, Lieutenant."

"Bet your fine Irish ass."

"Take care of my cop — and her face."

She gave him a nod in the mirror. "I'm on it."

When she left, Roarke glanced back and saw that while he'd been distracted, Galahad had made the most of it. He'd gained the table, and now enthusiastically licked the plates.

"I should call her back and have you arrested."

With a quiet belch, the cat sat and studiously cleaned the jam off his paws.

Once again, Eve — mostly — missed the morning traffic. Considering the raid the night before, she detoured to Jacko's, loaded up on cinnamon buns. She'd sampled one on a previous investigation, knew their magnificence.

Because they were there, she added in Danishes.

Even with the stop, she got into Central with plenty of time to set up for the briefing. Before she moved into the conference room, she swung by Evidence, checked out what she needed.

And since cop coffee felt like an insult to the cinnamon buns, she hauled in pots of coffee from her office AC.

Jenkinson and his tie came in first. A horde, a flock? A shitload of multicolored butterflies swarmed over screaming blue.

"LT, Reineke stopped to get —" He broke off, sniffed the air like a hound on the hunt. "That's real coffee. Sticky buns? Roarke's coming to the briefing?"

"No."

Jenkinson — fast on his feet — already had a mouthful of bun. "Sent 'em? Nice."

"No, he didn't send them." It griped, sincerely. "He's not the only one who can think of stuff."

"We got the best LT in the history of LTs." Very fast on his feet. "How's Peabody?"

"She's coming in unless I hear differently, so you can see for yourself."

Reineke came in with a couple of vending machine coffees. Like his partner, he sniffed the air. He dumped the coffees in the recycler, hit the pot with one hand, the pile of buns with the other.

"Roarke's the man!"

"I got the damn buns. I got the damn coffee. I'm the man."

"The man," Reineke said with his mouth full.

Baxter walked in with Trueheart, said, "Score! Where's —"

"Ix-nay on the oarke-ray," Jenkinson warned.

"How will I ever break your diabolical code?" In disgust, Eve poured herself more coffee.

Others wandered in, had their Roarke comments and questions stifled as the piles of buns and pastries depleted.

Then attention — even for sticky buns — shifted as Peabody came in with McNab.

Slight limp, Eve noted, because she favored the right knee, some NuSkin on facial cuts and scrapes, but all in all Peabody looked okay. Even a little flushed as fellow officers gave her high fives and fist bumps.

Trueheart poured her coffee, doctored it her way. McNab got her a chair, then pulled another over, lifted her bad leg onto it.

"Doc said it'd be good to keep it elevated when she's sitting," McNab explained.

"Fine." And sitting would be what she'd do until the knee healed. But she'd hit her partner with that order in private. "Let's settle down, get started. We've got a long one coming."

During the shuffle, Whitney came in. He raised his eyebrows at what was left of the sticky buns and Danishes. "Are those Jacko's? Roarke doesn't miss a trick."

Jenkinson cleared his throat. "We owe the glory of the sticky buns and the real, Commander, to the generosity of Lieutenant Kick-Ass Dallas. She's the man."

Applause followed.

"That's enough sucking up. Put your own kick-asses in chairs."

"Before you begin, Lieutenant — and let me add my thanks for the coffee and pastries — I'd like to say a word."

Whitney took a moment to scan the room. "First, I want you to know that Chief Tibble would have been here himself this morning but he's in East Washington attending a convention. He was, however, kept fully informed, and sends his congratulations and appreciation for a job well done. I'll add mine to his. Yesterday, you struck a hard blow against the lawlessness that has plagued two neighborhoods of this city. Through your actions and the investigation that led up to them, you've apprehended multiple suspects we believe are responsible for three murders, and others who have committed crimes of violence and intimidation against the people we serve.

"I have no doubt that what you do today will rid those neighborhoods, our streets, our city of nearly three dozen individuals who preyed on it. To each of you, good work. Damn good work."

He glanced at Eve. "I won't keep you from doing the work that needs to be done to close this out. We'll have a media conference this afternoon — time to be determined. Chief Tibbie will return from East Washington today and attend, as will I, Agent Teasdale representing the FBI, the prosecuting attorney, and APA Reo, Lieutenant Dallas as primary of the investigation, with Detectives Peabody and Strong, and Captain Feeney representing EDD."

He smiled at her. "No good deed, Lieutenant. Kyung will let you know the when and where later today."

"Yes, sir."

"I'll leave you to it. And I'm taking one of these." He walked to the table, picked up a sticky bun. "Good call on the pastries because what you've done is a big fucking deal. Carry on," he said and walked out.

"All right," Eve began. "That said it all, and I'll just say ditto from me. I'll summarize — briefly — both prongs of the op before assigning two-man teams to individuals for Interview. We'll be rotating to cover them all, with APA Reo available throughout."

Reo lifted a hand. "The PA and another APA will also be in house. As the commander said, this is a BFD, and we fully intend to charge and prosecute as many as we have in custody as possible. We're shooting for a hundred percent on that. We are reviewing, and will continue to review, the records of all those arrested in the raids, and will work with the interview teams as needed."

"We'll start having them brought up when we're done here. Okay, summary. Two prongs, no waiting," Eve began, and ran through the salient points before giving out assignments.

"Officer Carmichael, if you'd arrange for the first wave of interviewees to be brought up to their designated boxes, we'll get this party started. Everyone, review the sheets as well as the charges from last night as they come up. And nail them down. Dismissed."

She moved to the coffeepots, wasn't surprised to find them all drained. Oh well.

"McNab, don't you have work to do?"

"I was just going to help Peabody to the bullpen."

"Are you unable to walk on your own, Detective?"

"No, sir. I'm good." When Peabody started to rise, Eve gestured her back down, gave McNab a cool stare. "Dismissed," she repeated.

"Right. Later. Don't forget to —" Now Peabody shot him a look, with a little plea in it. "Okay, later."

When he left, with a last glance back, Eve took a seat. "How bad is it? And don't bullshit me. I'm asking as your boss, and I fully intend to contact Louise, so don't bullshit me."

"He's just being sweet," Peabody began, then shifted under the cool stare. "The knee's the worst. I've got to wear the brace for a couple days. Or a few maybe. And do a little PT. I didn't break anything, but there's a little tearing. Not bad," she insisted. "Not like they have to go in and do anything. Just the brace, icing, the PT, and elevation when I can."

"The shoulder?"

"Better — honest. Louise said it'll be sore, and I won't have full range of motion for a couple days. She gave me some exercises to do to help that. I banged my hip pretty good, but that's better, too, and bright side, I figure I banged it pretty good because I don't have as much padding as I did. Loose pants."

"The rest?"

"Just some bumps and bruises, I swear. She'll tell you the same. And if I can just say, boss, you look worse than I do."

"Concrete biceps on Zeus to the face. It might not look pretty, but it doesn't require desk duty."

"Oh, but —"

"You've got the interview assignments," Eve interrupted. "You can do those sitting down. When we nail them, Peabody, and we will nail them, you're riding the desk for the rest of the week, or until your doctor clears you for active."

"I knew you were going to say that," Peabody muttered.

"Then you should have already had your pouting time. And I want your word — don't fuck with me — that if you need a break, you tell me. This is the long haul. You need a break during the haul, you take one."

"I'm not sitting in Interview with my leg up on a chair like some invalid."

"No, you're not. So you take breaks as needed."

"Okay, deal. No bullshit, and no fucking with you."

"Then let's go. We take Washington first."

"Snapper. I reviewed the report, his sheet."

"I need you to start out good cop. Once we get a sense of him, get a rhythm, you adjust as you go, as you think, but start out sympathetic."

"Lull him, got it."

Eve stopped outside of Interview when she saw Mira.

"I'll be in and out of Observation," Mira told her. "I'll help when and where I can. I've cleared as much of my schedule as possible."

"Appreciate it."

"Good luck."

With Peabody, Eve stepped into Interview. "Record on. Dallas, Lieutenant Eve, Peabody, Detective Delia, entering Interview with Washington, Denby, on the matter of case files . . ." She paused, consulting her file, as if she needed to, then ran them through for the record.

"Y'all cops look beat-up." He grinned when he said it.

He had a hulking build, not as big as Aimes, but the sort who spent a lot of his time bulking up because he thought it made him look tough.

It didn't.

Acne scars sprinkled over his dark skin. His short dreads had fading red tips, and his jaw carried an impressive bruise from Roarke's fist.

His data set his age at eighteen. He looked younger — until you saw the mean in his eyes. That read old and bitter.

"You, too, Denby," Eve said as she sat.

"This here's from police brutality. I be suing first chance."

"Is that so? Strange, the record very clearly shows you incurred that injury while attempting to jack a police vehicle — while armed. That's one of the charges pending against you."

"Bullshit charge."

Below the table, his fingers snapped. Eve could hear the *snap, snap, snap.*

"I'm trying to warn the van people shit's going down, and dude sucker punched me, that's what."

"So when you were shouting — on the record —" Once again she consulted her file. " 'Get the fuck out the van or I kill you motherfuckers,' you were warning them? Because it sounds, clearly, like a threat to do bodily harm."

"That weren't me. Somebody else."

"It was confusing out there," Peabody began.

"Damn right. Shit's going down, and I'm just trying to get clear and warn people. I'm just walking down the street, and shit's going down."

"You were inside the building," Eve said flatly. "That's also on record. Inside, Washington, you lying sack, and when the shit went down, you ran outside like a coward."

"I ain't no coward, bitch." Now his hands jumped to the table in fists, and those old, bitter eyes flamed hot. "You take these cuffs off me, and we'll see who's the coward."

"Mr. Washington." In that reasonable tone, Peabody soothed. "We're trying to straighten out what did happen. It's best if you try to stay calm."

Shifting, Washington tried making his case directly to Peabody. "I run in to see what shit's going down, then I ran on out to warn people. That's it."

"You were attempting to keep bystanders out of danger."

"Yeah, like that." He shifted back to Eve. "Nobody calls the Snapper a coward. I don't run from nothing and nobody."

"Are you a member of the urban gang known as the Bangers?" Eve asked.

"Shit, yeah, and Bangers don't take no shit from anybody, don't take no shit from cops, sure don't take it from beat-up girl cops."

"As a member of said urban gang, have you engaged in any criminal activity?"

"We just living, that's all."

"Does 'just living' include possessing, distributing, selling illegal substances?"

"Don't know nothing about it."

"Several thousand dollars' worth of illegal substances were confiscated from the building that serves as Banger headquarters."

"Cops plant it there."

"Did they also plant the equipment and supplies used to generate false identification and to commit identity theft?"

"Don't know nothing about it."

"Did you, as a member of the aforesaid urban gang, participate in coercing residents and shopkeepers in your area to make payments to you or other members under the threat of property damage or personal injury?"

"Nuh-uh, people, they pay us to protect them. We keep people safe 'cause cops is wheeze."

Eve sat back. "You're off the streets, you're going in a cage. We have officers out right now in your neighborhood taking statements from people you threatened, coerced, intimidated, and physically harmed for profit."

"They liars."

"If you were protecting them," Peabody said helpfully, "they'll be grateful and say so."

"They know what's good for them they will."

Now Eve pushed forward. "What're you going to do, asshole, when they say how it really was?"

"People make trouble for me, I make trouble for them, got that? And I ain't afraid of going inside. I get out again."

"You think?" Eve took Rochelle's earrings out of the file, then Lyle's earbuds, set the evidence bags on the table. "Where'd you get these?"

"Bought those buds."

"Where?"

360

"Off the street. Some guy."

"Funny, some guy didn't leave his prints on them. You did, and Lyle Pickering — to whom these are registered — did."

"Don't know no Pickering. I bought those buds."

"When?"

"Like, last week."

"Are you that stupid? I just told you these were registered to Pickering, have his prints on them. And I can pull in a half dozen witnesses to attest he had these buds on his person the day he was murdered."

"They lie. I bought those buds last week from some guy."

"How about the earrings? Did you buy them from the same guy?"

She watched those old, bitter eyes try to calculate the best answer. "Never seen 'em before."

"They were in your pocket when you were processed. Keep lying, just keep lying."

"What's it to you?" *Snap, snap, snap* went his fingers. "I found them. No law against finding some stupid earrings."

"There is when you find them inside a drawer in an apartment you entered for the purpose of killing Lyle Pickering. There's a really big law against premeditated murder. The sort that sends you to a concrete cage off-planet for the rest of your ugly life. Coward."

"Fuck you. I don't kill nobody. I don't know no Pickering. I bought them buds off some guy. I found them earrings on the street. You can't prove no otherwise."

"Then how did your prints get inside Lyle Pickering's apartment?"

"Didn't leave no prints. We sealed up."

Idiots, Eve thought, a bunch of idiots, and this one might win top prize for falling for that line so easily.

"You sealed up before going in the apartment to kill Pickering. Who used the syringe on him?"

His fingers snapped faster, faster.

"It matters, Denby," Peabody said, earnest, almost kind. "If you didn't actually use the syringe, it could matter in the charges."

"Don't know what you're talking about. I don't have to talk to you no more."

"Lying coward." Eve shoved up, looked into those bitter eyes, saw the flare of hate and pride. "You used Dinnie Duff to get inside, and inside you attacked Pickering, stuck him with a tranq because you're a coward and wouldn't take him on man-to-man. Then you pumped him full of Go, overdosed him because you hated he was better than you."

He tried a lunge, but the restraints held him. "Motherfucker wasn't better than me. He got no loyalty, he turn his back on his *family*. Got no reason to live, got no right. Bolt says take him down 'cause Slice is too weak to do it, we take his ass down."

"Bolt, aka Kenneth Jorgenson, ordered you to kill Lyle Pickering?"

"Bitch cop trying to mess me up, but I did what had to be. Ain't no coward. I take on anybody comes at me," he spat out. "I take you on and we see who gets messed up."

362

"And did Bolt tell you how to do it? How to do what had to be? You, Barry Aimes, Burke Chesterfield."

"Fist and Ticker," Peabody said helpfully.

"Fist gotta prove himself, don't he, he wants to be a Banger. Ticker, too. Gotta prove worthy."

"By killing Pickering."

"Turned his back on his family. We took him out. I ain't afraid to say so."

"Dinnie Duff let you, Aimes, and Chesterfield into the apartment."

"She Bolt's bitch, so does what she told."

"And did she help you kill Pickering?"

"Don't need no bitch to help. Gonna mess you up." He snapped and rocked. "Mess you up good. Show you what bitches is for."

In the zone, Eve thought, she had him in that hate-filled pride zone. "So you sent her out. Only you, Chesterfield, and Aimes murdered Lyle Pickering."

"Executed, bitch. You feel? What had to be."

"Where was Pickering when you went inside to execute him?"

"In the kitchen. Fist, he gets a good hold, and Ticker jabs him with the takedown juice. I say that part's bullshit, and we should mess a fucker up, but Bolt, he says we gonna make it look like he OD'd. Like he was a liar."

"Who gave you the illegals to plant in the apartment?"

"Bolt can get what he wants. Man ought to be leading the Bangers. We put the junk in the fucker's room like Bolt say to do."

"What did you take from Lyle's bedroom?"

"Just some coin, man. Not like he could spend it." He snickered.

"Where were the buds?"

"In his pocket. He don't need 'em no more."

"And from the other bedroom?"

"Just some glitters, who cares? Fist, he liked this red purse. Thought he might trade it for getting laid. Boy's a dumb shit."

"Why did you kill Dinnie Duff?"

He sat for a moment, snapping.

"She helped you out," Eve reminded him. "Helped you do what had to be."

"Bolt say she whining. How she didn't know we gonna kill him or nothing. How she maybe tell Slice, maybe the cops. She Bolt's bitch, but she whining about cops? That ain't loyalty, man."

"You had to stop her," Peabody said. "She wasn't being loyal to Bolt of the Bangers."

"Bitch high all the time, run her mouth everywhere. So Bolt say we got to take her out."

"To beat and rape her in the neutral zone," Eve prompted.

"Ain't no rape. Bitch puts out for anybody anytime. We just take what she gives anyway."

"And beat her to death."

He shrugged. "Slice don't have the balls to take on the Dragons, to take back our turf. We take her out, we get the war. But even then, he's got no balls! He's the coward."

"So you need to push harder," Eve continued. "Why Fist? Why kill him?"

"His bad luck is all. Bolt don't think he's got what it takes, and how he's stupid with it, right? And lazy. Stupid and lazy don't make Bangers. We do him and do him good, me and Ticker and Bolt, and me and Ticker dump his lazy ass right on that fucker Fan Ho's door. That's what we did."

He bared his teeth at Eve. "Ain't no one take on Fan Ho like that before. No one but us."

She worked the details out of him, the murder itself, the transportation of the body. When he'd finished, he sat back, sneered at her.

"Who's a coward now, bitch?"

"I think you'll answer that for yourself after a couple years in a cage on Omega. Denby Washington, you are hereby charged with murder in the first, three counts, and other charges related to those crimes. You will be reprocessed and transported to Riker's to await your day in court. Dallas and Peabody exiting Interview. Record off."

"You think I'm afraid?" he shouted after them. "I ain't afraid of nothing."

After Eve signaled uniforms to take Washington, Peabody hissed out a breath.

"He gave us everything. Everything. We didn't even have to push that hard."

"Because he's not just stupid, he's proud of what he did. He flipped on the others, but doesn't see it that way. He sees them being proud of it all, too. Take a break."

"I'm good, really."

"Take one anyway. I need to check in with the other teams, see if the lab's come through on the DNA before we have Chesterfield brought up."

One down, Eve thought, and walked into Observation to check the status.

CHAPTER
TWENTY

Dealing with Burke Chesterfield took under an hour. Another big guy with his straw-colored hair worn in a stiff, high crown, a tat of a tear at the inside corner of his right eye, he started off Interview with a smirk.

Eve deduced that the cartoon bomb, fuse lit and sparking, on the side of his throat explained his street name.

He didn't have his murder partner's old, bitter eyes, but instead a flat emptiness she'd seen in stone-cold killers far too often.

"Our information indicates you're not yet a member of the Bangers."

Smirk turned to sneer. "Shows what you know."

"All right. When were you initiated?"

"It's coming, soon as I get out of this shithole."

Eve nodded as she continued to skim through the file. "So that's never — because you're going from this shithole to another shithole for the rest of your life."

"You got nothing on me. I walk today."

Eve plucked the crime scene still of Aimes out of the file. "How well did you know Barry Aimes, also known as Fist?"

"Don't know who that is."

"So you weren't well acquainted before you both, along with Denby Washington, also known as Snapper, entered Lyle Pickering's apartment with the aid of Dinnie Duff and killed him?"

For an instant shock cut through the empty eyes. Shock, Eve thought, that she'd connected him to the murder.

"Don't know nothing about no murder. Me and Snapper was playing round ball down the lot when that dude got down."

"Oh, you were with Mr. Washington," Peabody said helpfully.

"That's what I said. Ask, he'll tell you."

"We did." Peabody smiled now. "We've already interviewed Mr. Washington. You didn't mention . . ." Peabody frowned, leaned over to look at the file. "Right. A Kenneth Jorgenson."

"That's right." A hint of the smirk came back. "Bolt's there, too. We played some Horse."

"That's interesting. Detective Peabody, why don't we play back the portion of the interview with Washington that relates to Mr. Chesterfield's whereabouts and activities at the time in question."

"Sure. Just let me cue that up."

Peabody engaged the miniscreen.

Eve watched Chesterfield watch Washington give details, brag, and boast. Angry color flooded his face, then ebbed to ghastly white.

"He's lying."

"Why would he do that? Why wouldn't he tell us he was playing basketball with you and Jorgenson?"

"'Cause he's a liar."

"So he's lying about killing Pickering because . . . he wants to spend his life in prison?"

"I don't know what he did. He says do me a solid and say how I'm playing round ball with you, so I said how he was."

"Now you're saying he wasn't — that you lied."

"I did him a solid."

"Why would he implicate you after you did him a solid?"

"Fucker's crazy." Obviously warming to the theme, Chesterfield jabbed a finger at the miniscreen. "Hates me. Always looking to get me in the shit."

Arranging her face in a considering frown, Eve nodded. "So, he hates you, gets you in the shit, but you do him a solid over a murder? You're a very compassionate soul, I take it. So compassionate you pumped Lyle Pickering full of a killing dose of illegals to prove yourself worthy to be a Banger. Then stole his shoes. His Lightning high-tops."

"Those are my high-tops you assholes took from me. I bought them last week."

"A lot of buying going on last week," Eve remarked to Peabody. "A lot of buying — earbuds and high-tops — with Lyle Pickering's prints."

Something like inspiration lit on his face. "I bought them off Snapper."

"Right, the one who likes getting you in the shit, but you do solids for."

"He gave them to me for doing the solid."

"I see, so you didn't buy them last week as previously stated."

"I traded. The solid for the shoes."

"Who's trying to get who in the shit now?" Peabody wondered. "The only prints on the shoes are Lyle Pickering's and yours."

"I guess he used up his compassion," Eve said. "He didn't have any left when he gang-raped and beat Dinnie Duff to death with Aimes and Washington. He'd really used it up before he slit the throat of Gary Aimes. I mean otherwise, he's a goddamn humanitarian."

"I didn't do nothing. Snapper's just trying to twist me up, that's what. I never did none of those things, and nobody can say I did."

"You did all of those things, and we're saying you did."

"It's my word against Snapper's."

"More it's your stupidity against his, and I'd say they're running about the same pace. What do you think, Peabody?"

"Neck and neck from where I'm sitting."

"I ain't stupid. You guys are the stupid ones."

"Well, let's run that stupid race," Eve suggested. "You had the brooch you took from the Pickering apartment in your damn pocket and Lyle Pickering's shoes on your feet when we arrested you."

"He's pulling into the lead," Peabody decided.

"And we have a statement from the female who had the bracelet you traded her for sex, also taken from the Pickering apartment."

370

"I don't know what a fucking brooch *is*! And that Yolanda's a lying whore."

"A brooch is jewelry, a pin." Eve tossed the photo on the table. "And I didn't say the name of the female who had the bracelet. Adding, we found your DNA on Duff's body. You use a lot of product to get that vertical lift, asshole, but that doesn't affect the DNA on hair."

"Everybody's got hair."

"Jesus Christ, is basic science a foreign language to you? Everybody doesn't have your hair or your DNA."

Chesterfield tried a lip curl, but it wobbled some. "You don't have no DNA on me, my old lady wouldn't sign me up. She's smarter than that."

"Too bad she didn't pass the smarts to you. You drank a Coke during processing. We took your DNA from the tube, matched it with the hair on Duff's body. Like we took the knife you had when you were arrested, and we got Barry Aimes's blood off the blade and hilt."

"Then there's the bloody shirt he left in his flop at the HQ," Peabody pointed out. "Slitting throats is messy."

"That's not my shirt. I found that knife, and the pin thing, too."

"Where?"

"On the street." His eyes wheeled. "No, in Snapper's flop. They were in Snapper's flop."

"You want us to believe you're a thief but not a murderer? Explain why both the knife and the pin have your prints on them, and not Washington's? You can't," Eve snapped. "You can't lie fast enough, and he's already rolled on you. Bolt told you what you had to do to be worthy, and you did it. You pumped that syringe into Pickering, you raped and beat Duff and left her in the neutral zone hoping to start a gang war, then you cut Aimes's throat, transported him to Chinatown, and dumped his body outside Fan Ho's family restaurant."

"I was just there." His wheeling eyes filled now, with tears, to join the tat at the inside corner of his eye. "I didn't do any of it. I was just there. I was high. Bolt says we gotta do it."

"Start there, and be specific. What did Bolt tell you to do?"

When they'd finished, Peabody hit Vending for water for both of them.

"I don't know about you, but I need to hydrate. I thought, after we nailed those two, I'd want to high-five." Peabody cracked the tube. "But he was pitiful. I mean, God, he cried through the last twenty minutes. Not his fault, he was high. Not his fault, Bolt made him do it."

"So we'll take Bolt next." Eve rubbed at her eyes and the headache behind them. "Check on the team we sent out to get the van they used to transport Aimes. See if the sweepers have started to process it. Then take your break."

As they walked toward the bullpen, Eve spotted Crack and Rochelle sitting on a bench outside.

"Go ahead on the van," Eve said. "I'll take them."

"I can get updates from the other interviews while I'm on break. It's sitting-down work."

Eve continued toward Crack and Rochelle as they rose.

"Don't blame Wilson," Rochelle said quickly. "He's only here because he couldn't talk me out of coming. After I heard the reports about the arrests . . . You were hurt."

"Job hazard."

"Skinny white girl's tough."

"Yeah," Eve said to Crack. "We've got a lounge." Eve gestured. "Let's go in there."

"I know you're busy," Rochelle continued. "And taking time to talk to me adds to your day, but anything, anything you can tell me. I wanted to come in person because —"

"Less chance of me brushing you off."

"Yes. Yes, exactly."

Eve led the way into the lounge, nearly empty, as she had so many cops in so many interviews or transporting prisoners to and from. "Coffee's terrible," she warned.

"I don't need anything." Rochelle sat at a table with Eve, took Crack's hand in a strong grip. "Except whatever you can tell me."

She looked as if she hadn't slept in days, Eve thought, and in those exhausted eyes need lived.

"We have statements for the media later today, so what I'm telling you now can't get out. It could hamper the rest of the investigation."

"Is there something I can tell my family?"

"I need you to keep a lid on this until we're ready to go public."

"All right."

"Of the three men who killed your brother, we have two in custody and both are charged with his murder. First degree. The third's dead, at their hands."

"You have them." Rochelle's eyes swam. "You have them."

"There's a fourth individual, in custody. We'll interview him next. He's implicated, not in the execution of the murder, but in the ordering of it."

Rochelle let the tears come, let them roll silently down her face. "Is it Marcus Jones?"

"I can tell you it was not. I intend to put Jones away for a host of other crimes. But not for your brother. We've recovered the items taken from your apartment, and they'll be returned to you once this is finished. The illegals in your brother's room were planted there. We have full confessions."

"He didn't start using again." Rocking herself, Rochelle let out a shaky breath. "I knew he hadn't, but it helps that you know that, too. That everyone will know."

"Rochelle, your brother wasn't using again, or involved with his old gang. He didn't lie to you. He did omit something he'd done and was doing. Lyle was working with the police as a confidential informant."

As more tears fell, Rochelle pressed a hand to her mouth. "He was helping the police? You?"

"Not me. When I can, I'll arrange for you to speak with the detective he worked with. He didn't tell you because he couldn't tell you. He may have saved lives, he certainly passed on information that aided in arrests, in taking criminals off the street. He didn't just beat the

374

odds, he smashed them to dust. You're right to be proud of him."

"I am. I am. Is this why . . . Was he killed because they found out?"

"I don't know that yet. You need to give us time, and you need to keep what I've told you at this table until I can clear it."

"I will. I swear to you." With one hand still in Crack's, Rochelle pressed the other to her heart. "He was making amends, making amends to people he hurt before by helping the police. If you could tell the officer he worked with I'm grateful. I'm grateful he was given the opportunity."

"I will. I need to get back."

"Can we sit here for a couple minutes? I just need to sit for a minute."

"As long as you need," Eve said as she rose.

She strode back toward Homicide, paused when she heard Crack call her name.

"I'm not going to keep you, but I got one question."

"I went as far as I could already."

"No, this is personal for me. I want to know if you took down the motherfucker who did that to your face."

She had to smile a little, and more than a little fiercely. "Yeah, I took her down. And she doesn't look so pretty, either."

"Good enough." He stepped back, and as she walked away, called out, "I know some skinny white girls, but don't know any prettier than you."

She headed to her office, for coffee before she pulled in updates on the other arrests. Reo already had coffee, and Eve's desk chair.

"Sorry, I needed a quiet space for a couple minutes."

Eve waved her back down. "I'm just here for coffee."

"Well, while you're getting it, you might like to know that Donita Haver, or Tank as she prefers — and since you're you, you know that's the woman who tried to beat you with a bat — has confessed to the attempted murder of a police officer."

"What? Wait. She confessed not to assault with a deadly but to attempted murder?"

"Bragged about it, hopes to get another chance. She was actually smart enough, as a surprising number of them aren't, to demand legal rep. Then she coldcocked her public defender with an elbow when he was rattling off how she wasn't aware you were the police and tried to advise her to claim diminished capacity."

Reo held up a finger as she scrolled through her notes. "I quote: 'Knew that cunt was a cop. I'd've cracked her fucking head open and had a good taste of her brains if she hadn't had the fucking helmet. Next time I will.'"

Considering, Eve drank some coffee. "Does she know, in New York, that's forty to life?"

"She doesn't seem to care. Claims no cage can hold her, and she'll bust out, hunt you down, and eat your brains. However, during the interview — post-PD, as he required medical attention and she said fuck the lawyers — Baxter and Trueheart managed to get her to confess to a couple of other assaults, the beating death

— proudly with her bare fists — of an illegals dealer, and an assortment of others. We're going to put her in an off-planet cage for the rest of her life — she's twenty-four, by the way."

"The rest of her life works for me."

"Remember that, because we've made a few deals along the way, lower levels."

"They do short time, they'll end up back in. It's how it is." Eve thought of Lyle Pickering. "With rare and goddamn shining exceptions."

"We've also bagged a number for outstanding warrants. Jenkinson and Reineke pulled the location of a flop used to house more sex workers. You were in Interview, but Whitney sent a team out to scoop them up. Strong's working Ho now. She started with a couple of his underlings, worked up a nice file. A few deals made."

"Will they help her put him away?"

"I believe they will. He's lawyered — not a PD, but we're going to get him. Jorgenson has a PD, one who came to me proposing a deal." Reo examined her fingernails. "I scoffed and chortled."

" 'Scoffed and chortled'?"

"It goes like this."

Reo made a somehow ladylike snorting sound, then a low-throated, nicely evil laugh.

"Excellent."

"I practice. From what you got from Washington, there won't be a deal on this one."

"We just finished getting corroboration from Chesterfield, and a few more details." She checked her wrist unit. "I'm going to have Jorgenson brought up."

"I'll notify his attorney of record."

"Keep the desk. I still need to —"

Eve broke off as she heard footsteps — a smooth, steady stride. It didn't surprise her to see Kyung step into her doorway.

He was a tall, slick-looking black man, and as media liaison, not an asshole.

"Lieutenant, APA Reo, I'm sorry to interrupt."

"The commander said this afternoon, later this afternoon. It's not even afternoon yet."

"Nearly. I've just spoken with Chief Tibble, who is now on his way back to the city. He would like to target four o'clock. If this doesn't give you enough time, I can and will push it back."

Eve calculated. No point trying to wiggle out of it, so she calculated. She wanted to close out Jorgenson, Jones, and Cohen. "I can let you know by fifteen hundred."

"I can work with that. I will have a statement." He held up a hand before Eve could object. "Not for you to make, but for you to clear, to make sure we have all the facts in order, and if you choose, for you to spring off of during your time. In addition, I'm aware you rarely use facial enhancements."

"Screw that. I'm not going to —"

Again, he held up a hand. "I was going to request you not make this one of those rare times. Let's show them what our cops are made of."

Eve drained her coffee, set the mug down again. "You continue to not be an asshole, Kyung."

"I do my best to maintain that benchmark. APA Reo, if I could have a few minutes."

378

"Use the office," Eve told them.

Eve left them, used Baxter's desk to order Jorgenson brought to Interview, to text Roarke the next promised update.

Two for two now. On deck with number three.

A moment later, he responded.

Swing away, Lieutenant.

"For the fucking fences," she murmured.

Peabody swiveled around. "I can give you a running list of who's completed Interview, the charges, the disposition."

"Send it to my PPC." She started to rise when Baxter came in, but he shook his head, sat on the corner of the desk.

"We're taking a break. I told Trueheart to take a walk outside, get some air."

"Because?"

"We just finished with one. He's fourteen. His child advocate and his mother were both with him. The mother's begging us to help her, to help him. She says a couple of the Bangers started coming around the school a couple years ago, trying to recruit."

"We know that's true."

"Yeah. Gave some free illegals, talked trash. She said her boy stayed out of their way, or tried to. And one night she's coming home from work, she gets raped, beaten. We've got the incident report, so she's not bullshitting. She didn't know who attacked her. What else she didn't know is a couple of the gang cornered the kid after, told him if he didn't work for them, she'd get worse next time. Maybe end up dead next time. If he told her or anybody, they'd make sure of it."

"What did he do?"

"What he was told. They made a runner out of him, a delivery boy. He'd deliver illegals, pick up protection money. Up until six months ago, when this went down, the kid was a decent student. After, his grades take a dive, he gets in trouble in school, loses weight because he won't eat half the time. Even in there, he won't talk at first. Kid's terrified, LT, you can see it all over him."

"What was he doing at their HQ last night?"

"Delivering a package to Jones. Trueheart eased it all out of him, took some time, a lot of care, but he got it out of him."

"Can he identify the ones who threatened him?"

"Can and did. We're going to take them next. But he said he had to report to Jones once a week. And Jones said how they needed good young blood like him. How it was fine he wanted to protect his mother, but they were his family now. If he forgot that, well, his mother would pay for it."

"I want Mira to talk to the kid."

"Already notified her."

"Let's keep him under wraps, him and the mother. We don't know how many of these assholes are still on the streets. Any other relatives?"

"She's got a sister in Queens, parents in Brooklyn."

"She should pick one, go there, once Mira clears it."

"Same page. Dallas, he said they're pulling in girls his age for sex work. Either they find ones living on the edge, or use tactics like they did with him."

The headache that had never quite faded began to drum again. "We've got a location on where they keep sex workers. If there's more, if they have another place for minors, we'll get that, too. You push that in the rest of the interviews, pass the word. Push it.

"Peabody, break's over. Jorgenson's up."

"I'm ready. I'm freaking armed and ready."

He didn't look like much, Eve thought when she walked into Interview. On the short side at five-seven with that compact build. The spiked red hair flamed over a moon-white face.

He sat with his arms crossed and a look of boredom in pale green eyes while his overanxious public defender agitated beside him.

"My client has spent over sixteen hours waiting for this Interview. His due process —"

"Hold it. Record on. Dallas, Lieutenant Eve, and Peabody, Detective Delia, entering Interview with Jorgenson, Kenneth, and his court-appointed attorney. Please state your name for the record, sir."

"Paul Quentin."

Eve named various case files as she and Peabody took their seats.

"As I said, my client —"

"Had to wait his turn," Eve supplied. "Mr. Jorgenson —"

"I'll speak for my client, Lieutenant. My client prefers being addressed and/or referred to as Bolt."

"Is that so?"

Prissy-looking guy, Eve thought, and still green. Mixed race, skinny in his suit and carefully knotted tie.

She imagined he was still young enough, still new enough to be idealistic.

"Are you aware of the charges against your client?"

"Of course, and my client, of course, refutes them. My client can name two witnesses who will verify his whereabouts at the time Lyle Pickering died."

"First, your client is charged with ordering the murder of Mr. Pickering, not of carrying out the murder."

Eve aimed her gaze at that moon-white face, those bored eyes. "We're aware he doesn't do his own dirty work."

"My client, in fact, had no connection to the deceased and therefore would have no cause to order his murder. However, my client believes he may have some information that may help the police identify the individual who did, in fact, kill Mr. Pickering. He will offer that information in exchange for immunity on the lesser charges of assault, illegal possession, possession of —"

"Stop talking."

Quentin's mouth fell open. "I beg your pardon?"

"Stop talking." Time, Eve decided, to wipe some of that green away. "If your murderous fuck of a client thinks he can try to toss this off on Marcus Jones, you're wasting my time, my partner's time. And if you actually believe your scum of a client, you're going to last about six months as a PD."

"Speaking to me or about my client in such a way —"

"Stop talking," Eve repeated. "They rolled on you, Bolt. Snapper, Ticker — if we're going to use your lame gang names. They rolled, then folded you up and rolled some more."

Bolt leaned to his attorney, spoke low in his ear. Quentin nodded, cleared his throat. "My client and I are fully aware police officers are allowed to lie and mislead during an interview. Now, though my client is barely acquainted with the individuals you named, he did see them briefly at or about the time of Lyle Pickering's murder when they joined, for a short time, a casual game of basketball at a location known as the lot."

"That's interesting. Isn't that interesting, Peabody?"

"I'm riveted. I mean, sure, his lame-ass alibis both stated they were playing when he joined, but it's easy to mix up little details like that when you're lying."

"It's always the little things," Eve agreed. "And speaking of little things, I bet Washington, Chesterfield — and we need to add Aimes in here — didn't mention to your client the little things they took from the Pickering apartment after they carried out his orders and pumped a killing dose of Go into Pickering."

"There's no evidence my client —"

Eve rolled over him like his fellow gang members rolled on Jorgenson. "Like the shiny red purse from the vic's sister's closet we found in Aimes's pigsty of a room. And you know what? It had earrings inside with blood traces from where they'd been ripped out of earlobes. Dinnie Duff's blood, as it happened."

"My client's hardly responsible for or connected to —"

"Not finished," Eve said, and had to admit she enjoyed interrupting him again. "Washington had a pair of earrings, too." She shoved a photo from her file onto the table. "Taken from Rochelle Pickering's bedroom. He had them in his pocket, Bolt. I mean, Jesus, can't you find anybody smarter? Not Chesterfield, that's for sure, as he traded this bracelet — also from Rochelle Pickering's bedroom — for sex, and had on his person at the time of his arrest, this brooch, taken from Rochelle Pickering's bedroom. The asshole was wearing shoes he stole from Pickering's closet."

"If this is true, it has nothing to do with my client."

"I bet it pisses him off," Eve said, watching the muscles in Bolt's jaw tighten. "I mean, Jesus, they had one job. You sent three of them — four when you include Duff — to kill one guy. Get in, do it, plant the illegals, get out. But they had to take some shiny things."

"Actually, Lieutenant, he gave them two jobs that day. After Lyle, he ordered them to kill Dinnie Duff."

"That's true. Two jobs in one day. It's practically asking them to multitask. They screwed that up, too, ripping off her earrings, leaving hair and fiber on her body when they raped her. Now, we get the motive there. A junkie like Duff could blab, and doing her, leaving her in the neutral zone stirs up trouble with the Dragons. But I don't get the motive on Pickering. Why him, Bolt?"

"My client maintains, and will continue to maintain, his innocence in these matters."

384

"Then I guess he maintains same for the murder of Barry Aimes, and the subsequent transporting of his body into Chinatown. You know, Bolt, I figured you for the bright one of the group, because Washington and Chesterfield barely have half a brain between them, but using your cousin's van to haul the body to the alley behind Ho's family restaurant?"

As if in pity, Eve shook her head. "We're processing it now. Found it exactly where Chesterfield said we would."

Fury rippled over Bolt's face, but he again leaned to his attorney. This time it took a little longer.

"My client relates that if his cousin's vehicle was used in the commission of a crime, numerous people knew where said vehicle was kept."

"Yeah? How many of them had the access code to the garage where it was kept, or the codes to the van itself? How do you explain your client's prints on and in the van?"

This time when Bolt leaned toward Quentin, Eve rolled her eyes.

"For Christ's sake, just say it. Do you want to be in the box all day?"

"My client assists his cousin on a part-time basis in his delivery service, therefore his fingerprints could certainly be in and on said vehicle. Lieutenant, you have nothing but circumstantial evidence and supposition in regards to my client. I believe it's time to conclude this interview."

"Do you? Well, let's do one more thing. Peabody, cue it up and roll it out."

CHAPTER
TWENTY-ONE

Eve just sat back and enjoyed while Peabody ran portions of the interviews. Washington implicating Jorgenson, Chesterfield confirming the implication.

Back and forth, back and forth.

When Quentin tried to interrupt, Eve just pointed at him. "Stop talking."

She ended the screening after Chesterfield stated Jorgenson brought the van to the lot where they'd lured Aimes with the idea of getting high and shooting baskets.

Me and Snap can't drive, don't know how, so Bolt, he drives, then me and Snapper, we carry Fist down the alley and shove him behind the recycler. After, Bolt takes the van back so his cousin don't know nothing, then we go change 'cause we're bloody. And I traded that bracelet thing to Yolanda, got a BJ.

Then we go get some eats.

Eve signaled Peabody, then turned to Jorgenson. "Yeah, slitting throats and trying to incite gang wars sparks up the appetite. I've got cops at the diner now, talking to the staff. We'll nail you there, with the assholes you enlisted. Oh, and just another small detail. I guess you haven't helped out in your cousin's business in the last few weeks. He installed a security cam over the door."

Eve circled a finger in the air, then pointed it at Jorgenson. "Gotcha."

"I need to consult with my client."

"Bet you do. Dallas and Peabody exiting Interview. Record off."

At the door, Eve looked back at Jorgenson with a smile that could have sliced bone.

"Check in with the sweepers," Eve ordered once they were outside the Interview room. "I'll tag Officers Carmichael and Shelby."

"On it. I'm getting a fizzy — need a boost. Do you want a Pepsi?"

Eve only nodded. "Officer Carmichael."

As she listened to him her smile turned to one of pure satisfaction.

She took it with her into Observation, where Reo sat, coffee in hand, watching the screen split into various interviews. She muted the sound.

"You just missed Mira. She'll be back. We both agree you've got Jorgenson on the ropes. And she didn't see the last few minutes."

"I got more. I've got witnesses at the diner where he had 'eats' with Washington and Chesterfield after dumping Aimes and ditching the bloody clothes."

"You've got someone who puts all three of them there, together?"

"Two someones. My cops tracked down the cook and a waitress from the night shift. Both state all three came in, together, right about three-thirty. That works, given the time the witness from across the alley thinks she heard voices. Add the time for them to get the van back to the cousin's garage, change, for that idiot Chesterfield to trade the stolen bracelet for a quick BJ. Yeah, it works. And the waitress states Jorgenson paid for all three, said it was for doing what had to be done."

"That should put him on the mat. Not out, but down. His lawyer's going to want to deal. Call me in if and when he does. I'll enjoy shattering his dreams."

Peabody came in. "Hey, Reo."

"Sit," Eve ordered. "Put the knee up."

"I will, for a minute, while I tell you . . ." She sat, breathed slowly in and out as she lifted her foot onto a chair Reo moved over for her. "The sweepers are still processing, but they've got Jorgenson's prints as reported earlier. Driver's door, cargo doors, the wheel. No surprise there, or finding the other two idiots' prints. The new is they've picked up some blood in the cargo area. Not readily visible — laying the body on plastic was, at least, semi-smart. But it didn't catch it all. They're taking samples, doing an on-site comparison.

"Oh, and the cousin's pissed. He claims he cut Jorgenson off over the winter because he knew Jorgenson was stealing from him, suspected he took the van out for joyrides, or to have sex. It's why he installed the door cam."

"Why didn't he change the damn code on the garage?"

"He did, and that seemed to solve things. He caught Jorgenson trying to get in once on the feed, then that was it. He hardly checked the feed the last couple weeks, because no more trouble. Until he found out this morning Jorgenson threatened one of his drivers into giving him the code just a few days ago. She was too scared to tell him what happened, then let it all out when the cops came to the office."

"He planned it out. One of the three was always going to die."

"I think I see X's in his eyes," Reo commented.

Eve cracked the tube, drank, paced. "He'd have been smarter to do it all himself. Get Duff to let him in, deal with Pickering — though he wouldn't have taken Pickering out easy, and that's one reason. But he does that, does Duff, and if he needs more, he pulls out somebody like Aimes, does what he does. But he draws in three morons. Because he wants a following, he wants to be in charge. He goes low there because he can manipulate them. Once they kill for him, he's got them. And once they kill the weakest among them, they're sealed. That's how he saw it. You get the war started, whatever else it takes, and use it to take Jones out, one way or the other, and step in."

She drank again, gestured with the tube. "He sincerely believed they'd go down for him. They'd never flip. That's his arrogance, his own sense of self-importance. One flips because he thinks it makes them all heroes, because being a killer is a badge of honor."

"And he believes, probably sincerely," Peabody added, "that Jorgenson feels exactly the same."

"You got that. The second flips because he's not just stupid but scared. Take away his high, his gang buddies, he breaks down."

"I'll put in," Reo commented, "it strikes me Jorgenson lacks leadership qualities."

"You've got that right. We're going to hit him with Jones," Eve told Peabody. "The skimming, the partnership with Cohen, the whole ball. He won't take it well."

"You know, you need to start stocking popcorn around here."

"I'll keep that in mind." Eve turned to the door as a uniform opened it.

"Sir, Jorgenson's lawyer's ready to resume."

"Thank you, Officer. Come on, Peabody, let's finish this fucker."

Eve stepped into Interview, resumed the record, sat.

"Lieutenant, my client believes he may have some information that will apply to your investigation and perhaps aid you in it."

"We're all ears, right, Peabody?"

"We got four of them."

"In sharing this information, I've advised my client he may be in some legal jeopardy, despite acting without prior knowledge of any crime. We require assurances my client won't be prosecuted for these actions without knowledge, or the subsequent knowledge afforded during this interview, which has led my client to believe he has salient information."

"That's a lot of words to say you want to cut a deal."

"Lieutenant, since hearing the statements made by Washington and Chesterfield, and becoming aware they not only committed three murders but have attempted to implicate him, my client wishes to cooperate with the police in these matters."

"Lots of words to say your client's found himself in a hard corner and wants to try to slither his way out."

The PD sent Eve what she supposed he thought was a stern look. "You're required to inform the prosecutor's office that my client has information that may help in your investigation and in the subsequent prosecution of charged parties."

"Words, words." Eve rose, went to the door. "Officer, would you inform APA Cher Reo we have a suspect who's looking to deal?"

"Yes, sir."

Eve sat again, hooked an arm over the back of her chair, and met Jorgenson's stare with one of her own.

He looked away first.

As the uniform let Reo in, Eve spoke for the record. "Reo, APA Cher, entering Interview."

"Paul Quentin." The public defender extended a hand. "Attorney for Mr. Jorgenson."

"Tough for you." But Reo shook his hand before taking a seat. "So?"

Quentin repeated his pitch, almost verbatim, while Reo sat, folded her hands.

"How about the short answer? No deal."

"Ms. Reo, I don't doubt the prosecutor wants convictions on these murders. My client has information that will aid you in achieving that."

"Both Washington and Chesterfield have tendered full confessions for their parts in the murders, and in doing so, both — independently — implicated your client in those murders. No deal."

"My client maintains that his actions were done without prior knowledge of these crimes. Furthermore, he has information that will aid your investigation, your convictions of the perpetrators, and assist you in identifying others involved."

"Others. Now that's interesting."

"It's bullshit, Reo," Eve said.

"Maybe yes, maybe no. Here's what we'll do. If your client provides true and salient information that leads to the arrest of others involved in the murders of Pickering, Duff, Aimes, we'll talk deal."

"Immunity from all charges."

"Your green's showing, Mr. Quentin. You need to rub that off. Give me a nibble," she said directly to Jorgenson, "then we can talk — maybe — accessory after the fact on Barry Aimes — we know you provided the van and, in fact, drove same to transport the body of Barry Aimes. We could plead that down to five to ten."

"Is actually doing your job too much of a stretch for you, Reo?"

Reo turned her head, gave Eve a cool glance. "This is my job. Offer me something, Mr. Jorgenson, and I'll talk to my boss."

When Quentin began to speak, Reo shot a finger at him.

"He tells me. His words, not through your filter."

"They came to me." Jorgenson shrugged. "Had blood all over them."

"Who?"

"Snapper and Ticker. They came to me, and they said how they got jumped by Dragons, and Fan Ho killed Fist."

"That contradicts the statements they've given — independently — in their confessions."

"I'm saying what they told me. They said how they heard Slice was making a deal with Ho, to keep things down after Dinnie. And they didn't like it, got talking trash. They figured Slice put the Dragons on them. So they had the idea to get Fist over to Ho's place, prove the Dragons did him. All I did was get the van and drive it."

"Rather than report a murder to the police, you helped transport a body from the killing scene to Chinatown?"

"Bangers don't go to cops." He spoke defiantly. "We take care of our own."

"Uh-huh. And didn't it strike you as odd that neither of these men who survived an attack that killed Aimes had no injuries?"

"They had blood on them."

"Aimes's blood."

He shrugged. "How'm I to know? Blood's blood."

"And bullshit's bullshit. You went out for a big breakfast after disposing of the body, and both the other men had changed clothes — no blood showing. Yet you still failed to question the fact they had no injuries. Aimes's throat was sliced ear to ear, and showed no other injuries."

"I'm saying what they said, can you latch on? I figure they were working with Slice. Setting me up."

"Because?"

"Because he knows I'm smarter, stronger, and I'm going to take over."

"You." Laughing, Eve straightened in her chair. "You think you're smarter than Jones. Jones, who's been skimming off the gang's pool for over three years? Jones, who freaking owns the building you flop in — the one you pay rent to flop in."

"You're a fucking liar."

"Mr. Jorgenson," Quentin warned. "Please don't speak."

"Samuel Cohen. You know that name. You probably couldn't reach him to rep you here, probably figured he was too busy trying to rep a bunch of Bangers to get back to you. The two of them? They've been milking you and the rest. Buying real estate, for God's sake. Sure Jones wanted to keep it down — he didn't want the cops getting too close to his bank accounts. He's got a couple million socked away. And all that real estate with Cohen.

"And what does Cohen do? He comes along giving you some ideas once Jones backs off his percentage of the illegals, the protection racket, the sex workers. I bet he fed your delusions of grandeur."

Eve rose, circled the table, leaned down. "You can take him down? Is that what Cohen told you? I'll help you. Give me a cut when you're in charge, and I'll be your consigliere. Something like that? Don't worry, he didn't bump you back because he's working to cut Jones a deal in this. He's trying to cut one for himself, with the feds. Tax evasion, fraud, all kinds of goodies. And rolling on you? It's just part of the negotiation."

"They're dead. They're dead men."

"Mr. Jorgenson —"

"Shut up, you worthless piece of shit. Shut the fuck up."

"Would you kill them yourself if you could get to them, Bolt? Or would you order another couple of idiots to do it like you did with Pickering, Duff, Aimes?"

"They're dead. Slice, Cohen, Snapper, Ticker. Dead."

"Big talk, big talk from a guy who got his ass kicked by his own sister."

"You shut the fuck up."

"Did you know that one, Quentin? He physically assaulted his mother, and his sister gave him an ass kicking. You're here because, while the family didn't file charges, they kicked him hard to the curb, so he can't tap them for money for a lawyer."

"You don't know dick." Jorgenson snarled it, tried to take a swing at Eve, but the restraints stopped him.

"Temper, temper," she said. "I had a little conversation with your sister, Bolt. I know plenty. Oh, and the staff sergeant doesn't send her regards."

"She's a lying bitch, just like my lying whore of a mother."

"I don't think Bolt likes women much," Eve said pleasantly to Reo. "He might be afraid of them. You couldn't even take out the junkie you were having sex with, could you? You told them to rape the shit out of her, didn't you, to beat her to death and leave her where you figured Slice couldn't ignore it."

"I'm not the one afraid. Slice is."

He raged it out. In the zone, Eve thought again. But Jorgenson's zone was fury.

"If he had balls, Fan Ho and the rest would be dead. But he's got no balls."

"It's why you picked the neutral zone, but Slice didn't bite. Did you plan to use her, then have her killed back when you started banging her?"

"Don't —"

"Shut the fuck up!" he shouted at Quentin. "You think I'd stick it to that junkie whore, listen to her whiny ass because I liked it?"

"No." Eve circled the table again. "You did it because she had two uses for you. To help you get to Pickering, and to die bloody. I get that. I get that. What I don't get is Pickering. Why? He wasn't part of the gang anymore. He wasn't a threat, and I can't see how he'd be a tool."

"Slice let him walk, just walk away like he was better than us. Nobody walks away from us like that. I said we need to tune him up good, make him pay a price, and Slice? He says no. He says the asshole's off-limits, how he was a fine lieutenant, and how he'll come back when he's tired of living the bullshit life."

"And Slice, he'd have put him over you, wouldn't he? Put him at a higher rank."

"I said fuck that. Slice even goes to see him at his work sometimes, like friends. He wants a friend outside? I showed him what happens."

"So you ordered Pickering killed to strike back at Slice, to make an example, and because of their connection, to bring the cops sniffing around Slice."

"You came, didn't you? Cohen said it had to look like an accident."

Eve sat again. "Did he?"

"I said we'll cut him up good, plant the knife on Jones, but Cohen said make it look like he OD'd. The cops would still come. Slice would still look weak. So I told those motherfuckers what to do, and they can't do it right? Have to take shit out of the place?"

"You did tell them to mess Dinnie up though."

"Bitch had to go hard or no point. Cohen says now fucking just kill her like we did Pick, but I say it's going to be done right."

"He knew you planned to have her raped and beaten."

"Shit yeah. Said to make sure they suited up, so no juice in her for the cops to find."

"And still, after all that, Slice didn't call for war."

"Got no guts, got no honor. Stealing from his family."

"Why Aimes? Was it always going to be Aimes?"

"He's a dumb-ass, zoned out most of the time. He and Dinnie, always whining for more junk. I never killed any of them. You can't hang that on me."

Eve sat back. "Who's the dumb-ass now?"

This time Eve called for a break all around — and decided to pull another Roarke.

As she sat in her office, reviewing interviews, she smelled the pizza coming her way before she heard the clomp of Peabody's boots.

"Brought you a slice. Ah, the bullpen wants to know if you're okay."

"Why wouldn't I be?"

"Sticky buns this morning, pizza this afternoon."

"Special circumstances. You can tell them not to get used to it."

"Being smart cops, I think they know that. Did you talk to Teasdale?"

"Yeah, and sent her the interview. Cohen's going to be very sad when he doesn't get witness protection — ever."

"Instead he goes down for accessory before and after the fact, three counts."

"I'm going to ask for on-planet."

Peabody managed to look both surprised and disappointed simultaneously. "Why?"

"I think it'll actually be harder on the sleazy son of a bitch. Plus, Jorgenson and his idiot team are going off. If they end up in the same facility, Cohen *is* a dead man. I want him to live a long, miserable life. Go eat before the wolves leave a scatter of crumbs."

"They're being nice to me. They said I got the first slice. Let me know when you're ready for Jones."

"Yeah." Eve rolled her tired shoulders, texted Roarke.

Grand slam.

398

And smiled at his reply.

And the crowd goes wild. I hope to make it down to Central by four if you're still going to be at it.

She blew out a breath.

Supposed to do stupid media conference about then. Going to bag Jones, and leave Cohen for Teasdale. Jorgenson wrapped him up in a bow.

Then I'll try to make it down to see you tell the media and the people of New York the city's a safer place tonight. Eat something.

She started to tell him she had pizza, then remembered she'd had pizza the day before. He'd have something to say about that.

Breaking now. See you later.

After checking the time, she ate her slice, settled for water with a coffee chaser while she continued to review.

Then, calculating, tagged Nadine.

"Am I go? I need to head down to Central in a couple hours and join the rest of the media."

"Here's what you're go on now. Jorgenson, Washington, Chesterfield, Cohen, all charged."

She ran through the specific charges while she ate. "You can check with the PA's office on when, but they're all scheduled to be indicted today. You can add the federal charges on Cohen, but you should get confirmation from Special Agent Teasdale. If you wait about a half hour to break this, you can follow up with Pickering's CI status. I want Jones in the box before that hits. I don't want it to leak to him and maybe skew the interview."

"I can do that."

"Do me a solid — let Kyung know it's coming. He may be a little annoyed, but he'll get it."

"Don't sandbag him, got it." Nadine looked up from her notes. "We're going to do right by Rochelle's brother, Dallas."

"Counting on it. I'll let her know it's coming."

She clicked off, tagged Crack. "Are you with Rochelle?"

"Yeah. I'm helping her family with plans for Lyle's memorial. We're at her brother's."

"Good. Tell her she can share with her family what I told her this morning. And you should have Channel Seventy-Five on. There's going to be a major report in about thirty."

"Are they bagged, Dallas?"

"The five responsible won't see the outside again. Crack, I want to talk to Lyle's cop because I know she's carrying weight on this, but tell the family he wasn't killed because he was helping the cops. They didn't know he was helping us. They did it to punish him for leaving the gang, and to hit back at Jones for letting him. I'm sure of that.

"I've got to go finish this. Turn on the screen."

"I'll tell them. Thanks, skinny white girl."

"See you around, big black man."

She finished the slice, the coffee, sat for a minute studying her board.

So many lives ruined, wasted, ended, shattered. Because two men's greed pushed them to do ugly things for money. And another man's ego and rage demanded blood and war.

She walked into the bullpen and into applause over empty pizza boxes.

"Yeah, yeah. Now that you've stuffed your faces, get back to it. Peabody."

"Jones next, right? I'll have him brought up."

"In a minute." She moved to Peabody's desk. "I spoke with Agent Teasdale. She's giving Cohen the bad news."

"Aw. Even with all this, I sort of wish we could be there."

"We'll take our shot at him tomorrow. Teasdale and I worked it out. We're going to tie him to all three murders. And since his knowledge and connection to them were motivated by continuing the fraud, tax dodges, illegals dealing, he can do federal time for them, too. We tie him up, Teasdale locks him up."

"Sounds fair."

"Meanwhile, one left for today, here's how we're going to play Jones."

As she laid out the strategy, Mira came in.

"I'm sorry I missed you earlier," Mira began. "I wanted to tell you this marathon has been an education. Studying so many approaches, rhythms, reactions — one community, as it were, engaged with another within a confined space and confined time period."

"Engaged with?"

Mira set her medical bag on Peabody's desk. "I could say pitted against, but it is a form of engaging. Peabody, let's have a look at that knee."

"We're about to go into Interview."

"Call Jones up while she's doing what she does," Eve said. "It'll take awhile to get him here." As she spoke, Eve pulled over Baxter's desk chair so Mira could sit.

"Thanks. Of course, I've observed countless interviews before, but this has been a kind of microcosm."

In her gentle, efficient way, Mira rolled up Peabody's pants leg, removed the brace. "I think I'll write a paper on it. How's the discomfort level?"

"It's not bad. A little more when I'm walking around. But I haven't been."

"Good. I'm going to cold wand it."

Maybe the discomfort wasn't bad, Eve thought, but there was still considerable swelling and bruising.

Definitely riding the desk for the rest of the week, Eve reaffirmed. Longer if need be.

She waited until Peabody finished arranging for Jones to be brought into Interview. "I should have let you take the asshole who pulled you down into the box."

"Nah. Jenkinson and Reineke wrapped him up. Do you have time to do a little — maybe on my face?"

"Of course." Mira glanced over at Eve. "For both of you."

"After the media deal — her, too. We're going to show cops can take a hit."

Mira nodded as she treated Peabody's knee. "Your choice of outfit today makes you look like you give more hits than you take."

"That's the idea."

CHAPTER
TWENTY-TWO

Saving Jones for the last interview of the day hadn't just allowed Eve to close out three murders with three arrests — with Cohen to provide the icing on her justice cake the next day. It had given her the opportunity to gather more data from the three men who would spend their lives in cages.

She'd have all that in her pocket as she and Peabody "engaged with" Marcus Jones.

He sat alone in Interview when they walked in, started the record, read off the salient. He slouched — not out of despair, but to show how unconcerned he was. After his gaze tracked lazily over her face, then Peabody's, he allowed a hint of pleasure to show.

"Took you long enough, but I've got nothing to say."

"One of your rights," Eve returned as she and Peabody took their seats. "And I know you were read your rights, as I did it myself. You can sit there and be as quiet as you want. We still get paid."

"Got nothing to say," he repeated. "And I'm exercising another right. I'm waiting for my lawyer."

Eve gave him wide eyes. "You requested legal representation and your lawyer hasn't yet arrived? Must be a busy guy."

"Good lawyers are busy lawyers."

"Well then, we'll have you taken back to Holding until such time as your lawyer gets here." She started to rise, then angled her head. "Say, your lawyer doesn't happen to be Samuel Cohen?"

Jones's only reaction was a narrowing of his eyes. "That's my business."

"It is, definitely. It's just that if you're waiting for Cohen, well, you're going to be waiting, oh, about . . . forever. He's currently in federal custody representing himself against a whole . . . What's the word I'm after?"

"I think it's *shitload*," Peabody supplied.

"That's it. A shitload of crimes. You'll also be talking to the FBI when we're done here. But since you're exercising your right to remain silent, and wait for your attorney, we'll have you taken back, and notify the Special Agent in Charge."

"That's bullshit."

"Which part? Cohen hasn't returned your tags, has he? He can't because his 'link's been confiscated, and he has no access to it. The feds do — and, of course, the NYPSD did. We also accessed his electronics, his records. Yeah, the feds can't wait to have a nice, long chat with you."

"You think I'm afraid of a bunch of FBI suits?"

"You should be. Especially after Cohen spills his guts."

"Bring them in here." His chains rattled when he jabbed a finger at her. "They want Cohen, I'll make them a deal."

405

"Sorry, you have to deal with us first, and you're not talking to us, as is your right. We'll wait until you have something to say and/or engage another attorney."

"He'll need a public defender," Peabody pointed out as she and Eve stood. "Since all his accounts are frozen."

"That's his problem." Eve made a point of gathering up her files as she spoke to Peabody. "Just like the three charges of murder in the first are his problem, and that's before the feds get him."

"Murder my ass." Jones tried to shove to his feet. His chains rattled again, held him in place. "You're not going to pin murders on me."

"You either invoke your right to remain silent or you don't. You invoke your right to an attorney or you waive it. Decide."

"I'm saying you're not pinning murders on me."

"Are you now willing to speak, to answer questions, without the benefit of legal representation?"

"I'm not having some limp-dick court-ordered winding me up. I can handle myself, and you got no murders on me."

"Your former lawyer disagrees. He's laying them right on you."

"He's a lying sack!"

Eve sat again, waited for Peabody to do the same. "On that we agree. He's a lying, cheating sack. But he was pretty convincing when he laid out how you planned Lyle Pickering's murder, and how he tried to talk you out of it."

"I never killed Pick, and anybody who says so is a liar. Pick was a brother to me. I never talked to Cohen about Pick until after you came and said how he was dead."

"You did speak with Cohen about it?"

"*After*. He's a lawyer, ain't he? Supposed to be my fucking lawyer, so I told him you'd come sniffing."

"Reasonable," Eve said easily. "And what did he advise?"

"He said not to worry none. Sounded to him like you were trying to get a rise out of Pick's OD, out of Dinnie getting dead." Wrists cuffed, Jones beat a fist into his palm. "Now he's trying to save his own ass and using mine. Well, I can do the same. I know plenty about that mofo."

"I'm sure you do, and I imagine the FBI will be interested in what you have to say about your business dealings with him. But before they get their turn . . ."

She stacked the files, tapped them.

"We've got three murders, illegals charges, weapons charges, the matter of using unlicensed sex workers — including minors — for profit, extorting money — your protection racket. Oh, and there's the explosives materials found on your property, assorted firebombings, assaults, kidnapping, witness intimidation, related murders, and I can cap all that and other charges off with the attempted murder of a police officer. That would be me."

"I was defending myself."

"Ah . . . no. See, your property — and your name's on that property — was entered via warrant, you and your ... guests? Tenants? Were so informed. You resisted with force. You, specifically, aimed a stunner — illegal to civilians — on full at me, fired it while stating . . ."

She flipped through the file. "'You're done, bitch.'"

"If I had a stunner on full, why didn't you go down?"

Eve wiggled her fingers in the air. "Magic. So three murders, all the rest, and an attempted on me. I can tell you the courts take a really dim view of attempts to kill police. I know because I'm police."

"I never killed Pick or Dinnie or that dumb-ass Fist. I've been looking into that myself, figuring out about who did."

"That's amazing." Peabody widened her eyes, turned to Eve. "Dallas, isn't that amazing? He's been looking into it, and so have we."

"I'm almost speechless."

"You think you're smart?" Leaning forward, he spread his hands. "You ain't nothing. You get me somebody in here who can make me a deal — in writing — and I'll tell you what I know."

"You want a deal?"

"I want those feds off my ass for that petty bullshit, and I'll give them plenty on that mofo Cohen. You brush off the rest of this bullshit, mostly you can't prove, and I'll give you the murders. Simple as that."

"'Simple as that,'" Eve repeated, looked at Peabody. "He wants a deal."

"Yeah, like we haven't heard that one today."

The two of them went into fits of laughter, until Peabody gasped for air and wiped her eyes.

"You think you can laugh at me." His voice, dangerously low, shook with rage. "You think I won't mess you up?"

"It's not going to help you to threaten police officers, on the record, during Interview." Eve let out a huge sigh. "Boy, that felt good. Anyway, I repeat, police officers. Investigators. Freaking murder cops, dumb-ass. And if you think your suggestion that we need some rat-fucking gangbanger to help us close murder cases isn't hilarious, well, you need more humor in your life."

"We've made those arrests already," Peabody said helpfully. "But thanks for the offer."

"You tried to say I did the murders."

"See, we do stuff like that. Plus," Eve added, "some of the individuals we charged did claim it was on you. So we like to clear all that up, make it tidy."

"We know you didn't kill Pickering, Duff, or Aimes. You're not on the hook for those."

"True," Eve confirmed. "Three of your soldiers — well, I guess Aimes was a wannabe — and one of your lieutenants, they're on the hook. And your lawyer — disbarred lawyer — as accessory before and after the fact. They did it right under your nose."

"You're lying, trying to mess us up. It's Fan Ho and his did them. None of my people do *nothing* without my say."

"Really? So nobody shakes down the locals, does illegals deals, runs the sex operation, and so on without your go?"

"I run the Bangers, bitch." All derision, all defiance, Jones leaned forward again. "You get that?"

"Oh yeah. I get that, but it seems some haven't been real happy with your brand of leadership."

"They wanted to, you know, shake things up. Give you some incentive," Peabody explained. "So you'd call for war."

"You wouldn't take any action against Pickering, and he'd turned his back on the gang, he was getting his tat removed, living the straight life. Somebody didn't like how you handled that, and somebody got in a position to use Duff to set Pickering up."

"Let him guess who," Peabody urged, shoulders wiggling. "Let him guess, Dallas. I think I can see a glimmer."

"If Bolt went against me, he's a dead man."

"Yeah, yeah." Eve waved that away. "Lots of dead man threats with you guys. Bolt figures Snapper and Ticker are dead men for rolling on him — they did the actual murders, with Fist. Well, Fist didn't have much choice in his own murder. They turned on you, Jones. Duff, too. Fist and Duff paid a hard price for it already. And Bolt's hoping to make you a dead man — he'd hoped to take you out in the war he wanted. But now it's more personal."

"We might've let slip about you skimming from the gang pool, about hosing the gang for rent on the building." Peabody looked at Eve, pressed her fingers to her grin. "Oops."

"See, being investigators, we didn't have any trouble finding your lame-ass secret rooms, and being the NYPS-fucking-D, we have a whole division who gets off on going through electronics, records."

410

"That's my personal shit. You can't go into my personal shit. That's against my civil rights."

"Is that what your lawyer told you? Shows you what you get with one who's been disbarred. And one who got a little irked when you cut his take, so he threw in with Bolt. They tried to set you up. We're just smarter than they are."

"Doesn't take much. We're not charging him for the skimming, are we?" Peabody wondered.

"We'll leave some of that to the feds. We have a whole pile of statements and evidence, Jones, that — with recent exceptions due to dissent in your ranks — corroborates your claim that nothing goes down without your say-so. Like enlisting minors as runners, as recruits, and as bag boys by threatening their families. Beating and raping mothers. Forcing minor girls into the sex trade. Kidnapping the minor child of a previous victim to force her to recant, and lots more."

"You can't prove any of it."

"Oh, yes, we can. And already have in many cases." Eve shifted forward, spoke conversationally. "Do you know what a major raid and the resulting media coverage does? It brings people who've been afraid out, so they speak out. I'm going to tell you, you're not very well liked in your little neighborhood."

Peabody picked up the rhythm. "They're lined up to give statements, and to sweeten it, a lot of your gang, or those threatened into working for it, are rolling and flipping faster than we can log it in."

Peabody mimed wiping sweat off her forehead. "Whew! It's been a day!"

"And all this before the feds take their bite." Eve glanced at her wrist unit. "Cohen's spilling those guts about now. We don't need anything from you, *Slice*. You're done. You've got nothing left. No property, no money, no gang. And you can forget about Aruba."

"I'll get it back."

She could see him trembling now. Maybe some came from rage, betrayal-lit rage, maybe some was despair at the loss of everything.

"No, you won't. You're not going down for these three murders, but there are others you ordered, others you committed." Eve tapped her file. "And they're all right in here. Names, dates, methods, motives. You stole from them, you cheated them, you betrayed them. And once we showed them you had — and how — hell, they rolled on you like a flood.

"So." Eve opened the file. "We're going to talk about all of them. Every last one of them."

She had to send Peabody out, not only to take a break as the interview ran on, but to let Kyung know he needed to push the media conference to seventeen hundred.

By the time she wrapped, Jones had long since stopped trembling. He'd fallen back on pride — and that rage. She saw the murder in his eyes, and thought it would be frustrating he had no place to put it.

"And that," Eve said as she sent him to maximum with two guards, "is how it's done."

"I appreciate the break, but I'm really glad I got back for the finish."

"Take another. We've got about twenty before we have to talk to the media."

"He copped to it all," Peabody said as they walked out. "I didn't expect him to cop to it all."

"Under the skin he's the same as Bolt. The same as Fan Ho. Gang pride. He did what had to be done as he sees it."

"He stole from his own people."

"He wasn't going to end up like his father, brain damaged in a cage. If Bolt had pulled this off, taken over? I bet down the road he'd figure he deserved a little more, and a little more. I need coffee," she said, then saw Roarke come out of Observation.

"You made it."

"I did, yes, about a half hour ago. It was more than worth it. And how's my girl?" he asked and kissed Peabody's bruised cheek.

"Aw. I'm okay."

"She needs to put the knee up, and I need coffee before we deal with the damn PR portion of the day."

Roarke gave Peabody a gentle pat before he walked with Eve to her office.

"That's already started. I also had some entertainment watching Nadine's report before I got here. They're replaying it, or clips of it. It's the lead story, and I expect will be for a while."

"Good."

He moved to the AutoChef, so Eve went to her skinny window, stared out at the world.

"Sit." As he had with Peabody, Roarke gave her a gentle pat. "Drink your coffee, take your twenty."

"I've been sitting all damn day in a chair in the box. One after another, and none of them worth a bucket of piss. None of them much smarter than that, either."

"Where will these less than buckets of piss spend the rest of their lives?"

She drank coffee, looking for the jolt to get her through the next phase. "In cages. Reo and I talked some, and will again, but I'm going to push off-planet for Washington, Chesterfield, and Jorgenson. Jones, like Cohen, will do cage time in federal facilities. Separate. No point giving Jones an opportunity to cut Cohen's sentence short by shanking him."

"And yet you still have some of that sad in you."

"I'll shake it out. In the end, the system worked. And now there are a couple of neighborhoods and the people in them who'll be safer. My team worked this top to bottom, inside and out. Every interview I've reviewed . . ."

She drank more coffee. "Well, it's good work. Mira said she might write a paper on it." Now she turned to him. "We gutted two gangs. Gutted them. No leadership left now, and when the word spreads — and it damn well will — about the cheating, the betrayals, the lack of what they'd think of as honor and loyalty?" She shook her head. "They're done. Something else will spring up, that's the world. But the system will keep working."

He leaned down to kiss her because, whether she'd admit it or not, she needed it.

Strong stepped into the doorway. "Oh. Sorry."

"Not at all." Roarke eased back. "Coffee?"

"I, ah . . ."

"Why don't you get that, Lieutenant? I'm going to check on Peabody."

When Roarke stepped out, Strong still hesitated. "I didn't mean to chase him off."

"You didn't." Eve handed Strong the coffee.

"Thanks. I wanted a couple minutes before the media briefing."

"You've got it. I reviewed your interview with Ho. You worked him well. He's smarter than most of them, but he's got that quick trigger. You figured how to play him."

"He's got a little skim of polish, and under it, he's the most vicious bastard I've ever had in the box. Anyway, I got the word you wrapped Bolt, Snapper, and Ticker. Jones, too, but he wasn't —"

She broke off to look at the board. "He wasn't part of killing Lyle."

"No. And the ones that did bought concrete cages on Omega. They didn't kill him because he was your CI, Strong."

Strong's head snapped around, then she lowered into the visitor's chair. "You're sure?"

"I am. They didn't know, and that tells me you were both good at it. I gave them every opening, and if they'd known, they'd have taken it. It would've made more sense, given them some screwed-up prestige if that had been the motive. It wasn't."

"Then why?"

"Jorgenson ordered it to undermine Jones, to take a personal shot at Jones, and because it just pissed him off that Lyle walked away. The others, just following orders, proving their worth. Review the interviews."

"I will. If it had been because of working with me, I'd have to live with it. I've been working on how I would."

She stared down into her coffee a moment, then looked up. "I really liked him, Dallas, and I respected him. Is it worse that they killed him for nothing? Really for nothing?"

She'd asked herself the same question, and had no answer.

"We're cops. We live with that every day. His family knows now, but you might want to talk to them."

"I will. I want to thank you, Lieutenant, for bringing me into this, for giving me a part of it."

"He was yours."

"Yeah." Strong rose. "Yeah, he was." She started out, stopped in the doorway. "We still have his two-year chip in Evidence. Do you think if I had it put in a nice box, like a memorial, his family would like it?"

"I think they'd appreciate it. I'll clear you signing it out."

"Okay. I'll see you at the briefing."

Eve took her last few minutes alone, looking out her skinny window at the world.

The briefing ran long; then again, any media briefing more than five minutes struck Eve as long. Chief Tibble spoke first after making a point, as was his way, of thanking every officer involved in the arrests. Whitney followed him, speaking briefly, with both of them stating questions would wait until the end of the statements.

When it came to Eve, she took her place at the podium with her PPC in one hand. "The NYPSD, through the work, skill, and courage of the officers here, and with the cooperation and resources of the FBI, have made multiple arrests, confiscated many thousands of dollars' worth of illegals, of weapons, of fraudulent IDs and the equipment used for creating them. Our EDD has reviewed data from confiscated electronics documenting crimes including murder, the enforced sex slavery of minors, extortion, illegals distribution, destruction of property, fraud, and other crimes perpetrated by members of the urban gangs known as the Bangers and the Dragons.

"These investigations launched with the murder of Lyle Pickering. His murder didn't get much media attention. He was a former member of the Bangers, an ex-con, a recovering addict. He was also a man who rehabilitated himself, who learned a skill and used that skill to gain employment, who went to meetings, removed himself from his former gang ties, and lived a productive life. For these reasons members of his former gang plotted and carried out his murder.

"The investigation into Lyle Pickering's murder, and the subsequent murders of two others involved in it, led to the arrest of these individuals.

"Kenneth Jorgenson, murder in the first, three counts. Assault on a police officer, one charge; possession of a deadly weapon, two charges.

"Denby Washington, murder in the first, three counts. First degree rape, one charge. Possession of stolen property, two charges; possession of illegal substances, one charge."

She read them off, every one.

When she finished and stepped back, questions exploded. Tibble held up his hands, moved forward, took the first wave. Kyung caught her eye, nodded, murmured, "Well done, Lieutenant."

Maybe, she thought, maybe. But she couldn't yet shake out the sad.

When it finally ended, she let Roarke drive, and sat back, eyes closed. Roarke gave her silence. He thought she needed the quiet, and a bit of pampering. But he had an idea what might help lift that sadness that crowded her.

When he stopped the car, she sat up, opened her eyes. And frowned.

"I wanted a stop before home," he told her.

"I was just thinking about a really big glass of wine."

"We'll get to that, but first."

He got out, waited for her. She didn't know how the hell he'd found a parking place, but that was Roarke.

Then as she joined him on the sidewalk, the fog cleared in her brain, and she realized they stood in Hell's Kitchen.

The building still looked old, she noted, but in a classy, dignified way with its bricks cleaned and repointed, with new windows that would undoubtedly let in light.

He'd replaced the entrance doors with ones of deeply carved wood. Above them, a simple brass plaque.

"*An Didean.* 'Haven,' right? It works."

"Let's see what you think of the rest."

He moved to the doors. Excellent security, of course. She took the two steps up to join him.

"I know you'll think of the girls we found," he said before he opened the door. "The ones you found justice for. I hope what we've done here, what we'll do, might add some peace as well."

She remembered what she'd seen before, the crumbling interior, dirty walls, the hole in one of them Roarke's sledgehammer — ceremoniously — had opened.

And the remains of those young girls behind it.

Now, as Roarke called for lights, she saw a clean, fresh space, with walls a warm, sort of toasty color, with open archways leading to other rooms and spaces.

"You changed the —" She used her hands.

"Configuration, yes. It's more open, I think more welcoming. And even so, should be more efficient. Over here we have a common area, a place students can relax, hang. We'll have a screen in here, easy furniture, games, music, books. We have another common area, no screen, a quiet space for studying, doing assignments, reading, and that sort of thing. Some classrooms on this level, and administration offices."

She wandered with him, and what she saw equaled a lot of thought, a lot of care. Warm colors — not dull or institutional — the touches of crown molding, good lighting.

A room for computer science, a room for art studies, one for group therapy sessions, a smaller one for individual therapy.

A decent gym with a locker room and showers. Showers, she noted, with actual partitions between.

"It seems bigger," she commented.

"The configuration. It was considerably chopped up before. With this more open plan, it doesn't feel confining. The main kitchen," he said.

She could only stare. It was sleek and shining, as she would have expected. Yet it felt . . . homey. The colors? she wondered. The configuration again? Or did he just have some magic?

Maybe all of that.

"We have a nutritionist on staff, but she's not so strict they won't be allowed, well, happy food. And they can learn how to prepare their own in the classroom kitchen."

Smaller, but no less shiny, with a couple of island-type work spaces, a generous storage space — pantry, she remembered.

"I've asked Summerset if he'd come in and instruct now and again."

Her jaw actually dropped. "You — Summerset?"

"The man can cook, you'll agree. And he enjoys children."

"Summerset," she murmured as he led her back through, then up the new stairs.

Wide ones with sturdy rails.

He showed her bedrooms, each one with windows, with closets, with built-in study areas. She toured a game room, a space for music lessons, and one for dance.

She stopped, more than a little overwhelmed by what he'd done.

"When I was in school, state school, I marked the days. I swear to Christ, I marked the days from the time I went in until I could get out. I can look back and see it wasn't all bad. I learned things. It wasn't all terrible. But I marked the days," Eve recalled.

She paused to run her fingers over a wide windowsill.

"No privacy, no sense of self. You either ate what they put in front of you, when they put it in front of you, or you went hungry. The walls were the color of . . . They didn't have a color. One shower area for girls, one for boys. And both open, you know? No privacy. When I could, I'd sneak out in the middle of the night to shower.

"I marked the days," she said again. "The kids who come here won't. Unless they're serious hard cases, they won't mark the days until they can escape. It'll matter what you've done here, and what they're given the chance to do."

He took her hand, kissed it, then held it to take her to the roof.

They'd already started seedlings in raised beds, domed now against the threat of frost. Benches scattered to provide a place to sit and look or grouped together for a place to talk. And beyond the high safety walls, the city glimmered.

"We'll do more plantings — flowers, not just veg," Roarke explained. "And they'll finish the little fountain

421

soon. Some ornamental trees, and some that will fruit. Herbs, of course. The students can work the gardens, help harvest, and the kitchens will use what they grow."

She wandered, imagined what it would be like. Those voices, the sunlight, the music of the fountain, the smell of fresh things.

No, they wouldn't mark the days as she had.

She came back, looked at the memorial stones, already in place. All the young girls, she thought, all the doomed young girls she'd found, named here, remembered here. Even the one she hadn't been able to identify and had named Angel.

"You're right, about the peace." Now she took his hand, drew him down on a bench with her. "It's a good place, Roarke. It's a good chance. Whatever they've come from, they'll have a good chance here."

She tipped her head to his shoulder. "It's a good place. Let's just sit here awhile."

He slipped his arm around her, drew her closer so they sat with the city lights glimmering, and the future potential all around.

The sadness lifted.

Other titles published by Ulverscroft:

LEVERAGE IN DEATH

J. D. Robb

When Paul Rogan sets off a bomb at his office, killing eleven people, no one can understand why. He was a loving husband and father, with everything to live for. Then his wife and daughter are found chained up in the family home, and all becomes clear. Rogan has been given a horrifying choice — set off the bomb, or see his loved ones suffer and die. Lieutenant Eve Dallas knows the violence won't end here. The men behind the attack are determined, organised and utterly ruthless. In this shocking and challenging case, both Eve and her husband Roarke are heading into serious danger . . .

DARK IN DEATH

J. D. Robb

There's always a reason for murder. But when a young actress is killed in a swift and violent attack at a cinema screening, that reason is hard to fathom — even for Lieutenant Eve Dallas and her team. It's only when bestselling crime writer Blaine DeLano arrives at the precinct that the shocking truth is revealed. Someone is recreating the murder scenes from her latest series, book by book. With six more novels left in the series, Eve now knows how the killer will strike next. But why has DeLano been targeted? Could her abusive husband be involved? As fiction is transformed into bloody reality, Eve will need all her skill and experience to solve this unique case.

SECRETS IN DEATH

J. D. Robb

No one is going to miss Larinda Mars. A ruthless gossip queen with a lucrative sideline in blackmail, there's no lack of suspects when she's murdered in a fashionable New York bar. With so many people wanting her dead, it's going to be a tough case to crack. Lieutenant Eve Dallas may not like this particular victim, but it's her duty to bring the killer to justice. As she digs deeper into Larinda's mysterious past, it becomes clear the reporter had a unique talent for uncovering secrets. Including ones very close to home for Eve and her husband Roarke . . . Someone was willing to commit murder to keep their secrets hidden. And with Eve now working to uncover the truth, she and her team are heading into serious danger.

ECHOES IN DEATH

J. D. Robb

New York at night. A young woman stumbles out onto a busy street — right in front of Lieutenant Eve Dallas and husband Roarke. Her name is Daphne Strazza, and she has been brutally assaulted. Confused and traumatised, she manages to tell them one thing: her attacker wore a devil's mask. As Eve investigates this shocking case, she soon discovers a disturbing pattern. Someone is preying on wealthy couples, subjecting them to a cruel and terrifying ordeal. Worse still, the attacks are escalating in violence and depraved theatricality. Eve and her team are now in a race against time to find the man behind the mask before he strikes again. But for Eve, this case in particular has unsettling echoes of her own troubled past . . .